wildest dream

B.B. MILLER & LESLIE CARSON

Wildest Dream
B.B. Miller & Leslie Carson
© 2019
ISBN: 978-0-9982462-7-7

Cover design by: Jada D'Lee Designs
Cover Image by: iStock Photos
Editing by: Lauren Schmelz and Greg: Write Divas
Interior Design & Formatting by: Champagne Book Design

For the wild ones, the wanderers, the ones who march to the beat of a different drummer.

wildest dream

chapter one

Murphy's Law No. 261: If your bandmates get girlfriends, they quickly become dull and boring. AKA—Being the seventh wheel sucks.

Sean

"I'm going hang gliding." My announcement—an epic one, in my opinion—is met with the typical apathy I've come to expect from my Redfall bandmates over the last few years.

Kennedy Lane, lead singer and guitar genius; Cameron Chapman, our kick-ass rhythm guitarist; and Matt Logan, Redfall's fierce bassist extraordinaire, look more like teenagers unable to avoid the temptation of their smartphones than one of the biggest rock and roll bands on the planet.

Only Cam has the decency to lift his nose from the wonder of his beloved phone. "You're not going hang gliding," he grumbles. Since hooking up with the lovely Samantha, he's gone and got himself an instant family, and with that the parental instincts that go along with worrying about the fragile state of a five-year-old girl. Although, there is no debating how utterly adorable Hannah is. Talk about having someone wrapped around your finger. I think all four of us would move the earth for her.

Still, Cam's the last person I would ever expect fatherly advice from, but love apparently does things to you no one can predict. He and Sam are engaged now and beginning to plan their wedding. Wonders never cease.

"Damn right I am. *Adventure Wars* called Nic the other day."

This gets their collective attention, and I can't help but smirk as I lounge back against the sofa in the green room, stretching my arm across the back. Another interview, another city. They all start to blend together after a while. We're all feeling the toll of this tour, but there's a well-earned break on the horizon, and that can't come soon enough.

"*Adventure Wars?*" Matty looks more than a little impressed. "That TV show where celebrities battle it out to see which one is more stupid?"

My smirk fades a little.

"Last week, some pro quarterback went shark diving. The other contestant was too chicken-shit to try it. They all donate money to charity regardless," Matty adds.

"No shit," Kennedy mumbles before dropping his phone into the pocket of his leather jacket. "When's this taking place?"

"It's not." Tucker Pearson, our head of security, lurks at the door in that menacing way he has. "No fucking way are you doing that."

"But it's totally safe." Even I can admit that I sound like a petulant child.

Tucker snorts and shakes his head. "Throwing yourself off a cliff with only a kite holding you up isn't safe, Sean."

"Where's your sense of adventure, hmm?" I challenge them all. Pushing up from the sofa, I pace the room, keyed up and anticipating our next performance as always.

"I'm all for adventure, but—"

"But nothing!" I interrupt Tucker. "When's the last time we did something wild and crazy?"

"Last night," Kennedy deadpans. "Or did you forget the eighteen thousand people we played for?"

"Not talking about that. *That* is safe. It's what we know. What about pushing the boundaries a little?"

"Again, what about last night?" Kennedy continues. "Pretty sure no one has played a Stones tribute that way ever."

I grin at the memory of our latest concert. We blew the roof off Madison Square Garden for the fourth night in a row. There's nothing like that kind of adrenaline rush. "All right, I'll give you that, but I'm talking about taking real risks here. You know? Feel your heart pounding, pure adrenaline—not the kind we get when we play. I mean the unknown."

"Jesus, you need a hobby," Cam mutters, rolling his eyes.

"My point exactly. We can't all be in domesticated bliss. And what would I bring to the band if you all couldn't live vicariously through me?"

"I ask myself that question on a daily basis," Kennedy mocks with a grin, lifting his Gibson from the nearby stand and strumming a few chords.

"I really want—"

"No." There's no questioning the firmness in Tucker's voice as he cuts me off. "This wacked-out show must have other options, so find one."

"White water rafting in Ecuador?" Cam offers.

"Zip line over the rainforest in Costa Rica?" Matty chimes in.

Kennedy stops playing long enough to throw his two cents in. "New tattoo—on your forehead this time?"

"Yes. Yes. And are you insane? I can't ruin this pretty face for women everywhere. I'm our money ticket."

Cameron shakes his head and laughs at me.

"Whatever you do, it has to be something the insurance company will cover." Tucker passes me an energy drink from the table.

"Listen to you, old man. See? This is what I'm talking about. I want to spice things up, and all you lot can think about is not violating section twenty-four in our insurance policy."

"Finding a replacement drummer would be a pain in the ass," Cameron jokes. "Maybe we should start looking now?"

I level him a warning glance. "You wouldn't dare, Three." Cameron narrows his eyes at my nickname for him. Being born into an uber-rich, country club elitist family is something I'll never stop kidding Cam about. Cameron Louis Chapman, the Third... What a crock of shit. Who gives their kid a handle like that? So, to me, he'll always be Three. Sure, he pretends to hate the name, but secretly, I think he loves me for it.

"Don't die, and we won't have to," he fires back at me.

"Words of wisdom there." Matty pokes at my hair. I dyed it jet-black after experimenting with various shades of blue for the last couple of weeks. I like to change things up. Keep people guessing.

"And I thought we talked about this. Remember? When you channeled Spiderman at the hotel in Buenos Aires last month?" Kennedy glares at me, and I give him a one-finger salute.

"I was totally fin—"

"You could have died, Sean," Tucker reminds me. He's such a buzz-kill. "Climbing between the balconies like that. You're not invincible."

I wave him off. "I didn't die, though, did I? And the rooms were right beside each other."

"Yeah, Thirty-two stories up," Cam helpfully supplies while he shrugs on his leather jacket.

"Answer the door next time and we won't have to worry about it."

Cameron rests his arm across the back of the couch he's lounging in. "I was busy on a very important video chat with Sam." He ducks as I hurl a grape at him from the nearby fruit tray.

"Just think of the women you'd disappoint if you did die. Broken hearts around the globe," Matty says with a hint of amusement in his voice.

"I really do hate disappointing women." I throw a grape up into the air and catch it in my mouth.

Kennedy snorts. "Doesn't that happen every night?" I stick my tongue out at him.

A sharp knock on the door puts a stop to our limitless sparring. "Redfall! You're on in ten." Duty calls as always.

I'm not, nor have I ever been, what people define as normal. It's a blessing and a curse. My parents encouraged me to question everything and to never be complacent. They tried to do the same with my twin sister, Sydney, but she's always been the one on a more even keel, pulling me back to reality when I tended to run off the rails, which back in the day, was often.

We were *that* family—the ones who took backpacking tours to the middle of nowhere, whilst everyone else was lazing about on holiday. Sydney and I spent our tenth birthday helping my parents build a school in Tanzania. With my father being a director of the International Development Office, a government department that distributes aid to countries in need, summer holidays were taken wherever he happened to be dispatched: Nepal, Ghana, the Philippines. More than just a talking head, Dad is one of the rare ones who actually gives a shit; he rolls up his sleeves and digs in to help. He always wanted both Syd and me to get involved in political life, so near and dear it was and still is to him.

Sadly, for him, that dream was doomed for failure the moment I turned sixteen and made the miraculous discovery that girls would do just about anything if they found out you were a drummer—bless them many times over.

Politics wasn't for Sydney either. The artistic gene—that we still can't seem to place—bit her early. She's now an architect with one of the most prestigious firms in London. Those countless hours of drawing and sketching with my mum, who can't draw a straight line with a ruler, obviously came in handy.

Sydney, however, has never caused family embarrassment, something I've excelled at over the years. My stint in rehab doesn't shine as one of my finer moments. I don't think that's what dear old Mum and

Dad had in mind when they told me to spread my wings and explore. But for a while, I was weak and caved to the lure of seeking the ultimate high in an industry where drugs are offered around like appetizers at a glitzy party.

The press is brutal in ways you can't imagine when you're famous and make mistakes. Couple that with a by-the-book influential member of the government, and you've got yourself a scandal. That may be the only regret I have—causing my parents to be hounded relentlessly by the paparazzi, demanding their comments on my coke bender that landed me in rehab for a couple of months.

Thankfully, as these things often do, the next celebrity train wreck followed mine quickly, and my family was just a footnote on page ten within a couple of weeks.

These days, with my bandmates cozying up with their significant others, the dynamic in our group has changed dramatically. I had a tea party with Cam and Hannah a few weeks back, for the love of God. A proper tea party. Mind you, those pink sunglasses Hannah made me wear were fantastic, but still, it's quite the change in culture from our days gone by. My mates are blissfully happy, but our nights of partying and staying out unchecked until four in the morning are a distant memory.

All that partying we did in the past wasn't always a good thing. For a while there, all of us were in serious danger of taking things a step too far. Change is inevitable in life, a sign that we're all growing up, if you will, but if you asked me a year ago if I'd be hosting tea parties for five-year-olds, I would've told you you'd lost your mind.

But, that is the wonder of life. The unpredictability is what makes us want to get up and see what's in store. On days like today, when I'm held back, when I'm told I'm not allowed to do something, well, that just makes me want to do it more. Buy the shoes, wear the ridiculous outfits, take the jump. You're here to light it up, and I intend to do just that.

"Hey, London." My eyes snap open and I try to look over my shoulder in the direction of the melodic female voice. It's nearly impossible, as I'm strapped to a hulk of man who seems more than a little excited to have me sitting in his lap.

I'm currently hooked to a stranger to whom I've entrusted my entire existence. I've signed my life away—literally—on a myriad of forms, disclaiming the fine New York skydive organization from any liability should I plummet to my death. I've sat through the fastest instruction video in the history of the world, and been zipped into a fabulous blue jumpsuit that I would normally howl at wearing.

Right now, I'm not howling. My heart is literally in my throat, the deafening roar of the engine in my ears louder than most concerts I've played. Adrenaline pulses in my fingertips, firing harder, faster than ever before. A hint of burnt rubber lingers in the cramped cargo space eight of us are squashed into. The plane? Some rickety old number held together by duct tape most likely.

Metal clinks behind me, and I feel... Ted? Tim? Regardless, T-man tightens my harness across my rib cage, joking to one of the other experts about virgin jumpers. On any other day, I'd be all over that comment. Today? Breathing is hard. For the first time in my life, I'm actually questioning my sanity.

The reality of the situation grips me as one of the other instructors hauls the side door of the plane open. A gaping hole where a door should be. The brilliant blue sky stretches out for miles. At least it will be sunny when I plunge to my death. I let out a snort and try to calm down.

Growing up, Syd and I used to pretend to be superheroes. With blankets wrapped around our necks as capes, we would race through the yard in Knightsbridge, arms spread wide, me jumping into one of Mum's flowering shrubs just to see what it felt like. That was exhilarating. *This* is just pure insanity. I take another breath.

"London!" I twist around enough finally to land my eyes on the persistent woman in question. "Yeah. You." She smiles at me. "It helps if you remember to breathe."

"I'm all right."

Her eyes, pale blueish-gray behind her goggles, dart down to my perpetually bouncing leg and the corners of her mouth turn up.

"That's nothing. I'm always like this."

"Sure you are," she hollers over the deafening roar of the engine. The corner of her pretty mouth curves up. Typically, women tend to fall all over me. This one looks thoroughly amused. I can tell she's tall and hiding a significant amount of curves under the oversized jumpsuit. Her hair—blond, sleek, and cut in a funky, layered style—lands just under her chin. Color me intrigued.

"How did you know I was English?"

She rolls her pretty eyes. "Please. You were the loudest one in the waiting area. That accent is kind of hard to miss."

She's got me there. "You've done this before?" I ask as T-man shuffles us toward the door of death.

Tossing me a killer smile, she nods happily. "A few times."

"And you're not just the least bit scared?"

"Bigger things out there to be scared of."

"Such as?"

Her jaw sets, all amusement gone. "Never doing this. Having someone tell you that you can't." My heart stutters at her words, but before I can dig further, T-Man hollers in my ear.

"She's right. Just breathe, man. I've done this thousands of times. You're in good hands. It's the best thing you'll ever do!" T-Man sounds confident. I don't bother telling him I've played with legends—living and gone. I hardly think tandem jumping from a plane is going to top that.

More shuffling to a tiny, wobbly platform that sits between me and potential death. My legs dangling off the side of a plane seems surreal, and then we're rocking forward, back… What the hell was I supposed to remember? Cross legs, bend arms… No! That's not it, and what the hell were the taps on the shoulder meant to be?

I crane my neck to try to get another glimpse at my mystery woman, but it's too late. T-Man rocks forward once more, the air steals my breath, and we're free falling into the mind-blowing, great unknown.

"Sweetheart, I'm about to be inside you. At least give me a name." My voice is raw and needy as I arch against my mystery woman's palm.

We're outside, at the back of the hangar in the airfield, hidden from view. Adrenaline is, still coursing electric through my veins from the dive, from my blond beauty from the plane. This woman... she's killing me: a slow, torturous, but oh so delicious death. It's been a primal experience, unexpected and addictive.

I've made her come once already, her sweet taste tingling on my tongue. I'm pretty sure she pulled hair straight out of my skull from tugging on it so hard when I sank between her creamy thighs and licked my way to pure heaven. Praise the Lord for natural blondes.

"No names. Let's just pretend we don't know each other, London," she whispers against my ear. I can't help but groan when she glides her hands over my cock once more, drawing the condom down my hardened length as she nibbles up and down my neck.

It's maddening—she refuses to let me kiss her. I want those sweet lips on mine.

"But I *don't* know who you are." I groan, my hand tightening around the ample curve of her waist, pressing her against the building. She's going to have marks. So am I, and I'll wear them proudly.

"And that's the way it's going to stay."

I groan in frustration, and my fingers stroke between her glorious long legs once more. She grinds her hips forward. "You're aching for me, aren't you, love?"

"Fuck, stop talking. That accent..." Her words disappear on a whimper as my thumb brushes over her swollen clit. She throws her head back against the metal building, her short blond layers a tangled, freshly fucked mess, her pretty mouth parted, tempting me to taste it.

She claws at my hips, tugging me forward as my lips glide a hungry circuit along the curve of her neck. "Christ," I mumble against her thundering pulse, and she wraps her legs around my waist.

I'm not ashamed to admit I've had my fair share of women and experiences, but this? Out in the open, with the New York sun blazing over us, where anyone could find me buried inside her, is something else entirely.

She meets every punch of my hips as I drive into her with firm and unhurried strokes building to something rough and decadent. On a delicious cry, she wraps her other leg around my waist; her hands seem to be everywhere, clutching at my neck, fisting my T-shirt, drifting between us to tease her sensitive skin.

A series of unintelligible groans and curses are shared between us when we find a rougher rhythm. My hands tighten against her thighs on another powerful thrust. Her back slams against the building, the sound loud and echoing in my ears. She's a glorious, trembling mess, gently brushing her fingertips over my cheeks as my cock throbs inside her. She traces my nose, my jaw, everywhere but my lips, her gaze holding mine the whole time.

"God, right there," she murmurs, her hips churning to meet mine.

Then she takes my face between her hands, and her intoxicating blue-gray eyes meet mine and I'm lost. Lost in the electric burn that fires down my spine, in the sensation of her shattering around me, in the shudder that rips through me with my own release.

I can feel her heart pound, and her warm, wet pussy welcoming me home. I'm desperate to crash my lips to hers. She's still holding my face like I may break apart. She's pinned to the building, completely at my mercy, but somehow I'm the one who feels vulnerable. She's stripped me bare.

Her eyes burn with intensity before they drop to my lips. It's like she can feel the same fiery need as I do, but she turns her head to the side, avoiding my lips once more. I grip her hips, and gradually lower her legs to the ground. Her eyes widen as I glide my palm along her outer thigh, reluctantly easing from her. Fucking hell. I'm completely, totally wrecked. Not breaking my gaze, she wobbles slightly with a ragged breath, and I hold her steady before leaning back to deal with the condom. Turning away from her to tie it off, my heart races as I try to catch my breath. Can you actually die from an adrenaline rush?

"Now, I definitely need a name, love." I turn back to find her scrambling into her jeans, pushing her feet into the worn pair of trainers that hit the ground early on in our encounter, somewhere around the time she told me I had magic fingers.

"No. You don't." I frown as she runs her hands through her hair, trying to smooth it down. "No names, London. Don't follow me," she pants out. "Forget you ever saw me." Her voice is clipped and raw. She may as well just gut me for everyone to see.

She squares her shoulders and marches her fine self along the side of the building, disappearing around the corner. No looking back, no little wave, no name or phone number… just nothing, and all I'm left with is the lingering adrenaline of the ultimate mind fuck.

Cassidy

Sweet crispy Christ! I hit the steering wheel with my fist as I speed back toward the city. What the fuck was I thinking? Fucking a total stranger out in the open air, where anyone could've seen me? I suck in a ragged breath and try to calm down. This is out there, even for me.

Then again…I really couldn't help myself. Between that accent and those full lips I wish I could've tasted, I was done for. And his eyes…I haven't seen eyes that green in years. I wonder what color his hair is under all that black dye. Maybe he has a goth thing going on.

I shake my head. Stop it, Cassidy. It doesn't matter. You'll never see him again. I shift in the driver's seat, trying to ease the significant ache between my legs. As my granny used to say, he was touched by God, and knew what to do with the blessing. Good Lord, he was talented. It's good I'll never see him again, because I could become addicted to that kind of manhandling.

My cell phone rings and I jab the answer button on the steering wheel. My brother's voice booms throughout the car before I can even say hello. "Where the hell are you? Intermission is almost over!"

I curse under my breath. "I told Mom I wasn't coming."

"Oh, please. Do you honestly think she believed you?" I can practically hear his eye roll. "Besides, you *can't* make me face the snake pit by myself. I will never forgive you if you aren't here by the time they start serving hors d'oeuvres."

"You'll get over it." I change lanes and pass the Jeep that's been billowing noxious exhaust for a mile. Jesus. Hasn't he ever heard of emissions testing? "I have to put the finishing touches on a dress before Monday afternoon."

"You have all day tomorrow to do that. I *need* you here, Cass. Don't make me beg."

The touch of desperation in his voice makes me cave. My mother is, no doubt, trying to hook him up with another "suitable match." With a groan, I step on the gas. "Fine. I'll be there in an hour or so— I'm almost back to the city. I have to stop and get dressed first."

"An hour? Honestly, Cass, where are you? Aren't you home?"

I stifle another groan. Kevin is terrified of heights and hates it when I skydive, but I love it. The thrill of flying without a net is addictive. No one cares who I am or who my parents are, and I can just... be. All my everyday worries and stress disappear. It helps put things in perspective. "I had an errand to run this morning," I lie, not wanting to hear another safety lecture. "I'll see you soon." I hang up, cursing to myself. Being a player in my parents' dog and pony show today was something I'd hoped to avoid. But I can't say no to Kevin.

And he knows it. Jerk.

I fight my way over the Williamsburg Bridge and, a few minutes later, manage to snag a parking spot around the corner from my shop. The welcoming smell of fresh bagels greets me from the bakery across the street as I unlock my door and climb the stairs to my apartment. My shop and design studio is downstairs. I'm proud to say after five years, I'm starting to make a name for myself providing unique bridal creations to the pickiest of bridezillas and their mothers. I'm off the beaten path a bit—the garment district is about three miles away in midtown Manhattan—but I love my spot here in the East Village.

Casting a longing glance toward my sketchbook, I shake my head and rush to shower and change. Must look the part, after all.

"Cassidy! Finally!" My mother gives me a brittle smile, and I lean in to receive her air kiss. At fifty-five, Marilyn Skinner is the epitome of the political wife. Not a hair out of place, perfectly pressed suit dress, and pearls adorning her ears and neck. "We expected you hours ago." She waves at someone across the room.

As Kevin said, she obviously ignored me when I said I wouldn't be here. "Well, I'm here now," I say shortly, and shoot my brother an annoyed look as he strolls up to join us. He greets me with a hug and an admiring glance at my dress.

"You look gorgeous. This is one of yours, right?"

I nod and run a hand over my skirt. Made out of dark sapphire blue taffeta, my cocktail dress is a throwback to the forties, with a narrow skirt, belt, and three-quarter length sleeves. "Finished it last week." I wear my own creations to these events as much as possible—if I have to be here, I may as well get some free advertising out of it. I've scored more than one client thanks to my father's career.

Kevin leans in to whisper in my ear. "Thanks for coming. Dad was on a real tear earlier when you didn't show."

I roll my eyes. Our father is always on a tear about something. The senior senator from Wyoming, Robert Skinner is currently preparing for reelection. Today's little soiree, an afternoon performance by the New York Chamber Orchestra followed by drinks, dinner, and a chance to meet the great man himself, is sponsored by his party's national committee and Coleman Energy, one of dad's biggest supporters. If I remember correctly, seats were going for fifteen hundred dollars a pop.

Chump change for some of these people.

My mother touches my arm. "I have to go say hello to the

Bachmans. Don't wander off, dear; your father wants a word. Kevin, will you show her to our table? Dinner should be starting soon." She pats her blond helmet hair and flitters off, and my brother holds an arm out to me with a wry smile.

"This way," he says with a ridiculous flourish, making me smile. I can never stay mad at him for long. Two years older than me, he was my partner in crime growing up. Some older brothers would've considered a younger sister a nuisance, but not Kevin. He showed me how to climb trees, which fishing lures to choose, and the best hiding places in our grandparents' barn. We were inseparable until we went to college, him in New York and me in California—much to our dad's chagrin. Not only were they liberal colleges in blue states, but they were as far away from Cheyenne as we could get. Kevin stayed in New York and joined a law firm specializing in land deals. I had originally thought I'd stay in Los Angeles, but…things didn't work out that way.

"Does it ever strike you as hypocritical that Dad will happily spend all day lambasting New York's liberal ways but doesn't hesitate to raise money here?" I ask as we wind our way through the tables set with white tablecloths and little American flags.

Kevin laughs. "You say that like you're surprised. There's no way he could get what he needs for a run from just Wyoming donors. No one raises money solely in their own states. They go where the money is; you know that."

I do know that. It's disgusting how much money an election campaign requires. It's the way it is; I'm enough of a realist to know that. But that doesn't mean I like it. Political fundraising is a double-edged sword. Accepting money from wealthy donors and industrialists— like the ones in this room—means politicians are beholden to them, whether they want to admit it or not. It's virtually impossible to take their money now and then tell them to go fuck themselves later if they don't like how you're going to vote on a crucial bill. On the other hand, without the money to keep winning elections and stay in office, you don't get the chance to do what good you *can* do for your constituents. And that's the whole point of being there. Theoretically.

We reach our table and stand behind our chairs. A few people are already seated at other tables and more are making their way here. "Hey, what happened to your arm?" Kevin holds my limb up. There's a red scratch running the length of my right forearm.

"Oh, I caught it on a doorknob this morning." I rub the mark absently as I lie through my teeth. In truth, it happened when London slammed my arm up against the metal building he had me pinned against while he pounded into me. I grip the chair back and smile down at my shoes. I can't believe I did that, out in the open where anyone could see, but I can't regret it. When I'd looked into those amazing green eyes when we'd landed and saw the exhilaration and triumph that matched my own, we hadn't needed words. We both knew what we needed. And when he did speak, that *accent*…damn.

I hadn't wanted to shower his scent off of me so soon, but it's for the best. Maybe now I can stop thinking about him.

Kevin hums, accepting my excuse, and flags down a waiter to snag us both glasses of champagne. He's in the middle of telling me about one of his cases when I hear a familiar voice call my name.

"Cassidy—just the person I was looking for." Tall and distinguished with his steel-gray hair and pale blue eyes, my father gives me one of his political smiles as he leads two men over to our table. One I think is Mr. Coleman, and the other is about my age. *Uh oh.*

"Bert, you remember my daughter, Cassidy?" He eyes me like a prized mare. "Cass, this is Bert Coleman and his son, Jack." I shake hands dutifully with him, a practiced smile on my lips. I know my role.

"Mr. Coleman, so nice to see you again. It's been a few years." He's over sixty, with almost white hair and an impressive paunch. "I don't believe I've ever met your son, though." I turn toward the tall, dark-haired man waiting patiently to the side.

"Jack is set to replace his father as Coleman Energy CEO in a few years, once Bert finally decides to take life a little easier," my father adds, and Bert lets out a guffaw.

"I'm not ready to go yet!" He's full of good-old-boy cordiality, and claps a hand on Jack's shoulder. "But yes, Jack here is more than up to the task. He's my right-hand man now as it is. Coleman Energy wouldn't be where it is without him."

Jack gives me a self-deprecating smile, and I take his offered hand. He has classic good looks and a firm grip. "A pleasure to meet you, Cassidy." His deep voice is smooth and melodious, but it doesn't alleviate my growing suspicions about being set up... again.

Waiters begin to scurry about and more people have taken their seats. My mother joins us, two more people in tow. "Bob, let's take our seats," she says to my father, and beams at me. "Cassidy, I believe you're sitting here, next to Jack. It'll give you two some time to get acquainted. You have a lot in common!"

Bingo. I give my brother an accusatory glare, but he looks as surprised as I am. It's *me* who's being set up, not him. My father and Bert are giving each other congratulatory grins as they and the other table guests begin to take their seats.

Jack holds my chair out and gives me an expectant smile. "Cassidy?"

Mentally cursing a blue streak, I slide into my seat and try to pretend I don't feel the walls closing in around me.

chapter two

Murphy's Law No. 272: Wedding preparations turn otherwise happy people into stress bombs.

THE AIRPORT IS PERFECT FOR ONE OF MY FAVORITE PASTIMES: PEOPLE watching. I'm at the arrivals gate at LaGuardia, waiting for my twin sister's flight, which is delayed due to a storm or some other such nonsense. She's spending the week in New York with me in search of the ultimate wedding dress. No matter how much I protest, this wedding is steaming ahead full throttle.

I'm relaxed as I can be in one of the stiff chairs after having done a few walkabouts through the terminal. You can learn a lot about people, watching them handle the barely contained chaos of an airport.

The balding businessman in a three-piece suit paces relentlessly in front of the screens as if each pass will bring the plane in faster. He's wired tight, this one. A stress bomb waiting to go off.

There's a swarm of departing passengers hovering around the baggage carousel, jockeying for position. It won't get your bags here faster, that I can assure you.

A military man arriving from God only knows where drops his bags to the floor as he's greeted by his family. It's raw emotion at being reunited. There's real tears and genuine affection that's often lacking when you get busy with living the day-to-day.

The couple to my left refuse to speak to each other, sitting ramrod straight in their chairs, arms crossed with their scowls firmly in place. Life is too fucking short to be that unhappy.

Then there's another couple who can't keep their hands off each other. The man keeps his hand on his lady's lower back while they wait for their order at the coffee stand. He takes a squeeze of her waist and bends to whisper next to her ear. She looks at him like he hung the moon.

I don't have the faintest idea what that feels like—to look at someone like that or have someone else do the same, but it does make me think about my *fly girl*. I've been thinking about her a lot over the last couple of weeks. I don't have a name. I don't have a clue where she lives or what she does for a living, but fuck if I can't get her out of my head.

Every curve of her body, every single little breathy moan against my neck is etched in my brain, and there's not a damn thing I can do about it. She's a mystery. A mystery that makes me think about things other than my band and our next tour.

She was wild, a risk-taker with a spur-of-the-moment spirit. It's rare to find that. I'm also not forgetting those gray-blue eyes any time soon. The streets of Manhattan offer no answers. In a crowd of hundreds, I find myself looking for those eyes, for that silky blond, sleek-cut hair. Even now as I wait for Sydney's flight, I find myself lingering on every tall blonde that remotely resembles her. I'd call it pathetic if one of my bandmates were doing the same thing. Best to keep this mini obsession to myself, I think.

My phone chimes with an alert, and I grin at the message from Syd.

Syd: Look up!

I follow her instruction, and there she is, pulling her luggage behind her, smiling from ear to ear as she weaves through the dispersing crowd. Fuck, I've missed her. Syd and I are close, and between the insanity of her wedding planning and the Redfall tour schedule, we haven't had a chance to see each other as much as we typically do.

I'm up from the chair, lifting her off the ground as she barrels toward me. Her arms wrap around me, giving me a full-bodied hug before I set her down.

"Way to keep a low profile." She taps my sunglasses.

"Why is everyone always saying that to me?" I take the handle of her suitcase and start to lead her out of the terminal.

"Oh, I don't know. Maybe because bright yellow sunglasses in an airport tend to draw attention."

"Hey! Hannah picked these out, I'll have you know." I shove them on top of my head.

Syd nudges me in the side. "Of course she did. How is the poppet?"

"Utterly adorable in every way. She's got Cam wrapped around her finger." I move around a man carrying enough bags to make him look like a Sherpa.

"Mmm. I think that's probably fair to say for the lot of you, yeah?"

I grin down at her. "Absolutely. How was the flight?"

"Much better thanks to your upgrade to first class. You didn't have to do that, you know."

"I'm just sorry I couldn't send the jet. Kennedy's hoarding it again." I roll my eyes, taking us through the revolving door and out to the car park.

"Where's he off to now?"

"Visiting his parents in Minnesota with Abby. A little family time before the last half of our tour."

"You're back home next, right?"

"Indeed we are. London, Manchester, Dublin, a few other stops in there." I fish my keys from my jacket pocket just as Syd breaks into hysterical laughter.

"This is you, isn't it?" She shakes her head, stopping beside the VW van as she gives it the once over.

"How did you know that?" Opening the back door, she giggles.

"No one else in New York would want a pink VW van."

"I'll have you know, this is a hot commodity." I slap my hand on the bonnet. "The Pink Tornado has its own Twitter account and everything." I haul her bag into the back and slam the door shut.

"You've seriously lost the plot. Everyone will know where you are all the time."

I shake my head and open the passenger door for her. "They know that already. What's the difference?"

Closing her door once she's buckled in, I round the VW and climb in behind the wheel. "Besides, I get tired of being carted around in black SUVs all the time."

"Poor baby. Such a hard life you live," Syd teases and pats my head as I fire up the van and navigate through the car park.

I only get horned once turning out of the maze that is the airport, and then we're on our way. "What's on the agenda then? Let's hear it." Syd turns down the volume on the cassette deck, giggling under her breath.

"I can't believe you kept this radio. Who has cassette tapes anymore?" She leans back in the seat, putting her feet up on the dash. I can feel the tension rolling off her now that we're alone, and that's not normal. She lets out a long sigh, running her hand through her hair.

"They're making a comeback, and why are you avoiding the question?"

Sliding my sunglasses back on, I glance over at her. She looks tired. Worry lines crease her forehead. "I'm not avoiding, and I've got appointments at four dress shops." She lets out a frustrated sigh. "So far."

"Only four?"

"I've tried on over a hundred dresses!" She throws her arms up. "I can't find anything! They're all too poofy or—" Her arms flail. "I don't even know!"

"Maybe it's a sign." I'm only half joking.

"It's not a sign," Syd growls, and shoots me a withering glare.

"Sure it is. The universe is telling you not to get married." I change lanes, the VW engine complaining as I accelerate down the highway. Might be time for the good ole Pink Tornado to get looked at.

She punches my shoulder. Hard. Damn, twin. "You need to be nice to Philip," she warns.

"I'm trying. Honest to fuck I am."

"No. You're being an ass is what you are," she fires back.

"Tell me what you see in him. He's boring as fuck."

"He's a good man, Sean." Syd's voice softens, and I know I've hit a nerve. "He loves me."

"Everyone loves you, Syd. It's as easy as breathing."

"I know he's not Simon." Syd gives my arm a gentler squeeze than her punch. Simon was Syd's first husband. We went to the music academy together. He was one of my best mates growing up. He was always up for a good time, and typically, he was the one who suggested that we ditch school to sneak into a music festival we had no business being at, or ride the tube into the middle of the night, hopping off at random stops just to explore. We shared a love of wanderlust, a love that I'm still happy to indulge.

He came from a family with a rich military history. Simon joining the special forces was a given. Unfortunately, he didn't make it back from his second tour in Afghanistan. It devastated Syd and me. Even though that was years ago now, I don't think that's something you ever really get over, and I wonder if Syd's stressed-out mood has more to do with memories of Simon than it does with finding the perfect dress.

"You're damn right he's not."

"Sean…" I can hear the frustration in Syd's voice, and it kills me. I only want her to be happy.

"I'm sorry. But you should listen to your big brother, you know."

"We were born at the same time," she argues.

"I was born two minutes before you. That makes me older and definitely wiser."

Syd's laughter fills the VW, and I'm glad to be steering us away from conversations that will only serve to bring her down. Syd's right. I'm being an ass about Philip, but the guy just rubs me the wrong way.

It's like he's never colored outside the lines in his life. I don't get the attraction she has to him, but at the end of the day, I'm not the one who has to live with him, thank fuck.

"I'll try harder," I concede, if only to banish the gray cloud she's got hanging over her head at what should be the happiest time in her life.

"Goodness gracious." Syd glances over her shoulder at me as she stands in front of the panoramic windows. The Manhattan skyline stretches out before us in all its glory. Penthouse views are seriously worth their weight in gold. "Women must just eat this up."

"Now, you know the law, Syd."

"Never let them on your home turf," we repeat at the same time.

"Still, it's a shame not to share this." She drops into one of the sofas facing the view. "Nice touch with the Union Jack pattern here." She pats the soft leather. "Seriously, the lines in here are incredible."

"Ah, the architect in you awakens. You're supposed to be on vacation." I pass her a cup of tea, and she takes it between both hands.

"I am. That doesn't mean I can't appreciate a work of art when I see it. I knew this place would be amazing when you showed me the plans. Did you go with the privacy glass?" Syd glances up at the vaulted ceiling with a smile. I got Syd's opinion on a few places I considered purchasing last year. New York has always felt like a second home to me. I thrive on the energy and on how you can discover something new about it every day. It was a no-brainer for me to buy here.

I shrug, taking a seat in the chair beside her. "Of course. Just because I don't mind people staring at me during the day, doesn't mean I don't want privacy at home. Even if it's just a place to sleep."

"That cost you over fifteen million," she replies dryly.

"Real estate is a good investment. That's a law from the famous Chapman family. See? Cam's good for something."

She laughs, curling her legs under her, and settling in. "I'm glad you're here, Syd. Better yet, I'm glad you agreed to let me take you shopping. Maybe that's been your problem. I haven't been with you when you've been trying on these dresses."

She grins at me over her cup. "That must be it."

My leg bounces with pent-up energy as she sips her tea. "Are you absolutely positive you want to get married?"

She closes her eyes, dropping her head back against the cushions on the sofa. "Philip's mother is driving me crazy. She's got an opinion about everything! The lighting, the music, the length of the long-stemmed roses she wants. The guest list alone is enough to put me in an early grave."

I scowl, listening to her. "You're not exactly painting a convincing picture of this marriage business."

"You didn't let me finish." She takes a sip of tea before continuing, "Despite all of the craziness, and his semicontrolling mother, I love him. So yes, I'm absolutely positive I want to get married." She fingers the rim of the teacup. "I can't imagine my life without him."

"Then tomorrow, even if we have to scour every single shop in the city, we'll find you the biggest, best, most badass wedding dress we can find."

Her smile is everything I need to see. If it makes her happy, I swallow my damn opinion about Philip and marriage in general. For now at least.

Cassidy

Whistling to myself, I head downstairs to my shop. I watched the sunrise during my morning run, and helped a little old man find the bagel shop across the street. It's been a good morning so far.

I set the coffee to brew in the little break room in the back, and then make my way to the front of the shop to raise the window shades. The little old man waves at me as he leaves the bakery, and I wave back with a smile. Such a sweetie.

The bell over the door rings and I turn to see my assistant, Riya Patel, bustle inside. She's old enough to be my mother, almost as wide as she is tall, and a genius with clients. The enticing aroma of curry wafts from her lunch basket. Her grandparents emigrated to the States with their six children from a town near Mumbai. She grew up working in their restaurant on the edge of Greenwich Village and makes the best chicken curry I've ever had. Riya and her husband own the restaurant now, but Riya hasn't worked there since she went to accounting school. She's a whiz with numbers and has a marvelous touch with our many difficult clients. I'd be lost without her.

"Morning," she chirps, lowering her head scarf and sweeping past me to put her lunch in the refrigerator. "Today was a real winner. You'll never guess this time."

I cock my head and pause arranging the flowers in the salon. "Red-headed serial killer?"

"No. Besides, how would you know a serial killer to look at one?" She frowns at me as she comes back out of the break room, smoothing a wrinkle out of her long tunic. "That's the problem with serial killers, no? You never know until it's too late. Next guess."

"Bodybuilder carrying a cello?"

She rolls her eyes. "No."

"Biker with a poodle?"

"Nope. And you're displaying a shocking lack of imagination."

"Fine. I give up." I flop down into one of the comfortable satin-covered chairs surrounding the small riser where brides can model potential dresses. This is our usual game; I try to guess what outrageous or unusual thing she's seen on her morning subway commute.

"Bagpipes." She shivers with a grimace. "Being played by a man wearing a yellow poncho and black rubber pants."

I laugh. "Seriously? Isn't it a little early for bagpipes?"

"*That's* what you think is the weirdest thing in that scenario?" She shakes her head at me and fluffs one of the throw pillows. "And it's never a good time for bagpipes." I laugh again.

"Aw, come on. I like bagpipes. And rubber is very practical—it's supposed to rain later."

She throws the pillow at me, making me duck. "You're awfully chipper this morning. Did you get laid?"

I fire the pillow back at her. "Of course not!" I rise with as much dignity as I can muster. "It's just a lovely day, that's all. Why not be in a good mood?"

Chuckling under her breath, she moves to the front desk and flips through today's appointments. "Why not indeed?" She makes a notation in our schedule and taps the pen against her chin. "Hmm. Busy day today. Five fittings and three dress shoppers."

"Yep. And I'm not sure how many people the shoppers are bringing with them." Fittings usually only take thirty minutes or so, but dress shoppers can take hours depending on the size of their entourage, and the number of meltdowns the bride has. If the bride brings her mother *and* future mother-in-law with her, as well as a best friend, bridesmaid, or other family members, it can take forever.

She tosses the pen down and stops on her way back to the break room to straighten the collar on my blue taffeta wrap shirt. "I'll get the big dressing room ready if you'll prepare the snack plates."

"No problem." In the kitchen, I pull down the small china plates and get the storage containers out of the fridge. We don't offer snacks to everyone, but for longer appointments, finger foods and a glass of champagne add to the experience. It took a little experimentation, but I finally figured out the least messy items we could serve. Bite-size is the key. Tiny quiches and puffs from the bakery across the street, as well as cherry tomatoes, stuffed mushrooms, and grapes seem to work. I wrap up the various plates and put those that need to be cold back in the fridge just as my cell phone rings in my pants pocket. I answer without looking and regret it instantly.

"Cassidy. *Finally.*"

I groan mentally. "Mother."

"Don't you 'Mother' me," she snaps. "Why have you been avoiding my calls?"

"I haven't been avoiding you." That's actually exactly what I've been doing for the past couple of weeks. Ever since she and my father decided to set me up with a major donor.

"Baloney. Have you been avoiding Jack Coleman's calls, too? He's a very nice man, Cassidy. Would it really be that awful to go out with him? You seemed to have a nice time at the fundraiser."

Cringing, I sink down into a kitchen chair at the end of the counter and prop an elbow against a cabinet. I had, in fact, also been dodging Jack's calls. Not that he was awful; far from it. But I'm not in the mood for another one of my mother's attempts at matchmaking. "He was fine, Mom. But I'm not looking to get into anything right now—"

"Who says you have to 'get into anything'?" She huffs. "Really, Cassidy, it's just dinner. Why do you always overdramatize everything?"

I grit my teeth. "I'm not—"

"Besides, Jack and his father are some of your father's biggest donors," she continues, not listening to my protest. "Honestly, after *everything* your father has done for you, being friendly to Jack is the *least* you could do for him."

The sunshine streaming in the front window seems to dim. I knew it was coming. It always does. Usually she's more subtle; this thing with the Colemans must really be important to Dad if she's pulling out the big guns so soon.

I finger the crease in my black slacks and take a calming breath. "Fine. If he calls, I'll answer," I say softly, all my irritation at being manhandled by my mother dampened. "I have to get ready for my first client now."

"Thank you, Cassidy." She pauses, and just when I think she may actually apologize for playing their trump card, she continues, "You'll have fun with Jack. He's just the type of man you need."

"Right. Good-bye, Mother." I stare at the phone for a few minutes after ending the call. My earlier cheerfulness is replaced with the residual shame I can't quite get rid of, no matter how many counselors I've seen since California. Riya is singing to herself in the other room, and I imagine her setting aside the dresses I need for today's fittings. I close my eyes and picture the rows of dresses that will be tried on today, all of which are my own design. Women will come here today and find the dresses of their dreams. This shop has been *my* dream since college.

And none of it would've been possible without my father. And his staff.

I hear the bell ring in the entry, followed by Riya greeting my first client, and I immediately stand, plastering a professional smile on my face. Time to go to work.

"I thought she'd never leave!"

I smile at Riya's declaration. Mrs. Finch, our last fitting, had indeed been a chore. The dress is for the premiere of her husband's latest movie, and she felt the need to remind me *four* times that she chose me over more well-known designers the studio had encouraged her to use. By the time we were done, I'd almost wished she'd chosen one of them.

"Ah, well." I rub the small of my back, trying to ease the slight ache from bending over so much. "She'll look fabulous and everyone will know why." Directors' wives don't get much media exposure, but they do talk. All the women associated with the production will know who's wearing what and by whom by the end of the evening.

Riya bustles around straightening the already perfect salon area in preparation for our last shopper. Someone named Murphy-Kenton. In her email, she had mentioned that she had been on my website and had several dresses she wanted to try, but was open to whatever else I wanted to suggest. Eyeing the row of dresses lining the salon, I shrug. Without seeing her, there is no telling what will be best for her body type. I'll know soon enough.

The office phone rings, and Riya calls me to take it. I'm still mentally going over options for the mysterious Ms. Kenton, and am caught off guard by the male voice echoing down the line.

"Cassidy?"

My eyes fly open. "Oh, um, Jack." Good God, my mother works fast. "How nice to hear from you."

"I'm back in town this week and was wondering if you'd be free for dinner tonight." He sounds so polite. His Midwest twang is soft and familiar; I wonder if he knows my mother's using him in her latest Machiavellian plot.

"You just 'happen' to be back in town, do you?" I can't help the bite in my voice. "Are you really going to say that you haven't talked to someone from my father's staff today?"

"Uh, no, I wouldn't because I did," he says, surprised. "We had meetings about a bill he's proposing on drilling rights. We were supposed to meet last week, but I had to go to Dubai. Why?"

I rub my temple, trying to calm down. It's not fair of me to take this out on him. "No reason." I take a deep breath. "Yes, I'm free. What did you have in mind?"

"Excellent! Do you like Italian? There's a new restaurant in Brooklyn I've been wanting to try. What do you think?"

I grimace. He also 'just happens' to know Italian is my favorite food? My mother has been thorough. "Sounds good. Is seven all right? I have appointments until six."

"Perfect. Where shall I pick you up?"

I give him my address, and we hang up. Sinking down into a chair, I drag a hand through my hair, fingering the ends of my bob carefully. Time for another haircut. The predicted weather front has arrived, and I stare out the rain-streaked front window, trying to sort out my emotions.

My parents have shoved one man after another under my nose for the last few years, each one a dedicated member of my father's party and—surprise!—helpful to my father's cause. A senator's son, a powerful lobbyist, a campaign strategist, a media pundit, and several donors. They've done the same type of thing with my brother, except he doesn't mind as much. He looks at it as an easy dating service he doesn't have to pay for. Besides, they don't have the same leverage over him that they do over me.

It's not that I'm not grateful to my father; rather, I hate the constant reminder of why I'm in his debt. No one should have to relive that type of thing. A crack of thunder outside rattles the windows, but it's not the reason my hands are suddenly sweaty. I clench my fists, close my eyes, and try to push away the sudden images from years ago that had made my life a living hell. If only I'd gone into the bathroom with Sara, or if I'd encouraged her to leave the party sooner, or studied for my marketing class instead of going with her in the first place…

The phone jumps into the air with the force of my fist banging on the desk. "It's not your fault, damn it!" I growl softly to myself. I know it's true, but even so many years later, I can't stop my mental self-flagellation.

It's high time I get over this, I know. But just when I'm about to tell my parents that they can no longer count on me as a chip in my father's political games, I receive another report from the off-the-books web service my father employs letting me know of their latest efforts on my behalf. And I cave. I could never afford that type of ruthless cyber-maintenance on my own. I wish I could be sure he'd continue it even if I decided not to play ball any longer, but the sad truth is that I'm not. My father never does anything without expecting something in return. Period.

He wasn't always like this, though. I look up at the dust motes swirling under the overhead light. They remind me of the snowfall back home in Cheyenne when I was small and Dad would take us to look for a Christmas tree. He used to carry me on his shoulders so I wouldn't get stuck in the deep snow. It made me feel like the queen of the world. Sighing, I let me head fall back. I know my father loves me; he never would have done all he's done to help me if he didn't. He's just become so…hard over the years. I can't remember the last time he smiled when he wasn't in front of the cameras.

Folding my arms on the hard surface, I rest my forehead on my wrist. I'm so tired. Tired of the never-ending cycle, tired of being a pawn, tired of being afraid…just tired. Will it really kill me to spend a few pleasant hours with a nice man, regardless of how it comes about? Jack is certainly a better option than some of the men I've been paired with. He's well educated but isn't snobby about it, he can keep up his end of a conversation without constantly talking about himself, and he doesn't chew with his mouth open. What more could I possibly want?

A mop of silky black hair above a pair of vivid green eyes suddenly fills my mind, and I sit up abruptly, my heart racing. Damn, not again! It's been weeks since my British Bang. Why can't I forget that guy?

Oh, please. It's not that big of a mystery. I pick up a paper clip from the desk and lean back in my chair, twisting the tiny piece of metal between my fingers. Besides it being one of the hottest fucks I've ever enjoyed, it was completely spontaneous and entirely on my terms. I knew I was in for a treat from the minute he slammed my back against the wall of the hangar. Maybe it was the forbidden aspect of it. Anyone could've found us back there, and if they'd found out who I was, there would've been hell to pay. Or maybe it was just him—powerful, passionate, and so damn *present*.

I haven't felt that alive in ages. If ever.

My stranger has been front and center in several of my dreams since then. I startle awake, tangled in my bedsheets with my heart racing, and sure I can feel his strong hands on my body and his mouth on mine. Unlike our real tryst, I always kiss him in my dreams. It almost makes me wish I'd actually kissed him. Kissing is so intimate, though. A different kind of intimacy than fucking. Sex is an exchange of raw, mutual pleasure. But kissing—for me—involves emotions, and I can't afford those. Besides, I kinda loved he was frustrated that I wouldn't. He certainly found another way to use his mouth on me.

"What's that smile for?" Riya stands on the other side of the desk with a smirk. I quickly wipe said smile off my face and stand, dropping the now mangled paper clip on the desktop.

"Nothing." I smooth down my shirt, feeling my face flush. "Is the salon room ready? It's almost time for our last appointment."

Riya crosses her arms across her ample bosom, obviously seeing through my attempt at nonchalance. "Of course it's ready." She cocks her head to one side in amusement. "You don't want to talk now? Fine. We both know you'll tell me eventually."

She's right, damn it. "Whatever," I mutter, waving my hand in dismissal and ignoring her chuckle. "I, uh, need to run to the bathroom. I'll be back in a second." Her chuckle becomes full-fledged laughter as I walk away.

A few minutes later, feeling less, um, agitated, I head toward the reception area just as the bell rings. I can hear Riya's greeting and the response. Ah, our last client is English, based on her voice. I wonder if she lives here or is just visiting. Not sure why she'd come all the way to New York for a wedding dress, but stranger things have happened. Brides can be weird.

"Ms. Kenton? I'm Cassidy Skinner. It's a pleasure to meet you." I shake her hand, which is cold from being outside. She's slim and as tall as me, with a long neck and gorgeous auburn hair, and I immediately imagine which dresses and designs I'll show her.

"Please, call me Sydney. Thank you for fitting me in today," she says, her voice deep and melodious. "I'm at my wits' end, truly. But I saw your website and was immediately encouraged."

"Well, I have a few things in mind that should definitely interest you." I give her a warm smile, instantly liking her. "And you can call me Cass."

A whoosh of cold, rain-fresh air sweeps in the foyer as the door opens behind her, ringing the bell. I can see a shock of violet hair above her head and hear a low muttering that makes her grin. "I hope you don't mind," she says, an apology in her eyes. "I brought my brother to help me make up my mind. Sean?" She glances behind her. "Come meet Cass Skinner. Her designs are amazing!"

"Oh, aye?" He steps up next to her, shaking off the rain like a dog, and my mouth drops open when I'm faced with a pair of piercing green eyes staring at me in shock.

Sweet crispy Christ!

chapter three

*Murphy's Law No. 283: When fate surprises you, best
to hold on and enjoy the ride.*

Sean

"LONDON." THERE'S THAT BREATHLESS VOICE I'VE WHACKED OFF TO more than once.

"Fly-girl?"

"What's going on?" I barely register Syd's voice as my eyes meet my mystery woman's pale blue-gray ones. Those eyes and this woman have played hell in my head for weeks. It's almost like she's not real. Her eyes lift to my hair, and she gets a little crease on her forehead as she studies me.

"This is not happening right now," my beauty mumbles under her breath.

"I've been looking everywhere for you," I blurt out, taking a step closer to her. I inhale her scent and it's like coming home. Lavender and something sweet and tempting.

"Here I am."

"Cass? You said her name was Cass?" I turn to my sister who's got her arms crossed as she sizes me up. I recognize that look.

"You two know each other? Like, know-know each other? As in the biblical sense?" Syd sounds horrified, her arms flailing now.

"I don't think the folks in the good book would necessarily approve of the way we know each other."

"Oh God," my blond beauty murmurs, heat coloring her cheeks.

"Mmm. Pretty sure my name's Sean, but I do remember you calling me God. More than once." She doesn't return my smirk. "Keep doing that."

"You slept with my potential wedding dress designer?" I cringe at the tone of Syd's voice. Pretty sure that's a level designed only for wolves to hear.

"I wouldn't say we did any sleeping."

"Stop talking," Cass hisses, her eyes darting to Sydney before they settle back on mine.

"Come on in out of the rain, and we'll get you warmed up!" I turn to the sound of another voice. A smiling older woman waddles her way toward us. "Sydney, yes? I'm Riya. And who is this?" She's almost out of breath when she nears us, and she reaches up to poke at my hair. "What in the world was going through your head there?" She lifts her chin, with her hands on her hips, scowling at me.

"Aye, uh…" I rub my hand across the back of my neck under her scrutinizing gaze. I can't remember the last time I was intimidated by anyone. Not going to lie. This Riya woman kind of scares me.

"This is my brother, Sean," Syd grinds out. "Although I'm thinking of disowning him."

"Hmmm." Riya glances between me and Cass, who seems to be struck speechless. I'm happy just to stare at Cass. Fuck, she's beautiful. Even as she's looking like a deer caught in the headlights, the urge to touch her is strong. "Well, why don't we get you some tea, and we can talk about your big day," the helpful Riya so marvelously suggests, steering my sister in the direction of a smaller sitting area.

"That's a brilliant idea, Riya," I begin. "Don't you think so, Cass? What is Cass short for...Cassandra?" The corners of her mouth turn up at my voice, but then she grabs the sleeve of my leather jacket and tugs me forward.

"It's just Cassidy." She blows out a breath and turns to Syd. "If you'll just excuse us for a moment. Riya will get you some tea. This won't take long."

"Now, now. It might take long. I've been known to fu—" Cassidy's hand flies up to cover my mouth, and I take the opportunity to nip at her fingers.

"If you know what's good for you, you'll keep quiet," Cassidy warns, causing Sydney's laughter to fill the shop.

"You really don't know him at all, do you? Sean? Keep quiet? Good luck with that." Sydney all but snorts, and I can't argue with her. Everything she's said is true.

I don't mind Cassidy tugging me across the dark hardwood floor. It means I get to check out her round arse, perfectly kissed by those black trousers that make her sweet legs look even longer. I know what it feels like to have those beauties wrapped around me. Judging by the press of my cock against my jeans, it's safe to say he remembers too.

She whips open a dressing room door and shoves me inside and leans back on the door as it closes behind her. "What in the hell are you doing here? Who sent you?" she whisper-hisses, blowing her hair away from her face. I like that she seems to be all flustered.

"I beg your pardon?"

"Who's paying you to do this?" she rants in an accusatory tone, hands balled into fists at her hips.

"Do what now?"

"Find me! Stalk me! God, why can't you all just give it a rest?"

"Love, I don't know what you're—"

"Don't 'love' me. I can't... that accent." She closes her eyes and grips the handle of the door as if she can't quite trust herself and needs something to hold onto. I like it. I like it a lot.

"You like my accent. At least you did when I was buried inside you."

Her eyes flash with heat as she eyes me. "You really don't know who I am?" She squints at me, as if gauging my intentions.

"I could ask you the same question. Until five minutes ago, all I knew about you was that you were an incredibly sexy woman I can't seem to stop thinking about." I'm trapped in this pull between us that has me stepping forward. My fingers trail a path up her side. She leans into my touch slightly as I continue, "You don't know who I am, do you?"

"Until five minutes ago"—she throws my own words back at me—"all I knew about you was that you were afraid to skydive, but not afraid to fuck outside." Her hand on the handle of the door stays put, but her other hand reaches out to grip my jacket. "A man who knows what he wants."

"That I am, Cassidy."

Her eyes dart up to my hair. "Why dye your hair purple?"

"Because I can."

"It's that simple?" Her eyes are trained on my lips.

"It can be." I slide my hand against her neck, feeling her pulse thunder before I brush my thumb against her jaw. "I want to kiss you. I want to know what you taste like."

She swallows, her lips parting. "You already do. More than anyone has in a while." And doesn't that make me feel like a fucking god.

"And since?"

She shakes her head. "No. No one since."

"Me either. See? We have something in common."

"I have a date tonight," she blurts out. I take a step back, feeling as if she's slapped me in the face.

"Cancel it."

She turns her head, and I can see her reflection in the mirrors on each of the walls. The dressing room is large, a glow from a vintage overhead light softly dancing over her wicked curves. "I can't."

I hold her gaze in the mirror to the left. "You can't or you won't?"

"Both."

She ducks her head and I slide my fingers under her chin, tipping it up so she meets my eyes. "I'll take you on the best date you've ever had. Better than this yawn-fest dinner at a typical Italian restaurant with a git who has the charisma of a dinner napkin."

Those pretty eyes of hers widen. "How did you—"

"Because Italian's the safe place to take a date." I press my other hand against the door, framing her in, and lean forward to skim my lips against her ear. "Safe and boring. You're neither of those things, Cassidy."

"God…" It comes out strangled from her tempting lips.

"I like it when you call me that." She purses her lips, shaking her head as she releases my jacket and pushes against my chest.

"I don't even know you."

There's no way I'm letting her get away with that bullshit, so I lean forward, my lips hovering a hairsbreadth from hers. "We can rectify that." Fuck, she smells good. I want to bury myself in her scent.

Leaning back, I straighten up to my full six-four height and hold my hand out. "Sean Murphy. English. Thirty-seven. Musician. Drummer, actually, for the band Redfall. You may have heard of us. I'll try not to hold it against you if you haven't." That little adorable crease in her forehead appears again as she cocks her head. "I have a twin sister, Sydney, for whom I will hopefully drop an obscene amount of money in your shop, thus earning me a date and maybe if I'm extremely fortunate, more time with you. I've been to every continent on the planet—including Antarctica. I hate cruises as I get deathly seasick, although I've been on nine of them, and I would love nothing more than to spread you out on that chaise in the corner and fuck you until you can't remember your name."

She stares back at me, looking stunned if I'm being honest. "I… I just… I don't even know where to begin with that."

I reach around her. She takes a quick breath as I release her death grip on the handle and set her hand in mine. "Now, you would shake my hand and say something like: Cassidy Skinner." I drag my gaze down her delectable body. "Thirty-two?" She's having trouble fighting her grin as she nods. "American, although I can't quite place the accent. Kick-ass dress designer. You have a…"

I slowly tilt my head forward and she answers quickly, "Brother. I've never been anywhere outside the US, but I'd love to take a cruise because you'd be able to see so many islands all in one trip, and those buffets! I mean have you seen pictures of them? Who wouldn't love a midnight buffet at sea?"

I chuckle at her rambling, frantic description. "Who indeed?" I mumble, but the spell is broken, and she releases my hand as if it's on fire.

"I need to get to your sister." I nod and take a reluctant step back as she smooths back her sleek hair. "Try to salvage what's left of this appointment. If that's even possible at this point." She takes a deep breath and opens the door, pausing to look at me over her shoulder. "God, I can't believe this."

"Of all the wedding shops in all of New York, hmm? Must be fate."

She shakes her head, striding away from me again. Why does it feel like I'll always be chasing her?

Cassidy

This can't be happening to me.

New York has something like a billion people in it. How in God's green earth did he manage to fall into my life again? Clenching my fists, I try to get a grip on my churning emotions. Even as angry as I am right now—and I *am* angry—I have this weird bubbling feeling inside. Like I felt on Christmas morning when I was little, before we went downstairs to see all the presents under the tree. I don't know what to do with that.

His footsteps fall heavily behind me as I march toward the salon. There is no way I'm going to look back at him. He's a member of Redfall? Could he possibly be telling the truth? I try to dredge up what I know about the band, but my recall is shot—my thoughts are a jumbled mess. I have no idea how I'm going to save my current situation.

Disappointment wells inside me. Sydney seems so nice; I would've loved working with her.

Regardless, I plaster on a smile as I rejoin her and Riya, who's doing her usual wonderful job of settling a prospective client. Sydney sits on one of the satin-covered chairs with a cup of tea in her hand and gives me a wary look.

"Everything all right?" She glances over my shoulder with a slight frown, before refocusing on me.

"Certainly," I chirp, and sit next to her. "Now, then. I apologize for my...unprofessional greeting. Although I hope you're still interested in seeing what I can offer you, I completely understand if you're not."

"Why wouldn't she be?" Sean plops down on the other side of her, but I still refuse to acknowledge him. Strangely, so does his sister. "After some of the shite we've seen today, I'm looking forward to seeing something she'd actually consider."

Sweet crispy Christ, why can't he shut up for five seconds? Sydney glances down at her cup, a smile fighting to come out, and then back at me. "As much as I hate to admit it, he's right. Today's search hasn't been very fruitful." After a peek at her brother, who can't seem to stop staring at me, she tilts her head and gives me a cryptic smile. "I have a good feeling about you though, Cassidy, regardless of..." She waves her hand toward her brother, who pouts at her. "I still want to see some of the designs I saw on your website. Can we start over?"

Relief courses through me and I return her smile. "Of course."

Sean claps his hands together and sits forward. "Fabulous! Show us what you've got, Fly-girl."

I shoot him a look, finally making eye contact, which I immediately regret when he gives me another one of those sexy smirks that make my heart thump. Damn. With a shake of my head, I straighten my shoulders and try to focus on my client.

"Okay, if you don't mind spending a few extra minutes, I'd like to start by asking a little about you. I could slap you in a dress that would look fabulous, but if it doesn't fit your personality, you'll never be comfortable in it."

She looks surprised, but pleased, and nods. I wonder if the other shops she's visited just threw dresses at her. "Well, I'm an architect—"

"Not *just* an architect," Sean interjects, his chest puffing with pride. "She won a RIBA national award two years ago."

At my confused look, Sydney's cheeks color as she explains, "It's a national British architecture award."

"She developed a plot of affordable, sustainable, small houses. Super-efficient, clean designs. They were brilliant." Sean's green eyes glow as he regards his twin. Besides sharing eye color, the two don't look that much alike until they smile. Then, the likeness is really remarkable. "They're already building in London and Leeds, with two more sites in Manchester and Glasgow planned."

It's impressive, but what's even more impressive is her modesty isn't false. Considering the people who hang around my father, I've learned to spot the humblebrag from a mile away, and I avoid it like the plague. Sydney's soft-spoken acknowledgement of her brother's praise is refreshing…and reassuring.

"What kind of ceremony are you planning?" Riya glides up behind Sean with a fresh pot of tea in her hand. He startles, but she merely smiles sweetly, and I have to bite back a laugh.

"Oh, something small this time," Sydney comments with a wry laugh, flipping her auburn hair over her shoulder. "Assuming we can get Philip's mother to agree."

This time. So she's been married before. Good to know. Generally speaking, a woman's first wedding is all about the *princess dress*. Big skirt or ornate headpiece…something they've been dreaming about since they were little. Women who are getting married a second time have usually gotten all that out of their system and are looking for something a little simpler. Don't get me wrong—I can help a woman rock a princess dress. But simpler dresses can be more challenging. And I like a challenge.

There's a hint of sorrow in her eyes as she says it, although, that somehow strikes me more as grief rather than the pain of a divorce. Whatever her story, this isn't the time to dwell on it, especially if her first husband died.

I lean forward to draw her attention. "How did you meet your fiancé? Philip, correct?"

Her smile returns, her eyes crinkling at the corners, and the tension in her arms eases. "He's amazing. He—" She throws a glare at her brother when he snorts at her description, but then returns her gaze to me. "We met at a party…"

We chat a bit more and I learn her engagement has been longer than most I'm acquainted with—almost two years. It's not because of cold feet; just random circumstances causing delays. Her intended is a lawyer—*barrister*—with a London firm that handles a lot of civil rights cases. He does sound amazing.

Whereas her flamboyant twin wears his creativity like a second skin, Sydney seems to temper hers with a veneer of forthright civility. I take careful notice of her slacks and the soft scarf draped over her knit shirt. The ensemble is comfortable and stylish, feminine without being fussy. I have a good idea of what to show her and am happy that a few of the designs she shows me on her tablet match.

The hardest part is keeping my focus on Sydney and not on the violet-haired, larger-than-life persona at her side.

"Okay! Let's get started."

After a half dozen gowns, we have two solid front-runners, neither of which were on her list when she entered the shop. One is a fishtail with a boat neckline and narrow sleeves, and the other a sleeveless column dress with a lace ribbon at the waist. Both are stunning on her, but—surprise—her brother is the sticking point.

"I like this one better." He looks her over with a shrewd eye as she stands in the sleeveless gown. He holds his hands up in front of him and peers at her through his fingers, like a viewfinder. "But something's still not quite right."

Riya, holding the other gown off to the side, rolls her eyes at him.

"It was a mistake to do this with you." Sydney huffs with

annoyance and crosses her arms. "You're pickier than I am. What's wrong with this one?"

"I think it reminds me too much of a Grecian urn I broke a few years ago at a friend's house." He gives me a sly glance. "Elton was pissed."

I mimic his sister's stance. "Elton? Are you trying to oh-so-subtly infer that you're friends with Elton John to impress me?"

"Maybe. Is it working?" He stretches his arms above his head, letting me get a peek at his abs when his T-shirt rises a few inches. The sight makes me catch my breath, but I think I manage to keep my expression neutral.

"Not even a little." I turn my back on his wounded expression to address his sister, who just chuckles and shakes her head.

"You two are just too fun," I think she mutters, before raising her voice. "Well, I like it." She turns and looks again in the floor-length mirrors surrounding the small dais she's standing on. A small frown flickers over her lips. "I think."

"We're close, but 'I think' isn't good enough. You need to look at it and know—this is *my* dress." I run my hand through my hair, refusing to give up yet. "You mentioned you were thinking of maybe having an outdoor wedding, something simple, right? Does your dress have to be long?"

Her eyes pop open. "No, no it doesn't. What do you have in mind?"

"I'll be right back." I turn and practically sprint out of the salon, across the store, and up the stairs to my apartment. I cross quickly to my private studio and pull a sample off a mannequin. After watching *Breakfast at Tiffany's* for the hundredth time, I had a burst of inspiration for this one. Audrey Hepburn always had such grace and style. Classically beautiful with a hint of whimsy, this design just might work.

Rejoining them downstairs, I usher Sydney back to the changing room. "Okay, this isn't finished yet, but it will give you an idea. Slip it on. I'll have to pin you in, because it doesn't have a zipper yet." I hold up the muslin prototype in front of her shocked face. "Picture it in silk."

"O-kay," she drawls, not sounding convinced. When I hear her gasp from behind the door, I know I'm on to something.

"Let's see it, Syd!" Sean calls over my shoulder, too close. So close that I lose my balance and stumble back against him. His strong arms slip around my shoulders, holding me firmly to his rock-hard chest. "Steady on, Fly-girl," he whispers, sending a thrill down my spine. Despite the sudden heat flowing through me, I wrench myself out of his embrace and manage to regain my footing just as his sister swings the door open and steps out. The look on her face says it all.

It's a retro-styled sheath dress with a raised portrait collar and three-quarter length sleeves. Even in muslin, it's elegant. It's feminine without being fussy and shows her long neck to great effect. The prototype is a little big for her, but there's no doubt…it's perfect.

"Now, as I said, picture it in silk—kind of a toasted-champagne color." I step behind her and quickly insert pins, tucking in a little here and there. "Not because I have anything against second-time brides wearing white, but because it would look smashing with your hair." I move back in front and touch the edge of her sleeves lightly. "A row of pearl drop buttons here." I touch again at a spot on the collar. "And a cluster here."

Riya walks around behind Sydney and raises her wealth of hair from her shoulders so she can see the effect in the mirrors. "A simple roll would look marvelous. And you can adorn it with more pearls and a veil, if you'd like." Still holding Sydney's hair with one hand, Riya reaches over and plucks one of our sample veils off a table. She gives it a quick shake then fluffs the short sheath of tulle over Sydney's head so it floats down in front of her face. Sydney sucks in a tiny breath, staring at herself in the mirror.

"This is it!" Sydney's smile is like the sun coming up, and I reflexively grin back at her. There's nothing in the world like finding that one dress—the dress you *know* is yours.

All three of us turn to look at the tall man leaning in the corner who, for once, is quiet. Instead of the teasing smile or imperious glower he's worn while appraising the gowns she's tried, he's staring at his sister with a soft smile of affection that touches my heart.

"You're right, Syd. That's it." He takes two long steps and envelopes his laughing twin in a hug that lifts her off her feet. Riya claps her hands together, gives me a wink, and then starts to hang up the other gowns. Back on her feet, Sydney swings around to me.

"I'm just so, so… Thank you!" She grabs my hands, her face a picture of joy and relief. "So, now what happens?"

"The hard part's over. I need to take your measurements before you leave today. I'll send you some fabric swatches to approve, and then I'll get to work. I'll contact you for a final fitting. The whole thing can be ready—" I waggle my head back and forth, considering—"about two weeks before your wedding. How does that sound?"

"Let's do it!" Her enthusiasm dims, and she bites her lip. "Um, what's the price tag?"

"Never you mind. I'll take care of everything." Sean slips his arm around her shoulder. "I told you, it's my gift to you. Is there anything else you need? Shoes, slinky things that will make Philip lose his shit that I don't really want to know about, stuff like that?"

She laughs. "I'm just happy you said his name without yawning." She gives his side a poke of her finger. "No, nothing else now."

"Great! Let's get your measurements then." I pull a measuring tape out of my pocket and usher her into the large dressing room, Riya following with her notepad.

"So, what's the damage?" Placing his hands flat on the reception desk, Sean leans across the shiny wood with a devilish smile. I consider—for half a second—doubling the amount just to spite him, but can't do it. I slide a note card with the price across the desk for him to pick up and examine. His eyes widen. "That's all? Fly-girl, you're selling yourself short."

I purse my lips. There are several digits on that paper. I know exactly what a reasonable price for my work is, and it's not cheap. Or is he just trying to show off again? "Terms of payment are half now, the rest upon completion. You can either have someone pick it up, or you can arrange to ship it to London."

"We can discuss the details during dinner tonight. Among other things." He plucks a credit card out of his wallet and hands it to Riya, who scuttles off to process the payment.

I step back, needing to put more distance between us. "I told you. I'm busy tonight." Crossing my arms protectively, I try not to flinch when he swiftly steps around the desk and into my space.

"Cassidy." He stretches my name out, making it sound like liquid velvet. "Cancel the boring git. You know you want to. I'll take you on a cruise. Anywhere you want to go."

I look up at him through my lashes. "Are you serious? I can't afford to take days off for a cruise, even if I did agree to go with you. Which I did not. And didn't you say you hated cruises?"

He shrugs. "You said you wanted to go on one. I'll rent a boat just for us tonight. We can cruise the harbor. See the Statue of Liberty all lit up." He runs a finger from my shoulder to my elbow and smirks when I can't suppress a shiver. My resolve is slipping, and I lean closer to him, entranced by those hooded green eyes and purring accent. "After all, I just dropped an impressive amount of money in here. Surely that's worth a little of your time?"

The haze lifts and I freeze, my shiver morphing from one of desire to one of disgust. "That's the second time you've said that. Are you serious? You honestly think I'm for sale? That you need to *bribe* me to spend more time with you? Like I'm some escort?"

His eyes snap open. "What? No! I didn't—"

"Hey! Are we ready to go?" Sydney joins us, a sly smile curling her lips, until she sees my eyes. "What's going on?"

"Here you are, Mr. Murphy." Riya comes out of the back room and hands him the receipt to sign and his credit card. He grins as if she's a groupie asking for an autograph, and scribbles on the paper.

"Call me Sean." He tries to take my hand, but I snatch it away and tuck my hair behind my ear to mask the movement. "And we're not leaving until you listen to me."

Sydney sighs. "Sean, what did you do now?"

"Nothing! I was joking! It was a joke!" He holds his hands out, his eyebrows practically climbing into his hairline.

"Hysterical," I deadpan, checking the clock on the wall when I see a dark car pull up outside. Reaching under the desk, I grab my purse and slip the strap over my head as I move. "Sydney, it's been a pleasure, truly." I take her hands and give her a warm smile. "I'm so excited to be able to help you with your special day. I'll be in touch the next day or two to send you the swatches."

"Wait a minute," Sean sputters. "Fly-girl...Cassidy...you can't possibly think—"

I ignore him and keep talking. "I'm sorry to leave so quickly, but I have an appointment I can't break. Riya? Can you please help them with their coats and lock up?"

"Certainly." Riya gives Sean a scathing glare and then moves to the coat closet.

"Thanks, Cass." Sydney gives me a sad but understanding smile and squeezes my hands before releasing me. "Have fun tonight. We'll talk later."

"What the hell? Cassidy—"

The door closes on his stammering, and I walk quickly to where Jack is standing beside a car to help me inside. As we pull away from the curb, I look over my shoulder to see a tall figure staring after us, clutching a black jacket in one hand, and his violet hair glowing in the light of the streetlamp.

chapter four

Murphy's Law No. 294: Take chances in your life. You might just surprise yourself.

Sean

"SLOW DOWN! CHRIST, WE'RE NOT RUNNING THE LONDON MARATHON," Syd shouts from behind me as I stalk down yet another street in Little Italy.

Hauling open the door to a quaint restaurant, I scan the space and come up empty again. "What in the bloody hell are you looking for?" Syd pushes against my chest when I try to leave. "They all have the same thing," she hisses under her breath. "Pasta, pizza, and wine, which I would like about a vat of at the moment."

"It's just not the one."

Her lips twitch before she looks past me into the restaurant. "Maybe I should be asking *who* you're looking for, not what."

"Just one more, Syd. I promise."

She shakes her head. "It was *just one more* four restaurants ago. My feet are killing me."

I glance down at her boots. Not exactly the kind made for trekking through the streets of New York for any amount of time. "Wear Chuck Taylors and they won't be."

"Stop dragging me through Little Italy on a wild goose chase and I won't have to."

I throw my hands up, letting out a sigh. "Fine. Let's go across the street. There's an espresso bar and I bet it has cannoli with your name on it."

"There better be." Syd pokes me in the chest, glancing over at the café. "But after this, no more cannoli or I'll never fit into my dress." Syd's eyes light up. "I can finally say that now. *My* dress."

"It is pretty spectacular." Just like its designer.

"I had almost given up and then—" She gets this faraway look in her eyes. "Fate," we both say at the same time.

"It seems to be working overtime today," I mumble, steering her out of the restaurant and to the curb. Cannoli is required.

"I don't think I can move," Syd complains, leaning back against the booth, patting her stomach. "I ate my weight in these."

"They were damn good." I stretch my legs out under the table, glancing to the rain-soaked street outside. I wonder where Cassidy is. If she's actually enjoying her meal, the company. The thought of her spending time on a date with someone else annoys me.

"Just ask me for it," Syd says after giving my boot a swift kick, drawing my attention back to her.

"That hurt!" I rub my shin under the table. "What am I asking you for now?"

"Cassidy's number. I have it." Syd grins at me over the top of her espresso.

"Do you now?" I try to sound uninterested.

"Mhmm. You know? So she can give me updates while she works on my dress. You want it?"

I tear at the paper napkin on the table and shred it into tiny pieces. "Course I do, but I want her to want to give it to me. I don't want to have to pilfer it from you."

Syd shakes her head. "And you say women are complicated."

"You are! I mean come on. I'm standing right there, and she just leaves."

Syd tilts her head, regarding me in that shrewd way she's always had. "She had a date, it would seem." I scowl at her nasty reminder. "You know, the entire world doesn't revolve around you. People have lives that carry on just fine without you."

"Pfft." I toss a few bits of the napkin at her.

She leans forward, setting her mug down. "I don't want to know what happened between you two. Lord knows I've heard enough of your previous escapades; it's a wonder I don't need therapy. Maybe she just wants to leave whatever you had in the past, hmm? It's obvious she wasn't expecting to see you today."

"Well spotted there. What's your point?"

"My point is, sometimes, it's best to leave things. Not read too much into it. Maybe just let it go?"

"See?" I bang my fist on the table, causing the couple in the booth across from us to shoot me an annoyed look. "This is what happens when you start to settle down. You lose your sense of adventure. Is that what you did when you first met Philip? Just let it go? Would we be scouring New York for wedding dresses if you hadn't made the first move with him?" She opens her mouth to reply, but I forge on. "No. We wouldn't be. You grabbed that twist of fate by the balls and you ran with it."

"I did. But sometimes, Sean, doing that can cause a right ball ache. Remember that."

"You might be right. But, if you hadn't taken a chance, if you hadn't been the one to make the first move, you might have missed out on the sheer wonder of Philip."

"You're horrible. You know that?"

I try to hide my grin, but it's not easy. "Still, he's the reason I found her again. Liking him a bit more now based on that fact alone, to be honest."

"What was that?" Syd cups a hand to her ear. "I'm not quite sure I heard you correctly."

I lift my chin to the final cannoli sitting on the plate between us. "Just eat your cannoli, you."

She laughs, pushing the plate toward me. "No way. This one's all yours."

"We'll take it to go. Along with another dozen for tomorrow."

"No!" Syd tries to tug on my arm as I push up from the seat. "I'll need even more alterations on my dress."

I flash her a grin, moving to the display case. "Exactly."

She huffs in frustration and calls after me, "You're an evil, evil twin."

It's closing in on half twelve when we get back to my place. The rain stopped earlier, leaving the streets slick and glossy. Syd, wanting out of the Uber so we could wander home, insisted on riding piggyback for the last few blocks to the building. I'll happily indulge her. I've missed her these last few months. She retired to her room after tea, fighting jet lag, which means I have a gaping hole of time stretching out in front of me. The telly holds zero interest. Infomercials really are the worst at this time of night.

Posting to Instagram takes all of twenty seconds as I flash a photo of the view of the lights of Manhattan from my balcony with a slew of hashtags. The responding likes and comments range from, "Dude!" to the equally brilliant, "I'd do u there all night." A tempting offer to be sure.

I settle on another cup of tea and surfing the net, landing on Cassidy's website because I like to torture myself. There are no photos of her, only classic shots of flowy and elegant dresses set with the Manhattan skyline in the background, along with stunning models that would typically pique my interest. But, not tonight. Tonight, I'm playing back our time together on repeat in my head.

She's made it clear both times we've met I should know who she is. I hardly think it's because she's a dress designer, no matter how talented she is. Typing her name into the search engine is all it takes, and I finally understand why she told me to forget I ever saw her that first time.

Her father's a senator from Wyoming—a real conservative big shot with a reelection coming up later this year. I bet news of his daughter having sex outside with a rock star wouldn't go over well. If anyone understands how scandals can rock a political family, it's me.

I scowl at the screen of my laptop as I remember the brutality of the press when the headlines hit on my time in rehab. Shit like that, you remember. It was a total and complete invasion of my family's privacy. My father's pristine political record and parenting techniques called into question. If his son could fall off the rails, who was he to be making policy decisions at the International Development Office?

My dad weathered the shitstorm, taking it all in stride as is his way. Nothing rattles the man. It's one of the things I admire about him. I know how lucky I am to have supportive parents. It's one of the reasons I started donating to the music academy back in London. The academy is for gifted kids who have grown up without the kind of support I had. Kids who have been through hell, and yet despite all of it, still want to play an instrument.

Staring at the portrait of the quintessential American family on her father's website, I can understand her reluctance to get involved with me. No more sex outside then. I can be creative in other ways.

Powering off my laptop, I head to my soundproof music room. Thank fuck I had it put in. Without a gig to play, I feel a bit lost and unsettled. It's nothing a couple of hours won't cure. I pull off my shirt and toss it to the corner of the room. Judging by how amped up I am, I'm going to be here a while. Closing the door behind me, I cross the room to my kit. It's custom made, dark rosewood, a mix of stains and inks with brass-plated hardware, identical to the one I have on tour.

Bashing Zildjians is cathartic. Skating the edge of control is what fuels me; it fuels the band. It takes us to a different place every time we play. I'm proud of the fact people say a Redfall concert is never the same show twice. How fucking boring would that be?

I take chances. On stage and off. It's who I am. As I dive headfirst into the bridge for "Monster Down," I know I can't listen to Sydney and her suggestion to just let it go. I'm not going to be able to just drop this. I'm taking the chance that fate has dealt me, and I'm going to run with it.

Spring in New York is an interesting time. Having survived the polar vortex , gardens are making their appearance, pops of color dot window boxes, and kids shriek with delight in playgrounds. It's a bit of a rebirth.

This morning, the clouds are gone, and with Syd sleeping in, I find myself drawn to the East Village, with a container of cannoli from last night. It's almost nine. I'm trying not to dwell on the fact I know the hours of Cassidy's shop as I stand outside it. This ranks high on the desperate scale.

I'm not kept waiting long. I can hear the faint chime of bells on the door, and then those gray-blue eyes, wide and startled, blink up at me as Cassidy appears in the doorway. Fuck, she looks good. The hair that yesterday swept in front of her eyes is held back by a few little pins with bright red jewels. She's got a black knee-length dress on that does nothing to hide her endlessly long legs, and those shoes? Fuck me running. Simple, red, just high enough to put her almost at eye level with me.

"What are you—"

"Cannoli?" I clear my throat and hold the box out to her. She glances from the box back to me.

"It's not even nine yet."

"And your point is?"

"It's a little early for cannoli, isn't it?" She grips the side of the door.

"It's never too early for cannoli."

Her lips, stained in a blush gloss, curl up slightly, making me want to taste them. To taste her. I want her to want me to kiss her, and I'm afraid she might never feel that way.

"Is that a fact?" Her eyes dart to the tempting box of sweets.

I lean forward slightly, and she leans back. "Best breakfast you'll ever have."

"I'll take your word for it."

"Don't do that. Have one and be sure." I wiggle the box before popping the top open. "You know you want to."

Her eyes stay fixed to mine. "Tempting."

"You don't have to be tempted. It's right here. Just for you. Best you'll ever have."

She tries to hold back a laugh. "I have a fitting in a half hour."

"Loads of time, Fly-girl."

"I can't," she says so quietly, I hardly hear it.

"Can't or won't?"

Her grip tightens on the door. "A little of both."

Fucking hell. I think back to how I left things with her yesterday, about my asinine comment that she go out with me because I'm buying Syd's dress. Even though I was joking, I admit that it could have been taken the wrong way. I need to fix this. "Well, if you won't have cannoli, maybe you'll let me in for a fitting."

"A fitting?" She laughs, glancing back into her shop. "I'm not sure if you noticed, but I only have dresses here."

"Right, And I need a suit. You know, for the wedding."

"Ah... I don't design men's suits." That little crease in her forehead appears again.

"How hard can it be, really? I mean, there's no poofy layers, none of that lace nonsense, although I wouldn't be totally opposed to that, in moderation of course."

"Of course," she says through a grin.

"Think of it as a challenge."

"Oh, I think it's fair to say even without the suit, you're a challenge." She opens up the door a bit wider, and I take a step forward. I'm in her orbit; her subtle lavender scent drifts to me and locks in place.

She gazes up at me as I slip farther into the shop and close the door behind me. Leaning forward, I drop my eyes to her lips. Fuck, I want to kiss her, but instead, I just whisper, "I dress left. If that helps."

Cassidy

Without thinking, my eyes dart to the bulge in his worn jeans. Ah, yes he does, doesn't he? I wasn't really paying attention during our sky-diving tryst. The other things he did with his cock were much more interesting.

Meeting his gaze once more, I ignore his triumphant smile and step back. "Fell right into that one, didn't I?" I mumble, my cheeks heating. "Seriously, why are you here?"

"I told you." Moving with leonine grace, he inches me back into my shop. He's wearing a black leather jacket over an ancient Led Zeppelin T-shirt, looking like the prototype bad-boy rocker. "I brought you a treat."

The contents of the box make a soft shuffling sound when he wiggles it again. Cannoli. How could he possibly know that cannoli is one of my favorite pastries? "How do you know I didn't have some last night? During my date?" I'm playing with fire, I know. But I can't help myself. Not when he's stalking me like a panther and looking like he wants to eat *me* for breakfast.

His eyes darken. "Ah, yes, your 'date.' How was it?"

"It was fine. Riya will be here soon, you know." I bump into the table I use to lay out fabric samples when clients are here. Which will be shortly, I remind myself.

"But she's not here now." He takes another step toward me. "Just fine?"

"Fine. He's a nice man." The floor creaks as I take another step backwards.

"Nice," he scoffs. His violet hair glows in the early morning light coming through the front windows. "You deserve more than 'fine' and 'nice.'"

I raise my chin. "How do you know what I deserve?"

"I know you deserve more than undercooked veal in an overrated bistro."

Crossing my arms, I tilt my head and glare at him. "Jack's very intelligent and a good conversationalist who never suggests I should spend time with him because I owe him something," I snap. Sean rolls his eyes and looks at the ceiling, waving his arms. The poor cannoli sounds like it's being smashed to bits.

"Jesus, woman. I said I was kidding, and I was. Look, as I'm sure my sister and mates would agree, I'm a cocky bastard who rarely pays much attention to what comes out of my mouth most of the time." His lips curl into the confident grin I remember so well from my dreams. "Now, can we please start over? Hit rewind? Forgive me for my lapse?" He backs me up another step and holds the small box toward me again. "Consider this a peace offering."

Damn. That accent will be my undoing. It suddenly seems hotter in the room, and I run my finger along the neckline of my dress. We move deeper into my shop, toward the dressing rooms Sydney used yesterday afternoon. I'm not sure if he's steering me or if I'm leading him. Maybe both. He looks like a lion, ready to pounce. I can't tear my eyes away from his—I could drown in his twin pools of green fire if I'm not careful. The air between us crackles with anticipation, and I feel my resolve slipping. Dammit, who does he think he is? Showing up here and expecting...what, exactly? That I'd fall at his feet like a groupie?

Standing straighter, I stop and snatch the box from his hand, and pop the lid open. "Fine; let's see what you brought me." Surprisingly, the two desserts nestled inside look unbroken. Lifting one crispy tube to my lips, I close my eyes and scoop out a bit of the creamy filling with my tongue. Oh, so good. The faint taste of almonds balances the ricotta beautifully.

A strangled groan is my only warning. My eyes fly open as he grabs my waist, making me drop the culinary goodness. "Fuck, Cassidy," he growls, swinging me into an open dressing room as I cling to his leather jacket. His mouth descends, and I barely have time to avoid his kiss; I offer my neck instead and he takes it with a frustrated groan. My hands scramble to undo his pants as he pulls up my skirt.

"What do we have here? Silk knickers? Lovely." His nimble fingers easily slip my underwear down over my hips so they fall to my ankles. Cold hands on my warm ass make me gasp. His fingers tease between my legs where I'm wet and wanting, fueled by some base desire that flares whenever he's near.

"Condom."

"Back pocket. Wallet," he grunts, continuing to knead my ass with both hands. Reaching around him, I retrieve his wallet and pluck out a familiar packet, before letting it join the smashed ruins of the cannoli on the floor. Then I'm sheathing his hard, heavy length—oh, I remember this part well.

"Fuuuck." His eyes roll up in his head before his steely gaze returns to my own. "Wrap your legs around me, love; this won't be gentle."

"Good—ahh!" My head rolls back and smacks the wall as he thrusts home, but I barely notice the pain. He wasn't kidding—he sets a quick pace, pounding into me as if I might disappear any second. It's just like I remember, like I've been dreaming of since our first time against the hangar. His heavy, hot breath against my neck, his warm, musky scent, and the strength of his arms as he holds me…it's perfect. It's everything. He shifts me in his arms, and I can't help my cry when he hits even deeper. Sweet crispy Christ, he's amazing.

He snorts out a laugh. "Fuck, you're good for my ego."

Shit, I said that out loud? I tug at his wild hair. "I don't think your ego needs the help."

His eyes dart from mine, to my mouth, and down to where we're joined. Gripping his jaw, I bring his attention back to my face, but I'm not prepared for the intensity in his eyes. I feel like he can see right through me, and there's nowhere to hide. Suddenly, the levity is gone, replaced by a raw need that has us grabbing at each other even more. My nails rake down his neck, and I curse that I can't reach more of his bare skin. His fingers dig into my thighs so hard he's going to leave marks.

I can't wait to see them.

When he snakes one hand between us to stroke me, I'm lost. I bite the shoulder of his jacket to muffle my cry as I fall over the edge, feeling him shudder against me with his own release. I open my eyes to see him reflected in the mirror across from us, his strong form pinning me against the wall. I bite back a whimper at the sight. It's beyond hot. The man is a force of nature. As he sets me on my feet, I glance over my shoulder, surprised there's not an imprint of my back on the wall.

"Holy fuck, Cassidy." He bends over, bracing himself with his hands on his knees, and panting like he might pass out. He looks up at me with an impish grin. "At least I know your name this time."

"It might be better if you forgot it." My legs are wobbly, but I manage to retrieve my panties from the floor and pull them on. Jeez, I never took my shoes off. He's going to have marks on his ass from my heels.

He straightens and grabs my hand, waiting until I look him in the eye. There it is again, that intense focus that can bring me to my knees. "What if I don't want to forget it? What if I want more than a quick shag?"

My eyes meet his darkened emerald gaze in the mirror. "Sean—"

My head snaps toward the sound of the bell tinkling above the door. "Shit, it's Riya!" I hastily smooth down my dress and hop over the crushed cannoli to scuttle around the corner and toward the front. Riya is hanging up her coat in the small closet, her Indian tunic a gorgeous orange today. Her smile dims when she sees me.

"Good morning." She cocks her head to one side in confusion, making her silk pashmina rustle. "Are you all right? Have you been moving those heavy mannequins by yourself again?"

"Uh, no. Um…" I try not to fidget, but it's impossible. My whole body still tingles from Sean's touch.

"Riya, darling!" His booming voice comes from behind me. "How lovely to see you again. You're like a breath of spring."

Riya's mouth drops open and she stares as Sean's measured steps bring him alongside me. "Mr.… Mr. Murphy. We didn't expect to see you again so soon." She looks at me. "Did we?"

I shake my head quickly, but he simply shrugs. "I wanted to coax Ms. Skinner into taking a walk on the wild side." My eyes snap to his before I realize my mistake. It's like I'm trapped in some kind of sex tractor beam. How the fuck does he do that? Thankfully, he turns his gaze to Riya, and I can breathe again. "I know she hasn't tried to create men's clothing before," he continues smoothly, "but I think she'd do brilliantly. Do you think you could help me persuade her? Get her to step out of her comfort zone and make me a suit for my sister's wedding?"

Riya shoots me a look before plastering on an enigmatic smile. "I think it's an intriguing idea." She adjusts her scarf. "I've mentioned several times I think she should consider expanding her line."

"Brilliant!" He claps his hands together and beams at me. "See? Riya agrees with me."

Rolling my eyes, I try to herd him toward the front door. "Fine. But we'll have to discuss it later. Mrs. Hamilton will be here any minute." I hear Riya muttering to herself behind me as she wanders back toward the dressing rooms, and my eyes fly open in panic.

"Don't worry," he says quietly, but his smile is mischievous, and I can't help but smile in return. "I tossed the cannoli in a dustbin with the rubber. There may be a few crumbs, but no one should notice." At the door, he pauses and, after checking to see that Riya is still occupied, ghosts a fingertip down my cheek, smiling when I shiver in response.

He leans forward, his lips set to my ear. "I need your number."

Damn that accent. I bite at the inside of my lip to try to keep from smiling. "Do you now?"

"Absolutely. You know, there may be a wedding dress emergency that I need to help with." He adjusts one of my hairpins with a low hum that I feel all the way to my toes. "Mmm. This is pretty."

"Is that right?" I squeak out.

Reaching into the inside of his leather jacket, he produces his phone and presses in a code before holding it out to me. "That's right. And Syd's going to be in another time zone." His eyes drop to my lips for a moment and my heart pounds a little harder. "I'm right here. At your beck and call. Day or night in case of emergencies or… whatever."

He wiggles the phone and I glance down at it, chuckling at the case, which boasts a distressed version of the English flag. I take the phone with an exaggerated huff, trying to ignore his satisfied smirk as I add my number into his contacts. "Why do I have a feeling I may regret this?"

I turn the phone back to him and he waves it at me. "No regrets, Cassidy. Not ever. Not with me and not in your life. It's a horrible way to live." I stare at him, wanting to respond, but I can't seem to form words.

"Thank you for a lovely morning." He taps his phone and opens up the door. "I'll be in touch soon, Ms. Skinner."

We're kept busy for a few hours, and then I finally escape to my workshop upstairs. It's one thing to design these dresses, but I have yet to hire anyone on a permanent basis to help me make them. For big orders, I have a couple girls that help put the main pieces together so I can do the final touches, but I've been kind of gun-shy to take them on full time. It's a lot of responsibility. So, if I don't schedule time for my workshop, they remain dresses only on paper.

It's been impossible to hide the spring in my step from Riya. She's been giving me curious looks all day, especially whenever I walk past the dressing rooms, grinning like a fool. We haven't had time between clients for her to interrogate me. I gather my laptop bag and sketch pads and try to move quietly so I don't disturb Riya, who's doing the books at the front desk, but she has other ideas. "So, are we really go-ing to pretend that man was here this morning *only* because he wants you to design him a suit?"

Stopping in my tracks, I turn to face her with a sigh. She's peering at me over her reading glasses like an accusatory owl. "Yes, we are."

"And I don't want to ask why the dressing rooms smelled like a brothel this morning, right?"

I shift the load in my arms, avoiding her eyes. "That would proba-bly be for the best."

She frowns and removes her glasses, pinching the bridge of her nose. "Cassidy, that man is bad news."

"How do you know?" I slump in an opposite chair, holding my things in my lap. "Besides, he's the brother of a client. Be nice to him until the order is filled. Then we won't see him again." The realization dims the glow that's infused me all morning.

"Of course I'll be nice to him," she scoffs. "And I just know. I have a feeling about him. He reminds me of my uncle—you know, the crazy one who wasted his family fortune on a fig farm."

I bite my lips. "A fig farm?"

She waves a hand, almost flipping the pen from her fingertips. "He was the life of the party, and my aunt said he could fuck like a freight train, but he had no common sense. He didn't know a fig about figs."

I shake my head, trying not to laugh, and not wanting to hear an-other story about her crazy relatives. "Um, Riya—"

"How was your date last night? Now, *he* sounds like a good man." She folds her arms under her ample bosom.

"Jack's great." I wasn't kidding earlier; Jack is perfectly nice. It had been difficult to focus on him after my unexpected run-in with Sean, and even though he noticed my distraction, he didn't push me. Instead, he led me to safer topics, like our respective careers and goals for the future. I'd had a nice time. Surprisingly so, I suppose, since I couldn't stop comparing the two men in my head all through dinner. Jack is witty, very smart, and kind—and he has that familiar Wyoming connection going for him. Sean is like a party popper—loud, brightly colored, and you never know what you're going to get inside. One minute, he's blinking back tears when seeing his sister in her wedding gown, and the next minute he's growling like a tiger while he's pounding me into the wall.

"And..." Riya's thick eyebrows scrunch together, making her look like a caterpillar is crouching on her forehead.

"And, what?" I tear my thoughts away from wall pounding. "It was just dinner, Riya." Gripping my things, I rise and move toward the stairs again.

"Well, did he ask to see you again?" In fact, he had. He wants to meet me tonight and asked if I'd be willing to help him with a business opportunity he was considering. I don't know much—anything, really—about the oil and gas business, but he said that wasn't a problem. That a fresh pair of eyes is exactly what he needs.

Huffing in frustration, I give her a fishy eye. "Riya, I'd rather not—"

"Okay, okay. I'll shut up." She holds her hands up, and then gives me a fond smile. "I'll finish with these invoices, return a few client calls, and then I have a meeting with our CPA. Do you need me to come back for the Grafton appointment?"

Grateful, I return her smile. "No, that's fine. I can handle her and the late appointment with Harrington, too." She waves me off, and I finally escape to my apartment and private studio upstairs. I set my laptop and materials on my worktable, kick off my heels, and walk into my bedroom to flop on my bed. My mind whirls, images of Sean and Jack on a constant loop. Sean's green eyes staring into mine, Jack pouring my wine, the sound of Sean panting in my ear, Jack holding my door, Sean's delighted laugh, Sean's strong hands squeezing my ass, Sean's crazy hair...

With a groan, I fold my arms behind my head and stare at the ceiling. Okay, Cassidy, consider the facts. Jack's lovely, but there's no spark there. Besides, I only went out with him to make my mother happy. So that's done, right? Obligation met.

Except, I know my mother will want more. She always does,

especially when the stakes are this high. Coleman Energy is a multi-billion-dollar company. It's going to take at least three dates before I can convince her I've done my part for the family, and she'll leave me alone. At least, until next time.

A laugh escapes me when I picture my mother's face if she were ever to meet Sean. Holy Moses, that might be worth arranging. It'd be like telling Anna Wintour that she had to wear only things from Old Navy for an entire week.

My God, the things that man can do to me. My whole body lights up being near him. It's not just the sex—okay, *a lot* of it's the sex—but it's also his outrageous confidence, his take-no-prisoners attitude, that's so hard to resist. He's just so *alive*. Where does it come from? His sister is so, well, normal. Is it just a rock star entitlement thing, or has he always been so forward? Does he have an off switch? Surely, the man must do something to relax.

Soon, he said. Well… Sitting up abruptly, I slap my hands on my thighs, stand up, and move to my worktable. Whatever he can do to me, however he can make me feel, I'm not going to sit around and wait for a man. Period.

I've got work to do.

My phone chimes with a text, dragging me from my sewing machine. Shit. I still haven't responded to Jack. Bad form, Cass.

Dragging my cell from my pocket, I'm mentally composing a contrite message when I see the screen and almost drop it in panic. It's from my father's chief of staff, Dale Canton.

"Monthly report—one image captured and neutralized. Call for details."

Fuck. I slump back in my chair, swallowing thickly. It's been months. Months of reports where nothing was found. So many months I'd almost dared to think it might be over.

And now this. One image, captured and neutralized. I close my eyes and try to stop my racing heart. Where did they find it? Who had it? As much as I'm tempted, I never call for details. I don't really want to know. It's enough to know they're still out there. Little time bombs floating in the ether, just waiting to fuck up my life.

Taking a shaky breath, I delete the text and send up a silent prayer of thanks to my father. We never speak about it. Not since that first time. And even if we did, I'll never be able to thank him enough for his continued vigilance.

But there's one thing I can do to try.

Quickly looking up the number, I wait for him to pick up. "Jack? I'm sorry it's taken me so long to get back to you. Do you still want to get together?"

chapter five

Murphy's Law No. 78: *Meddling twins are dangerous.*

Sean

TOSSING MY KEYS TO THE TABLE NEAR THE DOOR, I FOLLOW THE heavenly smell of bacon. My kitchen rarely gets used unless I'm unpacking takeaway, so the smell is a welcome one. "Tell me that's breakfast."

Syd grins at me, stuffing a forkful of eggs into her mouth. "Mhmm."

"Did I mention you're the best sister ever?" I pull out a chair at the table and start filling a plate. She's got the doors to the balcony open, letting in the morning air. It breathes new life into the place.

"I thought you'd enjoy it. You were at it pretty late last night."

Scowling, I stack up a few slices of bacon. "You heard me? Damn, those walls are supposed to be soundproof."

"I'm sure for anyone else they are." She taps her temple. "Twin brain, remember? Plus, I'm still fighting the time change. I've been up since three thirty."

"Ouch. Sorry, Syd. I'll dial it back."

She laughs, leaning back, and cradling her cup of tea between her hands. "Right. Did we just meet? Dialing back is not in your vocabulary."

Shrugging, I dig into the meal. "I didn't even know I had bacon."

"You didn't. It's like Old Mother Hubbard's cupboard in there. I went to the shops this morning. Funny, you weren't in bed when I went to wake you." She eyes me warily as I devour breakfast. She's sizing me up. Damn twin. I can't hide a thing from her. "Where'd you run off to so early?"

"I had an errand."

She makes some dubious sound. "Does this errand happen to have anything to do with a certain tall blond?"

I can't help but grin. "Perhaps." She doesn't seem to share my expression; in fact, she's frowning. "What? I need a suit for your wedding."

"Because you can't wear one of the 200 suits you have hanging in your closet?"

"I need something special. It's your wedding, Syd. It's important." I bite into the bacon. Damn that's good. Bacon should be on everything.

Letting out a long sigh, she sets her cup down. "Please don't screw this up for me. You know how long it's taken me to find a dress? *My* dress?"

"And you'll be stunning in it." I point out the obvious.

"As long as Cassidy doesn't tear it to shreds because of some dumbass move of yours."

Irritation burns through me, and I reluctantly set the rest of the bacon down. "She's a professional, Syd. And thanks for the vote of confidence. I'm not a total arse, you know. Women love me."

She levels me a pointed look. "Cassidy doesn't strike me as the type to want to be lumped in with *all of your women.*"

"Christ, you make it sound like I have a harem."

She balls up her napkin and tosses it at me. It lands beside the plate. "Don't pretend like you're a saint."

"I'd never pretend that. I am who I am, Syd. You know this."

"Yeah I do. That's why I worry about you."

I finish off the scrambled eggs, feeling her staring at me. "I'm the last person in the world you need to worry about."

"It's just that you seem to spend a lot of time alone." Her voice is quiet.

I shake my head. "You're just talking crazy now. I'm hardly ever alone."

"Then there's the fact that the four people closest to you are…"

"Domestically unavailable?" I offer.

She laughs, pushing up from the table to carry her plate over to the sink. "That's one way of looking at it. Take Matt and Tess. You always thought he'd be alone forever, and now look at them." She spreads her arms wide as if emphasizing the point. "And you know, you're going to be thirty-eight this year."

I point my fork at her. "As will you."

She leans against the counter. "Don't you ever think about what's next?"

My throat feels tight. I don't like people questioning my life, particularly Sydney. She knows me too well. Always calls it how she sees it, and usually she's right, although I'd never admit it to her. "Right now, I'm thinking I'd like this conversation to be over."

"I'm serious."

"Syd, I love my life. Every single thing about it. I do what I want, when I want. I'm healthy, you're happy and about to be in wedded bliss. Mum and Dad are still going strong, and I get to do what I love with my best friends in the world. What's next? Nobody can answer that question. I'm just happy to see where life takes me; let the chips fall where they may."

I sip my tea as she studies me. "You'd make an amazing father."

So much for the tea. My mouthful spews across the table, causing her to laugh. "What in the hell are you on about?" Picking up the napkin she threw at me, I dab at the tea-stained white marble table.

"You heard me."

"Of course I'd be an amazing father. That's not even open for debate. If and when the time's right, it'll happen. Now is not that time."

She frowns, glancing out to the living room. "All this space and only you rattling 'round in it. What would you be doing if I wasn't here this week?"

I've about had enough of her mini interrogation. I'm an adult man who can make and own my own mistakes and run my own life, thank you very much. My chair scrapes across the floor as I push back from the table and carry my now sadly empty plate over to her. "It's New York, Syd. There's a million things I could be doing."

She folds her arms across her waist, not looking convinced.

"You want me to run down my diary then?" I don't wait for her to answer. "Today, I've got to check in on how the renovation is going at the music academy." Her smile brightens. I'm already funding a course at an academy in London, and plans to open a fully funded center in SoHo have been going strong for a few months now. It's a fabulous place Syd has helped to redesign. The loft is in one of the many historic cast-iron buildings, complete with a preserved fire escape and an expansive landscaped rooftop with strung lights and a stellar view I plan to make good use of.

"I'm so glad you're opening that up here," she says with a hint of pride.

Waving her off, I set the plate into the sink. "Yeah, yeah. We'll talk about my hero-like qualities later. I'm giving you a rundown of my day since you seem to be under the false impression that my life is lacking in some way."

She bites back a smile. "Please, do carry on."

Rinsing off the plate, I lean against the counter beside her. "After that, I plan on having lunch. Then, I have to check on a parcel that was supposed to arrive for Hannah yesterday but seems to be lost in a delivery vortex. I have a sync-up with Nicole." Syd's eyes widen. "Nicole Hays. Our *PR manager*, you know? About the details of the academy opening, and then I'm in the 5K mud run obstacle course tonight. Oh, and I have a gig at the Gramercy, which you're coming to, by the way, at the end of the week."

She hits me softly in the arm. "I didn't know the guys were in town. Why didn't you tell me?"

"No, not them. Grant Bishop, a buddy of mine, has an indie band. Bishops to Kings. Their drummer's girlfriend is having a baby. I said I'd fill in." I tug at the end of her ponytail the way I used to do when we were little. "So there, *Mum*. A jammed-pack day for Mr. Sean Murphy. No need for you to be filling your head with ridiculous scenarios about me sitting around in boredom and twiddling my thumbs."

"Now, just imagine how great all of that would be if you could share it with someone."

"I just shared it with you."

She shakes her head. "You don't get it yet, but someday you will. All of those little things—the day to day? Sharing it with someone who cares about it, someone who you know has got your back no matter what. It's everything." Syd lets out a little sigh of contentment. "Philip's the first person I want to talk to in the morning. The one I want to share everything with."

"Even though you're here with me?"

"Especially because I'm here with you. I want that for you. Someone you can't wait to talk to. Someone you miss. Someone who misses you. You deserve it." She pats her hand over my heart. "More than anyone, you deserve that kind of love."

I swallow back the lump that's made an appearance in my throat and sling my arm around her shoulder and ruffle her hair. "Enough of the sappy, Syd. Soon you'll be pulling out the rom-coms and forcing me to watch them."

She twists away. "Hey! You love some of those films. Don't even try to deny it."

"Wouldn't dream of it," I mutter, watching as she tugs her jacket off the back of one of the chairs.

"Where are you off to?"

"I'm doing a bit of shopping. I'd ask you to come, but what with your jammed-packed diary and everything, I know how busy you are." She purses her lips, heading for the door. "Even if I have no idea what a mud run is."

"It's exactly how it sounds. I'll send you the info and you can come to cheer me on. I'll see you later tonight?"

"Wouldn't miss it." With a wave, the door to the penthouse closes and I'm left alone with a canyon-wide silence I've never noticed before. She's good. She's making me question everything. Damn twin.

"Bloody hell," I mutter under my breath as the adrenaline floods my veins and my vision blurs from another round of mud splattered onto my face. I'm nearing the end of this sheer hell of a race, and while I'm caked in mud from head to foot, I couldn't feel more alive.

I'm battered and a little bruised, my back sporting scrapes from army-crawling under barbed wire through yet another deep mud puddle, but damn is it worth it. An A-framed cargo net and the inverted wall are all that sit between me and the sweet finish line.

The die-hards who actually train for this finished long ago and have joined the crowds to cheer the rest of us on. It's an inspirational and tight-knit community they have, that I'm just happy to play in once in a while.

Muddy shoes hit the slick ground and I lose my balance a little before sprinting to the damn inverted wall. Halfway up, I slip back down, landing on my arse, only to be hauled to my feet by some stranger who doesn't give me a second glance before he's up and disappearing over the top.

I return the favor for another participant who slips when we both reach the top of the wall. My arm shoots out, my hand catching his arm before he falls, and I tug him up and over with me.

He gives me a wave before racing forward and crossing the finish line ahead of me. I hear Syd before I see her, her loud cheers lifting above the crowd. I seek her out once I'm over the line, and ignore her shrill threats to not coat her in mud. Instead, I wrap my arms around her and lift her up from the ground in celebration.

She hits me hard in the chest when I set her down. "You actually meant mud race." She tries to wipe a glob of mud from her arm.

"That I did. You should try it with me next time."

"I think I'll take a pass," she says, handing over a gym bag full of clean clothes.

"Thanks for cheering me on." I take the bag and fish out my phone from the side pocket. There's an anxiousness running through me, something more than just finishing the race. I want to share this with someone other than Syd. I want to share it with Cass.

"I'll get us some water for after you're cleaned up." Syd gives me a wave, wandering toward the refreshment area. I don't waste any time taking a photo of my mud-stained face and sending it to Cass with a text:

Want to get dirty?

I hope she sees it before she goes to bed. I hope it gives her something to think about, maybe even dream about.

I'm kept waiting for Cassidy's response until long after I take a hot shower, trying to rinse away the mud. It's past one in the morning, and I'm lounging in the living room alone, Syd having packed it in once we were home and had a cup of tea.

My muscles ache, a sure sign that the mud race isn't something I should do more often. Although, I can't deny that rush is addicting. So is my phone when it finally chimes with a message. Even though she stored her name under Cassidy, I changed it to Fly-girl, and heat floods my veins when I see the name flash in the darkness.

Fly-girl: Do I want to know?

Sean: You're not afraid of a little mud, are you?

Fly-girl: I grew up around mud at the ranch. Never met a puddle I didn't like.

I grin, stretching my legs out against the sofa.

Sean: Tell me more. Did you fancy getting down and dirty with the cowboys?

I watch the little dots and wait for her reply. To my dismay, they disappear after a while, leaving me hanging with an unwelcome ache in my chest.

Sean: I take it that's a no.

More time passes, and I can't stop myself from trying once more.

Sean: Fly-girl? I meant no offense.

The dots appear once more and I feel instantly better. Something is better than nothing after all.

Fly-girl: Sorry. I'm just trying to finish up an alteration. No offense taken, but no to the cowboys.

I should probably be worried that I'm glad to hear that answer. The thought of Cass with anyone else before or now doesn't sit well. I glance out to the lights of Manhattan twinkling away.

Sean: You're still working? Isn't it late for that?

Fly-girl: Tell that to my bride who's getting married next weekend. And I don't mind. I work better under pressure.

Sean: "Under Pressure" is a kick-ass song. Shall I ring and sing it for you? Give you a little inspiration?

It doesn't take long this time for her reply.

*Fly-girl: *eye roll* Then I'd never get this done.*

Sean: Do I distract you?

I shift around on the sofa, more than a little intrigued for her reply.

Fly-girl: I reserve the right to remain silent... As should you. The little smiley face she adds at the end makes me laugh.

Sean: I've never been good at following that rule.

Fly-girl: Something to work on then? Goodnight, Sean.

I feel a bit crest-fallen that I'm being given the brush off, but I also understand. Cass's work is important to her, just as mine is. I'd never want to get in the way of that. So, as much as it pains me to, I bid her good night.

Sean: Sweet dreams, Fly-girl.

I follow up the text by sending a clip of "Under Pressure" from one of our concerts in London where we paid tribute to Queen. I shove my earbuds in and put the song on repeat. If I can't talk to her any more tonight, at least we can share the same song.

The morning dawns with breakfast that Syd has made and a welcome message from Cass that instantly puts a smile on my face.

Fly-girl: That's some performance! I think I need to see you play live.

Sean: *hand-to-heart* I'm wounded you haven't.

Fly-girl: I think you're doing just fine without me in attendance.

Sean: Yes, but I'd like you to be in attendance.

Syd clears her throat from across the table. "Important message?" she asks, eyebrows lifted.

"One of the most important."

Syd shakes her head at me as I enjoy the rest of my cup of the tea. I wasn't wrong in my original assessment that texting with Cass could easily become an addiction. I'm strangely okay with that.

Fly-girl: So much tulle… so little time.

The next day, I'm checking in at the music academy when I read her text, and I laugh at the photo that accompanies it. This time, it's piles of tulle in every pastel color imaginable that spill over a mannequin form in her shop. We've been exchanging quick texts and random photos, and I'm not afraid to say that I've started looking forward to them. Last night, she fell asleep mid-text conversation, no doubt exhausted from trying to finish up the adjustments for the woman she calls her "bridezilla from hell." She has the patience of a saint to deal with some of these women and their outlandish demands.

Sean: Is this an S-O-S that you need rescuing?

Fly-girl: No, no. I'm okay! She follows the text with a thumbs-up.

Sean: You just say the word and I'll whisk you away. Paris is beautiful this time of year.

Fly-girl: Paris in springtime? Sign me up!

I feel a jolt of excitement, wondering if Kennedy is hogging the jet, or if it's out of his clutches long enough to let me use it. I could make Paris work either way.

Sean: Done. When can you leave?

Fly-girl: OMG. No! Do not book a trip to Paris! I was joking.

Sean: I wasn't. I take a photo of myself pouting on the rooftop of the academy and send it to her.

Fly-girl: I know you weren't. How scary is that? I already seem to know you.

Oh, how I wish she did.

Sean: Ah, Fly-girl. You're just starting to.

Sean: Does this jacket make me look fat?

I fire off a photo of me trying on a dark green leather bomber jacket in a dressing room at a vintage shop in Brooklyn. Syd has been dragging me around whilst she finishes shopping for her honeymoon. Not that I need to be dragged to go shopping, actually. Typically, it's me leading the charge.

Fly-girl: Seriously?

I frown before replying.

Sean: Seriously, no? Or seriously, you look like a beached whale?

*Fly-girl: *eye roll* If you're fishing for compliments, you should try a different pond.*

Sean: But I don't want to fish in a different pond. You're the only one I want.

Fly-girl: Are you comparing me to a fish?

Sean: Never! Come over here. The dressing room has a lot of mirrors I'd like to put to good use.

Fly-girl: Brides are calling my name.

Sean: Lucky brides. I'd like to be the one calling your name.

She doesn't answer my last text.

I toss the jacket on the table at the register and spot a bowl of vintage hairpins and barrettes that remind me of the ones Cass had in hair when I was inside her last. That seems like a lifetime ago. I dump the bowl on the table and buy them all.

A few days later, finding a place to park near Cassidy's shop is a chore, but eventually I squeeze the Maserati into a space where I hope I'm not going to get towed. Even I know it's ridiculous to own this car in the city, but when I get to open it up? Man, what a rush. The open road, the boundless sky above, it comes close to the feeling I get when I play.

The midnight blue car tends to draws attention, but not as much as the VW. I was tempted to pick her up in the Pink Tornado but thought better of it. Baby steps, so they say.

The little bells on her shop door chime with my arrival, and I shut the door behind me. Her shop is quaint, a bit quirky with artfully placed gowns showcased throughout. I can hear muted women's voices in the room ahead. Lots of ohhing and ahhing. Studying one of the gowns draped on a mannequin, I know why. Fly-girl is insanely talented.

I slide my fingers over the lace silhouette. The amount of work gone into this is crazy, with sheer details and a fitted corset that's the perfect combination of classic and sexy.

I wonder where she gets her inspiration. I wonder what she'd look like in this dress. The thought is unnerving and has me stepping back from the mannequin as if it's on fire. I take a long breath in. My thoughts typically don't wander to women in wedding dresses, but Cassidy has me thinking all sorts of things I normally wouldn't.

"Can I help... You're back." I turn to the sound of Cassidy's voice, feeling that punch in my gut when I see her. Those hypnotic eyes, wide and wondering. The curious tilt of her head, every curve of her body highlighted in that skirt, and those legs. Fucking distracting is what they are. I imagine hiking that skirt up to reveal just how long and flexible they are. Maybe bending her over the arm of the chair in the corner.

"Free for a late lunch?" I finally rasp out after my blatant gawking. I have no idea if she's free, but I hope to hell she is. I've set up the rooftop at the academy with pillows and blankets and a hamper full of the best Thai takeout in the city being delivered in the sheer hope that she's free. If she's not, I'm eating alone.

She wets her lips, her eyes meeting mine. "I'm in the middle of something."

I take a step toward her. "I can wait. It's just lunch. Come."

The corner of her mouth kicks up in amusement. "You know women don't just come because the men in their lives tell them to."

"You know you just made me hard as a rock."

"What?"

"Mhmm. You just referred to me as the man in your life, Fly-girl." Can she hear the sound of my heartbeat? I sure as hell can.

As she shakes her head, those blue-gray eyes darken. "You know what I mean. I was just saying—"

I press my fingers over her soft lips, shutting her up. "Don't take it back. I like being the man in your life." Slowly, I slide my thumb against her lips, watching as they part. Fuck, I want to taste her. I want her to want me to.

"Just lunch," she whispers, taking a step back.

"Fair warning. A lot can happen at lunch."

Pulling in a breath, she backs up, nearly knocking over one of the mannequins. I try not to laugh. Honest to fuck I try.

She scrambles to steady the mannequin, muttering under her breath before she turns to face me, lifting her chin. "I'll just finish up."

"I'll just wait right here."

Minutes drag by like hours. She finally finishes with her clients, who leave in a flurry of excitement and pure joy she's brought to them. Then, I can hear creaking of the floorboards above the shop where she disappeared up the stairs. I have to fight the urge to go after her. I want to see where she lives and find out if the space smells of lavender, like she does. Fucking hell, she's got me twisted up.

It seems to take an age before she descends the stairs. I let my gaze drag over her, appreciating every single sultry step. She sails past me with that confidence that turns me on.

She starts to open the door, but I place my palm on the thick wood, closing it. The little crease in her forehead appears when her eyes flicker up at me.

"I want you to wear something."

Her eyes widen as I tug a blue blindfold from the pocket of my jeans. "What the hell is that?"

"Never seen one before?" I dangle it in front of her face.

"Of course I have. But why do you have it? Just where are you taking me?"

"I told you. Lunch."

She glares at me with her hands on her hips. "Lunch with a blindfold?"

"Cassidy, there are endless ways to have lunch." As I dangle the blindfold in front of her face, she ignores it, instead staring at me, neither of us wanting to break first.

"Trust me," I finally say.

"Okay." Her voice is clear, commanding, not wavering in the least. Fuck, that just makes me want her more. "Let me lock up first." Finding her keys in her bag is a challenge, but she finally does and locks the shop.

Turning to me, she tilts her head back. The afternoon sun catches her hair and makes it glow. "Darken my world, London."

Fuck this woman and the things she does to me. Slowly, I lift the blindfold over her head and position it over her eyes. "Don't let me fall," she whispers as I tuck her hair back.

"Never." I set my hand against the small of her back and guide her forward around the corner. "Steady now, up and over." She laughs as I steer her away from a lamppost.

"This is crazy. I have no idea where you're taking me."

"Does it matter?" She shakes her head, stretching her arm out to the empty air in front of her.

"Not even a little."

"This is us." I tighten my arm around her and reach down to open the passenger door. Her hand flails in the air and I see her frown.

"What is this?"

"A car."

Laughing, I help guide her into the seat. "Smart-ass. There's no top to the door," she says, her hands blindly searching the dashboard, the seat, the gear shift.

"No. There's not."

She turns her head to the sound of my voice. "It's a convertible?"

"That it is." I tug the seatbelt around her and fasten it into place. I can't resist letting my hand linger on her hip, tracing the belt across her stomach.

Pouting slightly, she leans back against the white leather. "I want to see it."

"You will. After lunch."

Closing her door, I move around the front of the car and slide in behind the wheel. It roars to life and her smile widens when I rev the engine. "What kind of a car is it? At least give me that."

Chuckling, I step on the gas and merge into afternoon traffic. "I think I'll make you wait." Her laughter is infectious as I swerve through the streets, winding my way to SoHo. I can't help watching as she lifts her head back to the sun, feeling the wind in her hair. I'm tempted to just keep going. Take us outside the city so I can really open it up. Maybe next time. Shit. I'm already thinking about the next time I'll see her.

She reaches out for the console, and I guide her fingers to mine on the gearshift. Her fingers mesh with mine, and I feel the heat from her skin with each gear change. Slowly, she traces my forearm, the little smile of hers growing the longer we stay in the car. It's erotic, causing my veins to hum in anticipation.

The drive to SoHo has never taken this fucking long in the history of time. Thank fuck the building has reserved parking. I swing into my assigned space and shove the car into park, causing her to laugh louder.

"You're a menace on the road," she says, touching the blindfold.

"I was completely in control of the vehicle at all times." Getting out of the car, I hurry to open her door.

"Can I take this off now?" She unbuckles her seatbelt and swings her legs out. I take her hand, tugging her forward against my torso. She melts into my arms, sending a shot of desire through me.

"Not quite yet."

"You're no fun." That damn pout again. I want to kiss her. I could easily. Claim those sweet lips as mine. But I want *her* to kiss *me*. And yes, I'm well aware of just how lame that sounds.

"You've had plenty of fun with me already and the day is still young." The little dimple deepens in her cheek from her smile. She's happy. Truly happy. And it makes me feel like a king.

"Lift's this way."

"Are people watching us?" she whispers, leaning into me as I guide her inside to the lift.

"I don't give a fuck if they are."

Pressing the button for the roof, I feel her sway as it grinds to life, sending us to the roof.

"This is crazy. Where are we?" she asks again as the doors open, and I brush my hand against her back, urging her forward to the land-scaped rooftop.

Slowly, I trace my hand along her cheek, lifting the blindfold off. "We're at lunch."

Cassidy

Breathing in the soft spring air, I blink as the fabric trails across my face. We're on a roof, high enough to see over the adjacent buildings, but low enough that a few skyscrapers tower in the distance. "Wow. This is lovely. Where are we?"

"New York." His rich voice in my ear is teasing. "We weren't in the car long enough to get out of the city."

"Be serious." He's created an oasis; there are a few soft lounge cushions placed on rugs, along with about a dozen throw pillows scattered around. A few strings of lights dangle above, winking softly in the late afternoon light. It's impressive. It's also touching; it's been a long time since someone has done something like this for me.

"SoHo. On top of my music academy, to be exact." He steps around me and walks over to a low table between two of the loungers. "Oh, good. The food is here. I hope you like Thai."

"Love it, as long as it's not too spicy. This is amazing, Sean. Thank you." I walk over to the edge and peer down. We're about six stories up, I'm guessing. "Wait—what do you mean by 'your music academy'?"

"Hmm, no plates. Sorry," he murmurs. He's pulling napkins and plastic forks out of a wicker basket and glances up at me before setting them on a low table. "It's a pet project of mine. The building isn't ready yet, but it will be a specialized school for young musicians who have passion and talent but can't afford to continue their lessons. It's no secret how school budgets are being stretched thin these days, and arts programs are often the first things cut, leaving hundreds of students twisting in the wind. My plan is to fill the gap."

"That's a fantastic plan." I sink down onto one of the lounges, slip my heels off, and help him pull paper cartons out of the basket. The tempting aroma of pad thai floats on the air. "So, like prodigies?"

He stretches over to a small cooler sitting beside the table and plucks a bottle of white wine out. "Not initially." Producing a couple glasses and a corkscrew from the basket, he starts opening the wine. "Mostly kids who have been squeezed out of their programs and don't have any other way to continue. But, yeah, I think we'll eventually establish another level for kids who are too advanced for the lessons available to them. Kids who could make a go of it if they had the resources."

"Raising the next generation of rock stars?" I accept a glass of wine from him and salute him with it. He laughs, and selects a carton of pad thai.

"Sure, why not? But we won't discriminate—jazz, classical, folk, whatever. They'll all be welcome. Music shouldn't have limits."

I take a spring roll from a carton and nibble on the end, watching his violet hair ruffle in the breeze. "That's important to you, isn't it? Pushing the limits."

He winks at me over the rim of his glass. "Always. Life's not worth living if you're not living on the edge."

Living on the edge. Even considering our short acquaintance, I can see that those words are the perfect descriptor for him. Stretching his long legs out in front of him, he leans back and raises his face to the sky, closing his eyes and letting the gentle breeze wash over his face. If it weren't for the hair, he'd look so normal. Well, if normal were a hot British musician wearing worn jeans, a white tee, and an old leather jacket... It's his energy that's different, that raises him to the next level. Even as relaxed as he seems now, it's there, pulsing under the surface. A constant live wire just waiting to be tripped.

It's captivating.

A high-pitched, little girl's laugh breaks the silence, and he grins as he fishes his phone out of his pocket. Laughing as he looks at the screen, he shows it to me. It's a video clip of a gleeful little girl with gorgeous strawberry blond curls doing a cartwheel in what looks like a home gym. "Who's that?"

"My poppet, Hannah," he says proudly, tapping out a message on the screen. "It's her first cartwheel."

My glass freezes midway to my lips. "*Your* poppet?"

"No! Not *mine*, mine," he corrects quickly, eyes wide in horror. "God, no. No poppets for me, at least not yet. She belongs to one of my band-mates—Cameron. I'm just her extremely-awesome-in-every-way uncle."

"I bet you are." I laugh. "You'd probably let her stay up too late, eat too much sugar, and play inappropriate video games that would give her nightmares before sending her home to her parents."

"You say that like it's a bad thing." He stuffs a ridiculous amount of noodles into his mouth and chews with gusto, making me shake my head. How does he fit all that in there and not look disgusting?

I pick up a carton of peanut chicken and a fork. "You can't blame me for asking, though," I say between bites. "You don't have any children or ex-wives somewhere in the world?"

He picks up his glass and takes a long sip before answering. "Definitely not." He eyes me over his glass. "You look surprised."

I shrug. "I am, I guess. You're a member of Redfall; you've had women all over the world, I'm sure. It wouldn't be surprising if you had formed some attachments along the way."

He barks out a laugh and sets his glass down. "Believe me, most of those women aren't up for that type of attachment, unless it means they can get an eighteen-year paycheck out of it. Who needs that kind of headache?" He sits up abruptly, almost spilling his carton of noodles.

I set my carton down and take a sip of wine. "I'm sorry. Sensitive subject?"

"No, I just…" He cocks his head at me. "I'll ask you the same question. No ex-husbands or little Cassidys running around?"

I shake my head. "Nope. I'm too busy for all that." That's as good an answer as any, I guess. And far better than the real reason.

A satisfied smile flickers on his lips as he picks up his glass to take another sip. "So, I'm playing a gig tonight—doing a favor for a friend. I'd like you to come."

"Really?" I lean back against one of the pillows. "I'd like a winning lottery ticket and no rain for the rest of the week. We'd all *like* something."

He smiles into his glass before looking at me, his green eyes sparkling. "Sorry." He clears his throat, making a spectacle out of himself. "Would you please, Miss Skinner, do me the incredible honor of joining me this evening at a soiree?"

God, that accent. It's irresistible. *He's* irresistible. And intense. He's got me off kilter. I never know when he's being serious. Like now. Unable to stand the intensity in his gaze, knowing I have to disappoint him, I look out over the city. "Thank you, but I can't. I have previous plans."

"Break them. Whatever you were going to do couldn't be as fun as spending the evening with me." He leans forward, drawing my attention again. He draws his finger across his lips, and for a wild second I imagine myself kissing those lips until we're both senseless. "Wait. Don't tell me you're going out with the sad Italian guy again."

"He's not Italian, and he's not sad," I snap. "He's a friend of the family and has a business opportunity he wants to discuss, not that it's any of *your* business."

"Isn't it?" Something flickers in his eyes that I can't quite name. Frustration? Hurt? Whatever it was, it disappears and he takes a deep breath. "You're right. It isn't. But maybe I'd like it to be."

I sit forward to hide my unease. "Sean, you barely know me."

"I know you well enough." He sets his food down and mirrors me. "And I'd like to know you better."

"Carnal knowledge isn't enough." I run my hand through my hair, trying not to remember the feel of him inside of me. It's impossible. "My life is complicated, and I'm sure yours is even more so with your touring, and recording, and academies, and…and whatever else rock stars do."

"I cornered the market on complicated. We share that, you know? Even if I wasn't in the band, my life would be scrutinized." I lean back studying him, unsure where he's going with this. "My father is the director of the International Development Agency." He pinches the top of one of the containers, shaking his head, and for the first time since I've met him, he's lost that easy-going attitude. "If there's one thing I regret, it's the embarrassment I've foisted on my parents over the years. Almost cost my father his position once, and dragged the family name through the mud back in the day. So, if you want to talk about complicated political nightmares, I'm your man."

I cringe inwardly. I've escaped one political nightmare in my life; I shouldn't court another. That's what my practical side is saying, at least. But there's that *other* voice in my head, the wild and reckless one that flares up occasionally, and is currently telling my practical side to fuck off and live a little. "But, there's so much more to know," I stammer, trying to hide my internal struggle.

"So, ask me something. Anything." My startled laughter rings out when he suddenly leaps over the table, almost knocking over the food, and lands on the pile of pillows next to me. "Look, I'm not asking for..." He shakes his head. "I don't know what I'm asking for, really. I like you and, based on your heel marks on my ass from the other day, it seems you like me. Let's have some fun. Let's see where it goes, yeah?"

God, I want to. Sitting here in the sunshine, looking into those mesmerizing eyes, I really want to. But... "You want me to be one of the worldwide women?"

His eyes shoot open. "No! I mean, there won't be other women. Not while I'm with you." He cups my cheek and I lean into him, savoring the feel of his hand on my skin. "Come on, Fly-girl. Trust me. I'm trustworthy. Ask Hannah—she's only five but she's a good judge of character. Come on. It'll be like an experiment."

I sweep my hand through my hair. "I'm not sure how I feel about being an experiment." Those hypnotic emerald eyes seem to see right through me. Any excuses I may have against getting involved with *anyone* seriously, much less someone like Sean, seem to evaporate under his penetrating gaze.

"Did you like this?" His arms spread wide to the lunch setup, and my irritation dims. I'd have to be an idiot not to like that he did this for me.

"Of course I did, but—"

"But nothing. We'd do more things like this, but with ground rules."

My lips twitch. "Ground rules?"

"Every good experiment has ground rules, Cass. That's just basic chemistry."

"Chemistry, hmm?"

"I was very good at chemistry." I don't stop him from wrapping his arms around me. He feels too good, too tempting.

"I just bet you were," I murmur. *You still are.* "Ground rule one: no other women."

He lets out a huff, rolling his eyes. "Did I not just say that?"

I try to stifle my smile and fail. His eyes lock to mine, his fingers drifting along the back of my neck send my pulse soaring. "You see, Fly-girl, you talk about other women, but what you don't realize is that the only one I can't stop thinking about is you. I wonder why that is."

That smug smile of his should annoy me, but it only causes my skin to prickle with heat. "Sex will do that to you." It's the only response I can come up with.

"It's not just the sex. It's you." His voice washes over me, raw and deep, and part of me yearns to believe him. I'm so tired of playing it safe and living with this constant fear of exposure, of always denying myself.

Fuck it. It's time I did something for me and not for my family. Excitement bubbles up inside me, like when I jump out of a plane. "Fine. We'll see where it goes. We'll do some experiments."

His startled grin is infectious. "Brilliant! So, I'll see you tonight." He leans in to kiss me, but I quickly slip two fingers over his lips.

"Wait. I'm not breaking my plans." He opens his mouth to protest, and I continue, "But I'll tell him I can't see him again. As a date, that is." Considering how tied up our fathers are, it would be next to impossible not to *see* Jack again.

"Fine," he mutters. God, he's cute when he pouts. "Then I'll just have to give you these now." He reaches in his pocket, pulls out a small, silky gift bag, and places it in my hand.

"What is this?" I poke at the lumpy bag like it has a live snake in it.

"Open it and see."

I pick it up and spill the contents into my hand; a bunch of pretty barrettes, some adorned with tiny crystals, wink up at me in the sunlight. A warmth fills my chest at his sweet gesture. "Sean! They're lovely." I look up to see a satisfied smile spread across his face. "Thank you!"

He plucks one out and leans forward to carefully slip it my hair next to the one I clipped there this morning. "There," he whispers, my heart pounding in my chest. "I saw these and thought of you. Only you. Does that tell you something?"

My stomach does a weird flip-flop at his words. I hum, feeling his kiss graze my cheek. But, when he tries to move his lips to mine, I move them just out of reach. "And what is it with you and not wanting to kiss me, Pretty Woman?" He sits back and folds his arms across his firm chest as my eyes widen. "What? Surprised I know about that film?"

"I didn't take you for a fan of nineties rom-coms," I say, trying to avoid his question, and carefully put the barrettes back in the tiny bag. The truth is, I'm afraid of a kiss. I'm afraid that if I'm not careful, I'm going to want a whole lot more than kisses from him.

"Please." He rolls his eyes. "Syd made me watch every single rom-com ever made. I'm a bit of an aficionado." He shoves one of the pillows out of the way and inches his way closer, the smell of leather and spice invading me.

"And something tells me you enjoyed every minute of it."

"I'll never tell." His eyes search mine, looking for answers.

"I just want to take it slow." Heat prickles my face. "I know that must sound crazy after we've…" I wave a hand at him. "You know."

His smile is contagious. I don't know if I've ever met anyone who is as at ease with himself. He radiates warmth, happiness, a carefree attitude I remember having what seems like a lifetime ago now. "Oh, I do know. And think of all the ways we can, *you know*." His eyes dart to my lips.

"I think we started this whole thing backward. You're supposed to get to know someone before you, *you know*," I counter, trying to hold back a laugh when he wiggles his eyebrows at me.

"I've found that what you're supposed to do rarely works for me. I was supposed to follow my father's path to politics. Can you imagine me hobnobbing with that stuffy old lot? I mean the wigs alone…" He shudders, scrunching up his nose.

It's the second time he's mentioned politics, and it dims the light that has started to burn in me. A constant reminder that regardless of what I may want, I always have to be careful. "Thank you, Sean. Truly. This was lovely. And thank you again for the gift," I say, wanting to steer our conversation away from politics for now. I lean in, inhaling his warm, spicy scent, and press my lips to his cheek. His arms instantly wrap around me, holding me to his chest, while he nibbles on my neck. I may not know him well, but my body obviously does; it melts against him, and my hands move to his hair. This pull between us is insane. I've never felt anything like it. He moans when I tug on his hair, sending a shiver through me. I'm about to pull him down to the cushions when I remember my next appointment.

With monumental effort, I push away, panting softly. My heart twinges at the confusion and longing in his eyes. "I can't. I have to get back to the shop." I tap lightly over his heart, and he flops back against the pillows, his hands clutching his chest dramatically. I can't help my laugh as I stand and start to put our lunch back in the basket. "Lunchtime is over. I have another client coming in, and I'm also sorting swatches to send to your sister."

His eyes crinkle at the edges. "Try saying that seven times fast. Sorting swatches sending sister, sorting swatches sending sister, sorting swa—" He ducks the pillow I chuck at him, howling with laughter.

"You're crazy."

"On the contrary, I'm one of the sanest people I know," he says primly, but can't hide his smile. Signing in resignation, he sits up and helps clean up our mess. "I'll let you go—this time—but only because you're working on Syd's dress. Next time, Fly-girl, you may not be as lucky."

"Another round?"

I thrust my empty glass out, not caring if it makes me look eager. Liquor is a necessity if I'm going to make it through tonight. Jack and I are tucked in a corner of the Jade Bar in the Gramercy Park Hotel. It's comfortable despite the swanky décor, and the bartenders are terrific. It's also a great place for conversation, no matter how full it is. Everyone is always so absorbed in their own dramas, a bomb could go off and no one would notice.

Jack laughs and signals our server, who makes a beeline to the bar. Gotta say, I appreciate her efficiency.

"Tough day?"

I tap my lips with a finger and consider his question. "Interesting day." Closing my eyes, I can almost feel Sean's lips on my neck. I wonder what he's doing now. He said he was playing somewhere. I wish I'd gone with him; I'd love to see him in his natural element on stage.

From the minute he surprised me in my shop this morning, he's all I've been able to think about. Oh, be honest, Cassidy—he's all you've thought about since you first met him on that plane.

Now I need to let Jack know that friendship is all I can offer him, but the conversation hasn't really given me an opening yet. So far, we've just talked about general things—a new project he's started in Alberta, family, my father's campaign. I wish we could get to this "opportunity" he wanted to discuss; that might make this easier.

Our drinks are delivered and Jack takes a sip of his scotch. "Well, I hope it's about to become even more interesting. Cassidy—can I speak frankly?" I nod, trying not to sag in relief. Finally. "I suppose it's no secret how *interested* our parents are in our personal lives." He leans a little closer. "And who we're dating."

I almost choke on my martini. Well, he said he wanted to speak frankly. "No, it's not," I manage, dabbing at the side of my mouth with a napkin. "I think I had three texts from my mother asking how our dinner went last night."

"My father sent me two." He chuckles, running his finger along the rim of his glass. Then he leans forward with a sheepish smile. "But, Cassidy, I've got to be honest—you're not my type."

A laugh bubbles up as a wave of relief washes over me. "Oh, thank God." I sigh, slumping back against the blue velvet banquette with a smile. "I've been sitting here trying to figure out how to let you off the hook, too."

He winks. "I had a feeling we were on the same page. But we can still be friends, I hope?" He raises his glass to me, which I clink with mine. We grin, reveling in our joint reprieve.

"I love my dad, but he's determined to marry me off before he retires and makes me CEO," Jack continues. "Something about securing a legacy, I think. Doesn't seem to care about my thoughts on the matter." He rolls his eyes, and I chuckle.

"I take it that you're not in as much of a hurry as he is?"

He draws a fingertip idly across his cocktail napkin and shakes his head. "I can't tell you how many women he's tried to set me up with over the last year. He's afraid I'm going to become a lonely workaholic when I take over and have a heart attack before I'm forty."

Giving him an understanding smile, I swirl the skewered olives in my glass. "Well, at least he cares."

"And I care about him. I'm worried; his health hasn't been good lately and his physician is trying to get him to slow down. But he just won't do it. For me." He frowns down at his drink.

"My parents aren't concerned with legacy as much as they are with my father's career. And politics are all about making connections—the right connections." I pop an olive in my mouth and eye him, wondering how much I should explain. "I owe my father a debt that I will never be able to repay." He frowns, but he doesn't press, so I continue, "Although I don't agree with his politics, I love and respect him. He has an honest desire to help the citizens of Wyoming. I also understand the role the whole family plays in a politician's success. So, when I find myself unexpectedly seated next to a key donor's son at a fundraiser…" I shrug.

He laughs. "I get it. How many unexpected dinner partners have you found yourself with?"

"Recently?" I tap my chin. "Well, in the last year, there's been a pharmaceutical lobbyist, the son of the Intelligence Committee chairwoman, a spokesman for the national committee—God, there's not enough alcohol in the world to get over that one—and the charming son of a big oil donor from my home state." I raise my glass to him and take a sip as he chuckles. "It's just politics."

"At least I'm the charming one." He grins. "Have your parents ever suggested a more permanent partner for you?"

Sean's face appears in my mind, and I shake my head to dispel the image. "Usually they're happy with a few dates—until whatever deal my dad's team is working on goes through."

He taps a long finger on the table. "Just dates?"

My gaze snaps to his. "They're my parents, not my pimps." I glare at him until he holds his hands up in apology. "Yes, I'm 'encouraged' to go out with some of these guys a couple of times, but that's it. As I said before, politics is about connections. They get to be seen with a powerful senator's daughter and enjoy the illusion of influence that infers, and my dad's team uses them to either push or block the legislation of the day. Everyone wins."

"Everyone?" His stare is penetrating, making me shift nervously. In truth, I hate being a part of my father's political ploys, but I can't say no. I owe him too much.

Jack clears his throat. "I have a proposition that I think could serve us both immensely." He leans forward. "What if I offered you a path to stop the revolving door of setups and still make your parents happy?"

"How?" I pop my last olive in my mouth and take a sip.

"Marry me."

This time I do choke. My eyes water as the vodka burns, and I try to suck in a lungful of air. Jack discreetly thumps me on the back. "Jesus, Cassidy," he blurts, as I accept a glass of water from the ever-helpful server. "That wasn't exactly the response I was looking for. Are you all right?"

"What the hell were you expecting, Jack?" I choke, my hand pressed to my chest, as I struggle to breathe normally. The few people who noticed have gone back to their conversations, since I'm apparently not dying. I glare at him and he leans back, hands held up.

"Hear me out." He pauses as I signal for another drink. God knows I need it. "I said I had a business proposition for you and I meant it. Consider it business."

I blink. "What are you talking about?"

"Look, I know how important your business is to you. You're damned talented. And my company is important to me. If we were to marry, we'd possibly save my father from a stroke, secure reelection for your father, and continue to do what we love without further meddling in our lives."

He crosses his legs and stretches his arm out along the back of the banquette, looking for all the world like he's talking about the weather instead of a life-altering event. "Are you crazy?" I shake my head. "Look, I get that my willingness to go along with my parents' political schemes doesn't make me a poster child for self-respect, but I do have some standards. I don't love you, Jack."

"And I don't love you." The server brings me my new martini, and I eagerly take a sip. "But I like you, Cass. What's more, I respect you. Our relationship would be purely platonic. Think about it; we could stay together for a few years, long enough for my father to retire and your father to be reelected for another term, and then we could part amicably. It's more than a lot of people have. I'd even invest in your business, maybe help you expand and hire more people, if that's what you'd like."

Running a hand through my hair, I stare at him. This is ridiculous. On one level, I suppose he's right; it would solve a lot of problems… but… Ignoring the sudden memory of a pair of teasing green eyes, I blurt, "I can't leave New York. It's one of the fashion capitals of the world. My business would shrivel up and die if I moved to Cheyenne. No one would want me except the wives and mistresses of oil barons and televangelists."

He snorts out a laugh, his scotch sloshing in his glass. "Who says you have to move back to Cheyenne?" He licks a drop of liquor off his finger. "You could stay here and we could live separately, or I could move my headquarters to New York to be with you. There's nothing that says I have to run the business from Wyoming. I spend half my time here, anyway."

"You'd do that?" I grip the glass of water tighter. He can't be serious about all this. Can he?

"New York has a special place in my heart," he says simply. My heart starts pounding and I feel a rising sense of panic. He makes it sound so simple, but it's anything but.

"Jack, this is nuts." I wave my hand at him. This is not the way this evening was supposed to go. "I came tonight because I wanted to talk business, but I was also going to tell you I can't see you again because..." I set my glass down and fold my hands in my lap, trying to force myself to focus. "Because I'm seeing somebody. At least, I think I am. It's new, but he's... I mean, he makes me feel..." I flounder, not sure how to describe this chaotic pull I have toward the crazy Englishman. I wish for the hundredth time tonight that I'd gone to see him play instead of sitting here listening to this.

"I'm glad. You're much too special to be alone," he replies, surprisingly unruffled by my revelation.

I just stare in confusion. "But—"

"Cass, when I said New York had a special place in my heart, I meant it." He runs a hand through his dark hair, and then takes a deep breath. "My father's worries about me becoming some kind of workaholic are unfounded. I know the importance of balance in my life. Except the balance—the *person*—I have in mind isn't the type of partner my father would accept."

My breath catches as the light dawns. "You're gay?" At his wary nod, I lean back in relief, so many things clicking in place. "Wow. Okay, I see your point." Then a light laugh escapes. "I'm really not your type at all, am I?" A smile ghosts over his lips as he shrugs. "How many people know?"

"Just a few close friends, and now you. No one in the business knows. And definitely not our board of directors or my dad." He shakes his head, looking at his glass.

I touch the back of his hand. "That's why you're in New York so often?"

"My partner lives here. I could introduce you if you'd like. If you take me up on my offer, the two of you will be seeing a lot of each other," he says with a small smile.

"How does he feel about this plan of yours?" My mind spins. From what I know of his father's conservative views, I suddenly understand the importance of Jack's proposal. It's awful to feel you have to hide who you are from the world, from your family.

"He understands. He came out to his parents a few years ago, and his relationship with them has been rocky ever since." Jack leans forward and signals for the check before placing a reassuring hand on mine. "Look, I know this is a lot to take in, and I know how it sounds. But it would be only for a few years. Take your time and think about it. Think about how it could benefit us both." He cocks his head. "You said you just started seeing someone; have you introduced him to your parents yet?"

"God, no!" I take a hasty sip of my drink. The thought of Sean meeting my parents is both alarming and strangely satisfying. "It's not like that. At least not yet. I just… I mean, he's not…"

Our server brings the check, thankfully interrupting my stammering. Jack pays before I can offer and gives me a charming smile. "It's the least I can do after dropping such a bomb on you. Let's walk and get a little air."

Our steps on the pavement are drowned out by the usual noises of the city that never sleeps. The rain has stayed away, so the sidewalks are full of people heading to their evening diversions. I'm emotionally and mentally worn out, but the fresh air helps. I have no idea what to think about any of this, except I can't believe any of it is happening to me.

There's a group milling around the entrance of the Gramercy Theater and the pounding rhythms of a live band filter out to us. Jack takes my elbow to help me navigate through the swirling bodies.

"Hey, Jack!"

A short man in a blazer with slicked-back hair jogs over to us, a wide grin on his face. "Peter," Jack greets him in surprise. "Good to see you, man. What's up?"

"I'm hosting a group of out-of-town businessmen for a couple days. They're inside acting like frat boys on a bender." He rolls his eyes. "I just stepped out for a smoke. Hey—why don't you come in for a while? It's sold out, but I can get you backstage to listen. They're really good."

Jack looks at me in question, and I shrug. As tired as I am, loud rock music sounds like just what I need to drown out the confusion in my head. There's a blast of noise as Jack's friend opens the doors and ushers us inside, waving at the doorman, much to the consternation of those waiting outside. We weave through the people in the lobby and through a door leading to a dim hallway. Jack takes my hand as we maneuver in the near darkness, the music making conversation impossible. We emerge backstage and stand in front of the fly rail, behind a handful of people who are swaying with the beat in the wings. The audience is packed with enthusiastic fans. I can only see two guitarists on stage, but I can hear drums and a keyboard. Peter is right—they're good.

Then the crowd of groupies shifts and my eyes pop open in shock when I get a clear view of the violet-haired drummer, banging on his kit as if his life depends on it.

Sweet crispy Christ!

chapter six

Murphy's Law No.94: Let yourself become complacent, and before you know it, you're swimming in a sea of mediocrity.

Sean

"I DON'T LIKE IT." THIS FROM BLAIR CAMPBELL, THE BASS PLAYER OF Grant's band, Bishops to Kings. Blair has been grumbling since we met at the Gramercy, and it's carried on for the entire sound check. Pain in the ass bass players. So damn moody all the time. Although Blair is talented in his own right, he'll never hold a candle to our own Matt Logan. I could use some of Matty's melodic bass lines at the moment.

Matty and I have been playing together for so long now, when we're on stage, we can read each other minds. I'm in his head and he's in mine. He knows instinctively where I want to go, and that organic ebb and flow is pure magic.

"You'd rather play it exactly how you recorded it?" I ask from behind my kit. We've been at it for over an hour now. Sweat drips down my back, and my arms are starting to burn.

"That's what they're coming to hear," Nick replies, adjusting his guitar. Punk kid. He doesn't really get it yet.

I point a drumstick at him. "No. They're coming for an experience. They're coming to have their minds blown. So, give them something they're not expecting. If they wanted to hear it the way you recorded it, they could just hit repeat on their phones."

Blair eyes me skeptically before glancing at Grant. Grant simply holds his hands up in surrender from behind the piano. "I'm kind of with Sean on this one. Might be nice to mix it up."

Grant looks over at Andrew Foster, their rhythm guitarist. "I'm up for whatever, man. I just can't believe we get to play with you." Andrew is a bit starstruck, I think. He and Blair are young: twenty-two or twenty-three. Grant, who's thirty-nine, definitely has his hands full with these two. Andrew kind of had a moment when I arrived. It was like he couldn't believe I actually showed up. He's been gushing ever since. It's getting kind of creepy, to be honest.

I wave him off. "It's not a big deal. Besides, I'm fairly certain I owe Grant here a favor."

Grant coughs. "Or thirty." I've known Grant a long time. We bailed each other out of a number of questionable circumstances back in the day when both of us were young and stupid and thought we were invincible. "'Mistress Nine' is meant to shake the roof off," Blair all but whines. "I mean, aren't you all about slamming the drums?"

I try to ignore that jab. "Not always. This song, to me, is about seduction. You want to entrance them, invite them in for a bit. Let them get drunk off the rhythm." Blair's eyes widen. Yeah, kid. I did my homework. I've studied every single song on the set list Grant gave me.

Kennedy, Redfall's taskmaster, drilled it into us to be prepared, and I never want to let him or anyone else I'm playing with down. I also watched a few of Grant's concert videos, and every gig seems the same. He's gotten into a bit of a rut. That's always a danger when you're in a band. Familiarity is easy, but it's also stifling, and before you know it, you're swimming in a sea of mediocrity.

One of the things I'm most proud of with Redfall is we don't follow a formula. The four of us are naturally curious. We want to explore new territory, and we take the audience with us on the journey each and every time. Which is why I know the audience is going to eat up a stripped back version of "Mistress Nine."

"Just trust me. Try it again; dial it back on the bridge. If you don't like it, I'm happy to go back to *'slam on the drums'* as you so eloquently put it."

That gets a grin out of Blair, and he shakes his head. "Sorry, man. I shouldn't have said that."

"You can say whatever the fuck you want. Just don't be afraid. If you're not willing to take a chance, to get stoked about pushing the boundaries, what the hell are you doing this for?"

Andrew chimes in with a faraway voice. "Murphy, man, you need to put that on a T-shirt."

Grant tries to hide his amusement, adjusting his microphone. "Watch it, Drew. Your fangirl is showing."

"Right then. Off we go." I count them in, quickly getting lost in a new sound, a new vibe, chasing the burn before it gets away from me.

No matter if I'm playing for a crowd of ten or ten thousand, warming up backstage brings the usual shot of adrenaline. My skin prickles with anticipation, and my heart rate pounds out a steady rhythm. The demanding crowd grows restless while I go through my warm-up for my wrists and fingers, and the cracking of my neck Cameron hates. It's a ritual, one that's second nature to me now. It clears my head, loosens me up, and I need that when I'm going to be playing for three solid hours.

Long gone are the shots of Jack Daniels I used to inhale like water back in the day. It's not to say I don't enjoy a pint or a good single malt whiskey after a show now and again, but I know firsthand what a temptress alcohol is, and so I leave the hard stuff that sits on the table in the green room to Blair and Andrew. I know it goes against convention. I know nearly every program out there tells you one drink is too many. I don't see it that way. I don't feel the need to adhere to what society dictates is acceptable. Everyone's addiction and recovery story is different. What works for some may not for others. I know from the brutality of experience what my triggers are, and there's not a white line of it in sight.

Grant used to have a bit of a love affair with coke ten years ago. In a strange turn of events, he developed an even bigger love for his substance abuse counselor who's now his wife, Caroline. The two of them are cozied up on a sofa beside me, their heads inclined, whispering to each other. Bishops to Kings is getting ready to embark on a grueling US summer tour, and despite the lure of the road, Grant hates to leave Caroline.

"I love my job, but touring has a price," Grant told me before Caroline arrived. "I miss being home. I miss her." It made me think about the fact I don't have anyone to miss. I don't know what it feels like—that longing Grant and the rest of the guys in Redfall have for the women in their lives. Kennedy once said he breathes easier when Abby is around. Spending time with Cassidy today gave me a glimpse of that. She opens me up, makes me think about possibilities, about ways to get her to smile, about having a connection with someone that lasts beyond a few hours or a single night.

"Hey." Sydney nudges me in the shoulder, grabbing my attention. She joined us an hour ago and has been avoiding the bowls of sweets the rest of the band is devouring. She spewed some nonsense about not wanting to gain weight before the wedding. I don't know what she's worried about. Syd and I share the same metabolism. We can eat like ravenous wolves and never have to worry.

Syd nods to the table in the far corner, lowering her voice. "You okay with all this?"

I glance over at Andrew who's passing vodka to Blair. "Come on,

Syd. You've been backstage a time or two. This is tame." She laughs, but it sounds hollow. "All is good. Is it tempting? Sure. Do I know what I can and can't handle now? Of course. Do I want to be caught up in chaos and tension again? Not in a million fucking years." I suck back an energy drink, its stark, manufactured taste stinging my tongue. I kind of miss the fresh fruit displays and protein-rich smoothies Tucker now insists we have before a show. It's a far cry from where we started out, when backstage was a hazy blur of excess and indulgence. Watching Andrew and Blair put a dent in the bottle gives me a flashback to those days gone by, but it doesn't make me crave it. My indulgences now are much different, and I know that's a good thing.

Syd gives my arm a squeeze. "I didn't mean to upset you." Her tone is soft, sincere.

"I know that, Syd. Thank you for caring enough to ask."

"Of course I care. When I think about what you went through in rehab…" A shadow of worry hangs in the air, threatening to choke us. My stint in rehab was a fucking nightmare—for my family and for me. What I put Syd and my parents through is always going to burn.

"Try not to think about it. I surrendered to the process. I did all the steps and then some. I still go to meetings if I need to. And if I'm feeling the itch, I have my sponsor who will pick up any time of day or night." Thank the Lord for Russell. He was on the receiving end of many a marathon phone call during the early days of my recovery. I haven't needed to call him in a long time, thank Christ.

"I will too, you know." Syd looks up at me, tears welling in her eyes. "I'm sorry. I shouldn't be talking about this right now when you're about to go on stage."

I sling my arm around her shoulder and ruffle her hair. "It's okay, Syd. It's never a bad time to remember that it's easy to get lost in your own selfishness sometimes."

She ducks away from me, trying to flatten down her hair. "You are not selfish, Sean."

"About some things I am. It's just not my center anymore."

She smiles at me. "I know that too. What you're doing tonight with these guys, how you insist on paying for everything for the wedding even though Philip isn't your favorite person in the world."

"Isn't that the tru—" Her death glares shuts me up, and I mock zipping my lips. I still can't quite wrap my head 'round what she sees in Philip. He's the most straight-laced, buttoned-up bloke you'd ever come across. Simon loved to take risks and thrived off adrenaline. Philip would be quite content watching paint dry. Maybe that's why she likes him—*loves* him. He's the exact opposite of who Simon was.

"Who knows how much money you donate to the music academy back home, and now you're starting one here." She shakes her head. "You may have your moments now and again where I'd like to throttle you, but you're one of the least selfish people I know."

Damn twin making me all emotional. I set the rest of the energy drink down and pull her into a hug. "Thanks for not throttling me, Syd. Think of how boring your life would be without me in it." Her laugh is muffled against my shirt, and she gives my chest a shove.

"Shouldn't you be out there now? That crowd seems to think so." Syd smiles at the impatient chants drifting to us. I see Grant push off the couch and move to the door, giving Caroline a kiss before he glances at me.

"You ready to do this, mate?" I give his shoulder a smack when I join him.

"Born ready, my friend. Born ready."

The Gramercy is small in comparison to the stadiums Redfall typically plays, but the intimate atmosphere adds a dimension that hooks me. A crowd this size is easier to read, and Grant plays off them with his instinctive charisma only the best front men have.

It doesn't take long for us to find our synergy, and soon, Grant drills the vocal, hitting the high notes that have become his trademark. He feeds off the crowd while I lead us into the haunting version of "Mistress Nine" we practiced this afternoon.

Blair falls into step easily, shooting me a grin halfway through. I'd like to say I told you so, but I don't need to. The crowd says it all. Their pulsing, electric energy fills the theater and pushes us to give them more.

Nights like this are what it's all about. That magic chemistry between musicians and the crowd is something I'm always seeking. I know how lucky I've been to share a stage with my own band when it happens. Tonight, I'm playing with an intensive authority that holds the audience captive, a passion that has every muscle in my body aching in the best way.

I feel like I've sprinted up Everest after we take our first standing ovation and head backstage to darkness. The crowd wants more, and we're going to give it to them. I'm dripping with sweat and reach for a towel perched on one of the amp cases when familiar, frantic squealing pierces through the constant buzz in my ears.

Through the muted glow cast by the recessed floor lights, I see two girls fawning over Andrew and Blair. Ah, the groupies. They're never far off. Caroline watches and ignores the random women who want a piece of her man. Grant is oblivious to the small group scratching and clawing their way to us. He's only got eyes for his wife, pulling her into his arms despite the fawning groupies.

I've never complained about women who can't get enough of musicians—bless them a thousand times over—but the arm snaking around my waist feels wrong. Glancing down, her eyes aren't that fascinating gray-blue I've started to crave. Her hair isn't soft or blond; it's ebony and rough against my exposed chest.

Grant leans away from Caroline, shouting so I can hear above the roar of the crowd. "You're on fire, Sean. Seriously. Thank you for doing this, man."

"You don't need to thank me." I can feel the hand at my waist drift down to the back of my jeans, into the pocket. I take a step to the side, knocking into a stack of equipment cases, but damn, if she isn't persistent.

"I'd like to thank you." The woman has a twangy voice. She won't let go as if she wants to climb my torso. This is all wrong. She's not Cassidy. It hits me; I want Cassidy here, and it burns to know she's out with another man. "Want me to show you how much?"

Gently, I pry Little Miss Determined's hand out of my back pocket. "Darling, you're lovely, but I've got an encore to perform." She gives me a little pout, pushing her tits forward. I do hate disappointing women. Leaning forward, I whisper next to her ear, motioning over to Andrew and Blair who have their hands full of their own distractions. "See these two over here?" She glances over in their direction. "They're the ones who could use a thank-you."

"But they're not you." She blinks at me all eager and ready to do whatever the fuck I want. I appreciate the enthusiasm even if it is shallow.

"Few men are, darling. Few men are." She huffs and then plants a kiss on my cheek and saunters her sweet ass over to join Andrew and Blair, preening her hair on the way. They can thank me later.

Satisfied I've done my good deed for the night, I turn to go in search for an ocean or two of water before we take the stage for the encore. I look over my shoulder to be wary of more groupies when I collide straightaway into curves I recognize easily. My hands itch to touch, to claim, to pull her against me, but she's not having it. Even in the muted light, those eyes of hers tell me everything I need to know. Cassidy's seen me with another woman, and she's not amused.

Those green eyes that have haunted my dreams since I met him widen in shock. I'm the last person he expected to see here tonight, especially considering his little black-haired friend over there. Ass.

"You came!" His grin could light up the city, and I can't help but smile in return. But then his eyes move past me to land on Jack's out-stretched hand.

"Great set, man." Jack's excited voice matches his eyes. "That was fantastic." When Sean leaves his hand hanging in the air and narrows his eyes to slits, Jack places his hand on my shoulder instead. "You never said you knew any musicians, Cass," he says, seeming to ignore the snub, but his voice carries a slight edge.

"Only one." Sean's eyes dart to mine at my flat tone, his jaw set. "Jack, this is Sean Murphy, usually the drummer for Redfall. Sean, Jack Coleman."

"Redfall?" Jack's eyes widen. "Holy shit. Why are you slumming it with these guys?"

"I don't consider it slumming," Sean shoots back, his eyes sparking green fire. "They're talented musicians."

Jack huffs a laugh and presses his free hand to his chest. "My mistake. It was a poor choice of words. So, are you the guest artist or something?" He slides his hand from my shoulder down to my waist, pulling me closer and out of the way of a stagehand who almost mows me down while carrying two mic stands past us. Jack's just being polite, but Sean's clenching his teeth so hard, the veins are popping on his neck.

"Just doing a friend a favor," he grits out. He waves a hand at Jack, but keeps his gaze on me. "So, this is the sad Italian guy, huh? The boring git you just can't say no to?"

Glaring at him, I take a step toward him and out of Jack's protective hold. "I told you at lunch, he's neither sad nor Italian. Stop being an ass."

"Ah, but he *is* boring, right?" He waves a hand at Jack, who's watching us with confusion and a touch of amusement. "I mean, just look at him. Christ. All buttoned up and not a hair out of place? You can't be serious about this tosser." He rakes a hand through his purple hair, looking skyward. "Jesus, what is it with the women in my life? First Syd falls in love with Philip-the-Damp-Squib, and now you show up with—"

"Would you shut up for five seconds?" I hiss, feeling my face heat in anger and embarrassment. Jesus, his lack of filter drives me nuts.

And I hate that his possessive outrage is kinda hot. "You have no idea what you're talking about."

"Have you told him?" He steps closer, making me look up at him. The shirt he's wearing is unbuttoned and looks like the sleeves were torn off, leaving jagged seams at the shoulders and exposing the swirling colors of ink that adorn his muscled arms and chest. Roses morph into musical notes, a lion is wrapped in the Union Jack, and a compass overshadows a map of Europe. He's a work of art and my fingers itch to explore each and every design. At the moment, glaring up into his stubborn expression, all I want to do is slap him.

"I'm not talking about this now," I grind out, mindful of the crush of bodies backstage. I don't really want to yell about my sex life in a crowd of strangers.

Sean leans closer, and I'm instantly surrounded by his warm, spicy scent. "Why not? He needs to know." He raises his chin in challenge. "Or didn't you mean anything you said today?"

"Okay, that's fucking it!" I shove at his chest, but it's like shoving a wall. "How dare you! You were cozying up to little Miss Thing over there?" I fling an arm out, pointing toward the hussy who was rubbing against him like a cat in heat a minute ago. "Or are you going to try to tell me it wasn't what it looked like?"

"Oh, it definitely was," he growls, that cocky smirk I hate to love sliding on his lips. "But—"

"But nothing." Propping my hands on my hips, I glare at him. "I was honest with you today, but all that crap you spewed about not wanting any other women?" I huff a scornful laugh. "You're all hat and no cattle."

Jack snickers behind me at my back-home comment as Sean looks like I've grown two heads. "All hat... what the fuck does that mean?" He reaches for my arm, but I jerk it out of his reach. "Fly-girl, I wasn't lying today. If you'd stop and think about what you really saw—"

"Cassidy!" Sydney appears out of the murky darkness, a bright, surprised smile on her face, and gives me a quick hug. "I didn't know you were coming! Sean didn't say anything."

"He didn't know. A friend got us in. I didn't know he was playing here," I say and quickly introduce Sydney and Jack. She gives my date a once-over, and then her eyes dart to her twin, her lips quirking with humor.

"Jack, nice to meet you," Sydney says over the noise of the chanting crowd. They're demanding another encore. "Don't mind my Neanderthal brother. He never was good at sharing his toys."

"For fuck's sake, Syd," Sean begins, his cheeks turning red, even in the dim backstage light. Before he can say any more, a man with a blond crewcut and goatee slaps his hand on Sean's shoulder.

"Come on, man, we need to get out there before they start pulling up the seats." He gives Syd and me a rakish smile. "You can hobnob with your ladies later."

Sean snorts out a laugh. "Right, mate. Let's do this." He turns and makes a grandiose bow to us. "Ladies. I'll see you *both* later." He jogs on stage, followed by a couple other guys who are slinging guitar straps over their heads.

"The guy with the goatee is Grant Bishop. It's his band." Syd leans closer so she can be heard over the roar of the crowd. "Their drummer is out for a couple gigs, so Sean is doing him a favor."

I nod, indicating I heard her, but can't take my eyes off the man settling behind the drum kit and twirling his sticks in his fingers like batons, much to the crowd's delight. His head snaps toward me, his eyes boring into mine, and then a smile curls his lips I feel in my belly. Giving a howl, he counts them in, and then the band bursts into a version of "Walk this Way" that sends the crowd into a frenzy.

Sydney and I bop and sway to the beat; it's impossible to stand still. "It's been years since I heard him play with a band other than Redfall," she yells in my ear. "They're like his brothers, and they share a hive mind when they play. But he hasn't missed a step with Grant's crew."

I let my eyes rove over the violet-haired maniac whose arms are flying with such skill and strength over his instrument. "He's amazing," I blurt. She shoots me a knowing grin.

"He is, isn't he?"

I give her a grudging smile in response, and she laughs, ducking closer to say, "You know, he thinks you're pretty amazing, too."

Humph. Maybe, maybe not. I nod to let her know I heard her, but don't reply. I can't focus on anything besides the man pounding out a driving, rock-solid rhythm that's propelling the band forward and thrilling the audience. A satisfied smile is never far from his lips, despite the intense look of concentration in his eyes. Based on the grins the guitarists throw each other across the stage, they look like they're having the time of their lives.

A warm glow forms in my chest as I watch Sean work his magic. The sheer joy he exudes is contagious, and I find myself mirroring his grin. Seeing him in his natural habitat is both a privilege and an indescribable pleasure.

Aerosmith gives way to Nirvana, and then to one of Redfall's biggest hits, making Sean howl like a fiend. The crowd is eating it up with a spoon, stomping and screaming and singing along for all their worth. Standing well out of sight of the audience, Sydney and I sway and clap along. Just when they've almost reached the end, a hand squeezes my shoulder, making me jump. Oh, jeez; I'd completely forgotten about Jack.

"Hey, I'm sorry, but do you mind if we head out now?" He leans close to my ear to be heard over the crowd. "It's almost midnight and I have some early meetings tomorrow."

Reality crashes down around me. Sneaking a look out at the stage, just as the guys come to a crashing end, I feel a flutter of nerves. As much as I want to stay, I don't really want a repeat of Sean being an ass to Jack. It feels like my worlds are colliding, and I can't quite handle it right now. I especially can't handle the pang of jealousy I feel when I see the herd of squealing groupies hovering offstage, ready to pounce. It makes my feelings for Sean all too real—more real than I want to think about now.

"Yes, let's go." I turn away from the lights as the guitarists onstage unplug, but Sydney grabs my arm. Jack pulls out his phone and mutters about texting his driver.

"You can't leave yet! He'll want to see you." Sydney's eyes implore me to wait, but I pat her hand and she releases me. The crowd roars for more even as the band saunters toward the front of the stage. Grant rises from behind the piano and waves at Sean, who nimbly jumps down from the raised drum platform; he joins the others and slings his arm around Grant's shoulders. He's giving the chanting crowd a cheeky salute when I look back at his sister.

"Tell him I'll talk to him later. Have a great evening, Sydney."

Sydney nods and gives me a resigned but understanding smile. "I will."

The journey back to my shop is mostly silent. My ears still ring from the volume of the speakers on stage. My heart thrums from watching the mesmerizing British man in his element. It was one of the hottest things I've ever seen. Ever. The sight of his biceps bunching as he pounded away, the drops of sweat that looked like gems caught in the stage lights when he shook his head...I suck in a small breath and try not wriggle in my seat to relieve some tension. As much as I hate to admit it, I can't really blame those damn groupies.

No wonder sex and rock and roll go together.

Jack breaks me out of my churning thoughts. "So, can I assume that was the man you were speaking of earlier? The complicated one?"

I sigh and meet his eyes in the quiet of the back seat, nodding once. He chuckles and shakes his head. "Wow. Sean Murphy." He leans back and crosses his legs. "You weren't kidding. Your father would have a coronary."

"I know." Closing my eyes, it's easy to imagine how red my father's face would be if I ever told him. And then he'd start sputter-swearing like he did when I told him I'd accepted a spot at UCLA. "Look, Jack, it's new, really new," I say, holding up a hand. "So new, I'm not even sure what it is yet, or what may happen. But I want to give it a try." I glance out the window at the New York evening. Even at midnight, there are people on the street. In Cheyenne, they would've rolled up the sidewalks hours ago. "Until I've figured it out, I want to keep it to myself."

"I understand. You can trust me." He takes my hand, drawing my gaze back to his. "And I can trust you?"

"You can. I promise." I laugh lightly. "I can't promise I'll agree to your plan, your proposal, but you can trust me to not reveal your secret."

"Thank you." The car pulls up outside my shop, and he swiftly gets out to come around and open my door. "I know I've given you a lot to think about tonight," he says, giving me a soft smile. "Don't dismiss it out of hand. Please. Given Redfall's touring schedule and such, an arrangement such as I suggested might work out well for both of us. Think about it."

I lean in and give him a quick kiss on the cheek. "I will. Goodnight, Jack. Talk to you later."

The only sound in my darkened shop is the muted ticking of the clock in the break room. I swiftly check the windows and doors to ensure they're locked and try to block out the conflicting voices in my head. Jack's plan shocked me…but I *can* see the benefits, to both of us. My parents would be over the moon. It would get them off my back until after Dad's reelection, and probably even after we separated, at least for a while. Besides, marriages of convenience happen every day, especially among politicians and celebrities. I've outfitted at least three brides—that I know of—who married for status or power rather than love. As far as his offer of investing in my business…I couldn't take his money outright, but I wouldn't be opposed to accepting a loan from him that I'd pay back. Then I could hire some seamstresses I trust and lessen the stress of meeting deadlines. From a practical perspective, my head is telling me it's not the worst thing I could do.

My heart isn't so sure. At all.

Rounding the corner near the front door, I start to mount the stairs—three sharp raps on the door scare the hell out of me and freeze me in my tracks. Sean's voice bellows from outside. "Fly-girl! Open up!"

"Oh my God," I mutter and jump down the steps to unlock the door. Swinging it open, my breath catches at the sight of him, standing tall with his amethyst hair glowing in the light of the streetlamp. "Shhhh! People live around here, you know. They're trying to sleep," I hiss, trying to ignore my suddenly pounding heart.

His smirk sends a delightful shiver down my spine. "There's only one person around here I care about." Without waiting to be asked, he moves past me into the foyer, closing and locking the door behind him. He changed after the show—he's wearing a tight black T-shirt under his leather jacket and looks like sin.

"What are you doing here?" My eyes search his in confusion. "And how did you get here so fast? I mean, I thought you had stuff to do afterward."

"Nothing is more important than you." He rakes a hand through his damp bangs, making them stick up all over, and takes a step closer.

"You don't say?" I hate how breathy I sound, and I rub at the base of my neck. As if that will help.

"I do say." He takes another slow step toward me. I'm hit with a wave of his spicy scent, and my heart starts racing. "You left. You left before I even got offstage."

I raise my chin at his accusatory tone. "There was no reason for me to stay."

"The hell there wasn't." Before I can blink, he grabs me by the shoulders and slams his mouth to mine. I can't breathe, I can't think...I can only feel the strength of his hands and the force of his kiss. He tastes of cinnamon and whiskey. My knees are weak and I slump a little in his grasp. I hate that this man can scramble my wits so thoroughly. Just as abruptly, he lets me go and I grab the door handle for support, almost collapsing on wobbly legs—damn him! His smug grin infuriates me, and I let my hand fly—the sound of my slap against his cheek echoes in the room. His eyes grow big and he presses a hand to his reddening cheek; he's as shocked as I am, I think. Then I'm moving without thinking, flinging my arms around his neck and pressing my lips to his.

"Fuck, Cassidy," he murmurs against my mouth, lifting me away from the door and pressing my back against the stairwell. I'm desperate for him, the irritation I felt earlier morphing into a need I can't explain. And he seems to feel the same. He peels my coat off and I grab at his leather jacket, both of them landing somewhere on the floor. I tug his hand and, between kisses, we slowly move up the stairs, removing clothing as we go. My Jimmy Choos clatter on the wooden steps, and I pull his shirt over his head.

"Hang on, Fly-girl." I can't help my giggle as he slings me over his shoulder and runs up the remaining steps. I cling to his belt loops and kiss as much of his bare back as I can. "Bed," he barks and I point as best as I'm able while hanging upside down. Then we're in my bedroom and he flings me on the bed as if I weigh nothing, leaving me bouncing on the mattress while he pulls his boots off. With a predatory smile that curls my toes, he crawls over top of me, and I sigh in satisfaction, savoring his weight pressing against me. Cupping his cheeks, I stare into those green eyes that seem to be able to see straight into my soul.

"What are you doing to me, Sean?" I whisper, feeling too vulnerable. Tears prick my eyes and his expression softens. His hand slides behind my head.

"I don't know, but you're doing the same thing to me, love." He kisses me tenderly, the urgency gone, but the desire as strong as ever. He trails his lips down my neck to my collarbone and reaches to remove my bra. "You should never wear these blasted things," he mutters, flinging the offending garment over his shoulder. "You're so fucking beautiful."

I slide my hands over his shoulders and around his biceps. "You're the beautiful one." Moonlight streams through my upper windows, allowing me to see him clearly. Tracing the line of the Union Jack as it curls around his arm, I press my lips to it. "I want to know about this," I whisper. "I want to learn about all of them."

He suckles and nips at my nipple, causing me to hiss and arch up off the mattress. "Good," he hums against my skin, his accent thicker. "Because that might take a while…weeks, months even."

"Well, I've never been a quitter." I gasp in delight when his teeth find another target. At this rate, I'm going to have hickeys everywhere—not that I'm complaining. All thoughts of Jack and fake marriages and political schemes fade away under Sean's skillful hands and lips. His skin is so smooth, with just a light smattering of golden red hair over his arms. Adorable freckles peep out between the swirls of ink, making me wonder where else he has them.

He helps me when I start pulling at the buttons on his jeans, and soon he's gloriously naked; his taut body kneeling over me as he rolls on a condom. "Are you ready for me, love?" he murmurs, his voice suddenly rough. In answer, I pull him down to me and guide his heavy cock to where I want him, *need* him. With one swift thrust, he claims me as only he can. I wrap my legs around him and squeeze, and he groans in appreciation before slamming his lips to mine. He sets a quick pace, sending my heart racing and my hands scrabbling for purchase on his shoulders, biceps, anywhere I can reach.

We don't speak, but words aren't really needed. With every thrust, every gasp, every whispered encouragement, we connect on a level I've never had before. This is how it is every time with him. Actually, it's better every time. I'm sure the number of partners I've had pales in comparison to his, but it doesn't matter. The desperation and need I see in his eyes tells me that he may just be feeling what I'm feeling. I'm out of control with him, and I'm not sure I really care. That's both terrifying and thrilling…just like he is. Sean is the giant coaster in the amusement park. The dangerous ride that taunts you until you finally get up enough nerve to strap yourself in, and then you have to remember to breathe while you're being scared out of your mind—and loving every second.

My climax seizes me without warning, and I gasp his name as my eyes squeeze shut, sparkles dancing behind my closed lids.

"Fuck, fuck, fuck," he chants, gripping my arms tightly as he spasms, every muscle straining, before collapsing on me. We're a panting, sweaty mess of limbs wrapped around each other, waiting for the world to right itself. Gradually, I come back to myself and slowly take stock; the bed looks like a cyclone hit it, and…yes, that's my lace bra dangling from my ceiling fan. How the hell did it get up there?

A series of sirens travels nearby, and he groans. "Is it always this loud here?" he complains, but I can see amusement in his eyes.

"This is New York. Yes, it's always this loud. Some of the bars start closing about now." My street isn't as busy as it is during the day, but you can still hear some traffic outside. I slide out from under his arms to get up and walk over to the wall above the front of my shop. I can feel his eyes on me as I move. Grabbing the long cords hanging down, I lower the blinds in my upper windows, plunging the room into near darkness. The sirens have passed us by, trailing off somewhere to the south. "See, they're already gone."

He grunts and pulls me back against him as soon as I return to the bed. "Why did you slap me?" he asks, surprising me. I stiffen in his arms.

"Well, you were an ass to Jack, for starters." I try to move away, but he holds me still.

"Hmm, well, maybe I was," he grumbles eventually. "He had his hand on you."

"Seriously?" I lean up on an elbow and look down at him in the dim light. "What about that groupie? She was on you like a Band-Aid." He starts to protest, but I cut him off. "Look—I get it. That stuff must happen to you all the time. And I'm not judging you—truly. But you can't get all up in arms when I show up with a guy you knew about *ahead of time,* not when you've got that kind of thing going on backstage." I flop back down beside him and allow him to draw me close again.

"I sent her away, though, didn't I?" His tone is reproachful. "If you saw her, you must have also seen that I didn't accept her offer."

"Yes," I admit with a sigh, and then look down, hiding my face. I'm not usually *that* girl, the girl who gets jealous over every little thing, and I'm not going to start now. "Like I said, I get it. I was more bothered by how you treated Jack. And…" I try to sound casual, but I'm not sure it's working. "I meant what I said at lunch. If we're going to try this, I can't be one of your worldwide women."

A car alarm goes off down the street and is abruptly silenced, but not before I hear Sean's aggravated grunt at the interruption. "You won't be, Cassidy," he says, his accent smoothing the hard consonants in my name. He lifts my chin with a finger and kisses me gently. His lips fit to mine as if they were made for me; I was crazy to wait so long before kissing him. "I sent her away because she wasn't who I wanted. I wanted *you*. And then, when suddenly you were there, with that—" I clear my throat as a warning, and he hums, considering his words. "That *Jack*, I overreacted. I'd like to say it won't happen again, but that would be a lie. Overreacting seems to be in my DNA. Ask Sydney."

I huff a laugh at his joke. "But I'll be less of an ass to your friends," he continues, trailing kisses down my shoulder. "That I can promise."

With a sigh, I relax into his embrace and stretch my neck out as his lips travel upward. Then the silence is shattered when another damn police siren blares, seemingly right outside the window before it heads off around the corner. "Fuck," he groans in frustration, dropping his forehead against my shoulder. "This is why I live in a fucking penthouse. You don't have to deal with all that rubbish."

"You live in a penthouse?" I shake my head—of course he does.

He hums in the affirmative, distracted, and then grabs my hand. "Hey, do you have to work tomorrow?"

"Well, I don't have any appointments, but, yeah, I have to work. You see, I have this wedding dress order from some posh Englishwoman and her overreacting brother," I quip, and he chuckles.

"It can wait." He rolls over me, and his voice drops to a devilish whisper in my ear, making me shiver. "I have just the idea to get away from all this noise."

chapter seven

Murphy's Law No. 7: Sex with no strings is safe.
Strings have a way of tangling up and choking you.

SEX WITH SOMEONE I'M ACTUALLY STARTING TO CARE ABOUT IS NEW. THAT sounds awful in my head. Of course, I cared about the women I was having sex with previously. I cared that they had an orgasm or three and so did I. I cared I was able to escape without any strings attached. There's already a hell of a lot of strings holding me to Cassidy. I have a feeling there's a solid chance they're going to become tangled and messy.

A woman disappearing at one of my concerts is also new. Someone who won't take any of my shit is new. I had asked her for "experiments," almost afraid of the word relationship. It's not something I understand. I used to think it sounded like a self-imposed prison, limiting yourself to one person, but I guess I didn't count on that person being Cassidy.

I didn't expect my chest to feel tight or for my heart to beat harder. It's singing to her as I pound into her tight heat: *Cassidy, Cassidy, Cassidy.*

When she comes, I feel like I'm spiraling out of control, losing my fucking mind over this woman. Every stroke of her hand over my skin, every hitched breath of hers I steal with a long, drawn-out kiss, reduces me to a raw, needy mess.

Now that I've tasted her and know what it feels like to have her sweet lips on mine, I can't stop. I don't know how long we spend kissing. Time doesn't seem to matter.

Her lips were made to be kissed by me and only me.

Her fingers find their way into my hair, and she's clutching so tight, I feel the sensation in my cock. Stroking my tongue against hers, she arches into me and seems to revel in the erotic journey of exploring my mouth. Finally being able to kiss Cassidy is pure bliss. I could get lost in the feel of her lips against mine. There's no more room between us. We're just a jumbled mass of limbs and urgent kisses. I'm drunk on her scent, on her lips, on any part of her she'll let me have.

Every so often, she drifts off into a boneless sleep, and yet the urge to bolt I usually have when I'm with a woman is nowhere to be found. The only place I'm supposed to be is here, with her messy blond hair splayed over my chest and my palm resting on the curve of her hip. That's also new, and the thought should terrify me, but it doesn't.

"You stayed." It's a sleep-warm, throaty whisper from Cassidy as the morning light spills into her room. Staying the night—another thing to add to the experimental list.

My arm is all pins and needles, likely from the weight of her sleeping on it, but I can't seem to care. I crack an eye open and take her in. She's fucking fabulous, turned toward me on her pillow with her hair all messed, her swollen mouth curled into what I can only describe as satisfied bliss.

"Did you want me to leave?"

She lets out a tired sigh. "No, but I should. I should want you to leave."

I rest my forehead against hers, tracing my thumb along her cheek. "Shouldn't you want your boyfriend to stay?" I grin to myself. Who would have thought I'd be someone's *boyfriend*? Who would have thought I'd actually *want* to be? Instead of being terrified, I'm strangely calm.

The corner of her mouth kicks up. "My boyfriend," she mumbles, her eyes still closed.

"Has a nice ring to it, yeah? Do I need to remind you of that fact?"

She groans, burying her face against the pillow with a groan. "No."

I start to work my hands over her shoulders.

"That feels so good." At least she can't see my smirk as I press harder, moving in slow circles over her back. My hands are strong from countless hours logged playing with Redfall, and that I can be useful for more than just drumming is a bit of a revelation. Or that I want to be more than a drummer is even more mind-blowing.

I drop a kiss to her creamy back. I get a shiver in response, but I don't bother covering her up. Now that she's spread out for me, there's no way I want her to hide away.

She murmurs into the pillow, "I just think I need to find a way to keep up with you. I need to be in better shape."

"I happen to be very fond of your shape." I trail my fingers up the length of her spine. It's the lightest of touches, but I hear her breath hitch. "It's the stamina. Comes with the territory."

"Lucky me."

"Three-hour concerts for over fifteen years. Sometimes they're longer depending on the crowd. And Kennedy is a perfectionist. Our rehearsals and sound checks are marathons."

"I'll have to thank him for that." Her deep groan as I work over her lower back causes my cock to stir again. "You know, the words scream that you're complaining, but your tone tells me you love it."

"I do love it. The high is just..." I brush her hair away from her face, trying to find the words. "There's little in life I've found that compares."

She gives me a lazy smile, her eyes still closed. "Not even sex?"

"Sex with you? Yes."

The color in her cheeks rises, and she drops her face into the pillow. "Silver-tongued Englishman." She tries to sound like she's grumbling, but I can hear the amusement in her voice.

"You finally kissed me last night, pretty woman," I whisper against the curve of her neck, tugging on the tiny wink of a diamond nestled against her earlobe.

"You started it."

"And it's a damn good thing I did. I'd hate to miss a minute of how sweet you taste."

Finally, those blue-gray eyes open to mine, and I can see the heat there. "I wanted to take it slow. That was the plan."

"Hmmm." Her lips part as I press my thumb over her kiss-swollen lips. "Think we're past slow now?"

"Maybe…" She pauses before continuing, "I feel like I know you, but I hardly know you." Her voice is soft, a little reserved.

"I'm an open book. Ask away."

"It's hard—"

I press my hips forward so she can feel the length of my cock. "Seems to always be around you."

She makes a feeble attempt to smack me. "I was going to say it's hard to ask questions when you're between my legs."

"Would you rather be on top?" I tighten my arm around her waist, bringing her with me as I roll to my back, ignoring her squeal of protest. "Is that better?" I rest an arm behind my head. "What do you want to know?"

She sits up and straddles my waist, laying her palms over my chest. She tucks a few strands of her hair behind her ear, and I let out a low hum. Christ, she's beautiful, and I just want to bottle up this moment and store it away. "Tell me anything. What was it like growing up with a twin? I have a brother and—"

"I want to meet him."

Her hand flattens over my chest. "You want to meet my brother?"

"It's the boyfriend thing to do, isn't it?"

Her lips twist, considering. "At some point—maybe."

I'm a little annoyed at that answer. "You've met my sister."

"Because she needed a wedding dress."

"Exactly! See? It's fate. It's meant to be, Fly-girl."

That little dimple in her cheek appears with her smile. "Tell me about growing up in England."

"Let's see. My father is in politics." That little crease at the bridge of her nose appears, and I brush my thumb over it. "I think I've told you, he's the director of the International Development Agency."

The heat of her palm warms my skin as she smooths over my bicep. "I don't know what that is."

"Ah, yes. Because only American politics matters, right?" I take a tug of her hair when she rolls her eyes. "It's focused on helping out in countries ravaged by poverty, disease, conflict. I saw the ugly side of the world with Dad growing up. He'd take Syd and me to build schools and help with relief efforts when disaster struck. Syd and I were twelve when he started bringing us along. He always wanted to make sure we knew there were people in the world who weren't as lucky as we were."

"That must have been hard to see sometimes."

"It was, but it's also an education they can't teach you in school. You don't really know what anyone is going through until you walk in their shoes." She hums a response, brushing along the inside of my arm, creating goose bumps over my skin.

"What about you? I know your father is in politics." Her eyes widen as she rears back.

"How do you know that?"

"Well, you see, when your girlfriend is dodgy about telling you things, you look to your friend Google to help you out."

It's meant to be a joke, but her hand covers her mouth. She looks terrified, the color drained from her face, her muscles tenses. "What do you know?" she asks, her voice guarded. Surely she can't be surprised I would find this out. It's not as if her father being in the senate is a secret she can keep. I don't know what's happened to have her do a one-eighty pivot on me, but I'm sure as hell going to find out.

"Just that he's a senator from Wyoming. Is that where you grew up?"

She relaxes, pressing herself against my chest on an exhale. "Yeah."

"Should I start wearing my hats more? I have about twenty of them. Save a horse, ride a cowboy?"

She shakes her head, her hands gliding over my sides, but I can feel her tension simmering just under the surface. I don't like it. "I'm an equal opportunity woman—cowboys, politicians, rock stars."

I growl at that. "Not anymore you're not. Only one rock star for you."

She drags a palm down my chest. "Only one."

"So, Wyoming? Is that where you went to school?" God, I hate I have to pry this information from her. I've been pretty damn open to this point, and she seems reluctant to share anything about her past or her family.

"No. I went to UCLA."

I can't help but trace my fingers along her thigh. So fucking inviting. Cassidy makes it hard for me to focus on an actual conversation. The fact she's starting to open up is the only thing stopping me from taking her again. "Now it's my turn to not know what that is."

"Tsk, tsk, tsk…and here I thought you were an international man of the world. It's in California."

"That's a ways from Wyoming. See? I know my geography. I should get a reward of some kind." I roll my hips forward, earning me a mild pinch to the side.

"Stop it… I'm trying to share here," she says, exasperated.

"Ah, we're having a moment. Got it." I wave my hand at her. "Please do carry on. Why California?"

"I wanted to branch out." She glances over to her workspace, her lips pressed together.

"Did you not enjoy it?"

"My education? Yes, it's where I fell in love with design."

"What about the rest? Were you a party animal? A freshman with newfound freedom and naughty ideas?" I can only imagine a young Cassidy flirting with senior boys. The thought makes my chest hurt with jealousy.

She shakes her head, her blond hair hiding her face from me. I brush it back and trace the soft contour of her cheek. "What aren't you telling me? Did something bad happen?" I grit my teeth. If someone hurt her, I will hunt them down to the ends of the earth and make their life miserable.

"I don't want to talk about it. Not yet, anyway. Maybe not ever." She lets out a long breath. "Let's just say when you talked about scandals? I know what that feels like."

"That's what a boyfriend is for, I understand. To be someone to talk to. Among other things."

"You know, for someone who claims to never have had an actual girlfriend before, you seem to know a lot about it." She's changing the subject, but I let her. For now.

"It's all the damn rom-coms Syd forced me to watch." She laughs, the sound lighting me up. "Even with all of those, you should know I'm fairly certain I'll do more than a few things to cock this up. But I do hear makeup sex is worth it."

"Is that what you hear?"

I glance over her shoulder to her large drawing table. It looks like she spends a lot of time here. It's chic and a little quirky—just like its owner. Endless pastel and blush rolls of fabric and lace all set into neat cubbyholes in the wall, dotted with the odd spark of color. There must be dozens of rolls of fabric.

Rows of crystals hanging off a rack near the window catch the early morning light through a break in the shades, throwing distorted rainbows on the dove gray walls. There's a whole shelf in the corner of her studio that seems to be devoted to feathers. And off to the side, three sewing machines, all with gowns on forms beside them in varying stages of completion. She's got different colors of tulips in mismatched vases throughout her workspace. I wonder where she gets her inspiration. Above it all her tempting lavender scent floats in the air. It's simultaneously soothing and calm, intoxicating and just a little wild.

I motion to her workspace. "Tell me more about this. Why you love it so much."

She smiles, settling against me. "I interned with Alexander McQueen."

Leaning back against the pillow, I grin up at her. "Alexander McQueen? Color me impressed, Fly-girl."

"Don't get too excited. It wasn't glamorous at all. Except for the one backstage show during fashion week, I was essentially a gopher who was barked orders at for a year in London. It's a wonder I tolerate your accent at all."

"You love my accent."

She ignores me, continuing on. "Did you know there's no less than 185 ways to have cappuccino?"

"Is that all?" I grin.

"I never could get it right. It was either too hot, too cold, too much sweetener, not the right design in the foam." She shakes her head against my chest.

My hand stills against the back of her neck. "You designed the foam?"

"No. But I got blamed for it anyway."

I tighten my arm around her. "They sound like bastards. I'll have to toss all the McQueen in my closet into the bin."

"Why am I not surprised you have McQueen couture in your closet. But don't trash anything. If nothing else, it's beautifully designed and impeccably made. Take away all the insane conflict and stress and, at the core, the label is all about tailoring. It's the attention to detail, the art of perfecting a silhouette I wanted to learn." I smile listening to her. It's obvious she loves what she does.

"Did you design anything for them?"

She lets out a wry laugh. "God no. They'd never let a lowly intern actually design something or have an opinion. The most I got to do was a buttonhole at two in the morning, and that was during fashion week because one of the tailors dropped out."

"I bet you rocked the hell out of that buttonhole."

I feel her smile against my chest. "Damn right I did."

"Best buttonhole ever."

"My hands shook the entire time, even though I'd probably done hundreds of them on my own by that point. There were eleven people hovering over me. It was torture, but I loved it."

"It sounds like you did."

"It also made my mind up about the kind of place I wanted. The big fashion houses? They're a machine. While the big names are partying on a yacht in Ibiza, the rest of the robots are working until their fingers bleed. And the show? It was just insane chaos backstage." She props her chin on my chest. "I bet it compares to backstage at a concert."

"And you didn't like that?" I ask, holding her gaze.

"No. I wanted a personal experience. I wanted to design and create everything myself. I want to know the stories about how a couple met, or why the bride wants to incorporate an heirloom in her dress. Interning at McQueen did influence my style, though. It's a lot of traditional blended with modern." She leans back, glancing over to one of the gowns. I follow her gaze. "That's charmeuse silk; some of the most expensive you can buy, but the shredded organza corset is what makes the statement. It makes it personal, more special." She shakes her head. "I'm just rambling now."

I tap the end of her nose. "Yeah, you are, but I know how it feels. To love something so much it consumes you."

She's quiet as she considers my words. "Is that how playing in the band is for you?"

"It is. I could play for days straight and never get tired of it."

She traces her fingers along my forearm, studying the ink closely. "As your girlfriend, I'd just like to tell you how much I appreciate these."

My lips twitch in amusement. "The tattoos?"

"Yeah, and your veins. I mean, come on. You're not even flexing and they're just… everywhere. It's like arm porn." She blows out a breath.

"Arm porn?" I bark out a laugh.

"What? You've never heard of it before."

"Apparently I've been missing out."

"No, you haven't. You could give a master class in arm porn."

"I'll take that under advisement. Maybe I could be your professor." I squeeze her waist and she squirms, not doing anything to calm my cock. It's hyper aware of every move she makes.

"You know, there are veins elsewhere on my body as well. You should check them out. It can be your first lesson as my student." I clear my throat. "Today, class, we will be examining the veins of the nether regions."

She throws her head back with a laugh. "The nether regions?"

"Are you unfamiliar with it? Well, we can't have that now, can we?" I guide her down my torso, and she complies, shimmying her way, her soft hair a caress over my skin as she moves. "You see? Many veins to explore."

I feel the warmth of her breath on my thighs as her fingers tease my length. "What happened here?"

"Where now, love?" I glance down at her, the sight of her examining my cock too much to take. I have to swallow before answering. "Ah, I was pierced."

She lifts her head, her eyes wide. "Why on earth would you pierce yourself?"

"Well, several reasons, really. I had a bet with Matty; he's our bass player. And it just so happens that the sensation is mind-blowing."

"Huh. I've never been with a guy who's pierced," she says, almost in awe as she pulls her thumb over the flared head of my cock.

"Never? Hmm. Do you want me to put it back in? It's painful as fuck when you get it done, but it's worth it." She hums, glancing up at me as she pulls me into the warmth of her mouth. I drop my head back with a groan. "Tell me I get to have you all day. You don't have to work on Syd's dress. There's plenty of time."

She releases me with a pop, her tongue teasing the crease of my thigh. "There's not, actually."

"Come on. Just the day, oh and overnight. Call it another experiment." I sound like I'm begging.

"Where are you taking me?" My little tease strokes over my length at a long, languid pace.

I roll my hips as her hand tightens at my base. "It's a surprise," I croak out.

"Pretty sure surprises aren't part of experiments. Or if they are, I missed that part of chemistry class."

"Hey now, some of the best discoveries in the world have come from a surprise."

She runs her tongue across her bottom lip. "Really, professor? Please do school me."

I'm a panting mess. Desire flares with white-hot heat. "Play-Doh, for example."

She lifts her gaze to mine again, all the while continuing to pump my length. "Play-Doh?"

"Mmm. It was supposed to be wallpaper cleaner. That was an epic fail that turned into the joyful surprise that is Play-Doh."

She lifts her hand to mine, setting it at the back of her neck. "I'm pretty sure that's an urban legend."

Gripping her hair, I guide her forward. "So am I, Fly-girl."

"You have to at least give me a hint on where you're taking me." She's quite the negotiator while she's denying me her mouth until I give her what she wants.

I take a firm tug of her hair, enjoying her little groan in response. "No hints. Other than dress casual."

"I have to be back tomorrow by eleven."

I lean up as she takes her time gliding her tongue against my abs. "You know, I'm hearing blah, blah, blah, when all I want to hear is, 'Yes, my amazing boyfriend. I can't wait to spend the next twenty-four hours with your undivided attention.'"

She nips at my hip, making my muscles tense. "I mean it. Eleven tomorrow. I have to be back here, Sean. I have a final fitting with a woman whose main goal in life seems to be getting on the top of the bridezilla list."

Threading my fingers through her hair, I concede. Mostly because it means she can focus on my cock, but partially because I think compromise is probably a good thing. "Fine, Cinderella. I'll have you back by eleven. I swear on the queen."

She gives me a satisfied smile. "Thank you."

"I know how you can thank me." Grinning, I reach over to my wallet by the nightstand, scowling. "I'm out of condoms. Tell me you have some." Good God, I didn't realize my voice could actually sound this pathetic.

"Afraid not, London. I don't exactly have a lot of guys over like this."

I flop back to the bed. "Fuck me."

She laughs, her hand resting on my arm. "Sorry, no can do."

I lean up again, taking her face between my hands. "I'm clean. I swear to fuck I am. I'm always telling the guys to wrap it more than once if you can. I've never done it without one."

"Be that as it may, better safe than sorry," she whispers, her hand tightening against the back of my neck.

My cock practically cries in protest. "Isn't every woman on the pill or some other form of birth control?"

She shakes her head, her fingers continuing their path along my bicep. "Every woman probably tells you that. And I am on the pill, but I think we should probably wait. You know? Get tested?"

I glance at the ceiling. "I promise when we're back, I'll get the works. Every single test there is."

She smiles, resting her forehead against mine. "Me too."

"In the meantime, there's plenty we can do, Fly-girl."

Two hours later, I'm greeted by a casually sexy Cassidy, looking at me like I'm crazy as I stand on the sidewalk outside of her shop.

"What's this?" She waves her hands frantically in front of her.

"Did you live a deprived childhood in the wilds of Wyoming? This is a bicycle. More precisely, a six-three-zero beach coaster, super soft seat, and cruiser tires." I sweep my hand across the seat as if I'm in a telly advert.

Her smile widens. "I know it's a bike, but why do you have them?"

"Where we're going, we don't need a car."

"So you rented me a pink bike?"

"Ah, yours is the green. Mine is the pink and black one. And they're not rented. I bought them."

Her mouth drops open as she adjusts her backpack. "You had time to buy bikes this morning?"

"It took like ten minutes. The biggest time suck was waiting for them doing a safety check and putting the baskets on. But I used that time wisely to pick up supplies. Not to worry." I push the sea-foam green bike in front of her with a helmet. "Your chariot, Miss Skinner."

Cassidy

Fresh air blows my hair in my face. Leaning forward over the rail, I can see the water curling into foam as the ferry plows through New York harbor. "So, you're taking me to Governors Island?" I point at the rapidly approaching boat dock.

He grins. "Ever been here?"

"Once. I attended a boring political fundraiser held at Fort Jay years ago." I raise my chin and close my eyes, savoring the feel of the wind and sun on my face. "Something tells me this isn't going to be boring, though."

"Smart girl." Maintaining a grip on his bike, he wraps his free arm around my waist and pulls my back to his chest. "I'm the least boring person you'll ever meet," he whispers in my ear.

"Ain't that the truth," I mutter, and I can feel his lips curl into a smile against my cheek. My body still aches from the *unboring* workout he gave me last night. This man just might kill me if I don't start doing Pilates or something.

He nips at my earlobe, sending a shiver down my spine. "You weren't meant for boring, Fly-girl." He straightens and pulls away slightly as another couple walks past with steaming lattes in their hands. Besides a few looks at his hair, no one has paid any attention to us. "The woman who can jump out of a perfectly good airplane with nothing but a bit of silk to stop her fall will never be satisfied with *boring.*"

I have a feeling he's talking about more than dreary fundraisers. Neither of us has mentioned Jack or what happened backstage since we went upstairs. My stomach churns with the secret knowledge of Jack's proposal. I need to tell Sean, but when? My skin seems to burn under the weight of his hand on my hip. It's guilt, although I haven't done anything to feel guilty. Yet.

As the ferry pulls into the dock, the passengers surge toward the exits. Sean claps his hands together and gives me an excited grin. "Time to get this party started!" He helps me shoulder my backpack again and gestures grandly for me to go first with my bike. Gripping my handlebars, we join the line forming to disembark.

Shaking my head, I put aside all thoughts of proposals and guilt. I'm going to enjoy this while it lasts.

"Stop! Stop, woman!"

I brake and coast to a stop off to the side of the bike path. Sean catches up and comes to a jerky stop behind me.

"I thought you said you hadn't been on a bike in years?" He glares at me, but his panting ruins the effect. I look down at my feet to hide my smile.

"No, I said I hadn't been on a *moving* bike in years." I squint and look up at him, finally letting my grin out. "Haven't you ever heard of spin class?"

He huffs and looks around, as if getting his bearings. "I think you played me, Fly-girl."

"Maybe. I thought you said you could go all day." I give him my best innocent look. "We've barely gone five miles."

He narrows his eyes at me, but there's a smile lurking on his lips. "Five miles after you dragged me around that damn museum all morning." There was an exhibition of avant-garde sculpture at Fort Jay I'd read about in the *Post*. It was fabulous, made even better by Sean's lively, impromptu commentary, and then we toured the historical exhibit about the island itself. Now, after a quick lunch from a food truck, we're on our way to the other side of the island to see "the real surprise."

"Suck it up, buttercup." I look over the field of lavender blooming next to us and inhale deeply. The soft scent fills my lungs, giving me a sense of peace. "So, are we close to wherever we're going?"

"Just around the bend." He points ahead and pushes off, giving me a challenging look. "Come on, slowpoke. Try to keep up."

"Ta-da!" Sean waves his arm in a grand gesture for me to precede him through the drawn tent flap. "I told you I was going to find a quieter place for us."

I feel as though I'm stepping into a page from Arabian Nights. The tent is huge and looks like something from a movie, with its white canvas forming neat corners and erected on a wooden platform. There's a real bed—an enormous king-sized bed—and even a funky chandelier mounted at the peak. Off to the side is an attached bathroom, also with canvas walls but with cabinetry boasting all the regular bathroom amenities—even a shower. I run a hand over one of the fluffy towels. It feels like a cloud. There's even a front porch with Adirondack chairs positioned to take in the sight of the harbor and Statue of Liberty.

"This is amazing! What is this place?"

He walks over to the mini fridge and pulls out two bottles of

Perrier. He opens one and offers it to me. "It's an 'urban camping experience,'" he quotes meticulously as I accept the proffered bottle and take a sip. "They'll bring dinner when we're ready, and there's a fire-pit not far away we can sit around later if you'd like." I can't help my laugh.

"Camping?" I look wide-eyed at the furnishings. "This isn't camping. This could be a layout in *GQ*."

He takes a long drink. "There's a tent." He gestures to the pristine white canvas overhead. "What more do you want?"

Chuckling, I step closer and clink my green bottle against his. "Well, it's a far cry from the nylon tents and sleeping bags I grew up with. And the mini fridge is way more efficient than a cooler filled with ice. Thank you." His eyes crinkle with humor and he nods in acceptance. "But, come on. All those trips with your parents when you were a kid to help build schools? You can't tell me you 'camped' like this."

Slipping his arm around my waist, he pulls me close and whispers in my ear, "Of course not. But why not have a little luxury when you can?" His lips on my neck send a bolt of warmth down my spine. "You deserve to have the world laid at your feet, Cass. I want to do that for you."

How I haven't dissolved into a puddle at his feet, I don't know. My pulse thrums in my throat when I look into those wild green eyes that seem to devour me in a glance. "Thank you. Truly."

He grins and steps back. "Anything for you, milady," he says, joking again, and makes a sweeping bow. "Shall we go survey the rest of your kingdom?"

We leave the bikes parked at the tent and stroll toward a grove of trees. We pass a few other tents on the way, but they seem deserted. "Where is everyone?" I toss my empty bottle into a recycle bin along the path. "I wanted privacy." He shrugs and drains his bottle before tossing it in the bin. He holds his hand out to me and I take it. "I don't want anyone else hearing you scream my name tonight."

I stare at him as we walk. "You rented out the whole place? But, but, what about the people who already had reservations?"

"They were well compensated, I'm sure. I just asked how much it would cost and I paid. I didn't worry about the details." He squeezes my hand and leads me into the thin grove of trees. Light filters through the leaves, speckling the ground.

"I must be getting used to you." I shake my head at his extravagance—it must have cost him thousands. This is so him: over the top, and I have to admit, I like it. "I'm not as shocked by that as I should be."

"Good." His impudent grin makes me laugh as we emerge from the trees into a sea of red rope hammocks strung on sturdy poles. There are dozens of them, swaying gently in the breeze. I finally spy a few other tourists, but they're leaving the hammocks and heading away on their bikes.

"Did we scare them away?" I ask, confused, and then narrow my eyes at his overly innocent smile.

"I 'spect they're on their way to the docks to catch the last ferry. They don't want to be stranded here; there's a fine."

This time I gape at him. "Wait—we're all alone? On the whole flipping island?"

He leads me to a hammock that's in the shade and helps me in. "Well, besides the camp manager, caterer, and assorted park rangers, we are."

I flop back on the woven ropes, laughing helplessly. "Holy crap, Sean. That's...that's...I don't know what that is."

"It's fabulous, obviously. Scoot over."

He makes shooing motions with his hands, and I shift awkwardly to one side as he grabs the ropes. "Will it hold both of us?"

"It'd better." He climbs on, but a shrill chirping from his phone stops him. "This had better be important," he growls, pulling it out and looking at the screen. His eyes shoot open. "What the ever-loving fuck?"

I sit up, setting my hand on his arm. "What is it?"

"It's a text from Kennedy fucking Lane, that's what!" He jabs at the phone and holds it to his ear, scowling. "And now he's not answering, the prick. I can't fucking believe it." He shakes his head and quickly scrolls to another contact. "Damn it, Matt's not answering either," he grumbles. More scrolling, and then he yells into the phone, digging his free hand into his hair. "Where the fuck is everyone? Three! Call me as soon as you get this! Did you know what our illustrious leader was planning? Why the fuck didn't he tell us?"

With his face screwed up in exasperation, he taps out a text, and shoves the phone back in his pocket. Then he starts pacing and shaking his head.

I stare in fascination at his display. "What did he do? What happened?"

"He got *married*, that's what. He and the lovely Abigail went off and eloped, the little shits. *And* he's also apparently knocked her up." He waves his hands as he talks and paces. "How could he do this and not *tell* us? Tell *me*?"

I cock my head to one side, trying not to laugh at his righteous indignation. "Don't you like this Abigail?"

"What?" He stops in his tracks, staring at me. "No! Abby's smashing. Kennedy's happier than I've ever seen him and his songwriting has been even more incredible than it usually is. It's a fucking match made in heaven."

"Then what's the problem?"

He heaves a sigh, his shoulders sagging in defeat. "We're his family. His brothers. How could he do something so…so fucking *life changing* and not tell us? And he's not answering his phone!"

His dejection makes me want to pull him onto my lap like a child. "Maybe he's talking to someone else," I offer. "His parents, maybe. If they ran off without telling their parents, they'll probably have some fast talking to do." I know I would. My mother would skin me alive if I eloped and prevented her from having my wedding splashed on the society pages.

"Maybe," he grunts. "Fuck. First Syd, then Three, and now our dear leader. The world's gone crazy." He crams his hands in his pockets and kicks at a clump of grass.

"You sound like marriage is the worst thing in the world." A knot forms in my belly, the secret of Jack's proposal weighing on me.

He looks at me, his eyes troubled, and then frowns toward the trees. "Of course not."

I pat the edge of the hammock in invitation and he climbs in after me. We wriggle around until we're comfortable, wrapped around each other. The edges of the hammock stretch up around us, creating our own little bubble. We're quiet, absorbing the gentle rocking of the hammock, and his tense muscles relax. "Are you more upset that they got married, or that they didn't tell you first?"

He huffs a chuckle. "Isn't it written somewhere that you have to tell your nearest and dearest when you get married?"

"He did. He just waited until after the fact." I rest my head on his shoulder. The hammock is incredibly comfortable, but as he relaxes, my nerves are jangling. Then the words are out before I can stop them. "Jack proposed to me."

"What?" Sean's entire body stills; his fingers stroking my arm freeze. "When? What did you tell him?"

His voice is calm, but I can tell he's anything but calm. A frisson of fear spikes through me, and I take a deep breath, forcing myself to answer him. "Just before I saw you backstage last night. I told him I had to think about it." My stomach churns and my palms begin to sweat. "I thought I could wait to tell you until I'd decided, but... I can't keep it from you. You deserve to know. And you need to know why I'm considering it." He twists away from me and grabs the edges of the hammock to get up, but I clutch his arms. "Wait. Please. Will you listen?"

My heart is in my throat as I wait an eternity for his answer. When he finally looks at me, the turmoil swirling in his emerald eyes hurts my heart. "Listen to what?" he mutters, his jaw set.

I pick at the edge of the hammock. Everything in me wants to stay silent, but I can't. Of all people, Sean needs to know. "I told you I went to school at UCLA," I begin, my voice just above a whisper. "Everything was great. I'd found my calling, I had friends, and I loved being so close to the beach. I was happy. Then, in my junior year, I went to a party with a friend."

The wariness in his eyes softens, curiosity getting the best of him, and he lies back into the hammock. His body is rigid, but I wrap an arm around his waist and lay my head on his chest anyway, yearning for his acceptance, and praying I'm not making a mistake.

"It was at a frat house. My friend, Sara, had a brother there." I try to swallow down the lump in my throat, but it doesn't work. "We did everything right. We stayed together, got our own drinks from the keg instead of accepting any from strangers, and stuck to the public areas where everyone was gathered. Around midnight, I started to feel sick, so we'd decided to go home. Sara needed to go to the bathroom first, so I waited outside the door. Just in that short space of time, things started spinning and I was so tired; I remember sliding down the wall and calling out for Sara, and then...nothing."

He grips the edge of the hammock, his knuckles white, but he doesn't move. I take comfort from the heat radiating from him and glide my hand over his stomach, his T-shirt bunching up under my palm. Golden red hairs glint in a shaft of fading sunlight that finds us through the leaves above.

"When I came to myself, I was back in my apartment. Sara was crying, kneeling beside my bed, and I was draped in a blanket. Underneath, I was naked." My voice is soft, but matter-of-fact, as if I'm discussing the weather instead of the event that changed my life. "Apparently, when Sara got out of the bathroom, I was gone. In a panic, she grabbed her brother and they searched until they found me. They burst into a bedroom to find three of his 'brothers' groping me and taking pictures. They'd removed my clothes. They hadn't raped me yet, but one was inches away from it. They stopped him."

With a strangled noise, he breaks; wrapping both arms around me, he holds me tightly, his face buried in my hair. "Cassidy...how... what..."

"They hadn't targeted me. We found out they'd painted a few random cups with rohypnol and waited to see what would happen. It was just dumb luck that I'd picked one," I continue, my voice muffled by his T-shirt. "I hid away for a week. I took endless showers. They'd marked me; hickeys and fingerprints where they'd pinched me. I almost scrubbed myself raw, trying to get rid of them, trying to feel clean again. My brother, Kevin, kept calling but I couldn't answer—we talked almost every day, so I knew he must have been worried. But I couldn't talk to him or anyone. I turned everyone away. I just felt powerless."

"Didn't you call the police? You or your friend?" His voice is rough, and I feel him lay his cheek against my hair.

"I didn't want anyone to know. I was ashamed and terrified what they might do with the photos they'd taken if I provoked them. And I was worried that if I got the police involved, it would hurt my dad. He was in his first term and still trying to establish himself."

"They assaulted you! They were going to…to…" he chokes out, his body vibrating with outrage. His arms feel like steel bands, both protecting and comforting. I want to curl up in a ball and let him sooth me, but I have to get it all out now or I may never be able to.

"The end of the week, Kevin showed up on my doorstep. As soon as I saw his face, I lost it, started bawling, and blurted it all out. He was madder than I'd ever seen him. I begged him not to call the police—I didn't even want him to call my parents. He finally agreed about the cops, but he called my dad and explained what happened. I couldn't speak to him myself; I was a mess. The next day, Dad's chief of staff, Dale Canton, showed up. He talked to my brother, said he'd take care of it and left."

Sean huffs out a breath, blowing strands of my hair around. "What did he do?"

"That night, all three of the fuckers ended up in emergency rooms with broken bones and concussions. But they wouldn't say a word about what happened to them—they were scared shitless. I can only assume that Dale arranged something. I don't know for sure." I swallow the lump in my throat. "I don't really want to know."

"They got off light," he snarls, his voice deep and dangerous. "What happened to them then?"

"Their frat kicked them out, and they all ended up dropping out of school. One is a teller in a tiny bank in Bakersfield and has been divorced twice, one is homeless after declaring bankruptcy, and one died of an overdose about five years ago. Kevin keeps tabs on them."

"I want to know who they are." His voice is soft, but filled with so much anger I can't help my shiver.

"Why? It doesn't matter, Sean. It's in the past."

"Like hell it is," he snaps, and then takes a deep breath, as if forcing himself to calm down. "I'm sorry. So, what happened then? How long did it take you…how did you…manage?"

I roll on my back, but he keeps me in his embrace. The leaves flutter above us and I hear ship horns in the distance. "It took about six months, but I finally started to relax. I stopped looking over my shoulder, expecting to see someone who knew what had happened, or who had one of those photos. My internship with McQueen came just at the right time. I graduated, went to London, and never looked back. Until I got a call from Dale about a year later."

Sean swears under his breath. "The pictures?"

"The pictures." The breeze picks up and a wave of goose bumps rises on my forearms. "He'd heard they were being shopped to one of my dad's political opponents. I'd only been in New York a few months. I was trying to establish my shop and it was slow going. My first clients were friends of my parents and their recommendations were helping get the word out. The photos would've ruined everything, everything I ever wanted as well as my father's career."

"But, again, my father handled it. He had Dale retain a cybersecurity team to destroy those copies, and they're still on the job. They scan constantly. Every once in a while, I'll get a text from Dale, letting me know another image was found and deleted. Because of my father, no one knows what happened; no one will see me… like that." I swipe at my suddenly blurry eyes. "I owe my father everything."

"I can see why you feel that way." He sighs, shifting against my body, and I can feel his eyes on me. "But, Cass, some would say he's only doing what a father would do. What a father *should* do. He's protecting his daughter. You don't owe him anything."

"But I do!" I twist in the hammock and grab his shirt as I look at him. The concern and worry I see swimming in his emerald eyes almost kills me. "In my family, we were raised on doing things ourselves. Being accountable and responsible for our own actions. It was drilled into us. If you get yourself into a mess, it's on you to sort out. Don't expect anyone else to fix it. During that week after, after what happened, it was killing me that even after all my precautions, it still happened. And I couldn't see how to fix it, how to protect my family. That my father had to step in is so...humiliating. Almost more than what happened was. I'll never be able to repay him."

A frown tugs at his lips. "Not sure I agree with that, but we'll set that aside for now. How does all this fit in with what's-his-name?"

"Jack." I huff in frustration. "Marrying Jack would solve everything. It would pay my father back for everything he's done for me, and it would solve Jack's own family issues. It's a win-win."

"Oh, for the love of God. And I thought Three had the worst family guilt I'd ever seen," he mutters and climbs out of the hammock before I can stop him. But instead of leaving, he wheels around to face me, eyes alight with...something. "Do you love him?"

"What? No. No, but that doesn't matter. He—"

"Of course it matters!" He rolls his eyes and looks heavenward for a moment. "I may have been upset Kennedy ran off and got married without telling me, but I can't fault him, not really. He and Abby are meant to be together. The same as Matt and Tess, and Cam and Sam. My parents. Even Syd and that git, Philip." He rakes a hand through his hair and fixes me with an intense stare. "Are you telling me your perceived obligation to your father is truly big enough to marry someone you don't love?"

A shadow falls over me. "Well, I did, kind of," I mutter, sitting up awkwardly in the hammock. "Hearing you say it like that though..." He grunts in satisfaction and crosses his arms. I glare at him. "It would only be for a few years. Lots of people get married for worse reasons.

I like Jack. He's kind and smart and would never do anything to hurt me. And we wouldn't even need to live in the same city."

Sean gapes at me. "Why the hell not?"

"We wouldn't be, um, intimate," I say primly, staring at my hands gripping the edge of the hammock. With every word, the realization of how ridiculous this is hits me square in the face, but I keep going. Out of stubbornness or denial that Sean's right, I'm not sure which. "He'd go his way and I'd go mine. Discreetly, of course."

"Oh, of course. Discretion is the better part of valor, after all." Sean stomps a few feet away, waving his arms. Thank God we're alone. "You can't possibly think he's serious about that. He'd have to be an idiot not to want to sleep with you." He whirls around, narrowing his eyes with suspicion. "Or gay." I keep a blank expression as I fight to keep my promise to Jack, and he shakes his head and stomps back, still flailing. "Whatever. You're not thinking straight, Fly-girl. A sham marriage to make your parents happy? This isn't the sixteenth century, you know."

"Lucky for you." I wave a hand at him standing there with his hands on his hips like a petulant twelve-year-old girl. "They'd lock you up for having hair like that."

He squints at me, a slow flush creeping up his neck. "So what happened to experimenting, just you and me?" he demands, and I feel a twinge in my heart. "Are you expecting me to creep into your bed at night when no one's looking? Will I be your dirty little secret on the side?"

"Of course not. I know you could never do that." I twist the rope under my hands, my stomach churning. "Look, I didn't mean to just blurt everything out like that. Only a handful of people know what happened to me. Not even Riya knows. But, you needed to know why, why I'm considering this," I say, knowing I sound like I'm begging. I want him to understand, even if he can't agree with me.

He purses his lips. "Considering. Not decided?"

"Not decided," I say, wondering what's whizzing around under that violet hair. "But—"

"Fine." He grabs my hand, hauls me out of the hammock, and roughly swings me over his shoulder before I can blink, knocking the air out of me.

"What the hell are you doing?" I squawk, after sucking in a breath.

Spinning us around, he stalks off through the trees toward the tent. "Seizing the day," he announces, and then smacks my bottom, making me yelp. "Since you're so fond of ancient courtship rites, I thought I'd remind you what I have to offer. Think of it as a duel for your favor—and I think you'll like how I swing my sword."

chapter eight

Murphy's Law No. 21: Sometimes, you need to be hit over the head with a different perspective.

 Sean

"You know, I've got the perfect solution to your problem," I mutter against Cassidy's ear as she arches her back, her hand slipping down the headboard.

"If it involves stopping what you're doing, you can shut up." Always such a cheeky girl. Even with me, fucking her from behind in this tent, she finds a way to keep up the sass.

I tighten my hand against her plump arse before delivering a firm slap; the sound magnified in the confines of the tent. "I'm being serious."

"Hmpfff. Oh God, do that again." She's all breathless and in this moment, all fucking mine. Only she's not really. Not even remotely mine. Not when there's this cloud of a sham proposal hanging over us.

"You mean do this?" My teeth sink into the buttery smooth skin of her shoulder, right over the little mole that sits there as my palm smacks over her delicious arse once more.

"God, yes."

"See?" I whisper under her ear. "That's the answer I want. It's the answer to my perfect solution."

Her fingers claw at my hip, trying to tug me faster against her. "Less talking, more of this."

"You love my voice. You can't get enough, and you know it." Maybe this time, she'll actually agree with me. Her meeting each thrust of my hips tells me she has to feel something more than she lets on.

"You're so full of it," she grinds out, and I can't resist landing my palm against her backside again.

"I'd say you're the one full of it at the moment, sweetheart." I'm trying to hang on to a thread of control, but it's slipping. I feel her shudder around my throbbing cock, and I know she's close. She's a muttering, incoherent mess as my fingers reach around to strum a beat against her clit.

Heat surges through me as she cries out in that moment I crave; where she falls apart and lets her guard down. I lose myself in her. Clutching at her hips, my muscles are wrought with tension, and I try like hell to keep us both from falling—into where and what, who the fuck knows.

We're panting, shattered, and spent; the sweat trickles down my back. She lets me have her lips. It doesn't take long for her to move, pressing forward as I roll my hips back to ease from that sweet pussy and deal with the condom. I'm wrecked, unable to form a coherent thought, and she carries on just fine, reaching over for a glass of sparkling water as if we haven't just fucked like my world is coming to an end.

"So, about that solution you mentioned?" she asks, all business. She pushes up and leans back against the headboard; the sheets fall to reveal those sweet breasts. She's trying to act all nonchalant, but that flush to her cheeks, her hitched breaths, and the way her eyes rake over me as I move back to the bed and kneel beside her, give her away.

"Marry me."

That stops her dead, the glass stilling in front of her lips. Those blue-gray eyes that slay me widen in shock. And then, she bursts out laughing. "You really are a nut job, you know?"

"I'm serious." Perhaps for the first time in my life—one hundred percent serious. This woman has fallen into my world and rocked it. I'm not prepared to let her go—not now, not ever.

"Sure you are." She leans back, taking a sip of water, making her nipples perk for me. I can't help leaning forward to pull a sweet bud into my mouth.

"One hundred percent serious," I mumble against her heavenly scented skin. Her fingers grab into my hair, and she tugs my head up, her eyes searching mine.

"You've lost whatever was left of your mind."

"Come on. You feel some sort of insane obligation to pay back your father. He's picked this twit—"

"*Jack*. His name is Jack." She smiles behind her glass.

I wave her off. "Whatever. His name is irrelevant. He's picked him because he's rich, politically connected, and wants to donate a fuck-ton of money to his campaign, but you feel nothing whatsoever for the bastard."

"Thanks for the update." Her voice is hollow as she leans over to set the glass down. She stares back at me; the fire in the pit outside crackling.

"I'm a much better plan."

"You're a drummer in a rock and roll band, followed by the paparazzi and screaming fans daily. Right… that wouldn't attract any attention at all."

"Do I need to remind you of who my father is?"

She reaches between us, tugging the sheets up to cover that perfect body. She tucks the sheet in under her arms, crossing them over her chest. Another coat of armor donned.

"Does it matter?"

"Course it does."

She rolls her eyes and lands her gaze deliberately at my cock. "Cover that up."

"Can't concentrate, love?" I can't hide the grin as I straddle her hips.

I can see her hesitate, her eyes searching mine, and I grab onto the only glimmer of hope I have. "If you'll recall, my father runs a political office in the UK." She narrows her eyes in suspicion. "You want political connections? I know the queen. I could introduce your father. Maybe start some sort of Wyoming-British collaboration."

"Bullshit you know the queen."

Setting my hand over the tattoo of the flag on my chest, I stare back at her bewildered face. "I swear. Even named one of her corgis."

She shakes her head. "There is no way you named one of the queen's corgis."

"Damn straight I did. Also, I hosted her grandson's bachelor party a few years back, you know? The future King of England? The world will never know what happened that night. You want to talk about a scandal. I can totally keep my mouth shut when it's warranted."

I wish I had a camera for her expression. "You did what?"

"Attended the wedding as well. A bit over the top for my tastes, and the meal was subpar, but our wedding will be epic."

She juts her chin out, tightening the sheet against her chest. "We're not getting married."

"But it's the perfect solution."

Her lips twitch in amusement. "Two proposals in a week. Not in a million years could I have imagined that happening."

"I could. Just look at you. A man would be a fool to not want to be your husband."

She slides her hand against my cheek. "You know, when you're not being completely ridiculous, you're incredibly sweet."

I turn my head to press a kiss to her palm and hold it in mine. "Come on. It will be fun. Think of it as another experiment. A lifelong experiment."

"Marriage isn't an experiment. It's not supposed to be fun or a joke, Sean. It's serious, and I don't think you have a serious bone in your body."

"I like how you're talking about my body. Keep doing that." I pluck the sheet from her hand to tug it away, exposing her to me once more. "And if it's not fun, why the hell do it? You want to be miserable your whole life?"

She tips her head, amusement in her eyes. "It's interesting how your mind works. I appreciate the offer, even though it's beyond insane. But, I'm not ready to marry anyone."

I sit back, holding her gaze. "Not even Jack?"

She blows out a long breath. "No. Not Jack. You're right about that. I need to stop thinking I owe my father." Her fingers trace absently along the ink of my forearm, tracking the veins I know she loves so much. Relief floods through me; the jealous rage that took over when we were on the hammock and she told me about Jack's asinine proposal fades away. "I'm grateful to him, of course. I'm not sure I'd be where I am without him."

"Now that's just bullshit. You're an amazingly talented designer. That's got nothing to do with your father."

"If he hadn't stepped in, those pictures would've been out there. It could've ruined me before I even got a chance to start."

Shaking my head, I tighten my hand against hers. "The thing about scandals is: there's always another one, lurking around the corner." I can't resist reaching to brush back her messed-up hair. "Darling, it would've been a shitshow, but I guarantee you it would be forgotten just as quickly. No scandal can take away from who you are. Not if you don't let it."

I can see how much this still hurts her. If I'm not mistaken, there are tears threatening in those eyes of hers and that kills me. I want to take this away, make her forget—permanently—about what happened to her, and make her understand it wasn't her fault.

"Whenever you're ready, I'd be a kick-ass husband." I can see her bite back a smile, and I tighten my hand against her hip. "Sex whenever you wanted. I'd buy you shit, could take you around the world. Money is no object."

She lets out a little laugh. "I have money. I can buy my own shit, as you so eloquently put it, and can get sex whenever I want it now." Her voice drops to a whisper. "Those aren't the reasons people get married, Sean. Not even close."

"Neither are the reasons good ole Jack gave you. You tell me, then. Why do you get married?" I slide in beside her, biting back a groan as she tucks in under my arm, her fingers resting against my stomach. "What is it you want?"

She peeks up at me and rests her chin on my chest. "To share my life. I don't need a piece of paper to do that. It's not that I'm against marriage… I'm just not sure what I want right now."

Cupping her face between my hands, I lower my lips to hover against hers. "We'd have a great life, you know."

"I know." Her voice is so quiet, I almost can't hear it. Somewhere along the way, any notions of "experiments" have been blown away. This is real. She feels it just as I do. The question is what the hell are we going to do about it.

"You'll tell him tonight?" I ask against her lips. I can feel her smile into the kiss before she pulls back. I'm leaning against the bike outside her shop. She's been delivered back and in time for her fitting with the bridezilla as requested. See? I can be responsible.

Sleep-warm morning sex is the best, I've decided. I wanted to wrap her up in that bed in that tent and never let her leave. The ferry ride back was torturous, with my chest pressed to her back as we watched our little island oasis get farther and farther away.

"Reality waits," she kept saying this morning. I don't think she realizes this could *be* our reality. Her and me and whatever we want to do—all day, every day.

"Tell Jack, you mean?" she teases, and I give her side a pinch. She jumps away with a squeal.

"Don't test me, Fly-girl. That man needs to know you're not now, nor will you ever be, his." It's almost a growl. "I thought that was established last night."

"Aren't you the possessive one?" She backs up and tugs her bike from me.

"Who knew, hmm?"

"Oh, I had a feeling," she calls back to me over her shoulder. "Thank you again, Sean. I had an amazing time." She's said that more than once, but fuck if it doesn't make me feel like a champion. "I'll text you later on." Giving me a wave, she steers her bike into the shop, the little bells chiming above when the door closes and shuts me out once more.

"And you couldn't have waited? I mean, where's the fucking loyalty, mate? We have been waiting forever for you two to tie the knot, and we're just shut out! Cast aside like commoners!" I wave my hand at the camera as I sit on video conference with Kennedy, Matty, and Cameron.

"Calm down, man. It's not a big deal." The asshole Kennedy smirks... he actually smirks at me from whatever tropical paradise he's currently lounging in on his honeymoon. *His honeymoon!* Goddamn bastard.

"Not a big deal? Not a big fucking deal? Are you hearing this, Matty? You know what, Lane, fuck you. Fuck you hard! This *is* a big deal. Life changing, if you want to know the truth. How could you not invite us?"

"Jesus, would you take a breath?" Matty chuckles at me.

"Wise words there, Matty," Cameron chimes in. "Sean, look at it this way: we can have a party when they're back."

Cameron's suggestion gives me pause, and I glare at the screen. "A party?"

"Yeah, you know? The whole gang together. There's a lot to celebrate," Cameron says.

"And you had to go and knock her up." I shake my head. "Shit."

"It wasn't planned, if that helps. Turns out the pill isn't a hundred percent all the time." Kennedy slides his sunglasses on the top of his head, and I can see the gunmetal band that now sits on his ring finger.

"At least we know your boys can swim," Matty says from behind his coffee cup.

"Well spotted there, genius." Kennedy holds back a laugh.

I throw my hands up. "I'm being an ass. Congratulations, mate. On both counts. She's an amazing girl and this baby will have kick-ass uncles."

"Amen to that. And I'm sorry I didn't tell you guys. We just didn't want to make a big deal out of it. The press, the pictures." He lets out a long breath, glancing away from the screen. Pretty sure I can hear the surf pounding on the shore. "That kind of chaos? That's not what I want for Abby. Not on a day like that. It was just us on a beach in the middle of nowhere. Not even our families were there, and it was fucking perfect."

"I'm glad it was. Three's right."

Cameron sticks his tongue out at me, and I flip him off in return.

"We'll have a party when you're back to celebrate. We can have it here."

"I do have to come to New York to do Ravine's show in a couple of weeks." Kennedy frowns.

"A promise is a promise after all. That may just about send you over the edge, spending any amount of time with the asshole," Matty replies. There's a long-standing feud between the arrogant prick Landon Ravine and his band, but Ravine was there for the charity concert for Parker a few years ago, and Kennedy promised to do his ridiculous find-the-next-big-star show in return for his appearance.

"Don't fucking remind me," Kennedy growls. "Why did I agree to this again?"

"Because he brought in a fuck-ton of money for What's Your Dream," Cameron answers, and Kennedy rolls his eyes.

"Not to worry; we'll balance out your time in hell with a celebration of all things love and mushy."

"Hey, there's nothing mushy about me," Matty says.

"That remains to be seen," I fire back at him. "I'll get going with plans then. Let us know when you're gracing New York with your presence. You guys can stay here if you want. The music academy is probably going to open around that time. Maybe we can do a few numbers with some of the kids."

"Perfect plan. See? So much better than crashing my wedding."

"Not even remotely, Lane. You're still on my shitlist, but I'm willing to forgive because you knocked up one of my favorite people in the world."

Kennedy grins. "Speaking of which, gentlemen, I have a new wife that needs my attention. Something about a massage on the beach."

I point at the camera. "You're an asshole, married man."

Kennedy gives me a salute. "I love you too, Sean."

All talk of unplanned pregnancy has me doing what I promised Cassidy I would. I'm currently sitting in the clinical exam room of good old Dr. Perez in downtown Manhattan getting the works.

Dr. Perez is pushing sixty with stark white hair and the obligatory lab coat that seems to be busting out a bit more than it did when I saw him a little over two years ago.

Physical exam over—an experience as awful as it sounds—I'm listening as he goes over the various tests they'll be taking once they extract enough vials of blood to keep a vampire going for a while.

"Let me ask you a question, doc." He looks at me over his wire frame glasses. "How effective is the birth control pill?" At that, his bushy white eyebrows rise. "I mean, a friend of mine just got his girlfriend—wife now—knocked up and she was on it."

He gives me a half smile. "When taken properly, it's ninety-nine percent effective. However, there are many factors that can impact that."

"Such as?"

He pulls his glasses off and cleans the lenses on the edge of his lab coat. "Forgetting to take it, if you're on other medication, if you don't take it at the same time every day, just to name a few."

I drum my fingers against the edge of the chair. "Holy shit. No wonder men aren't in charge of it."

Doc laughs. "Surely you've heard this before?"

I wave him off. "Yeah, of course. It's just good to hear it from an expert."

He nods. "They're working on a pill for men. At some point we'll see how well that goes."

I grimace. "I think I'll take a pass on that."

"Probably a wise decision." He passes over two cups and two paper bags left in the room by the nurse.

"What's this?"

"Urine and sperm." He points to each cup.

"I'm sorry, what?"

"You wanted the works. We're giving you the works."

I try to hand him back one of the cups. "There's nothing wrong with my sperm. I can assure you of that, doc."

"I'm sure you're right. But you're thirty-seven. We'll test just to make sure."

I glance at the cup and back at him. "So what? I'm supposed to whack off? Like now?"

He clears his throat, straightening the file on his desk. "There's a room down the hall that's used for this." He must see the surprise in my face because he follows that up with, "Don't worry. We have men using it all the time."

"Is that supposed to make me feel better about this?" He shakes his head. "That you have a steady stream of men masturbating in some private room?"

"Sean, it's normal. And if you're having trouble, there're magazines in the room."

I laugh, pushing up from the chair. "Doc, trust me. I don't need magazines. I got this."

"Just drop them off with Susan at the front desk when you're done. We'll call you if there are any issues with your results." At least Susan is pushing sixty and not a fan-girl.

"Always entertaining seeing you, doc." I give him a salute and open the door before heading down the hall.

I didn't imagine I'd be whacking off into a cup today. It's tempting to call Cassidy to see if she's free. Probably not the best date idea I've ever had.

The hall is a long one, and I have to pass behind the reception desk on the way. Susan glances up from her computer, and I hold up the little paper bags with a shrug of my shoulder. She grins back at me. "Third door on your left. Take your time."

Fuck, how awkward is this? Thank God there's a barrier that separates the hallway from the waiting room so people can't see me.

The door she indicated is open slightly, and I peek in, slipping inside and quickly closing the door behind me. Fucking hell. What in the world is this bullshit? There's low lighting, a chaise lounge in the corner with a crisp white sheet draped over the back. Jazz music... fucking *jazz music* playing softly from a machine set up on a table. And right under that table, the magazines that the good doctor promised. There's a *Penthouse* on the top of the stack. I don't even want to know what else is hiding under there. I don't want to touch anything, even though the distinct smell of disinfectant permeates the room.

There's a little sign tucked into a frame on the table with instructions. What to do if there's an accident. Bloody hell. I rake my hand through my hair. This is hands down officially the weirdest doctor's appointment I've ever had.

Right. No time to waste then. I promised Cassidy the works, and that's what I'm going to do. I set the bags and one of the cups on the table, twisting the top off the other. I glance at the label on the plastic container, seeing my name in big, bold letters, along with some barcode underneath. No mistakes to be made then.

I release my belt, the sound echoing in the empty room. I can hear muffled voices in the hall, reminding me an audience lingers just outside the door. Not intimidating in the least. Right, Sean, suck it up. I bark out a laugh. If Cassidy were here, she would. Hell. Time to get to work.

Cassidy

"What do you mean you'll have to charge me extra? We have a contract! I've already paid half!"

Riya takes a prudent step back from the fire-breathing bridezilla who's practically vibrating with hysteria. Taking a deep breath, I steel myself and maintain my most professional smile.

"Yes, indeed, you have. But that was based on the original design and fabric," I say with excruciating politeness as I slip her dress back on the hanger and place it on one of the racks in the fitting salon. "I've complied with all your requests, Ashley, but to change fabrics now when all the gowns are almost finished goes beyond our original agreement."

"That's, that's outrageous! Mother, are you listening to this? She wants to charge us more just for a few scraps of cloth!" As a pampered daughter of a prominent hedge fund manager and his wife, Ashley has been getting increasingly louder for the past hour, changing her mind about this or that adornment to her half-completed silk taffeta gown, sometimes at lightning speed. Her mother has been glued to her phone, only paying scant attention. I've been going along with Ashley's whims, determined just to ride out the storm, until she demanded a complete redo of her dress and the three bridesmaids' dresses that are almost complete.

Mrs. Pitt raises her face from her electronic addiction, quickly assesses her daughter's red face and fiery eyes, and does the only thing she can that won't make her the next target. "That's absurd! I thought your customer's happiness was paramount," she says, rising to stand next to her daughter and looking down her nose at me.

"It is. And it seems your daughter's happiness is going to cost you an extra fifteen thousand dollars." I keep my tone neutral and extend a hand toward the dress forms adorned with the bridesmaid dress. "We're talking three rolls of yarn-dyed silk taffeta at a cost of twenty-five hundred each. Plus, I'll need to hire two extra people in order to make the timeline—unless, of course, you want to delay the wedding."

"Don't be ridiculous," Ashley snaps, waving her hands in the air. "The invitations have already been sent. We can't delay!"

"Well, then you have two choices at this point: you can stay with the fabric you selected originally, or Riya can draw up a new agreement right now for the extra material and work." I take comfort knowing Riya stands right behind me, a witness in case Ashley does something really stupid. I don't think I've ever seen a face that red.

Instead of exploding, an evil smile curls her lips. "I have another choice. I can walk out right now and you won't get another penny. How 'bout that?"

Tapping a finger on my chin, I take in the triumphant gleam in her eye. Poor girl is punching way above her weight. "Perhaps that is for the best." Riya clears her throat behind me, and I can only imagine the indigestion I'm giving her at the thought of losing thousands of dollars, but I stand tall.

"Wait, what?" Ashley stutters, clearly not expecting me to agree with her, while her mother's eyes widen with the beginnings of panic. She and I are on the same page.

"I'm obviously not able to meet your needs, so perhaps you should take your business elsewhere. Of course, with only two weeks until the wedding, you'll be stuck with something off the rack unless you want to pay another designer three times what I'd charge, even with the extra fees."

"Now, now, there's no need to be hasty," Mrs. Pitt interjects; the thought of her precious daughter walking the aisle in a mass-produced dress causes her face to pale. With her ash-blond hair, it's not a good look. "Ashley, dear, you've loved everything Cassidy's done for you so far—"

"We'll...we'll sue for breach of contract," Ashley blurts, trying to regain control that she never really had.

"You can try." I smile politely and start to slip a muslin bag over her gown. "My brother drew up my contracts; you'll find the fine print is rather thorough."

Ashley takes a step closer, shaking off her mother's hand on her arm. "You're so willing to lose all this money? And what about your reputation? When I'm done with you, you'll lose half your potential customers!"

I hum, considering. "Maybe. It's funny; just a few days ago, a bride came in—Brittany St. John—and she's taken quite a liking to a few of my designs."

"*Brittany?*" Mother and daughter freeze in their tracks, but I continue, pretending I don't notice. "Oh, you know her? Such a small world. Anyway, since you're no longer interested in this, I'm sure she'll be happy to learn it's available. She's about your height, if a little slimmer. It wouldn't take much at all to alter them for her and her maids."

At that, Mrs. Pitt finally regains her voice. "Oh, no need for that, Cassidy, my dear." She gives Ashley a hard look that makes her gulp. She looks like she's swallowed her tongue. "We'll continue with the original fabric—no need for any further changes. Ashley, gather your things. We have a spa appointment in an hour."

"Warn me the next time you do that. I almost had a heart attack."

I give Riya an apologetic smile. "Sorry. She was never going to walk. There wasn't a chance in hell she'd let her ex's new fiancée have those dresses."

She laughs. "The competition between women like her is worse than *The Hunger Games*." She shakes her head, and then she peers at me over the dress form we're wrestling into place. "So, what's had you grinning like a Cheshire cat all day, bridezilla attacks aside? Can I assume it has something to do with that bicycle in the kitchen?"

"Sorry about that. I haven't had time to clear a space for it in the storage room." We finally get the dress form in the right spot and, when it begins to wobble, I kneel and jam a sock under the leg to stabilize it. "We need to get a new one of these," I grumble. "I'm tired of having to prop it up all the time."

Riya grunts in agreement. "Where did the bike come from? That purple-haired demon?"

Rising from my knees, I almost stumble at her statement. "He's not a demon!" I burst, laughing. "What are you talking about?"

Folding her arms, she appraises me. "He must be some kind of a supernatural being if he's been able to make you smile like that even in the face of bridezilla."

"He's just a nice guy." I wish she'd drop it, but she snickers.

"Ah, a unicorn, then," she says, and I can't help my laughter. Considering the way he makes me feel in bed, a unicorn doesn't seem that far off. My phone chimes with a reminder and I swallow my groan.

"Will you be all right here without me? I need to meet Kevin."

She waves a hand and gives me a fond smile. "Go. I have some bills to prepare. I'll lock up behind me. Say hi to your brother for me."

"Thank God you're here." Kevin gives me a one-armed hug, and I laugh at his overly relieved expression. "If you'd been much later, I would've been forced to eat with Darcy Hamilton." He shudders at the thought of spending one minute alone with the jewelry heiress.

"That would be interesting. I think she only eats to give herself something to purge later." He huffs in agreement, and I eagerly accept the martini he hands me. Closing my eyes, I savor the ice-cold vodka as it slides down my throat. It's the only way I'm going to get through tonight. This time, it's an "intimate" dinner in a private Brooklyn dining room with my parents and about fifty other politicos and lobbyists.

When I open my eyes, I'm surprised to see Kevin frowning at me. "What?"

"What, yourself—something's up with you, little sister." He grins at me, tapping his lips with a fingertip.

"I don't know what you're talking about." I blink innocently and try to distract him. "What do you think of this?" I slide a hand over the skirt of my plum-colored dress. "It's out of this fabulous stretch silk I got from Italy. The twist at the neckline works for me, don't you think?"

"Fabulous." He takes my elbow and steers me over to a recessed doorway along the paneled wall. "Now start talking. Ah, ah…" He gives me a look that stops me midprotest. "It's no use. Something is tying you in knots, and I know it's not having to spend another boring evening entertaining lobbyists. I can see it in your eyes. Besides, you keep sneaking peeks at your phone and trying not to laugh, so spill."

"Sweet crispy Christ." I hastily take another sip. Sean is never far from my thoughts, whether I'm dealing with bridezillas, donors, or meddlesome brothers. It hasn't helped that he keeps sending me hilarious texts…something about whacking off in public…and funny photos of himself and Sydney.

"Cassidy…" I look up into Kevin's sympathetic eyes and suddenly begin talking, needing to confide in someone. I tell him all about Sean—his music academy, the band, the day on Governors Island—and then I tell him about Jack's offer. As I talk, his eyes get bigger and bigger, and he slumps against the doorframe in disbelief. Finally, he laughs out loud, doubling over.

"Holy fuck, Cass," he says through his chuckles, holding his stomach. Straightening, he takes my martini and drains it. "Sean Murphy is insane. And a genius. Above all, he's guaranteed to make Mom and Dad's heads explode when they find out."

"I'm not sure if I want them to find out. At least, not yet." I take my glass back, pluck out the toothpick with olives, and pop one in my mouth. Oh, so good. "Look, all this is new. New and scary and…" I chuckle in disbelief, still amazed that such a wild and passionate man has fallen into my life. "Kevin, I don't know how to describe it. When I'm with him, I feel like one of those silly debutantes I see in my shop…

all melty and giggly inside. It's pathetic." He barks out another laugh, and I give him a playful shove. "Stop it. I'm serious."

"I am too. Sounds like love, Cass," he says, his eyes serious, and I swallow nervously. I want to deny it, but I can't quite form the words. "What about Jack? As ludicrous as his idea is, he's right that it would kill two birds with one stone. Mom and Dad would be over the moon at the prospect of Jack Coleman as a son-in-law."

"Tell me about it." I sigh and twirl the empty the glass between my hands. Even though I know Kevin would keep Jack's secret, I made a promise to Jack; I don't make promises lightly. "Jack is…lovely. He's kind, smart, successful, and handsome. He makes me laugh and he's good company. Normally, all things I'd look for in a partner, unless…"

"Unless." Kevin twists his lips in a frown and look at his toes, thinking. "I know Jack, and he's a great guy. He's all of those things and then some. But, regardless of anything—any*one*—else, you can't marry when you don't love, Cass. Even if it's just for a few years. Could you?"

A waiter walks by with a tray, and I give him my empty glass. "No," I murmur, watching the waiter walk away. "A month or so ago, I'm afraid to say that I probably could. But now? No." Sean's beautiful green eyes and roguish smile come to mind. "One day, I will probably get married. But I can't right now, no matter how attractive Jack Coleman's proposal is."

The door next to us creaks open a few inches, and Kevin swiftly swings it wider, popping his head in the next room. He shrugs. "Just an empty hallway. Come on." He slings his arm around my shoulders. "Let's go get another drink, and you can tell me more about this crazy musician of yours."

About an hour and another martini later, I'm relaxed but impatient for the evening to be over. Kevin and I have done our duty, hobnobbing with our father's well-heeled crowd and smiling at jokes we've heard a hundred times. We're seated at yet another round banquet table, watching our parents move to take their seats across the way. My mother has been in an unusually good mood, which is nice to see. She's the perfect politician's wife, always with the perfect smile, the perfect story, and not a hair out of place. But occasionally, she lets the real Marilyn Skinner show, the woman I knew growing up; daughter of a rich cattle rancher who wasn't afraid to get on her hands and knees and play with her young children. As much as she drives me nuts sometimes, she's been a great mom.

"What's up with Mom?" Kevin murmurs in my ear. "Both she and Dad have been acting like they won the lottery all night." I shrug, and he raises his glass to his lips.

"I don't know. Maybe she let Dad talk her into a quickie in the bathroom," I muse. Kevin snorts into his drink, which leads to a coughing fit and a few stares.

"Jesus, Cassidy!" he mutters, as I snicker behind my hand. "I'm going to get you back for that. Ugh, what an image."

A gentle tapping against a water glass quiets the crowd and draws our attention to where our parents are standing. "Good evening. I just wanted to thank our hosts for the lovely evening and, with their indulgence, make a small announcement," my father says, his craggy voice full of satisfaction. Kevin and I exchange curious looks, and then I realize my mother is staring at me with a triumphant smile. "Marilyn and I are pleased to announce the engagement of our daughter, Cassidy, to Mr. Jack Coleman, of Coleman Energy."

There's a smattering of applause and general happy chatter as my heart freezes and Kevin chokes out a curse beside me. Clutching his forearm so I don't fall out of my chair, the good wishes of the others at our table sound muffled and far away.

What the fuck?

chapter nine

Murphy's Law No. 29: Embrace reality, especially if it burns you.

Sean

"IT LOOKS INCREDIBLE," I SAY ALMOST IN AWE, STARING UP AT THE fifteen-foot ceiling of the loft at the music academy.

"It's come together nicely. Sydney was amazing to work with," the interior designer who has worked with Sydney on the redesign of the SoHo building replies. How can he not be impressed? Syd is a brilliant architect and her lean toward the funky yet functional is evident in the space.

Syd offers only a shy smile as she drifts away, holding up her phone. "I'm going to call Philip and show him." Never one for the spotlight, something I'll never understand, she wanders off.

The loft is enormous, taking up the entire top floor. Six cast iron columns anchor the lounge, complete with exposed brick walls, and a functional juice bar the kids can take full advantage of. It's grandiose, but there's a warmth and style distinctly Sydney's. She's made sure there are multiple sitting areas with large inviting leather chairs and sofas for the kids to relax in. Cubbies made of reclaimed barn wood with custom metal accents and ample storage for instruments are strategically placed throughout the impressive space.

Resurfaced matte black oak floors now gleam in the late afternoon light spilling in from a row of arched windows. Iconic views of the New York skyline could provide a distraction to a lot of people, but these kids won't be here for the view.

He leads me past the rehearsal rooms and down the hall to the recording studio, and I spot the Redfall logo etched lightly into the frosted glass on the door. It's the only sign I'm behind this place, and that's exactly how I want it. Sure, we'll have the grand opening and the band will be here to promote it, but after that, I want the focus to be on the kids, not on me.

I push open the door as the designer explains the state-of-the-art studio equipment he's sourced. "You guys could record here, if you wanted to. It's that good." He glances at me hopefully.

"A valid offer, but no. We record at Kennedy's place." I clap him on the shoulder, and his phone rings in his pocket.

He tugs his phone out and glances at the screen. "Sorry, I need to take this."

"No worries. I'll find my way through the rest." He gives me a nod and moves quickly down the hall, setting the phone to his ear.

At the end of the hallway is the exit to the fire escape, and I climb out to take a seat on the iron stair. The city bustles below as usual, perpetually in motion. I know how lucky I am to be here. How many people would kill for this view, for this life I have. I never want to take it for granted. I've done a lot of questionable and, quite frankly, illegal shit over the years, but this academy? It's one of the things I'm most proud of.

Looking across the skyline makes me think of Cassidy working away in the East Village. It's not even been twenty-four hours, and I already miss her. I think about Syd, whose first instinct was to call Philip and show him what she's worked so hard on. I'm starting to understand her comment the other day about wanting to share things.

I want Cassidy to see this, to understand how important it is to me and to be here to share it. Tugging my phone from my pocket, I call her, but it goes to voice mail. I'm slightly deflated; not a normal feeling for me. I snap off a few photos of me on the fire escape and send one to her before I post a more generic one to Instagram that just features the skyline.

"Sean?" I turn in the direction of Syd's voice, seeing her poke her head out of the window.

"Yeah?" I push up from the hard metal of the stair, but she holds up a hand.

"I'm coming out." I crack up, watching her almost fall out of the window before I can get to her, but she rights herself and plops down unceremoniously beside me.

"Well done." I pat her knee, and she smacks my shoulder. "How is Boy Wonder?"

"*Philip* is doing just fine, thank you for asking. He's drowning in a case at the moment."

I lean back against the stair. "Mmm. The exciting world of mergers and acquisitions."

"He doesn't deal with mergers and acquisitions, Sean. He's prepping for a human rights case."

I glance at her. "Huh. Who knew? Got to say, that's a little impressive."

She beams at me. "Just a little. And I'm going to remind you that you said that when you start complaining about him." Blowing a few strands of hair out of her face, she takes in the view. "This is incredible."

"You did an amazing job."

She shakes her head. "No. Not that. This whole thing." She motions to the building. "You're going to make a difference to so many kids, Sean. I don't know if you understand what you'll be bringing into their lives."

I nudge her in the arm. "I mean, it's not a human rights case, but at least I'm good for something."

"Stop doing that. You need to take credit when it's due. Not everyone would do something like this."

I shake my head, glancing at the rooftops across the street. "It's not like I'm some hero, Syd. I don't look at it that way."

She slings her arm around my shoulder. "I know you don't. That's what makes it even more special."

"You've got it all sorted then?" I ask Nicole Hays, Redfall's PR manager, aka the one who keeps us in line, or tries to. Honestly, she deserves a medal for having to deal with some of the shit we've put her through over the years.

She rolls her eyes, tapping the webcam with a scowl. "Hello? Have we just met? Of course I have it sorted. TV crews and radio will be on site the day before the opening. That's the twenty-fourth. I'll update your schedule so you don't miss any interviews."

"I never miss—"

She points an accusatory finger at me. "Don't even try it, Sean. You've missed your fair share of interviews before. Do I need to remind you about the Madrid debacle of a press tour back in 2004?" I open my mouth to defend myself, but her glare has me wisely shutting up. That year was nothing but a blur. I have zero defense on this one. "You can't miss these interviews."

"I won't. I won't!" I hold up my hands in surrender. "Scout's honor?" I hold up four fingers, having no clue what the sign for a scout actually is.

Nic snorts a response. "I think you missed the whole Boy Scout phase, but nice try."

"This is important to me, Nic. You don't have to worry."

"Famous last words," she mutters, adjusting her dark red glasses. She pretends to be annoyed, but Nic loves us. She wouldn't have stuck around for over fifteen years if she didn't. "Let's talk about the contest."

"Ah yes. How's it looking?" Nic gives an update on the contest one of the radio stations is having. While normal entrance to the music academy will be handled via applications and scheduled auditions to the director we've hired, we decided to hold a contest for one of the openings.

The radio station, WBER, has been flooded with video submissions to the point where they had to hire additional staff to vet them. One of the first tasks the director will have with me is selecting the winner.

Nic hit that particular task—hiring the director for the academy—out of the park. After a series of brutal interviews, some with questionable candidates, we found Nari Johnston, and we knew she was the one.

Originally from Korea, Nari started playing classical piano at the age of six and won several prestigious competitions before graduating with a master's of music from Oxford. She went on to perform with the London Symphony and moved to New York two years ago to pursue teaching gifted students at one of the private schools in Manhattan. She's driven, smart as a whip, and doesn't take any of my shit. In other words, exactly what we need to keep me in line.

She's been an integral part of our planning sessions since she signed on the dotted line last month. Nari has taken over interviewing instructors and planning the curriculum; things I have zero understanding of. I'm not sure what we'd do without her.

"Some of these entries are a joke," Nic says. "Nari has had a good laugh, particularly at the ones sent in by grown women in bikinis dry-humping various instruments."

I scowl at the screen. "What are you on about? They did advertise this correctly, did they not? The academy is for kids under the age of seventeen."

Nic lets out a laugh. "You think that's going to stop some of your crazy fans? It's been entertaining to say the least."

"I was wondering why you hadn't sent me any entries to review."

"You'll get them once we've narrowed it down to twelve. Trust me when I tell you, you don't want to see most of these. I need brain bleach and a raise." She grins at the screen.

"Done. Just let Kennedy know."

"You're all way too easy. I should ask for a raise on a weekly basis," she says with a laugh.

"And we'd give it to you."

She waves her hand at the screen. "You're all pushovers now. A few years back? Not so much. I had my hands full. That's when I should've been asking for a raise."

"We're all in line for sainthood now, Nic. Your biggest worry is how to break it to women around the globe their beloved lead singer is officially off the market."

Nic blinks, slapping a hand to her forehead. "I'm sorry, what?"

"Oh, did his royal highness not inform you either? Mr. Lane is married, darling. And has knocked up Abby."

Her mouth drops open for a moment before the rant starts. "That son-of-a—" Nic's face turns a nasty shade of red. "I'm going to kill him. I swear to God, I'm going to kill him. When? When did this happen, and why am I always the last to know?"

I can't hold back my laugh. "Apparently a couple of days ago in some tropical undisclosed location. They were alone, with just a minister and a couple generic witnesses. If it helps, there aren't any photos."

"That you know of." She props an elbow on the desk and drops her forehead to her palm. "Just when you think you have them under control. I should've known better. Why? Why do you guys do this to me?" Nic's mumbling and that's never good.

"Just think of it this way, it's a good news story. Love and babies, and all that. It could be a hell of a lot worse, you know."

Her eyes lift skyward. "I know. I know." She lets out a long sigh. "Some warning would've been nice, though." She grits her teeth.

"Nic? You know that raise that you mentioned?" She glances at the webcam. "Just ask for triple when you finally do reach the proud papa-to-be."

I can hear the faint sounds of the telly in the living room whilst I get tea ready for Syd. It's been a long day for her between spending time at the academy this afternoon and dealing with wedding plans back in London.

I don't know why Syd didn't take me up on the offer to hire a planner. She's doing the whole damn thing herself, spouting off about not wanting someone else to be in charge of the most important day of her life, blah, blah, blah. I'd almost suggest she and Philip go off and elope like Kennedy and Abby did, but there's no way, no how, I'm missing her wedding in London.

As is her evening routine, she's nestled into the corner of the couch with the late night news. It's been fun having her here. I didn't realize how empty the place was until she came to stay. I'm so used to either just crashing here or playing until all hours of the morning. Everything else in between just seemed like white noise.

She's heading home in a couple of days, and I'm not going to see her until she flies back for the grand opening of the academy next month. Seeing it all start to come together, I'm getting excited for this. I'm hoping Cassidy will be able to join me. Syd was right, not that I'd admit it to her. Sharing something you love with the people who are important to you makes the experience sweeter.

Cassidy is fast becoming important to me. Although why she hasn't texted me back is a bit of a mystery. I've sent her a few photos and texts throughout the day, but so far, silence.

I scowl, checking my phone before pocketing it once more. "Sean?" Syd's voice drifts through from the living room.

"Your tea is ready, madam," I tease, setting two cups on a tray along with a plate of biscuits.

"You need to see this," she calls out, her voice a little harder.

"Hang on. You're like a bulldog chewing on a wasp. You can't rush tea."

"Just get in here!" Syd yells. She never yells.

I gather the tray and head into the living room, setting it on the table in front of the sofa. "What's going on?"

Syd's posture is rigid and in stark contrast to the relaxed state she was in a few minutes ago. She's got the telly paused, and she waves the remote at me. "Sit. You need to sit."

I glance at the telly, frowning at the image on the screen. It looks like a posh dining room filled with people dressed in their Sunday best. I have no idea what she's on about. "Why do I need to sit?"

"Just do it!"

"All right, all right." I drop into the chair beside the sofa. "Geez. What is this?" I nod to the flickering screen and she lets out a long breath.

"I'm not sure. Just, please promise me you won't do anything rash."

My skin prickles. This isn't like her. "Syd... What's going on? Is something wrong with Mum or Dad?"

"No! Nothing like that. Just... Just watch."

She clicks the remote and a female voiceover begins; the screen switches to a snap of a stuffy-looking man in a suit. "In what can only be described as an American royal wedding, Wyoming Senator Robert Skinner officially announced at a fundraiser in Brooklyn tonight the engagement of his daughter Cassidy to Jack Coleman of Coleman Energy." I blink at the screen, my fingers digging into the leather arm-rests while my heart takes a nosedive. What the bloody hell? This has got to be a mistake.

The screen changes to a headshot of Cassidy beside one of Jack, and the female voice continues, "The senator's daughter has made a name for herself in bridal couture, with a shop in the East Village that creates one-of-a-kind dresses." A few shots of random wedding dresses sail past on the screen. "Jack Coleman is set to take over for his father, Bert Coleman, at the end of the year as CEO of the multibillion-dollar energy company, Coleman Energy. The company made headlines last year in a pipeline oil dispute that pitted environmentalists against the energy giant."

I try to get a fucking grip, glancing over at Syd. She just shakes her head and gives me a look reserved only for the pathetic and down-trodden. "A spokesman for Senator Skinner confirmed Mr. Coleman had asked permission before popping the question to Miss Skinner earlier in the evening. The spokesman said that while a date hasn't been set, there will be a formal announcement on the details in the coming weeks."

It hurts to take a breath; a stabbing pain slashes through me. I can hardly look at the screen as some panoramic shot of an oil refinery in the middle of the ocean is shown. "This is the first marriage for both Mr. Coleman and Miss Skinner. It's not known how long the couple has been together, the spokesman only saying that the couple preferred to keep their relationship private. We'll continue to bring you updates as the story develops."

The screen switches back to an anchor desk shared by a man and a woman. "Exciting news there. Our own version of a royal wedding," the man who is obviously a certified idiot says.

"Coleman Energy is a household name, and Senator Skinner is no stranger to the American people. A decorated war hero and successful politician. There's been talk of a presidential run for him. There will be a lot of famous people attending this one," the perky blonde agrees.

"A hot ticket indeed," idiot man says. "Turning now to international news—"

Syd freezes the telly once more, silence engulfing the room.

"Sean..."

I glare at her, pushing out of the chair. "Did you know about this?" My voice sounds gritty, edgy, a little violent if I'm being honest.

"No. Of course not. This is the first I'm hearing about it."

Stalking across the room, I shove my keys from the console table at the door in my pocket. Syd is on my heels. "Sean, wait. Don't go—"

"This is bullshit, Syd. Utter bullshit. You don't spend the kind of time we have together and then go off getting *engaged* to someone else." I haul open the door, punching the button for the elevator.

"Please be careful. Don't do anything—" I scowl and she shuts up. "Call me if you need anything. I'm here, okay? And don't drive, please." Unfortunately, those words do nothing to calm me down, but I do take her advice. Even I can recognize driving in my amped-up state isn't a wise move.

By the time the Uber reaches Cassidy's place, I'm beyond angry. This level of rage isn't normal for me. I don't even bother thanking the driver, who doesn't recognize me, thank fuck. I pound my fist on the door of her shop, glancing once again at my unanswered messages. Not hearing this from her first is like a blade to my heart. How the hell could I have been so wrong about this? About her?

"Cassidy! Open up!" I punch my fist again and rest my forehead against the cool metal. "I swear to fucking God if you don't open this door right the fuck now…" Backing up to the edge of the curb, I look up, seeing muted light in the windows of her loft above the shop.

"Cassidy!" I bend down, finding a couple of rocks on the ground and firing them up to her window. They only hit lightly, pathetically falling back to the sidewalk. Pacing is no use either. I put the phone to my ear, calling her once more. Voice mail it is, and I unleash a message. "Open your fucking door right now." Fucking hell. I tug at my hair in frustration.

Fine. She wants to play it that way? I lean my back against the door and slide down, settling in. She has to open it at some point. It's her home, her shop, her livelihood, and I'll stay here all goddamn night if I have to.

I pull my knees up to my chest and clutch my phone, resisting the temptation to go to a news website. Fucking engaged! How does that happen? It guts me to think I've been played by Cassidy. Was I just a good time for her before she settled into domestic bliss? If that's the case, why wasn't she just honest about it? Fuck knows it wouldn't be the first time a woman only wanted me for sex.

A few drops of rain bead on my phone and I turn my face up to the blackened sky. "Can't give me a break, can you?" A crash of thunder is the answer as the sky opens up and a deluge of rain unleashes on the street.

It rains for a long time. Long enough my T-shirt is soaked through and there's a shallow puddle forming under my boots. The rain is unrelenting, coming down in sheets, amplifying that unique New York earthy scent while I slowly lose my mind.

About an eon later, a dark town car pulls up to the curb, and I feel my jaw set as the back door opens. If he's with her, I swear to fuck I will not be responsible for what I do.

In the light cast from the streetlamp, I see those familiar legs drop out of the car first. She's got sky-high heels on and a flowing dress that steals my breath and hurts my heart.

She raises her clutch over her head, shielding herself from the rain after closing the door. She hops over the puddle on the street and hurries to the door as I slowly rise up. I'm drenched, dripping water as she stops short when she finally sees me.

"Sean." Even after the clusterfuck I've seen on the news tonight, just my name on her lips has me all twisted up. Her eyes widen as she takes me in. Clearly, she wasn't expecting to find me here.

I fold my arms across my chest. It's not nearly as intimidating as I want it to be. I'm a drowned rat at this point. "You got something you'd like to share with me, *love?*" My words slice through the night.

"What?" She lowers her clutch, and shakes her head.

"Don't bother with the innocent act. I saw, all right? I saw it all. What I want to know is why. Why didn't you just tell me?"

"Tell you?" She takes a deep breath and closes her eyes. "It's on the news already?"

I let out a huff. "Good news travels fast, apparently. Congratulations, by the way. You're the royal American wedding dream come true." Her eyes flash at me.

"That's not what this is." Lights from an oncoming vehicle practically blind us as it comes to a screeching halt at the curb. "We shouldn't do this here. Please. Just—"

"Why not out here? I mean, if you're going to destroy me, this is pretty damn apropos, don't you think?" I motion to the rain-soaked street.

She reaches for my arm, and as much as I want to pull her into me, I just can't. Not until I understand what the fuck is going on. When I lean away, I can see the pain in her eyes, but I'm not sure I trust it. "Please just come inside." She opens up her clutch and digs around for her keys. "We shouldn't do this here." She nods to the town car, and I see a flash I recognize as a camera. Perfect. Just fucking perfect. The goddamn paparazzi have started to descend.

I stand behind her, blocking both of our faces, even though it's pointless. They obviously know it's her shop, and my hair is easy enough to figure out for any scumbag photographer out there who knows anything at all about music.

She fumbles with the keys, but eventually unlocks and pushes the door open and quickly steps into the shop. I slam the door shut behind me and tighten my hand on the handle to ground me. The only light in the store is muted from the recessed flooring that highlights her perfect designs. She's standing close to one, a gentle glow making her look like a rain-soaked angel. It's an effort to clear my throat. "Start talking. Now."

"We need to get you dry. You're drenched and I don't want you catching—"

"Oh, now you care about me? When I'm dripping all over your precious hardwood floor?" I'm practically roaring.

"Stop it. Yelling at each other isn't going to solve this." She waves her hand between us, that fiery spark we make igniting as it always does.

"Then you tell me what is. Tell me why, after the time we've spent together, do I find out on some crappy news channel that you're engaged to another man. A man you told me less than a day ago you didn't want to marry." She stares at me, brushing her damp hair away from her face. She's wet from the rain, her hair a little messed up, but she's also perfect. Perfect for me in every single flawed way. "Fuck, you look amazing right now."

"I'm drenched!" she yells, motioning at her dress, and then throws her hands up in frustration.

"You're beautiful. You're always so fucking beautiful it hurts. It's hurting me right now not to—Fuck." I palm the back of my neck, pacing away from her. I stop at one of the mannequins draped in an intricate lace dress, letting my gaze fall over the design. I know how much each and every one of these dresses means to her. How she pours her heart and soul into them. She's showed that side of herself to me. The fact that I know that gives me just a bit of hope. "Was this real at all for you?" I turn to her, standing my ground, resisting the temptation to go to her.

Her expression softens. "Of course it was. It is."

"So, what happened then? Tell me and don't give me some line." I'm dripping water all over the floor. This whole thing is a colossal mess.

"I'd never do that, Sean."

"But you must know how this looks, Cass. I mean, I'm used to two things when it comes to women. The ones who play games and the ones who just want to say they fucked a rock star. I didn't think either one of those was you."

She's quiet, my words hitting her hard, I think. When she does speak, it's hushed, reserved. "It's not. My dad, he...he spoke out of turn tonight. Jack did propose to me. I told you that." Her hands tighten on her clutch purse, her knuckles turning white.

I level her with a look, and she glances away. "You also said you weren't ready to get married."

"I'm not. Mom overheard me telling Kevin about it tonight and she told Dad. She either didn't hear me say I couldn't marry him, or she ignored it; I don't know for sure yet. Dad took it upon himself to tell the world tonight. I had no idea." I frown, listening to her. She's been blindsided by this just as much as I have.

"Why the fuck would he do that?"

Her shoulders lift. "I don't know! Why does he do anything? To gain an advantage, to push his agenda. He sees something, and he acts. That's the way he's always been."

"Without talking to you?"

"He just assumed…they both did." She takes a deep breath. "They brought up what happened at UCLA again tonight." I can see the pain in her eyes, and I cross the room to her to grip her shoulders.

"For Christ's sake. You don't owe him anything. Why can't you see that?"

Her eyes well with tears that rip at my heart. "You weren't there. You didn't see what it did to me, to him. What it would have done to his candidacy. The press is lethal. You know that better than most."

"I don't give a rat's ass. He's your father. He's supposed to defend you, and not expect anything in return. Even I know that's what a good parent does." My voice echoes in the store, making her flinch.

"He's a good parent."

I stalk away from her, glancing out the window to the town car still parked on the street. "Sean, he is. He protected me when no one else would have."

"And now he thinks you owe him something, and that's not right, Cass. Not even remotely." I turn away from the window to look at her.

"I know."

"Do you? Do you really know? Are you seriously considering this sham of a proposal?"

Her eyes search mine. "No! But I didn't have a chance to tell them yet."

I stalk back through the trail of water on the floor to her and take her face in my hands. "Cass. I want you to really think about this. If doing this for your father is more important than your happiness, then you should really make sure you realize what you're giving up. I want you. All of you. Not for some fling or for some experiment." I can feel her smooth skin and tiny shivers under my fingertips as I caress her cheek. "All day today, I was at the music academy, and all I could think of was sharing that with you. Do you understand? That's never happened before. Ever. So as crazy as that sounds, and as inconvenient as that might be for you and for your father, that's how I feel. I'm crazy about you. I don't care about your past, or about how long we've known each other. I only know this is something special. I don't want to lose it. I don't want to lose you." Her breath hitches, and she swallows as I brush my thumb over her lips. "But I will, if Jack's proposal is what you want. If it's really what you need in your life right now. But you have to decide that."

"Sean…" Her hand slides against my neck, and I close my eyes, savoring her touch.

"Don't decide now. Think about it. Really think about it, and when you decide, you know where to find me." The lump in my throat threatens my breathing, but I swallow it down, press a lingering kiss to her forehead, and despite everything in me telling me to stay, I leave her to think.

Cassidy

The ache in my chest is so painful, it feels like it will never go away. The quiet click of the door closing behind him sounds like a death knell in the silence of the room.

Like I'm wading through mud, I walk to the door and see Sean getting blinded by flashes. I lock it before making my way upstairs. Shoes are kicked off automatically, and I leave my wet dress in a purple puddle on the floor with my bra and underwear before flopping on my bed and drawing the comforter around me like a cocoon. My head is pounding from all the alcohol I drank at dinner and the hurt I saw in Sean's beautiful eyes. I want to shut my brain off, but the unbelievable events of the evening keep playing on an endless, excruciating loop.

After my father made his staggering declaration, I had sat frozen as well-wishers and waiters serving dinner swirled around me. The social smile plastered on my face felt like a macabre mask. Kevin, bless him, handled the conversation for both of us and intercepted any question asked of me so I didn't have to talk, but kept shooting me worried looks like he was afraid I'd burst apart. I'm surprised I didn't.

I didn't eat. I don't think I even picked up my fork. But they couldn't refill my wine glass fast enough. Alcohol was the only way I could control the rising flood of panic and anger at my parents' smug smiles across the room. At least they'd had the sense not to sit at the same table. I'm not normally a violent person, but if they had been within range of my cutlery, we might have given people even more to talk about.

As soon as things started to wrap up, I was out of my chair and shocked the hell out of my mother by practically dragging her into an adjoining storage room. Things got ugly from there.

"What the hell was that?" I'd demanded with my hands on my hips and fire in my eyes. There wasn't much room between the stacks of extra chairs and row of tables on their sides, but I didn't care. "Where the fuck did you get the idea I was going to marry Jack?"

"Cassidy!" She stared at me like I'd grown a third head. "Language! Someone could hear you."

"I don't care if all of New York hears me," I ground out. "Tell me! And what gave you the idea to blurt something like that out without consulting me first? What the hell were you thinking?"

She crossed her arms, the vision of the perfect politician's wife in one of her many polished suit-dresses, and frowned in disapproval. "I stepped out to the restroom and heard you talking to your brother tonight. You sounded over the moon for Jack, but hadn't told him yet. I know you, Cassidy," she said, softening her tone and shaking her head with a tiny, affectionate smile, as if I was five again and asking to drive my grandfather's giant tractor. She spread her hands and gave me one of her motherly know-it-all looks that always pre-cedes a lecture. "You always overthink things and need a little push to get off the dime. From what you were saying it's obvious you love Jack, but you were tying yourself up in knots over committing. So your father and I decided to help."

"Help!" I laughed, but it sounded hollow. "You decided to 'help' by tak-ing away my right to choose? In front of all those people?" I flung my hand toward the door, almost hitting a stack of chairs; angry tears pricked at my eyes. "You're helping yourselves, that's what."

The door opened, making us both jump, and my father strode in, looking even taller in the cramped space. But he didn't look happy. "What's going on in here?" He quickly shut the door behind him. "What the hell are you doing in a closet? Dale is keeping the Pfizer people busy, but we have to get back in there. Marilyn." He looked at my mother, but I spoke.

"How could you make an announcement like that without asking me?" I demanded, wheeling to face him. He frowned, looking between my mother and me. "How could you, Dad?"

"Your mother said Jack had proposed," he said, as if that was the only part of the equation that counted. "We weren't going to take the risk of you eloping. Your mother has dreamed of your wedding for a long time."

"That's…that's your excuse?" I sputtered, stunned by the absurdity of it all. "I haven't even accepted, and you're worried that I would elope?"

He actually rolled his eyes at me. "For heaven's sake, Cassidy. Why wouldn't you accept? Jack is a stellar match for you."

I gaped at him. "You're kidding, right?"

"And tonight was a perfect time to announce it, before the new poll numbers come out. I just got a text from Bert Coleman, and he's over the moon." He acted as if I hadn't spoken. "So, stop all this drama. It's beneath you."

"We were just helping you, Cassidy." My mother takes his arm, forming a united front. "Besides, time is marching on. You're thirty-two, honey. You and Jack will make amazing parents."

I was so angry, I'm surprised I didn't catch fire. It felt like I was trapped in one of those floaty prison squares in the old Superman movies; spinning through space and silently screaming into the void. They both stood there frowning, as if they'd done me this huge favor and were confused because I wasn't falling to my knees in gratitude.

Then, as I opened my mouth to tell them I wasn't going to marry Jack and that they could both go to hell, my mother lowered her chin, her eyes boring into mine, and fired her final salvo. "It's time to grow up, Cassidy. You're not in college anymore. Thank goodness."

Pulling my knees to my chest, I let the tears finally fall against my pillow. It felt like a punch to the gut when she'd said that. Seeing the distaste in my father's eyes at the reminder of my past shattered me. Kevin had come in then, but I don't remember what he'd said, just that my parents left. He promised to talk to Dad and get him to issue a correction, but I couldn't talk about it. I wanted to pretend it was just a bad dream. That my parents hadn't done what they always did, and assumed I'd go along with whatever they wanted.

With a groan, I punch the pillow and roll on my back, a ball of rage forming in my belly as I replay my parents' words in my head. But I'm just as frustrated with myself as I am with them. Because honestly, I've allowed myself to be used for so long, why would they think this time was any different?

Being confronted by Sean was the final straw in this hellish evening. He was all I could think of on the long ride home. I never dreamed he'd be camped outside my door like an avenging angel, his soaked T-shirt plastered against his chest, and practically vibrating with anger.

Flinging an arm over my eyes, I swallow a sob. His anger was understandable, and it matched mine, but the hurt in his eyes tore at me. That he would question how serious I am—I press my fists to my eyes and snort derisively. Of course he questioned it. I can't blame him.

He's right—I don't owe them anything. But he doesn't understand what it's been like for me all these years. He thinks he does, with all his years of dealing with the media and paparazzi and gossip blogs, but it's different for him. His lifestyle uses them as much as they use him. He was prepared, hell, he *expects* to be the center of attention. He *courts* it…thrives on it.

I was *forced* into my situation. Sean can't truly understand the days of terror I felt after it happened. Wondering if that day was the day a picture of me, naked and drooling with some guy ready to shove his dick into me, would be posted somewhere my friends would see it. Where my *family* would see it. Days of imagining what my dad's opponent's campaign would do with it—nothing is off-limits in politics. Wracking my brain to figure out what to do without going to the cops because all it would take is one enterprising reporter on the local beat to find my police report and realize I was Senator Skinner's daughter for all hell to break loose. How I wept out of sheer *relief* when Kevin had told me Dale took care of it and I didn't need to worry anymore. And he takes care of it to this day.

"Fuck," I groan, slamming my fists into the mattress. "Fuck, fuckity, *fuck!*" I glare up at the ceiling and swipe the wetness from my eyes. Time to pull yourself together, Cass. You've wallowed enough. I know what I have to do, despite the chaos it's going to cause my dad. As much as I owe him, I can't allow that to keep me living in the past.

Never in my wildest dreams have I ever imagined a man more perfect for me than the whirlwind that is Sean Murphy. He's bold, he's unpredictable, he's...everything. An incredibly talented, vibrant man with a generous, passionate soul. His music academy is going to help so many kids, and I don't think he wants any credit for it at all. That's so incredibly rare, at least in my experience. He's fearless and if he wants something, he does what he has to do to get it...like owning my heart.

I can't believe he came all the way over here when he heard the news, but...that's Sean. He wears his heart on his sleeve, and it's one of the things I love about him. There's no subterfuge, no hidden agendas. My heart jumps when I remember the intensity in his stormy emerald eyes when he held my face between his hands.

"He's crazy about me," I whisper in amazement, and then snort a laugh, shaking my head. "He *must* be crazy." Maybe so, but I can't take the risk of him walking out of my life.

Because I'm just as crazy about him.

A muffled ringing coming from under my ass startles a yelp out of me. After a few seconds of fumbling, I pull my forgotten clutch out from under the comforter and retrieve my phone. It's probably Kevin, checking up on me...but no. Damnit. "Hey, Jack."

"So..." His wary drawl speaks volumes. "I hear we're engaged?"

"No, we're not," I growl. "My parents went rogue in front of about fifty donors, and the media picked it up before I could do anything about it."

"Holy shit."

"That's putting it mildly. Did your dad call you?"

He heaves a sigh, and I think I hear ice tinkling in a glass. "Yeah.

He was more excited than he's been in years. Pissed that I hadn't told him, but that passed when he started talking about grandbabies. How did your parents find out?"

I roll my eyes at the thought of the earlier debacle. "Sorry about that—Mom overheard me talking to Kevin about it tonight, and she and Dad decided to seize the day."

"So, no engagement, then?" He sounds resigned, and I sigh in agreement.

"Jack, I just…can't." I grab a fistful of hair, hating everything about this. "You're a wonderful man and six months ago I might have agreed. But it would've been just as wrong then as it would be now." I take a deep breath and smile a little as the weight on my heart lifts. "We don't love each other. It would be wrong for us to get married only to make other people happy. I'm sorry."

He sighs. "I know. You're right, of course. I just thought…" He huffs a laugh. "Well, it sounded like a good idea at the time. I'll make sure my dad doesn't issue any kind of a statement. I told him to hold off until I'd spoken to you."

A sad smile colors my voice. "I'm sorry; I know this kind of puts you in a bind, but…" Even in the dark room, I can see the rain streaking down my skylight. In my present mood, it feels like even the sky is crying. "I bet your partner will be glad to hear it's not really happening."

"He will. Adam. His name is Adam," he says, his voice warming, and I hear the ice clink again. "What about your friend? Sean? What does he think?"

"He basically thinks I—well, both of us—are 'bloody fucking idiots' for even considering it, or words to that effect." My heart clenches when I recall Sean's own proposal. For whatever reason, the thought of that doesn't scare me like it did before. "Tonight…well, he didn't take tonight's debacle well." The memory of Sean standing there, dripping water on the floor, and shaking with justified wrath, chills me.

"Well, hell, Cassidy." A hint of his Wyoming twang shows in his soft chuckle. "Why are you still talking to me? Get your ass moving, girl, and fix it."

His words snap me out of my gloom. I sit up abruptly, clutching the comforter to my chest. "I…I have to go, Jack. Bye." I can hear his laughter and a faint "good luck" as I end the call and toss the phone on the bed. Jumping up, I quickly dress in casual clothes and swipe a brush through my hair. I grab my phone and dial quickly, listening to it go to voice mail as I shove my feet into flat boots.

"Answer, you stubborn Brit," I growl and hang up when it goes to voice mail. "Fine, have it your way." I jam it in my jeans pocket and grab my purse, knowing it's useless to call back. He's not going to answer.

Pacing the room, my frustration comes to a boil when I realize I don't know where he lives. All I know is that he's in a penthouse some-where. Fuck! He may not have even gone back home, I suppose, except Sydney is still staying with—Sydney!

My feet barely touch the stairs as I run down to my desk and flip through my customer book until I find the one I want. My eyes dart to the clock; it's ridiculously late, and I pray she'll forgive me.

"Hello?" There's not a trace of sleep in her voice, which actually worries me a little.

"Sydney, it's Cassidy Skinner." Her relieved hum emboldens me. "I'm sorry, I know it's late, but I need to see your brother. Is he with you?"

She sighs. "Yes, he's here. He's… Cass, are you okay? He couldn't talk to me when he got back." Her concern is almost palpable, and I take a ragged breath.

"I will be. Can I come over? How do I get there?"

Her brief hesitation sends my heart plummeting to my feet. I'm sure she only wants to protect her brother, and I pray she doesn't shut me out. I wonder if she hears the desperation in my voice. "Yes. Yes, I think that's a good idea," she says after what feels like an eternity and rattles off an address near Central Park. "Text me when you get here, and I'll ring the doorman to let you in the lift."

"Thank you, Sydney." I can almost hear her smile at the relief in my voice.

"No problem. Hurry, Cass."

I summon a Lyft, and while I'm waiting, there's one more thing I have to do before I leave.

"Cassidy? What's wrong?" My mother sounds exhausted, but too damned bad.

"Nothing is wrong. I'm not marrying Jack. You and Dad need to issue a correction. Pronto."

She heaves a sigh. "Oh for heaven's sake… Look, we just boarded a red-eye back to Washington. I have to turn off my phone. We'll call you tomorrow."

"You can call tomorrow, but it won't change anything." I step outside as I see the Lyft round the corner; I scan the street before locking the door behind me. It looks like the photographers have called it a night, thank God. "Issue a correction or I'll do it myself. I don't think you'll like that option, so I suggest you don't dally."

"Cassidy—" I hang up and quickly climb in the car.

The elevator doors open, revealing a spacious room with soaring windows and an exhausted Sydney. She's wearing leggings and a thermal shirt, clutching a throw around her shoulders. "I'm sorry to bother you so late—"

"Don't worry about it," she says quickly, cutting me off. She gives me a wry smile, her bare toes flexing against the hardwood. "You look like I feel."

I laugh weakly. "That bad, huh?" I push my hood back and run a hand through my damp hair. It's still pouring outside. I let her take my coat and nervously look around as I set my purse on a glass-topped table. "Does he know I'm here?"

"No. He's taking out his frustration in his studio." She hangs my coat on a peg by the elevator and leads me through the gorgeous room; she pauses at the bottom of a curved staircase. Her eyes search mine. "Do you know what you're going to say?"

I tug down my T-shirt and play with the hem. "Not entirely. But, there's really only one thing *to* say. If he'll listen."

She gives me a knowing smile. "Good."

We climb the stairs, my nerves building with each step. I've never been this nervous about talking to a man in my life. Then again, I've never felt this way about a man before, either.

As we walk down a short hall, a rhythmic pounding penetrates my senses the closer I get to the closed door—I feel it more than hear it. "It's soundproofed, but I think the stripping around the door is beginning to go." We stop in front of a door that seems to be vibrating. "In you go." She pats me on the shoulder and heads back downstairs.

My palms feel clammy, and I wipe them against my jeans. "Okay, Skinner. Don't chicken out now," I mutter. "If he won't listen, then fuck him." Taking a deep breath, I square my shoulders and swing the door open.

The blast of sound hits me in the face and I blink. It's like a cave—the light from the doorway slices across the floor, cutting through the darkness of the room. Then, I realize there's a single candle on the floor by one of the drum kits.

His back is to me, and he stops almost immediately. He's sucking in great breaths as if he's run a marathon. "Fuck, I'm sorry, Syd," he says between pants and begins to turn. "I'll tone it dow—" The sticks fall from his hands with a clatter. "It's you."

"It's me." I step inside and close the door behind me. I can't see anything, and I jump when I hear his stool creak.

"Damn meddling twin," he mutters, his voice coming from a different place—closer and to my left. I swallow down my nerves and peer into the darkness, willing my eyes to adjust.

"Don't blame Syd. I told her I had to see you."

"Did you now?"

His voice is soft, almost a purr, to my right this time, and I can't help my flinch. His accent curls around each word, making my entire body tingle. I feel like prey being stalked by a tiger. When my eyes finally adjust, he's mere inches away. My back hits the door behind me.

"What do you want, Fly-girl?" He leans forward, planting his hands against the door on each side of my head, his eyes boring into mine, his spicy, sweaty scent enveloping me. I'm breathing as heavily as he is. When I finally manage to speak, my voice is barely a whisper; my hands flatten against his bare chest.

"I want you."

chapter ten

Murphy's Law No.38: If it's easy it's probably a trap. Nothing worthwhile in life ever comes easy.

Sean

THAT FAMILIAR LAVENDER SCENT INVADES MY SPACE, MY ENTIRE FUCKING being.

She's here and I'm hanging by a thread. My arms burn from who knows how long at my kit. As is often the case, I've been lost to the one thing I know best. It gives me clarity, doesn't make me feel like I'm floundering. I know what to expect when I sit down. It's automatic and cathartic, allowing me an outlet for all this pent-up emotion.

Cassidy's got me all twisted. For so long I've been all about women with no strings, but with Cassidy it's like a thousand symphonies of them all twisting and turning.

Tonight was unexpected, and normally I'm up for that. When it makes me feel like there's a dagger to my heart, I'm not quite a fan.

I couldn't even speak to Sydney when I got home because there was something more important that I needed to do, something that pulls me away from the edge when I'm in danger of tipping over it. Despite Syd's protests, and assurances she's here for me, but this isn't something I can talk to her about.

"Sean, you're scaring me. I'm here. You can talk to me." Her voice was nervous and filled with worry. I was a dangerous live wire when I left Cassidy at her shop. An intense desire to erase the last hour or so from my brain was the overwhelming goal.

In the past, there had been one sure way to do that, and in the good city that never sleeps, it's easy to find a little something to take the edge off.

That temptation was always one bad decision away from something I knew I had to live with for the rest of my life.

Ignoring the fact that it was blowing a gale, I actually walked in the direction of a place where I knew I could score what was guaranteed to obliterate the last few hours along with some brain cells in the process. It would be so easy to fall back into destructive and dangerous habits. Which was one of the many reasons I didn't follow through. Nothing worthwhile in life ever came easy.

Instead, I stalked home, drenched. I brushed off Syd and surrendered myself to my studio. Calling my sponsor, Russell—I'm not even sure that's his real name—was the only option. He picked up on the third ring; relief flooded through me when I heard his gravelly voice.

"Sean Murphy. It's been a long time, man. How are you?" His Texas accent was a balm to the chaos raging inside.

"I've been better, to be honest." Greeted by silence, swamped with shame. I'm not sure I'll ever get over that feeling. "Do you have time?"

"Always. I don't have to be at work for another half hour."

Pacing a hole in the hardwood seemed like the best course of action. As always, Russell just waited. In the beginning stages of kicking my coke habit, calls to Russell were marathons. He's a fabulous listener, a sounding board, a beacon of light and information. He's one of the many unsung heroes of the program. Like most sponsors, he doesn't want attention, no fuss or muss. He's been through his own hell and now he just wants to help.

"Have you used?" he asked after an eon.

"No." I ran a palm across the back of my neck.

"Do you have anything with you that you could take?"

"Outside of a few headache tablets, no."

"But you'd like to?"

"Fuck." My fingers dug into my skin, trying to beat down temptation. "No. I wouldn't like to. I know where it leads, mate, and I'm not going back there. Fuck would I ever love to erase the last couple of hours from my memory, you know?"

"I do know. I know exactly what you mean."

I pressed my back against the wall and glared at my drum kit. "I know you do. And I was horrible to my sister."

"I'm sure that's not true."

"I told her she wouldn't understand."

"She wouldn't, Sean. She can't understand if she's never been there herself."

I took a quick glance at the door, knowing Syd was probably waiting right outside it, sick with worry. "Logically, I know that. Doesn't mean I don't feel like shit about it."

"It's okay to feel that way, but you can't control how anyone else feels about you, Sean."

Pushing off the wall, I moved to trace the curve of the high hat. "I wish I could."

"But you can't. You can only control yourself. Your reactions. Your decisions."

I tapped on the brushed gold surface, anxiety twisting in my stomach. "You sure you're not a mystical philosopher, Russell?"

He laughed a little. "Positive."

"I shouldn't need to call you." I let out a long, slow breath, regretting the words instantly. "Sorry, I don't mean to sound ungrateful. I'd probably be high as a fucking kite right now if I didn't have you."

"No you wouldn't."

"I thought about it." I know this was part of the never-ending recovery journey. It's not rational. The urge to wipe out reality hadn't hit me in a long time, but seeing that news report tonight, knowing there's a possibility Cassidy might never be mine, sent me right back to wanting to escape for a while.

When you've experienced the warm buzz that lets you drift high into nothingness it's easy to give in and want to feel it again. The intensity of emotions currently flooding my system is in stark contrast to that empty feeling. That's the irrationality of the situation I'm in. I've never been in a better place, but it's also terrifying.

"We've all thought about it. The thing to focus on here is that you only thought about it and now you get to hear my angelic voice in your head." That made me laugh. Russell was probably the only person who could do that right now. "You want to tell me what happened?"

I slid the stool behind my kit back with my foot. "I'm not even sure myself. There's this woman."

"Ah."

"Exactly. Ah."

"She do a number on you?"

"Not the way you probably think." I swiveled a bit on the stool. "I don't want to lose her." Saying those words sparked something in me: a determination and fire. "I gave both her and me space tonight, not wanting to escalate an already tense and emotionally charged situation. The proverbial ball was now firmly in her court, and that doesn't sit well with me."

"Why not?"

I gave him the truth because I could. Because I needed to. "I like who I am with her."

"And who is that?"

"Not a selfish bastard. I want to make her happy. It's all I want."

"And that scares you?"

"It terrifies me."

"Why?" Damn, Russell was good at that, at pulling the truth out of me.

"Because it means I care about her."

"Are you afraid she doesn't feel the same way?"

"No, mate, I'm afraid she does. But it's all new, you know? The way I feel about her is different and that's terrifying. It's all consuming, and I'm afraid it's slipping away from me at the same time. I don't want to lose her."

Russell was quiet for a minute, his voice full of that determination I'm used to hearing from him when he spoke again. "Just remember to keep a balance, Sean. One day at a time. Don't forget that."

"Why do you think I'm calling you?"

"You just missed the sound of my voice." I let out a half laugh.

"You see right through me, Russell."

"Isn't that why you keep calling me?"

"I'm going to let you go now." Which was our code for, "I'm okay and I'm not going to do anything stupid, thanks to you."

"Any time you need me…"

"I know. Thank you, man."

"No need to thank me." And then he was gone, and it was just me, my studio, and a whole lot of excess energy that needed to be set free.

As Cassidy speaks the words "I want you," I almost think I must be dreaming, still caught in that perfect place when I'm playing, and time and space and the chaos in my head ceases to exist.

I lean forward, my lips pressed to the sweet curve of her neck. Her skin is so soft and perfect it makes restraint nearly impossible. I grip the doorjamb harder, leaning back to catch her gaze in the soft light. "Does that mean no Jack? I don't want to share you, Fly-girl, even if it is a sham relationship you've got going with him."

Her hand gently trails up my arm, her fingers pressing against my bicep before she rests her palm on my neck. "No Jack," she whispers.

"How are your parents going to deal with that?"

She shakes her head, and moves her fingers across the back of my neck as I dip my head and brush my nose against her warm skin. "I don't know." She's a little breathless. I like that I can do that to her.

"There'll be pictures of us at your place out there soon enough. Mystery man who was obviously not Jack at your doorstep late at night? Screams of a scandal to me."

Her fingers press against my lips, and I can't resist taking a nip of them. "No more talk of Jack or my parents. Right now, I want you. Only you. We can do that, right? Forget the world for a while?" There's an undertone of vulnerability in her words.

"The world will still be here in the morning, Fly-girl, won't it? And we're going to have to deal with it at some point."

"We will," she whispers against my neck. "Now, touch me. You haven't touched me yet."

"Well, that's a damn crime, isn't it?" I murmur and my hands abandon the wall for much better places.

"More tea?" Sydney glances at Cassidy across the breakfast bar, trying to be all nonchalant and casual. As if a woman staying the night at my place is normal.

"You're a star, Syd." I push my cup across the marble countertop. "Fill me up."

Syd bites back a laugh and ignores me. "You can get your own tea."

Cassidy gives me a lazy smile, pulling her silky strands of hair into one of those messy bun things with a hair tie. "I'm okay, Sydney. Thank you for breakfast. It was delicious."

Cassidy's dressed in her clothes from last night, even though I tried to convince her wearing mine would be a much better idea. Actually, wearing none would be stellar, but the presence of my damn twin nixed that idea before it even had time to take wing. As much as I love my sister and the short amount of time we get to spend together, she's put a damper on morning sex in the kitchen.

Last night was intense. A frenzied, wild fucking in the studio giving way to slow and easy once we made our way to my bedroom. If we slept a total of two hours, I'd be surprised. Waking up to Cassidy's perfect lips wrapped around my cock also needs to happen more often. Christ, the woman is insatiable, and I'm more than happy to indulge her.

"I need to get going." Cassidy pushes off the stool.

"You should stay." I stand with her and brush a lock of her hair behind her ear. She leans into my touch.

"I can't. I have three clients today, and I have to work on Sydney's dress."

I scoff. "Her dress can wait. You can postpone the wedding, right, Syd?"

Syd glares at me over her teacup. "I'm going to pretend you didn't just say that, and that it's lack of sleep talking, what with all the racket I heard last night coming from your bedroom."

"Oh, there was lots of coming in the bedroom." Cassidy's cheeks flush pink even as she gives my chest a swat. "What? You're not exactly quiet." I cover her hand with mine and turn it over to kiss the palm.

"Neither are you," Syd fires at me.

"I'm so sorry," Cassidy mumbles under her breath as I press her against my side.

"It's fine." Syd waves us off, glancing at my phone when it buzzes on the counter. "You should probably get that. It's been going off for a while now." She nods to my phone, and Cassidy slips out from under my arm.

"I'll get going and you guys can get on with your day." Cass moves to the door.

"Hang on." Picking up my phone, I frown at the myriad messages from Nicole, our PR manager. Maybe there's something happening with the academy schedule.

I scroll through the texts while I walk to the door with Cassidy. Nic is in full panic mode, ranting at me in all caps with escalating degrees of annoyance. Her last text contains a picture from some tabloid site I know is from last night. The photo is dark and blurry, taken outside Cassidy's shop with a clickbait headline, "Engaged Senator's Daughter Already Cheating." I grimace at the photo of us glaring at each other as the rain pours down. I knew this would happen, but could we not have at least twenty-four hours of peace before the sharks start circling? "Bloody hell."

"Everything okay?" Cassidy glances up at me.

"Afraid not, darling." I pass the phone to her, watching her eyes widen.

"Already?" she squeaks out.

"Welcome to the shitshow."

Cassidy

"Sweet crispy Christ."

As the Uber heads down the street, I can see a few photographers camped out by the bagel shop across from my studio. Ah, crap; there's a local news van, too. I guess I should've taken Sean up on his offer of a bodyguard. Judging by my phone that's currently blowing up with messages from my mother and Kevin, Sean's right. This is a shitshow.

I jump out of the car and hurry to my door, but a fresh-faced reporter and cameraman pop out of the van and intercept me. "Ms. Skinner! Congratulations on your engagement! Could we have a few words?" He jabs a microphone in my face, smiling like a shark. I get my key in the lock just in time.

"Sorry, no time now. Please call my father's office and make an appointment." I enter and slam the door in his face, leaning against it. Well, this day just got more interesting.

"Cassidy!" Riya comes around the desk, her eyes wide. "Are you all right? What the hell happened last night? Why didn't you tell me you were getting married to that Jack?"

With a groan, I push off the door. "I'm not marrying Jack." I run upstairs to change, Riya hot on my heels.

"Are you marrying the crazy one, then?" She's breathless and holds her ample sides at the top of the stairs while I rush to my closet.

I strip off my clothes and slip on fresh undergarments. With a shiver, I inhale the spicy smell of Sean's bodywash he anointed me with this morning in his ginormous shower. That man will be the death of me, I swear. Shaking my head to dispel thoughts of Sean's magical cock, I suck in a deep breath. "No, not him, either." At least not yet. Rolling my eyes at myself, I pull on a pair of black slacks and grab a burgundy silk shirt.

"Well, then why did I see an engagement headline with your picture in the *Times* this morning?" she calls, lowering her voice when I emerge from the closet, pulling on my shirt.

I quickly update her while brushing the tangles out of my hair. Slipping my feet in black heels, I face her, ready for the day. I'm not ready for her angry expression. "What?"

"What do you mean, what?" She throws her hands in the air. "How could your parents do that? They can't tell you who to marry—this isn't one of those stupid reality shows. What are you going to do about it?"

"I told Mom they needed to issue a retraction, or I would." I shoo her toward the stairs. "Come on. We have to get ready for our first appointment this morning."

"I've already prepared the salon," she replies, but she descends the stairs anyway with me following. "Did you give her a deadline? You know your mother, Cass."

She's right. Mom will try to pretend she thought I wasn't serious or, if I was, that I could be talked out of it. And, I need to deal with the texts from her and my brother. "Could you get the tea ready? I need to call my mother."

"You're welcome, Cynthia. Mrs. Evans," I say with a bright smile as I show our last appointment and her mother to the door. "Your special day will be glorious. I'll have the gowns messengered over tomorrow, if that's agreeable."

"Perfect, Cassidy." The banker's wife follows her daughter. "And congratulations again on your own engagement. I saw the blurb on Page Six."

My smile becomes brittle. "An unfortunate misprint, Mrs. Evans. I'm not engaged to anyone. Have a lovely day," I say, giving them a friendly wave that I don't feel as they bustle out the door. I close it firmly behind them. The photographers seem to have left, thank God. After sending me a barrage of texts this morning demanding to know who that 'weird-looking' man was in the pictures and why I was embarrassing them after they'd 'helped me out' with Jack—because, of course, it's only about how it makes *them* feel—my mother hasn't answered her phone all day. I was able to catch Kevin between meetings to reassure him everything was fine, and learn that he'd been trying to reach our parents too, to no avail. They're dodging both of us, apparently. Time to step it up.

I grab my phone.

"Cassidy! How nice to hear from you. Congratulations on your engagement!"

"There is no engagement, Sylvia," I say, barely keeping myself from snapping at my father's office admin. "Can I please speak to my father?"

"He just left for a floor vote. That new prescription drug bill?" she says, as if I should know all about it. "He won't be back for an hour, at least. What did you mean about your engagement? Your father was all smiles about it this morning."

"I'm sure he was, but I'm not engaged." I look out the window and my heart sinks when I spot the photographer lurking across the street by the bagel shop. How long has he been there? I hope he hasn't bothered any of my clients. "When he returns, Sylvia, please tell him that if he doesn't issue a retraction before six tonight, so it can get on the evening news, I'll do it myself."

Poor Sylvia is clearly confused. "A retraction? About what?"

"He knows. Thanks, Sylvia. Have a nice evening."

With a dry smile of satisfaction, I slip the phone into my pocket. That should light a fire under someone. If not, I guess I can always step outside and let Mr. Industrious Photographer have a scoop. I huff in grim amusement. The parents would love that.

Barely thirty minutes pass before my phone rings. Wow, that was faster than I expected, actually. Frowning at the display, it's not who I expected. But maybe I should have.

"Dale? What's up?"

Riya cranes her head to peer at me around the rack of gowns we were arranging; I give her a reassuring smile and walk into the kitchenette for some privacy.

"Hello, Cassidy." His smooth voice does nothing to ease my apprehension—it's the voice I've heard him use a millions times before when he's handling a difficult lobbyist or reporter. "Congratulations on your engagement."

"How can I help you, Dale?" As much as I owe my father, I also owe thanks to this man. I'll never forget the look on Dale's face when he and Kevin showed up on my doorstep in California. It had shocked me, even through my haze of terror and panic. I had only seen him as my father's affable and effective right hand. That day, he looked like an avenging angel, wearing a face of cold resolve that still chills me when I think about it. As much as I'm thankful for what he did, all I want to do now is cut to the chase.

"I heard you called. Your father is on the senate floor. Can I help you?"

"No, I don't think so." I sink down into a chair. "But thanks for asking."

He hums softly. "Sylvia said something about a retraction? Concerning what?"

"The engagement announcement." I take a deep breath. "My parents were mistaken last night; I'm not marrying Jack Coleman. He needs to issue a retraction. Today, before this gets any messier."

"I see."

There's a silence, and this awkward conversation feels even more awkward. I clear my throat, tapping my fingers on the table in front of me. "Um, yes, so if you'll let my father know—"

"Are you sure you want to do that? Jack Coleman is a great guy."

My fingers still. What the hell? "Yes, he is, but I'm sure," I state, barely managing to keep my sudden irritation out of my voice.

"Are you? Your union with Jack is one of the best things that could happen for the campaign—for your father. And you want to help your father, don't you?"

"I think I've helped him plenty." I sit up straight and frown down at the table. "Look, Dale, this is bigger than a campaign. This is my life—"

"Did you get the text I sent you a few weeks ago?" His voice is quiet but firm, and the blood freezes in my veins. "I was just about to send you another one. We intercepted two images this morning. I suppose your recent notoriety has sparked new interest."

I try to swallow down the sudden lump in my throat, but my throat is dry. "Two?" I choke out finally.

He hums. "I'll let my team know to be extra vigilant in the coming weeks. It would be a shame if any images slipped out. The last two were particularly…unfortunate." I hear a chair squeaking in the background, and I imagine him leaning back. "Your mother would be devastated," he murmurs, a note of sympathy in his tone. "There was…a birthmark."

I gasp and instinctively squeeze my thighs together where my birthmark colors my skin. The thought Dale has seen it—that he's been seeing *any* of the photos they find—curdles my stomach. "What, what are you saying?" I whisper, the hair on the back of my neck standing up.

"Besides the embarrassment to your family, can you imagine what would happen if your clients saw those photos? You'd be ruined. It's a tricky business, you know, cybersecurity. It's so easy *to let things slip through*, no matter how thorough you are. There have been so many over the years. I mean, what if *someone were keeping a file of all of them?* You know, for a rainy day." A strangled squeak escapes me, and I clap a hand over my mouth. When he speaks again, he's all business, any trace of sympathy gone. Closing the deal. "I think it might be wiser to let the engagement stand for a while. Perhaps indefinitely. The wedding can wait. For now." He pauses, and when I don't respond, he prompts, "Don't you agree, Cassidy?"

The thought of that night and what those photos could contain being plastered all over the news and gossip sites is terrifying. I swallow thickly, the words sticking in my throat. "Yes."

"Excellent. I'll let your parents know it was just a misunderstanding. On your part." His smooth voice makes me want to vomit. "Have a good evening."

When the call ends I stare in disbelief at the phone, my gorge rising. I don't want to believe it, but his meaning is clear. This is more than playing on my guilt. This is sinister.

I make it to the sink just in time.

"Are you sure you're all right? You're still a bit pale." Riya tenderly brushes my hair out of my face, her brow furrowed with concern. After she found me doubled over, it took me fifteen minutes to convince her it was just a touch of food poisoning. Then she watched over me like a mother hen for the next two hours while we prepared the Evans' gowns to be messengered tomorrow.

"Yes, I'm fine." I give her a soft smile, full of affection for this woman who has always treated me like one of her own children. "I promise, Riya. I'll just take it easy tonight."

She crosses her arms over her chest, not convinced. "Are you sure you don't want me to stay?"

"No, I'll be fine." When she squishes up her face in disbelief, I laugh. "Honest! Go home to your husband. I'll see you tomorrow, okay?"

"Fine," she says finally. She slips her laptop in the desk to do the accounts tomorrow and gathers up her tote bag. "Why won't you tell me who was on the phone? It was your mother, wasn't it? Is she the one who upset you?"

My heart twinges with fear at the reminder. "No, it wasn't Mom." I sigh and look at her, begging with my eyes. "Please, let it go."

Reluctantly, she nods and gives me a kiss on the cheek. "See you tomorrow. Get some sleep."

I lock up after her and lower the front blinds. I'm not sure if the photographer is still out there, but I'm not taking any chances. In the silence of my bedroom, I sink down on my bed and finally let my mind turn to my problem. The fear of those photos slipping through—of being *let* through—is almost choking. But I told Sean the truth last night. I choose him. And that means I can't let this threat stand.

Mixed with the fear, however, is a boiling anger. If I'm going to break away, I need to take matters into my own hands. I've let others protect me, preferring not to know the details, but all that's done is prolong my guilt. Nibbling on my thumbnail, I try to remember everything I've ever heard about cybersecurity. I don't understand it, but I know it's always expensive.

I look around my workroom: the racks of lace and ornaments; bolts of fabric leaning against the wall; and the dress form in the corner, draped in pieces of my latest creation. Whatever it's going to cost, it will be worth it. I can't let what happened back then destroy what I've built for myself, and I refuse to let anyone threaten me again. It's time—*more* than time.

The rain has started again, a spring squall pelting angrily against the windows. I'm terrified, but I know what I have to do…and I think I know who can help.

He answers his phone on the second ring. "You aren't going to believe this, but I was just about to ring you." His voice is like a balm, and the tension in me eases. "Have you eaten? I know a nice, quiet Russian place in the Village that makes the best piroshkies you've ever had. And then I want to get you naked and—"

"Sean, I need to take control of my own future…and past," I blurt. "Do you know someone who has experience in scouring the internet?"

There's a silence, during which I think my heart will fly out of my chest. When he speaks, his voice is full of resolve. "Have you seen any paparazzi today?"

"Um, there was a photographer earlier, but I'm not sure if he's still there." I get up and look out the rain-streaked window, but I can't see anything. "What's that got to do with—"

"Doesn't matter. I'll send a car to pick you up—my driver can shake anyone following. We'll have the piroshkies delivered."

I smile at his take-charge tone. "Can you help?"

"Of course I can, love. I know just the man."

chapter eleven

Murphy's Law No. 42: You can either hit the dead end, or turn and take a different path.

Sean

TUCKER ISN'T TRYING TO HIDE HIS AMUSED SMILE AS WE SIT ON VIDEO chat. "Well, well, well. Better stock up on parkas; hell has officially frozen over. You've got yourself a girlfriend, Sean."

"Fuck, why did I call you?" I mumble, taking a sip of tea.

"Because I'm the best and you love me." Our head of security just grins at me.

"I will neither confirm nor deny my love for you, mate. She'll be here any minute. Just tell me you can do something about this."

He narrows his eyes at the camera. "Of course I can. Let me get this straight. You said her father is a senator?"

"Yes, from Wyoming."

Tucker doesn't even try to cover his laugh. "You fell for a cowgirl?"

"She's not a cowgirl, you oversized mammoth. She's been through a lot, and it would be really nice if we could get rid of these damn photos for good."

His amusement is obliterated as he stares at the screen. "You really like this girl."

I run a hand down my face. "I really do. There. I said it. Happy now?"

"You have no idea. Okay, I'll look into these pictures, but, Sean, if I find anything I'm not going to show you. Got it?"

I scowl. "Why the hell not?"

"Because if it's as bad you're making it out to be, and you really care about this girl, I don't think you want those visuals in your head. Shit like this can change things."

"She was taken advantage of, Tucker." I blow out a long breath. "Drugged and almost raped. Whoever is still holding onto the photos needs to be dealt with."

"And this was at UCLA? Do you have a date or any names of these frat-boy assholes?"

"I don't have an exact date. It would've been about ten years ago. No names, although she did say her father's chief of staff, I think his name is Dale something, dealt with it. There may be records at the hospital. Apparently, these fuckers had the shit kicked out of them once this Dale character got into the picture."

Tucker nods, writing something in his book. "Give me a couple of hours, and I'll have something."

"Thanks, Tuck. I know this goes outside of your typical duties, but…" My throat tightens with some weird emotion. "I owe you."

"Famous last words, man. If I had a dime for every time you guys said that…" He taps the screen. "And I'll always help you, Sean. No questions asked."

"I know. Even though we are a pain in your arse."

He lets out a laugh. "You have no idea. I'll get back to you soon." The screen goes dark before I can thank him again.

I stare at the computer, thinking of how much my life has changed in the weeks that Cassidy blazed into it. That I want another person outside of my family, the band, and their significant others to be safe and protected is new. But, that's all I want. To be the person who takes this nightmare away from her.

"Give me your mouth," I whisper-rasp into Cassidy's ear as she flattens her palms against one of the panoramic windows. The Manhattan night skyline has never looked as good as it does now, with Cassidy naked, her desperate cries filling the penthouse as I drive into her from behind.

Thank God for that privacy glass.

We started shedding our clothes the moment she stepped foot into the apartment. Both of us seem to be driven by raw need, by the insane desire to get lost in each other. She turns her head; her warm lips meet mine in a kiss so intense it makes my heart leap.

I feed her my tongue with each sharp roll of my hips and take a tug of her hair. I smile against her mouth as she pushes back to meet the frantic pace. "You like it this way, don't you?" She answers by biting at my bottom lip. "Spread out and open for me." Her lips trail across my jaw, hovering against my throat. I can feel the warmth of her hitched breaths as she chases down euphoria.

"That's right, Fly-girl. Feel all of me." I wish she fucking could. I can't wait for these test results to come in so I can feel her bare. I might just lose my mind in the process, but what a way to go.

The window reflects every dip and curve of her glorious body. Her creamy skin, those peaked, delicious nipples, reddened from every lick and suck I gave them. And then her lips draw away from my skin and her head drops forward, and I feel that perfect moment when she crashes and shatters around me.

My own orgasm barrels through me, electric heat making me press her against the cool glass with my face buried between her shoulders. I keep one arm wrapped around her and drop a lingering kiss on her shoulder blade.

Lifting my gaze, I can see the glass fog with each of her panted breaths, making me feel like I'm the king of the fucking world for wrecking her like this. I glide my hand up the curve of her back, along her arm, and cover one of her hands still anchored to the glass. "Fuck, you're amazing," I whisper against her neck, unable to stop the press of my lips along her sweet skin.

"You're not too shabby yourself." Her voice is shaky, and my heart stutters with her vulnerability. She's put a hell of a lot of trust in me today, and I don't think she does that lightly.

It's agony pulling out of her to deal with the condom. I want to stay buried in her for a lifetime. By the time I pull on a pair of jeans and return, she's already out of the loo and standing at the window with my Union Jack blanket wrapped around her. Manhattan lights sparkle in the inky sky behind her, but she outshines them all.

"You really are trying to kill me." I take her face between my hands and trace the gentle slope of her cheek. "This is guaranteed to make me hard again."

"I don't think that takes much," she whispers against my lips.

"Not when you're around." Her hand finds the back of my neck and she coaxes me forward, her lips pressing to mine. It's sweet and slow, and nothing like the desperation of before. She hums against my lips, making them throb with need.

"You taste like tea," she murmurs against my mouth.

"Had some before you got here, after I talked to Tuck. Fancy a cup?" I tighten my arms around her, pressing her to my chest. She feels like home.

She shakes her head, leaning back to look up at me. "I'm okay right now. Maybe you can make me dinner later."

I laugh, unsure if she's serious or not, and I press a kiss to her forehead. "The only thing I make are reservations, love. I'm afraid you've found something I can't do."

"Impossible. Sean Murphy can't do something?" I kiss the corner of her upturned mouth. "I don't believe it."

"Believe it, but don't tell anyone. Wouldn't want people to think less of me." Her eyes light and her fingers tug through the short strands of my hair. "I can, however, order those piroshkies I was telling you about."

"Sounds delicious." She shuffles backward, the edge of the blanket getting caught a bit on her feet. She gathers it up with a grin. "I should get dressed."

"You should stay exactly like this." I follow along after her like a man possessed. When I reach her, I run my fingers along her shoulder, exposed from where the blanket has drifted down.

"Won't Sydney be home soon?" She glances at the door and the trail of her discarded clothes.

"She's out for a bit. Some last-minute shopping before she flies home tomorrow."

I frown as she ignores me and starts picking up her clothes. "Still, we've broken every single client rule there is at this point."

"I'm not your client, Sydney is," I remind her.

She tips her head to the side. "I thought you wanted me to make you a suit?"

"Will you?"

"I'm thinking about it." Little tease. She clutches her clothing against her chest.

"Will you do it naked?"

She laughs, the sound lighting the room. "That really would break all the rules." I trail behind her to the loo, and she slips inside, trying to shut the door. I slap my hand on it, stopping it mid-close.

"I've been known to do that now and again. Break the rules."

"I never would've guessed that," she deadpans. "You order food. I'm getting dressed."

"Bossy thing, aren't you?" She just smiles, steps back into the loo, and pushes the door shut. It should probably worry me that I'll do just about anything she asks.

Two hours later, Cassidy is on my sofa, complaining about one too many Russian puff pastries. Although, I'm not sure there is such a thing. These are delicious, melt-in-your-mouth goodness.

"It's ridiculous how good these are." She groans, waving her hand at the coffee table. She's currently got her legs stretched out over my lap and settles in. Her being comfortable here spreads like a wave of contentment through me. This feeling goes against everything I've ever known, everything I've told the guys in the band to avoid. *Never bring them to your place.* Even Syd knows that's one of my rules, but here Cassidy is, tucked in and sated, and I'm struck with the overwhelming feeling of never wanting her to leave.

"So, have another." I lean forward to pluck one from the container, but she presses her leg against me.

"No. No more. I can barely move as it is."

"Not to worry, love. You can just lie back and enjoy. I'll do all the work." She laughs as I lean over her and press my lips to hers. I groan at the sound of my phone buzzing from the table. "Bloody hell."

She smiles against my lips, her palm flattening against my chest. "It might be important."

"Is anything more important than my lips on yours?" Her cheeks rise with color, and she leans back against the arm of the couch.

"It might be your security guy." It's barely a whisper from her, but it derails my plans instantly.

"Right. Tucker." I reluctantly pull away from her lips and reach for my phone. It is indeed from Tucker.

Tuck: Let me know when you have a minute. I've got info.

I fire him back an answer.

Sean: Video chat or text?

Tuck: Video.

Sean: Give me 5.

I feel Cassidy sit up and she leans against my side, her hand trailing over my bicep. "He's got info for us."

Her eyes widen. "Already?"

"Told you he was the best." Her expression flips instantly, fear replacing the relaxed bliss she was just in. God, I hate this look on her face and the worry etched in her forehead. I set my hand against her neck and stroke the curve of her cheek. "Whatever it is, we'll deal with it together, okay?"

She nods, her fingers digging into my arm.

"Let me get my laptop." I retrieve it from the study, and return to find Cassidy gnawing on her lips and twisting her fingers together. Her anxiety ratchets up my own as I fire up our chat app, and Tucker's face appears.

"Hey, man." His eyes widen as he sees Cassidy. "Oh, hey. It's nice to meet you, Cassidy."

I take her hand, giving it a gentle squeeze. "You too, Tucker. Although I'm sorry it's this way. Thank you for doing this." Her voice softens. "Just let me know how much it costs and—"

Tucker looks confused. "Ah, no. There's no charge for this."

"I wouldn't feel right about—"

"Hey"—I press a kiss to her temple—"discussion over, love." I turn back to Tucker's expression. He looks caught between amused and dumbfounded. "What do you know?"

"First, there are no pictures," he says, dropping into that familiar matter-of-fact mode he always operates in.

"What? Yes, there are," Cassidy argues, glancing between us.

He shakes his head. "There's not. We've done every possible search and then some. If there ever were any, they're gone now."

"That's not... What?" Cassidy's eyes widen in confusion as she looks at me. "Dale said there were pictures as recently as this morning. He talked about my birthmark." She closes her eyes, suppressing a shudder before she continues, "How... how is that possible if there aren't any pictures?"

My brain seems to have faltered with the knowledge this Dale fucker seems to know about the birthmark hidden on her inner thigh. I've run my tongue over it and traced the contour of the edge when her legs are over my shoulder. That some prick has seen it stirs up a sea of rage inside me.

"Dale Canton. Your father's chief of staff, yes?" Tucker asks.

"Yes. He's been with him for fifteen years." I slide my arm around Cassidy and pull her closer to my side.

"He's a slimeball, for starters. The guy was into some sketchy shit a few years back." Cassidy's hand flies up to her mouth. "Canton was dipping his toe into the world of sexually suggestive instant messages to some former support staff of other senators." Tucker pauses, his mouth smashed into a firm line before he continues, "And there are photos of him. The kind of stuff that would ruin a career if they ever got out."

Cassidy looks to be in shock; the color drains from her face as she listens in horror to Tucker. I can only run circles on her back, feeling helpless to the cause. What a clusterfuck. "But he said—" Cass curses from behind her hand.

"A lot of crap, I'm assuming. These pictures aren't anywhere, Cassidy. Not on the dark web, not anywhere we can find them. We'll keep looking, but I think he's been lying to you. Why? I have no idea. Who knows how these bottom dwellers work."

"To control me," Cassidy blurts out. "That's what he's been doing. Trying to keep me in line, when he's the one who's out of control!"

"All it would take is a phone call to one of the reporters I know, and Dale would be out on his ass by morning. It at least deserves an investigation." He shakes his head. "He's as good as gone. Just give me the word, and I'll make a call."

"What if he does have pictures and releases them, though? I can't have that out there." Panic flares in Cassidy's eyes. "It would ruin me and my dad. The election is coming up. He wouldn't survive the scandal."

"I could talk to Canton. Give him an ultimatum. If he has pictures, he turns them over and walks away from your father's staff quietly or I'll release what I have to the press. Trust me, Cassidy; if people saw these pictures and what he wrote, he'll be done. He'll never work in politics again, and he's got to know that."

"What will I tell my father?" she asks, her voice a hoarse whisper. "This doesn't feel right. It's blackmail. I'll be just as bad as Dale is."

"Hey." Even over video, Tucker takes on that commanding presence that causes everyone in his general orbit to pay attention. "First, nothing. You tell your father nothing. As a senator, the less he knows the better. Canton hands over the photos to me, and then he resigns. Even if he doesn't have pictures, what he's been doing to you is wrong. He can give whatever excuse he wants on his resignation, as long as it doesn't harm your father or his campaign. And blackmail is what *Dale's* been doing to *you* for ten years. I prefer to call what I'm doing karma."

"I don't know about this." Cassidy glances up at me as if I have the answers. "I need to think about it. Is that okay?"

Tucker nods. "Absolutely. Take as long as you need. In the meantime, we'll keep looking, and if I find anything, I'll let you know. But, Cassidy?" She glances back to the screen. "Whatever bullshit he's been telling you is just that—bullshit."

Cassidy tightens her hand around my arm, her eyes glassy. "Thank you, Tucker. You don't know what this means to me."

Tucker shrugs, his half grin back in place. "Just look after this one over here." He nods in my direction. "You taking him off my hands is actually a good thing. I should be the one thanking you."

That gets a laugh out of Cassidy, and she leans into my side. "I don't think he's nearly as bad as you make him out to be."

Tucker scoffs. "No. You're right. He's worse, but we'll keep him around."

"Your life would be as dull as a burned-out light bulb without me in it, mate." Tucker laughs but doesn't dare disagree. He knows the truth all too well. "Thanks, Tuck. I'll give you a ring tomorrow, yeah?"

"Sounds like a plan. Talk to you then. Take care of him, Cassidy."

"I will," she says, meeting my gaze. I'm aware of the chat window going black, and then her mouth is on mine. Despite the seesaw of emotions we're both dealing with, she does a damn fine job of taking care of me.

Cassidy

"What color is your hair under all this dye?" I drag my fingers through his soft hair. The vibrant purple has dulled a bit, making it look like the color of evening shade against the mountains in Wyoming where we camped when I was a child.

"You don't want to know. Besides, it's been so long since I've seen it, I think I've forgotten." We're stretched out on his sofa, luxuriating in the afterglow of the blowjob I just gave him. I swear to God, his cock is magical. Watching him fall apart with my mouth around him makes me feel like a superhero.

After talking to Tucker, I needed what I always seem to need lately. Sean. The shock of hearing there were no pictures—and the implications of that—was almost too much, and he centers me like no one else ever has.

"I do want to know." I finger a silky strand. "Considering your twin's hair, I'm guessing it's red."

He sighs and opens one eye to peer at me. "Where did this sudden interest in my hair come from?"

I shrug. "Just wondering. I find your hair fascinating. And I like red hair." It's also helping me delay dealing with my problems. I slide my hand over his chest, toying with some of his reddish-gold hairs, and he covers my fingers with his. "Why not let it go natural for a while? Is it this color? Kind of golden red?"

"Keep guessing." He looks up at me. "You like red hair, huh? Harbor a secret love for gingers, Fly-girl?"

A giggle slips out and I kiss his chin. "Maybe. You never see Prince Harry complaining about his hair."

He barks out a laugh. "That's because he's a prince, love. You should've seen him at his brother's bachelor party. He—" The trilling of his phone interrupts him and he scowls at it.

"You'd better get it." I look at it like it's a rattlesnake. "It might be Tucker again."

He gives me a quick kiss before helping us both sit up. Snatching it off the coffee table, he frowns at the screen. He taps it and holds it out in front of him—he must be Facetiming. "Hey, Matty, what's up?"

"Hey, uh, how's it going, man?" a deep voice answers him.

"Peachy." Sean cocks an eyebrow at the screen. "What's going on, mate? Are you...are you fucking *blushing*?"

"Fuck you. Of course not." Sean rises and walks over to sit at the kitchen counter. "Um, Tess was just asking about you, so I thought I'd check in."

"Oh no, you don't!" A woman's amused voice rings through, and Sean smiles at the phone. "Don't you dare pin this on me, Matthew Thomas Logan!"

Sean laughs at the grumbling from his friend. "Just a second." I hear what sounds like footsteps on wooden stairs, and the woman's merry laughter fades.

"What the hell are you doing?" Sean demands, amusement coloring his voice. "Why the fuck are you going down to your garage? Are we plotting a coup or something?"

"So, I was just, um, talking with Tucker about the setup for the next show, and I thought I'd see what you thought about it." I don't know this man, but even I can hear the false note of nonchalance. Sean rolls his eyes.

"About the next show. Which isn't for eight months," he says flatly. "Bullshit. He fucking told you, didn't he? He called you and you two gossiped about me like a couple of fishwives, didn't you?"

He sweeps his hand through his shaggy hair, and I can't help but giggle at his aggrieved expression. I uncurl from my comfy spot on the sofa and saunter toward him, smoothing down my sweater.

"No! He, uh, just mentioned..." I hear a deep sigh. "Fuck it. Yes, fine. He may have mentioned something about a girlfriend. I accused him of having a concussion or something because the Sean Murphy I know doesn't have that word in his vocabulary. He told me to do something anatomically impossible, so I figured he was serious, and that I'd better check to see if you've been abducted by aliens."

"Oh, for fuck's sake." Sean groans, palming his face. His phone chimes twice, and he taps at the screen. "Brilliant. Now the other two are texting. Bunch of nosy gits. I swear to God, you lot are like a gaggle of twelve-year-old girls." He sets the phone on the counter, propping it against a small basket of apples.

"Please. Like you aren't always in all of our business?" Matt's sarcasm is tinged with humor. "What is it you always say—that you're just looking out for us? Well, right back at ya, big guy."

Sean looks at me wide-eyed as I approach and waves his free hand at me, as if to ward me off. Screw that. I laugh softly and come up behind him, slipping my arm around his waist, and propping my chin on his shoulder so I can see the screen. "Hello, I'm Cassidy Skinner. May I assume you're the Matt Logan I've heard so much about?"

An attractive man with short, dark blond hair, and scruff covering a sharp jawline is grinning from the screen. "That I am. Nice to meet you, Cassidy. And whatever stories he's told you about me are no doubt exaggerations. Just bear that in mind."

I laugh. "I will." Sean twists so I move from behind to stand beside him and he slings his arm over my shoulders.

"Okay, okay, so you've met her and can report back that she's not an axe murderer or something," he says, but Matt seems to scan the screen, and his eyes open wide in awe.

"Wait—are you at *your* place? *She's* at your place?" he asks in disbelief.

What's this? I glance at Sean, who scowls at the screen, but shoots me nervous glances out of the corner of his eye. "Of course we are. Where else would we be?"

Running his hand through his hair, Matt laughs, his eyes bright with glee. "Holy shit. That's one of your top ten Murphy's Laws! I can't believe it. This is a momentous day."

"Murphy's Laws?" I ask, my head swiveling between them. Matt huffs a laugh.

"You haven't told her about your laws yet? Cassidy, he's been lording them over us for years. Got 'em for everything, although most of them revolve around sex. Right now, he's breaking number eight, I believe."

Sydney's voice rings out behind us. "Actually, it's number five." I look over my shoulder to see her toss an armful of shopping bags on the sofa we'd vacated. Her long auburn hair is piled on her head, and she's wearing a long paisley-print tunic over jeans. "I believe it's 'never bring them back your place,'" she recites, walking over and leaning in so she can see the screen. "You wouldn't believe how many laws he's breaking these days. How are you, Matty?"

"Syd! It's nice to see you, gorgeous. Tess was wondering if you'd picked out a dress yet."

She chuckles and pats me on the shoulder. "I have indeed. Cassidy is creating it just for me. She's a brilliant designer."

My cheeks heat from her praise as Matt grins. "You don't say? So is that how you all met?"

Sydney and I begin to answer, but Sean snatches his phone off the counter and hops out of his seat, striding away from us. "Yes, yes, that's enough show-and-tell for now. Say hello to the lovely Tess for me, eh? And you can tell HRH and Three I won't be answering their texts. I'll see you all for the taping of your buddy Landon's show, yes?"

Matt snorts. "He's not my buddy, and you know it."

"Keep telling yourself that, mate." Sean sticks his tongue out at Matt. "See you in three weeks." He pockets his phone and turns to face us; Sydney and I are both standing with our arms crossed. "What?"

"Who's HRH and Three?" I ask, curious.

"His nicknames for Kennedy and Cameron," Sydney answers for him. "He has nicknames for everyone, except me."

"Yes I do." He smiles sweetly at her. "Demon twin." He ducks her sudden swing easily, laughing as she rolls her eyes at him.

"Asshat," she says, allowing him to pull her into a hug.

"I know, but you love me anyway. You have to. It's in the twin contract." He smacks a kiss against her cheek and laughs when she shoves him away and wipes her face with a hand. "Did you accomplish all your shopping goals?"

"I did. Did you achieve your goals?" She looks between us.

Her question brings back the subject I've been trying to forget. I clutch the back of the chair Sean had left and swivel it side to side. "We made a good start." The anger wells again; I take a deep breath and force a smile for Sydney's sake. "So, what are these laws you're breaking?"

Syd laughs; her brother ducks his head but can't hide the rosy glow on his cheeks. "I'm going to let you explain this one." She gives him a playful shove on the shoulder. "I need to add all this to my luggage for tomorrow." She waves toward her purchases and then walks over to me. "Do you need anything from me until I come back for the bash?"

We'd planned for her first fitting in three weeks when she returns for the opening celebration of Sean's music academy. "No, I'm good." I manage a more real smile. "You selected the perfect shade of cream. I can't wait to see it on you."

She beams. "I can't either!" She folds me in a tight hug, and I welcome her sweet, soothing scent. "You're very good for him, Cass," she whispers in my ear. "Thank you."

Surprised to be blinking back a few tears, I give her a crooked smile and nod when she pulls away. Sean's soft smile tells me he knows exactly how I feel, even if I don't.

"What are you thinking?" We're entwined in his huge bed, lying on our backs and watching a cloud scud past the moon through his skylight. I sigh and snuggle closer in his embrace.

"Right now, I'm thinking I need to take up Pilates or something to keep up with you." I'm deflecting, but not much. I used to think I was in shape; it's amazing how being drilled by a certain British sex god on a regular basis can change your perspective.

His soft chuckle is warm against my neck. "You know what I mean. Do you want to talk about it?" I tug the sheets up over us. I usually dread talking about this, but Sean makes it easier. He's genuinely concerned and just wants to help. Opening up to him feels cathartic in a way I haven't felt before. I don't feel like I'm in this alone any longer.

"I still can't quite believe there aren't any photos—that there *never* were." The anger still simmers just below the surface, beginning to boil again. I shift in his arms, my hand tightening on the sheet. "I need to find out what my father knows."

He grunts and shifts next to me. Above us, the clouds shroud the moon, dimming its glow. I bet it starts raining again soon. "Are you sure you want to do that?" he says finally. "Why should you spend one more minute with that fucker Canton? He doesn't deserve to breathe the same air as you. I like Tucker's idea. Just have him deal with it and leave you out of it."

"I can't," I whisper, shaking my head. I move around until I'm facing him. "I've let others deal with things for me for too long."

He brushes some hair out of my face, his eyes searching mine. "I understand. I hate the idea of anything more happening to you, but I understand."

"I don't want to spend any time with Dale either, but I have to find out if my father was part of this, or if Dale was acting alone. It's…hard to fathom Dale would take a step sideways that my dad didn't know about." I frown, thinking of how Dad and Dale have always moved in lockstep. "Dad trusts Dale implicitly. That's why I need to talk to him. And I need to do it in person."

He cranes his neck to press a kiss between my eyebrows and then rests his forehead against mine. "When?"

"Not as soon as I'd like." I kiss him gently. "He leaves soon for a diplomatic trip to Australia and Japan. I'll have to wait until he returns."

He slips his hands around my waist and pulls our hips together while nibbling on my neck. "When will that be?"

"I'm…oh, that feels nice." My fingers tighten on his shoulders as his lips send little jolts of electricity running under my skin. "I'm not sure." I'm about to let myself go when another thought occurs to me. "You and Matt seem pretty close."

He hums, and I can feel him nod as his hands slide over my body.

"We're all close—like brothers. The brothers I chose. But you're right; there's a little something extra between Kennedy and Cam, and between Matty and me."

"Why did you get so upset about them talking about us?" While it was funny to see him get so flustered, it was confusing, too. He was so calm and determined with Tucker, but Matt threw him off his game.

Sean sighs and pulls back a little, flopping his head on the pillow. "I wasn't upset, not really." He twists a strand of my hair between his fingers. "It surprised me, that's all. Matt was right—usually it's me getting into their business, not the other way 'round." He huffs a soft laugh. "I guess I should've expected it. I know I shocked Tucker, so it stands to reason he'd bring the others into it."

Some of Matt's words come back to me. "Shocked him by your request or with my situation?" I take a deep breath. "I know it's embarrassing—"

"Shocked him by being so obviously serious about taking care of you: a beautiful woman I'm also obviously head over heels for." His hand travels the length of my spine, making me shiver. "Believe me, love, nothing you could ever do would be as embarrassing as some of the shit the band has done over the years. It's that I have a woman in my life besides my sister that's shocked them."

"Oh, come on. We've already talked about your not-so-saintly past," I tease, tracing his lips with a fingertip. "Surely there've been women who—"

He cuts me off again with a quick kiss. "Nope," he whispers, pressing his forehead to mine again. "There's only you, Fly-girl."

Warmth seeps through my veins, lighting me up inside. My God, I may be falling in love with this man. My heart leaps with the revelation, and I don't know what to do with the sudden rush of emotion. So I change the topic.

"Are you going to explain these laws of yours to me?" I pinch his ass playfully, and he laughs, grabbing me and rolling us until he's looming over me in the darkness.

His voice in my ear is a wicked purr. "Let's break a few more first."

chapter twelve

Murphy's Law No. 17: *If you live in a bubble for too long,*
it's bound to burst.

Sean

"Don't you have some place to be?" Cassidy's eyes never move from the intricacy of her work. She's been at it for hours, and I can't get enough of being with her in her space while she creates something beautiful out of a mere idea in her head.

"Right here's the place to be."

"Watching me work?"

"Mhmm." From the bed, I prop my hand under my chin and adjust my position.

She shakes her head. "You really are a nut job."

"Keep talking about my nuts."

A small smile plays at her lips. "Behave."

"I'm sorry. I don't recognize that word."

"Sean…"

"Cass…"

"Sixty-five hundred Swarovski crystals aren't going to hand sew themselves."

I blow out a long breath, glancing out to the rain pelting the windows. "Don't I know it. I've probably seen you sew 1,400 of them."

"You've only seen 840. Stop exaggerating."

I scoff. "I never exaggerate."

She snorts, and it somehow ends up sounding cute and sexy at the same time. "I guess you don't need to." Her eyes lift to mine from behind her sexy as all hell dark blue framed glasses she's got on. It's only for the briefest of moments, but her eyes widen as she takes me in on the bed.

"Really? Again?" She looks pointedly at the tented sheets. I push them down deliberately.

"Always seems to be in this state around you, love."

"You're insatiable."

I laugh, taking a long, slow stroke of my cock. "Ah, pot, kettle? I wasn't the one waking you up in the middle of night."

"Is that a complaint?" She pushes her glasses up the bridge of her nose.

"Merely an observation."

She hums, focusing back on her task. I know this dress is important, just like all of the others she creates. I also know she's behind the deadline. She hasn't exactly come out to put the blame on me, but I've been spending nearly every waking and sleeping moment with her for the last two weeks. I like distracting her, and she has yet to complain.

Since the revelation from Tucker a couple of weeks ago about the photos, or lack thereof, things have been intense. The concept of having a woman take over my life was inconceivable to me only a few months ago, but I now understand what's happened to the rest of the guys. Having someone to look forward to at the end of a day, to share the little things with, makes life infinitely more fulfilling.

She's been to the music academy, which is almost ready for our grand opening. She's met Nari Johnston, the academy director, and the pair of them got on like a house on fire. Nari tried to teach Cass a few bars on the piano, but that was hopeless. Cassidy's artistic flare is well routed in design and couture and ends there. Her pout was adorable when she couldn't figure out the keys, and she promptly declared she'd leave the music to me.

Her father is still overseas at a political conference, which I think he's using as an excuse for not issuing a retraction on the faux engagement. But, with Dale's threats hanging over her head, Cass hasn't pressed it with him. If she keeps haranguing her father to issue a statement, Dale—that fucker—would find out. In this case, silence is golden.

Her father is arriving back next week, so she's finally going to be able to confront him about his involvement in Dale's deception—if he was involved at all.

The fact that Dale is blackmailing her to try to keep her in line is something I'd like to knock him into next year for. But, I've been good. Although Tucker is still digging and keeping an eye on him.

Even though we're trying to be discreet, we've started frequenting the café where I picked up those mouthwatering cannoli for her what seems like a lifetime ago. There have only been a couple of blurry photos that surfaced of us at the café, fueling further speculation around Cassidy's engagement. Those photos prompted a few calls from Dale, which she ignored. I can't deny that all of this sneaking around is starting to get old. It's putting a strain on both of us.

I was down with it in the beginning. My adrenaline spiked when we started sneaking into alleyways to steal a kiss, or disguising ourselves under bland ball caps to avoid being recognized, but I'm ready to move on. I want the world to know that Cassidy is mine.

Thankfully, as is typically the case, the paparazzi are random. Some days, they camp out in front of her shop, making it difficult for her brides to get in the door. Other days, they are nowhere to be found. God bless the bastards in the spotlight those days.

For the most part, her brides haven't minded the attention. In fact, some of them welcome it and have added photos on Insta of them in her shop. Despite the PR rule of any news is good news, I know it's not the type of attention that Cassidy wants.

Still, there's not a moment that goes by I'm not thinking about her, wanting to be inside her, or needing to hear her coming apart because of me. It should be scaring the shit out of me that someone has taken over my life this quickly, but I'm strangely content. It's not a feeling I'm used to, but I learned a long time ago if life isn't surprising you, you're not really living it.

I reach down to the floor for my jeans and tug them on. "Do they appreciate it? All the work you put into this?"

She smiles, reaching into a glass container beside her for another crystal. "Some more than others, but that's not why I do it." I find my T-shirt and head over to lean against her desk. "Being part of someone's dream and having it come to life…" Her voice trails off as her fingers work delicately over the expensive fabric. "That moment when a bride tears up at that first glance in the mirror, or the look on their partner's face when they see them for the first time is something I'll never get tired of seeing."

"Do you go to all of the weddings then?" I pick up a tiny crystal, rolling it between my fingers.

"I'm not invited to them all, but I do try to go to the ones in the city. I remember the first dress I did." She glances up at me with that smile I crave. "It was a big deal. Half of New York was invited to that wedding. Riya and I were there with an entourage of about a hundred people to help the bride get ready. None of us were actually worthy of the guest list, but I slipped into the church to watch her walk down the aisle. It was about four miles long, that aisle. It took forever." She glances up wistfully at the photographs of her brides that line her wall. "I was so worried about every single thread: Had we tied them off properly? Was the veil falling just so? There were gasps when she finally came into view, and I was so worried about the dress, I almost missed the groom's reaction when he saw her." She looks back at me, her hand covering her mouth for a moment. Even now, I can see how emotional she is about this, how much it means to her. "He just melted. This big burly marine, so stoic all of the time it was like…" She waves her hand in the air.

"Magic."

She nods slowly. "Yeah. Like magic."

I lean over her desk and cup her cheek, letting my fingers brush against her smooth skin. "You're a magician of dreams, Cassidy." My head fills with other words I have yet to say out loud. They're right there, knocking on my heart, perching on the tip of my tongue, but I don't say them. I don't want the bubble we're in to burst and float away.

"Vampires need more fuel, doc?" I drop into the chair across from Dr. Perez's large desk in his office. A phone call this morning was a bit unexpected, asking me to come in for additional tests, so here I am.

He gives me a tight smile and opens up the folder on his desk. "Something like that, Sean." He clears his throat and glances at the file before looking at me. He adjusts his glasses. If I didn't know better, I'd say the man is nervous.

"As you know, when you were here last time, you gave us some samples."

I grin at him. "I remember it well. Not exactly the most romantic orgasm I've ever had." Doc seems to bite back a smile.

"I know the setup is… less than ideal," he says.

"You got the sample; I'd say it worked regardless of how creepy that room is."

"Yes, well, you're all clear from a STD perspective," he announces in his clinical tone.

Music to my ears. "Of course I am. I always wrap it, doc."

He gives me a tight nod and clears his throat. "We've found some other… anomalies."

Heat prickles the back of my neck, and my heart slams against my chest. "Anomalies?"

"Yes. As you know, we gave you 'the works' as per your request. Your semen was sent to a lab to measure the number of sperm present and to look for any abnormalities in the morphology and motility."

My knee bounces, annoyance rising. "You want to start speaking in English, Doc? Not whatever Yale mumble-jumble that just was?"

"I went to Johns Hopkins, Sean." He glances at the degrees on his wall. "We've had this conversation."

My fingers tighten on the armrest. "Whatever. Just explain it to me like I'm a person, not in whatever code you use when you talk to your mates from *Johns Hopkins*."

"It means they tested for shape and movement of the sperm as well as volume, vitality." I narrow my eyes at him. "The percentage of sperm that is active and alive."

"Okay, *and?*"

"The tests showed poor motility and a low sperm count."

I just blink at him, white noise seeping into my head. "I'm sorry, what?"

He turns the file around and points out what appears to be hiero-glyphics to me. "You have sluggish sperm and under a million in the sample we tested."

Sluggish fucking sperm? I swallow back the lump forming in my throat. "A million seems like a lot."

"Normal sperm density ranges from fifteen million to over two hundred million per milliliter. We don't really start worrying about fer-tilization until the levels dip below fifteen million."

"There's nothing *normal* about me, doc." I run a nervous hand through my hair. "And what do you mean, fertilization?"

"To father a child, Sean." I push up and out of the chair, pacing in front of his desk.

"Are you telling me I can't father a child?" Doc just looks at me. "I mean, come on! Look at me. If anyone's designed to procreate, it's me." I spread my arms wide as he stares back at me as if I've lost my mind.

"Your looks, what you do for a living, has nothing to do with this,

Sean. The truth is sperm counts have been declining globally for de-cades. And some men with low sperm counts like yours successfully *do* father children. Then, there are other men who have normal counts that are never able to father a child. There are many factors involved."

I grip the back of the chair, my knuckles whitening. "So what are you telling me, then? That I may or may not ever be able to have a child? Isn't that true for everyone?"

"Well, yes, but the findings in your sample are something you need to know about. It may be a challenge for you to father a child. Is that something you're thinking about for the future?"

"I don't know!" I yell at him, making him lean back in his chair. "I haven't really thought about it. Maybe? Is there anything I can do? Some pill I can take or something?"

Doc regards me thoughtfully. "There are things you can do to try to increase the likelihood. A healthy diet and exercise, not smoking or doing drugs helps." He pauses, giving me a pointed look.

I hang my head, letting out a heavy breath. "I haven't done any in a long time. I've been clean for a while now."

"Good. Keep it that way. Steer clear of hot tubs. There's some research that suggest exposing your testicles to heat decreases sperm production."

"Right, no hot tubs. Wise advice there," I bite out.

"In men of your age…" he starts, and I lift my head, pinning him with a look, cutting him off.

"Men of my age?"

"Over thirty-five, things start to change. When you're eighteen, you can ejaculate daily and recharge quickly. It tends to take a bit lon-ger after that," Dr. Perez says, matter-of-factly.

"You obviously don't know me, Doc. I have no problems recharg-ing or ejaculating for that matter. Christ. I can't believe I'm having this conversation." I round the chair and drop back down to the seat. I feel numb. I'd be less shocked if Kennedy, Cam, and Matty told me they were running off to get married to each other and live a threesome.

"I'm talking about your sperm counts. They can fluctuate, so we'll take another sample, do the tests again." The room tips along with my stomach as the possibility of never having a child starts to plant itself in my brain. I get a flash of Cass pushing a stroller, and it just about brings me to my knees.

"I've never really thought about children." Doc nods as he listens and closes the nasty file. "I mean, I'd move the earth for Hannah if I could. And Kennedy just has to look at Abby and she's knocked up." I shake my head, feeling empty and raw. "I don't know how to feel about this, Doc."

"I know it's a lot to take in. If it helps, this is more common than you think. For about half of couples, it's the man that has the fertility challenges." Fertility challenges. The words rumble around in my head. "I've seen hundreds of patients with challenging results." He pushes some pamphlet across the table to me. It's light blue with a leaf pattern on the front. "Male Infertility, What You Need to Know" is emblazoned in a big bold font across the top. A flashing sign that I'm suddenly not man enough. "But there are steps we can take."

I can't look at the mocking pamphlet. "Such as?"

"Hormone treatment, assisted reproductive technology. Of course, there's always IVF, adoption if you wanted to go that route, sperm donors." His words are fuzzy. The thought of needing a sperm donor because I'm apparently shooting blanks emasculates me. "We can do a testicular biopsy to look at—" I cringe, rearing back.

"No way in hell are you coming anywhere close to my junk with a knife, doc." My cock seems to recoil with the mere suggestion.

"Right. Let's just get another sample and see what comes back. We can talk about it further once we have additional results."

My mind clears enough to think about Syd. "Wait. Does this mean Syd may have issues as well?"

"You're talking about your twin sister?" I nod and he grimaces. "I'm going to give you an answer you're probably not going to like."

"Well, why baulk the trend now? I haven't liked much of what you've had to say so far today, doc."

He smoothes out the lapel of his lab coat. "Obviously the anatomy is quite different." I glare at him. "It would probably be a good idea for her to get her own tests done. We don't have a lot of clear-cut answers in male fertility, and with twins, even less."

"Perfect. So no real answers then."

"I can only go by the research, Sean. I wish I could give you a definitive answer on all of this, but the truth is, we just don't know enough about it." Such a clinical, bullshit nonanswer. Fuck, the medical profession pisses me off.

I lean forward, anxiety firing through me. "Give it to me straight then on what you do know. Of all the hundreds of patients you've said you've had with this type of thing, how many have fathered children?"

He shakes his head. "Every case is different, and there are extenuating factors in all—"

"How fucking many?" I'm shouting now, probably causing the poor man more white hair.

He pauses, leaning back in his chair. "None of them with levels like yours."

The world seems to drop away along with my stomach. "None?"

"No. None." I sink into the chair, deflated. "But as I said, every patient is different, and there are men with levels like yours that *have* fathered children. Try not to think about the odds right now. Let's get this second round of tests done, and we'll go from there."

I hear none of what he's saying after that. It's a fog from that moment on. Some sort of unseen force propels me forward through the motions like a robot.

The sterilized room, where I'm to produce yet another sample, taunts me. It takes forever to get hard. I'm even tempted to open up one of the dodgy magazines. But I don't, and it takes a millennium for me to do what I need to.

When I finally have the sample and all of my *sluggish sperm*, Susan at the front desk says nothing. She takes the paper bag with the plastic cup inside and sets it into a wire bin with a few others. I wonder how many other men are walking around Manhattan with this light blue pamphlet feeling like this. Confused. Emasculated.

I find myself in a park near Cassidy's shop, surrounded by prams, and the sounds of kids playing. Sure, I notice kids from time to time, but now it's like they're everywhere. A reminder of something I may never be blessed enough to have.

I'm stuck in a foggy unknown chasm. How is Cassidy going to feel about this? She's the reason I even know my systems aren't firing as they should. If I hadn't met her, I'd still be walking around unaware. Would that be better?

I watch as a man pushes a toddler in a swing. The little one squeals in delight as the man runs underneath the swing and falls into the sand. He waves up at the little man as the swing passes over him. The toddler yells for him to do it again, and my heart clenches.

Would it be better if I'd never met Cass? That's one thing I know for sure. I can't imagine not having Cass in my life. She's become my center, the one I crave, the one I want to spend every moment with. I want it all with her—even if *it all* doesn't include a child.

Too much time passes and the ache in my chest gets progressively worse, spreading through me like a rapidly moving virus. I'm hot and cold, angry and confused, resigned and annoyed at the same time. I don't know what to feel, or how to process the last few hours. I imagine this is infinitely harder for men who are actually trying to have a baby.

I make my way to Cassidy's, trying not to think about how many little poppets I see along the way. I pause at a flower shop and a baby store just down a few stops from Cassidy's; the cycle of life all laid out in order in this one stretch of street.

I can hear Cassidy's soft voice as she works with one of her clients, and I climb the stairs to her loft above the shop. I'm engulfed with the now familiar scent of lavender, but everything feels off.

Pausing at her desk, I lift her sketchbook, and trace my fingers over the unexpected design. It's a man's suit. I reckon it's the one she claims she can't or won't design for me. It's all neat, trim lines, hugged close to the body, with a flare of fabric in the chest pocket. She's got a few different swatches of color affixed to the page; a vibrant steel blue and a more subtle light gray pinstriped. Does she realize how talented she is? She could probably design a men's line in a heartbeat and make a killing.

I leave the sketchbook on her desk and head to the shower. I want to wash away the day and the antiseptic feeling that has numbed everything in me.

Her shower isn't as high tech as mine, but I fiddle with the taps until the water scalds and pounds down on me.

I stand there, looking up at the spray, letting the room fill with steam. My skin is red and raw, and I can't bring myself to care. I don't know how much time passes, but I eventually feel her arms wrap around me from behind. Her lips on my shoulder kiss me back to life. Her soft voice asks me what's wrong, and I don't have the words to answer.

She tugs on my shoulder, coaxing me to turn around. I do, but I can't look at her. I just lower my neck and press my forehead against hers. "Please talk to me. What is it?" Her voice comes out all whispered and uneven.

I just shake my head, tightening my arms around her, pinning her to my torso. I don't even know how to begin to have this conversation, or if it's even one that matters to her. Surely it's too early to start thinking about the potential of children with Cassidy. I worry it's a conversation that could very well end this, and I don't want what Cass and I have to end. That bubble we were in is about to not just pop, but explode.

So, we stand there, with her palms gliding over my skin, trying to soothe me but only making the ache intensify. Finally, one of her hands leaves me and the water abruptly shuts off. I'm ushered out of the shower and swallowed up in a soft towel. Christ how I love this woman. I must look a wreck, but she's here caring for me regardless. "Crazy man. You're waterlogged."

She runs a second towel through my soaked hair, pausing when she lifts it away from me. Her worried eyes find mine as she steps closer and tugs the towel around us both. She rests her chin on my chest, looking up at me, all soft and wet and perfect. I know she's waiting for me to explain. I'm rarely quiet and I haven't spoken a word to her yet. It's just her and me and the sounds of traffic outside until I finally find my voice.

"Have you ever been gutted about losing something you never knew you wanted?"

Cassidy leans back, a frown pulling her lips down. "Everyone has disappointment in their lives. It's part of what makes us human."

"Fly-girl, you're a philosopher to boot."

She lifts up on her toes and brushes her fingers over my lips. "Just let me help. That's all I want," she says before her lips find mine. I don't bother stopping her. I let her help ease the ache, even if it's just for a little while.

Cassidy

Sluggish sperm? The phrase sounds like it should be the punch line to a joke, but as I brush a strand of hair from Sean's forehead, I know it's no laughing matter.

Finding him standing in my shower, unresponsive while the steam billowed around him, unnerved me. He was obviously struggling with something, something that struck him virtually speechless—which was the disturbing part. Sean always has something to say; it may not always be appropriate, but he's rarely left without words. So I did what I could to show him that I was there for him, that I cared, and whatever it was would be okay.

Sex with Sean is amazing…frequently loud, sometimes reckless, and always passionate. Tonight was on an entirely different level. Slow and sweet, we loved each other with a thorough tenderness that took my breath away. Caressing with lips and hands, we said everything that needed to be said without words. When he finally fell apart with an anguished cry, I held him tightly as he shuddered and collapsed around me.

Eventually, in a dull voice, he was able to tell me about his exam results. I listened quietly, cradling his head against my chest as he struggled to give voice to his confused emotions. It was a stream-of-consciousness rambling, and so Sean-like, it actually eased my worries in spite of the difficult subject. So here we lie, snuggled together, his breath warm against my breast while my thoughts bump around in my head.

With a soft sigh, I stare up at the shaft of light streaking across the ceiling from the streetlight outside. Memories of films about reproduction during health class flicker through my mind…scads of wriggling, industrious sperm racing to their goal and frantically trying to break through the ovum wall to the promised land. What would a sluggish sperm look like? One that saunters up to the egg and asks it out for drinks?

He hums as I trail my fingers through his silky strands of hair, marveling at his masculine beauty. His long dark eyelashes lie on his freckled cheeks, one of the few areas of his body that are unadorned by ink. A straight, almost too long nose. He must not have shaved today because his sharp chin is covered in fine dark scruff. One muscular arm is outside the sheets, lying across my body and trapping me in place. Although the Union Jack is elsewhere on his body, this arm bears the red and white English flag, a Tudor rose, and a gorgeous rendering of a medieval sword. The man is a living, breathing homage to his country.

"What are you thinking?" His soft voice is muffled against my skin. "I'm sorry to dump all that on you. You must think I'm mad."

I tug the sheet up over his shoulder, and he shifts to move his head to the pillow next to me. "Not mad." He leans forward and kisses me softly. "You had a lot to get off your chest."

"Who knew mental anguish was so taxing?" He gives me a lopsided smile, and I huff a laugh. "So." He draws out the word, his smile fading. "I suppose it *is* a bit mad to be worried about something I never thought I'd want until I couldn't have it. I just… What *do* you think? Have you ever wanted, I mean, thought about having, you know—"

"Thought about children of my own?"

He nods, his green eyes searching my face as I consider the question.

Children. I like them, and I'm good with them, if my experiences with a few dozen flower girls and ring bearers are a measure. I've only ever thought of them in the abstract. As in, one day in the distant future, I'll probably have children. I'm only thirty-two. I have several years before pregnancy starts to get a bit dicey. I've never really pictured myself with them...until the last few weeks.

Sean has been a revelation to me. A real shock to the system. Since I've met him, I've been thinking about a lot of things I've never thought about before. If I'm honest, that's one of the reasons I was curious about his real hair color. The thought of a tiny ginger-haired toddler wobbling around my workshop and rearranging all my thread spools out of order, makes me go all warm and gooey inside. But now...

"Not really," I whisper, averting my eyes to focus on my fingers entwined with his between us. "At least, I hadn't..."

"And now?" He gives my hand a squeeze. "Tell me."

I sigh and look back at him, afraid to hope about why what I want is so important to him. "Sean, this diagnosis isn't carved in stone," I say instead. "Didn't you say your doctor suggested some options?" He nods, a frown flickering on his lips. "Then don't let your mind dwell on it now. It's like I said: this is just part of being human. Some people have a stutter, some are dyslexic, some have red hair." He huffs a laugh, and I continue, "None of it is *bad*. None of it makes anyone less than or deficient. It's simply a part of being human. Everyone has their unique differences. So don't worry; you never know what the future could hold. When—or if—you reach that point in your life where you want children, you'll have options." With a gentle fingertip, I trace the side of his face. "Whatever you decide, any child that could call you daddy, biological or not, will be lucky. You'd be a great dad."

"Do you really think that?" The vibrant emerald green of his eyes softens to a mossy warmth.

"Absolutely. Especially the part about you being a great dad," I say with complete conviction. Then I give him a teasing smile. "Don't tell me the indomitable Sean Murphy is having doubts about his abilities as a father?"

He laughs, a flash of his usual exuberance sparkling in his eyes. "Never. I'd totally rock that shit." His grin softens, and he tucks my hair behind my ear. "So would you. You'd be the best mum a kid could hope for."

My heart twinges. "Sean—" I whisper, but he suddenly rolls us so he's above me, looking down at me with an intensity that makes my breath stutter.

"So tell me, Fly-girl. Does this make a difference between us? You keep saying 'whatever *I* decide in the future.'" He slides his hand up my side deliberately, claiming me, and making me shiver. "Don't you know you're a part of that future? I'm so yours it's not even funny." His hand reaches my face, gliding to cup my jaw so I couldn't look away if I'd wanted to. "I love you, Cass. Whatever decision I make about anything in the future, you will make with me…if you want."

My vision is blurry, and I blink to clear it. I didn't even know I was crying. He loves me. To hear those words, to know absolutely that he means them, is…everything. "I want," I whisper, and the hope in his eyes sparks a fire in my veins. "I love you, too. We'll figure it out together. You're stuck with me, London."

His lips cover mine in a bruising kiss I feel down to my toes. "You know, there is one silver lining in what the good doctor told me," he murmurs against my lips and pulls away to give me a devilish grin.

I reach between us and give his hard cock a firm stroke, making him groan in pleasure. "What would that be?"

He leans closer, his delicious accent a growl in my ear. "No more condoms."

chapter thirteen

Murphy's Law No. 135: Heavy conversations are exhausting.

Sean

My throat feels dry as I wait for Syd to pick up on video chat. Having a conversation with my sister about reproduction ranks pretty damn low on my list of things to do, but I just have to suck it up and do it. If I keep this from Syd and it turns out she does have challenges—as dear old Dr. Perez so eloquently puts it—in this area, I'd never forgive myself.

After what seems like an eon, her face appears on screen. Her smile takes an immediate downturn when she sees me. "What's wrong?" Damn twin. I can't keep a thing from her.

"Why do you immediately assume something is wrong?" I take a sip of tea. Stalling seems like the way to go.

She throws her arms up in the air. "This is me, Sean. I know when something's wrong. Just tell me if you're okay."

Setting my cup down, I pinch the bridge of my nose. "I'm okay, Syd. Well, as okay as I can be."

"You're seriously killing me. Just tell me. Whatever it is, we'll deal with it."

"I saw my doctor today," I start and her eyes widen.

"What? Are you ill?"

"No, Syd. Nothing like that." I lean back in the chair, glancing out the windows of my penthouse. Manhattan is spread out like a dream at my feet as I'm about to drop this bomb.

"Sean…" God I hate hearing the worry in her voice, seeing her face pale. Her eyes dart around on the screen in that way she has when she's trying to figure out what's going to come out of my mouth next.

"Okay, I'm just going to say this. It seems I have a fertility problem." She blinks, confusion marring her face. "The boys apparently are swimming in circles, and they don't know if this is something that might affect you too. I mean, obviously not the sperm part." I cringe, seeing her lip tremble before rambling on. "There's not a lot of information on twins, but Doc told me you should get checked out." I palm my forehead. "I'm sorry, Syd. It might only be me with this bullshit, but I couldn't keep it from you. You know"—I wave at the screen—"with this marriage business with Philip and everything."

Her face leans closer to the screen. "That doesn't… What? Are you sure?"

"Yeah, Syd. I'm sure. Believe me, I don't want it to be true, but it seems I've got a snowball's chance in hell of having a baby someday."

She's quiet for a moment, studying me, and I can't bear that look of sympathy in her eyes. I take another sip of tea. "That can't be right. I mean, there's got to be something they can do."

"Oh, there is. If I want to go under a knife, or eventually try IVF or something off the laundry list of medical miracle treatments out there. It's not a lost cause, and you might be completely different, Syd, but you need to get checked out."

"I have been." Her quiet voice takes me back. "You know Philip—the barrister in him wanted to cover all the bases, so we both got all worked up a few months ago. We're both fine."

"You are? I mean…" I drop my head, letting out a long breath. "Thank Christ. Bless Philip and his stuffy legal mind." Syd laughs, but I can see the pain in her eyes when I glance back at the screen.

"Do you want me to come back? You shouldn't be alone right now."

I wave her off, swallowing down the lump in my throat. "I'm not alone, Syd. I've got Cass. She knows, and she still wants to keep me 'round. Talk about a miracle." I let out a laugh, but it sounds flat and forced.

Syd shakes her head. "Crazy girl, that one."

"Crazy enough to love me. Not sure I'd ever see that day." I think about how Cass sent me on my way this morning, and can't help but smile. Lazy morning sex is definitely the best.

Syd's smile lights up. "She said she loves you?"

"It was quite the moment we had. I'd tell you about the details, but I'm pretty sure I've pushed my overshare for the day—probably the year."

"I'm so happy for you. She's fabulous and you deserve that kind of love, Sean. You deserve it more than anyone." I try not to get emotional listening to her. I'm still trying to come to grips with this twisted reality I'm in. Having options taken away from you doesn't sit well, but at the end of the day, I can either wallow in it or move on. You can't change facts, but I can decide how to deal with them.

"We all deserve love, Syd."

"What are you feeling about this, honestly?" Syd scans my face before continuing, "I know we've only ever talked about kids in the someday sense but—"

"Somedays can change. And it's not like I'm giving up. That's not who I am. Like Doc said, there are lots of options." Syd tries to stealthily wipe her eyes and I forge on. "If it's something Cass and I decide we want to do there are treatments or even adoption." Syd nods, her smile watery. "And don't forget luck and karma. Those have gotten me where I am, and I'll never give up believing in them."

Cassidy

"Are you sure it's okay for me to come?" I ask again as Sean helps me out of the hired car in front of Rockefeller Plaza. We're quickly greeted by a staffer who whisks us inside the stage entrance.

Hand in hand, we walk briskly through the lobby, although Sean waves gaily at a few people who stop in their tracks to gawk at him. His hair is a freshly dyed vivid green that matches the emerald of his eyes.

"Of course it is," he states. "It'll be fun. My compatriots are bringing their better halves. We all need to give Kennedy moral support to get through this ridiculous taping." He snorts. "And we need to keep Matt from punching Landon Ravine in his little weasel nose. *Rock to the Top* will never be the same after tonight, I guarantee it." A buzz of energy surges through me. Landon Ravine's popular show, *Rock to the Top*, has churned out three chart-topping bands in the last couple of years. It's something of a phenomenon, and I can't help getting caught up in the excitement.

We enter an elevator, and I nervously pick some lint from my navy blazer. "If you guys don't like him, why is Kennedy doing his show?"

"It was the only way we could get him to perform at a charity concert we gave a few years ago for a cancer patient. Remember? I told you about Parker."

I nod, remembering. Sean has shown me pictures of the cheeky little blond boy whose cancer is in remission, thankfully. "Yes, but I thought everyone was happy to participate in that concert?"

"Oh, they were." He huffs a laugh as the steel box we're riding in rises quickly. "But Landon's not the sort to give without getting something in return. Bit of an arse, really."

Eventually, the doors slide open, revealing a busy hallway. Following our guide, we dodge people scurrying around; you can feel the preshow excitement in the air. Finally, we reach a set of industrial double doors, and our guide holds one open for us.

"Wait here with the others, please." He gives us a bland look. The guy must have seen so many famous faces he's become jaded.

Unfazed, Sean gives me a grin and tugs me after him. "Come on. Time to see the magic behind the curtain."

We enter a green room, and a group of women and men I recognize as his bandmates rise from some uncomfortable-looking sofas and chairs. "Let's get this party started!" Sean declares, strolling in like he owns the place. A man I recognize as Kennedy Lane steps forward, flanked by Matt and another man I assume is Cam Chapman.

They look between us, smug smiles on their faces, and then Kennedy clears his throat, running a hand through his dark hair. "It's about time you got here."

chapter fourteen

*Murphy's Law No. 36: Some things are better left unsaid. Sadly,
I typically remember this right after I've said them.*

"Isn't it a little early for St. Patrick's Day celebrations?" Cameron pokes at my hair, and I swat his hand away.

"Shut it, you." An array of fist bumps and back pats are thrown my way while Sam and Tess look between Cassidy and me with something akin to wonder.

"Where's the missus, then?" I ask Kennedy as he leans against an overstuffed leather chair.

"The what?"

"Your wife, genius. Is she reacquainting herself with the wonders of Landon Ravine, bless his little cotton socks?"

Kennedy snorts. "He wishes. She's in the ladies room."

I glance at the door. "Is she all right?"

"Mostly. Random things turn her stomach. And there was sushi in here when we walked in." Kennedy grimaces, wrinkling his nose.

"That's backstage rule number one: no fish in the green room." Cameron shakes his head.

"Ravine probably did it on purpose," Matty says with a snarl.

Tess smacks my arm with surprising force. "I'm sure you weren't born in a barn. Introduce us." She waves her hand at Cassidy, and I frown and rub my bicep. Tess and Sam inch their way toward Cassidy. Cass gives them a little shy wave.

"Forgive me, love." I cross back to take her hand, bringing her into the fold. "Everyone, this is Cassidy Skinner. Cass, this is my second family, as dysfunctional as we are."

"Don't listen to him," Tess says, enveloping Cassidy in a hug. "He's the dysfunctional one. We're normal… mostly. I'm Tess and this is Samantha." Sam likewise gives Cassidy a hug.

"It's so nice to meet you," Sam says as they both corral Cassidy away from us and stop in front of the food table, babbling away.

Matt nudges me in the side, lifting his chin in the direction of the girls. "She's actually real. I thought maybe you had her created in some lab." Kennedy claps his hand over his mouth, stifling a laugh.

"Mate, I couldn't have had anyone more perfect created if I tried." I watch Cassidy throw her head back and laugh at something Tess says, the overhead lights catching the golden sheen of her hair. She really is fucking perfect. I'd like to rip that buttoned-up blazer she's rocking right from her body and bury my face between her breasts. "Even dropped the L word a couple of weeks ago."

Cameron steps up beside us. "Well hell. I would've bet money on this day never coming."

"I think you did bet money on this day never coming," Kennedy pipes up. "Pretty sure you owe someone some coin."

Cameron laughs, slapping me on the back. "Does this mean your days of living the single life are over?"

"That it does, Three. That it does."

"No more late night wall pounding?" Kennedy asks as I reach over for an energy drink and twist the top off.

"Not sure what kind of sex you're having—" I start.

"The kind that gets my wife pregnant," Kennedy says proudly.

I bite back the bitter sting of annoyance. It's been a couple of weeks since the good old doc dropped the bomb that my little soldiers aren't marching with purpose. Those two weeks have done nothing to dull the nagging feeling I'm somehow less of a man. "Well, I'm not dead. There's plenty of wall pounding," I say a little too forcefully. I take a long sip of the energy drink, the lime coating my tongue. It would be nice to have something a bit stronger at the moment if we're going to be talking rounds of babies and impending fatherhood.

"No more Cherry Riddle?" Matt asks, almost causing me to spit out the drink. I wipe my arm across my mouth with a laugh.

"You just had to bring her up, didn't you?"

"We're in New York. Of course I did. You never know when she may make an appearance," Matt reminds me.

"That's a riddle that will forever remain unsolved," Cameron helpfully supplies. "Does Cassidy know about the tattoo you have dedicated to Miss Cherry?"

I rub my forearm where the cherry skulls sit. Cherry Riddle, fangirl extraordinaire, managed to get backstage at most of the shows we've played in New York. Try as I might to stay away from her, those luscious lips of hers have been far too tempting, up until now. The tatt is a result of a lost bet I had with the guys two years ago. They had bet me I would cave to her desperate, often colorful begging to suck my cock. I tried. Honest to God, I tried, but a man has his limits, and she was just too tempting, too eager. And she brought actual pom-poms last time to sweeten the deal. I didn't want to disappoint.

I give my head a shake because a meaningless encounter like that can't hold a candle to Cassidy. The fact some random, persistent groupies were the norm for me is a bit mind-boggling when I think about what I have with Cass. "No, she doesn't know, and that's the way it's going to stay," I mutter under my breath.

Cameron laughs and takes a sip from his water bottle. "Next thing you know you'll be hitched and have her knocked up. Who wants in on this one?" Matt and Kennedy both raise their hands, the bastards. It's on the tip of my tongue to tell the lot of them to go fuck themselves, but I can't. The last thing I need is the guys knowing about my *sluggish* goddamn sperm.

"You know, not everyone follows the traditional relationship society demands," I snap at them, my emotions still raw.

"Amen to that, brother," Matt says. "I have no plans on changing anything with Tess. We don't need a piece of paper or a kid to prove we're together."

"Yeah? Well, we didn't plan on getting pregnant either, and look what happened," Kennedy reminds me, all smug. "Sometimes, the universe decides for you."

Not being able to stomach any more from either of them, I turn my attention to the girls. "Sammy! Where is my poppet?"

Sam looks over from her deep discussion with the girls. "She's having a sleepover with Victoria and Louis."

I cringe at the mention of Cameron's parents. They may be one of the richest families in the country, but having money doesn't mean they've been stellar parents. Cameron was raised by nannies, if the truth be told, and his mother is the original Ice Queen. The introduction of Sam and Hannah into their lives brought on an almost Disney-like thawing that still astounds me. "Blimey. Bring Hannah next time, yes?"

"I will. She was upset when she found out she wasn't coming with us."

"Nothing two days with Midnight and the rest of the horses can't cure," Cameron slides his arm around Sam's waist as the girls join us once more. Cassidy glances up at me with that smile that makes me crazy.

"Cameron's family owns a stable and about a thousand horses. Hannah, Sam's daughter, is learning how to ride," I explain.

Cameron rolls his eyes. "Not a thousand horses, but yes, and she's getting really good."

"She'll be donning the polo kit before you know it."

"I sure hope so," Cameron says as Sam leans into his side.

I stop middrink as the door flies opens and Abby steps in with Tucker towering behind her. My eyes fall to her stomach. Her very swollen, very pregnant stomach, and my own bottoms out. She's looking a little knackered, but her smile widens when she sees me.

"You're here!" My throat tightens and I can't seem to look away from her obvious addition. She's probably five months along now, judging from the timing Kennedy provided us, and she's definitely showing as plain as day. Another reminder of something I may never have. I want to be happy for Abby and a man I consider a brother, but an unexpected ache lingers, darkening what should be a celebration.

I feel all eyes on me. I'm quiet, staring like some stunted git. I throw my arms wide and try to give them what they all want and expect.

"I am. The party can officially start." My voice sounds flat and forced. Abby cocks her head at my less than enthusiastic greeting and gives me an awkward side hug, her belly getting in the way. "Congratulations, Abby, on both counts. Although you're going to have to name the little one Sean either way."

She smiles at me, her hand settling over her bump as Kennedy moves in to kiss the top of her head. "And why is that?"

"Because you didn't invite me to the wedding."

She gives me a sheepish smile. "It was…"

"Last minute. I've heard." I give them both a mock glare. "Doesn't mean I'm going to forget it any time soon."

Abby ignores me, her eyes brightening as she takes in Cassidy. "And you must be Cassidy. You're a brave woman to take this one on." Abby nudges me in the shoulder.

"Hey! I'm not that bad," I protest, but it gets lost in another round of girl-hugging.

"He's not, actually. It doesn't take much to keep him in line, if you want to know the truth," Cass replies, her lips twisting in amusement.

Matt laughs. "I like her. We're going to keep her."

"That we are, Matty." I sling my arm around Cassidy's shoulder, and she gives me a playful pinch to my side.

"You're making Sydney's wedding dress, right?" Tess asks.

Cass nods. "I am. It's coming along nicely."

"I'd love to see it," Abby says.

"You should come to the shop if you have time while you're in town," Cassidy offers.

"Cass has her own shop in the East Village." I tighten my arm against her.

"That's amazing!" Samantha says. "I do need to start looking for a dress." Cameron presses a kiss to the modest ring on her left hand.

"Yeah, you do, Miss McKenzie." The man is a bazillionaire and could afford an Antarctic-sized ring on Sam's finger, but Sam isn't like that. She's as down to earth as you can get, preferring the simple things in life. Her engagement ring is a reflection of who she is, and of what Cam loves about her. It's simple and classically beautiful without being ostentatious.

"Is that how you two met then? At your shop?" Tess asks.

"Yes!" "No," we both say at the same time, and I glance down at Cassidy in confusion as she covers my mouth with her hand.

"We're going to leave it at yes," she announces to the group, earning a laugh from Abby.

"Why do I have a feeling there's more to this story?" Abby folds her arms across her chest.

I nip at Cassidy's fingers and tug her hand from my mouth. "Let's just say she fell after me… literally."

"Or how about we just say nothing." Cass pins me with a dark look.

"Ah, the mystery. Yes. Let's leave it and have them draw their own conclusions, love." I glance back up, getting a few amused looks from the group. "Cass is also making my suit for the wedding."

"I never said I'd make your suit," Cass reminds me.

"Really? I saw a sketch of it a couple of weeks ago."

Cass glares at me. "You weren't supposed to see that!" God, I love it when she's feisty.

"Then don't leave it out on your drawing table." I'm pushing, but bantering with Cass is akin to foreplay for me, and I can't seem stop myself.

"Can't leave home without an entourage, I see." Landon Ravine steps into the room, and our jovial mood is instantly dampened. He's looking for all the world like he owns the place, and rightfully so—this is his hit television show after all. His entire outfit screams rock and roll, he smells like he's spent the night in a brewery, and he reeks a bit of desperation.

Kennedy moves to a protective stance beside Abby. "Well you know, have band will travel." Kennedy pauses before continuing, "Oh wait, you don't know, do you. Didn't your band kick you out?" Kennedy tries to hide his cocky grin, but it's impossible. "Again?"

Ravine's jaw ticks. By not checking his entitled attitude at the door, he doesn't make it easy on himself. His latest band fired him following a rather public meltdown after a show in Paris where he accused them of not bringing their A game, which was bollocks. "That was a mutual breakup," he grinds out.

"Ah, let's see if I can paint the newsworthy article." I step up beside Kennedy, pinning Ravine with a stare. "It's with a heavy heart we announce our separation. We'll always have a mutual love and respect for each other, and our music will forever bind us together. Please respect our privacy in this troubled time." Matt tries to cover his laugh with a cough. Ravine shoots him a glare. "Have I got it right?"

"Six bands in five years. Going for a record?" Cameron asks from somewhere behind me.

Ravine casts a slow gaze around the room, his lips curling into a sneer. "I see there's some new additions, and that you've been busy, Lane." He nods in Abby's direction and Kennedy's shoulders tense.

"Watch it," Kennedy growls as Tucker moves beside him.

"Relax. Both of you." Tucker fires his usual forceful warning. "Remember why we're here." Tucker claps his hand over Kennedy's shoulder, easing him back. "Let's try to get through this without punches being thrown this time, hmm?"

Landon holds Kennedy's gaze and takes a wise step back. "Aren't you going to introduce me to your new friends? I know Abby, and of course do I ever remember Tessa." He rakes his eyes over Tess like she's his next meal, and Matt coaxes her behind him.

"And who's this?" The bastard leers at Cassidy.

"Hey!" I snap my fingers in his face. "That vampiric glamour you try to wield won't work, Ravine. Best to quit while you're ahead."

"Can we just get this over with?" Kennedy asks, his voice hard. "The only reason we're not bolting is because I made a promise to you in the name of charity. You've ten seconds to tell me where you want me, and what I'm going to be doing, or we're out of here."

Landon holds his palms up, giving us a fake laugh. "I'm just teasing. Fuck, you guys need to relax. I meant no offense."

"Bullshit," Matt says. "Show some fucking respect."

Landon shakes his head and takes a deliberate deep breath. "Let's start this again. Welcome!" He spreads his arms wide. "I'm glad you guys could make it. We're in the semifinals of the show and down to twelve contestants who are fighting for a spot on the four-member band we're creating."

Tucker relaxes his stance but stays beside Kennedy.

"How much experience do they have?" Kennedy asks.

Landon crosses to the table of food, scanning it before selecting a handful of chocolate-covered somethings from a bowl. He jiggles them in his hand. "Some of them have come close to getting record deals. But you know how it goes." His mocking glare doesn't go unnoticed.

Back in the day when we were first starting out, Landon and his band at the time slime-balled their way into our slot at a label audition. They won the favor of the record producer and the feud between us was born. Redfall ultimately won out at the end of the day, with Landon's label going bankrupt shortly after the release of their first album, which was a bust. Since then, he's earned a reputation as a cutthroat pain in the arse who can barely hang onto a band. His die-hard fans don't care. They're sucked in by the illusion of the glitz and glam punctuated by his success on the show. Editing can do wonders at hiding someone's real personality, but we haven't forgotten just how dirty he can be.

Landon shoves the handful of candy in his mouth and chews before continuing, "A few have never played in front of an audience before. It's quite the mix. Your pretty faces are here to mentor them. Give them tips on their performance. Show them how to rev up a crowd." Landon pauses for a moment. "Maybe change up the songs a bit. Give them a different arrangement."

Kennedy studies Ravine. "Isn't that what you're doing with them?"

Landon is quiet for a moment, studying Kennedy thoughtfully. "Truth is, I'm not all that good in that area." Landon rubs the back of his neck. I think we're all in a bit of shock. That's as close to a compliment as we're ever going to hear from Landon. At our stunned expressions, he rambles on. "Can I play the hell out of any song you give me? Fuck yeah. Can I breathe new life into them like you can? Make them relevant for a new audience? That's a bit of a challenge."

"And here I thought you were all about challenges, Ravine," Matty mumbles.

Ravine shoots him a look.

"What songs are you doing?" Kennedy asks.

"This week it's seventies rock."

"Hell yes," Cameron says.

"It was the audience's choice." Landon shrugs.

"Clearly your audience has *some* taste," I remark.

"We didn't bring anything. Your PR people didn't mention playing," Kennedy replies, and Landon huffs a laugh.

"I've got an entire studio full of instruments, Lane." He glances at Matt. "Even got a vintage Rickenbacker in there. It's almost as if I knew you'd all show up." Matty tries to look like he doesn't care, but I know he jumps at a chance to play any Rickenbacker.

Kennedy glances at us in silent question, and Cameron gives me a slight nod. "Okay. We'll work on a few arrangements with them, but I don't want the show to be about us. It's supposed to be about finding new talent."

Ravine flashes an evil smile. "You guys *are* getting older. Aren't you forty soon, Logan?" The bastard just can't resist getting in another dig.

"Do you want our fucking help or not?" Matty grinds out, his body tensed with contained anger as he takes a step forward.

"Okay, okay. I get it, Logan," Ravine starts. "It's a sensitive subject. And yeah, I'd like your help." He glances back at Kennedy. "I'd appreciate your help."

"Then lead the way." Ravine grins like the Cheshire cat and starts out the door. "You know if this works out, maybe we can talk about collaborating on something else."

Kennedy slaps Landon on the shoulder with more force than necessary. "Not a snowball's chance in hell. But I appreciate you being the eternal delusional optimist." Kennedy presses a kiss to Abby's lips. "We won't be long, baby."

"There's a viewing room of the studio if you'd like to come this way," says a tall brunette dressed like she's going to a dance club. She ushers the girls into the hallway and motions to the right. The girls file along behind her.

I tug on Cassidy's hand as she passes, bringing her against my chest. "You'll be watching me?"

She lifts up and presses a chaste kiss to my lips. "I'm always watching you."

"Stalker," I mumble against her lips. "I like it."

"Just go do your thing. If you're any good, I might reward you later." She nips playfully at my bottom lip, and I tighten my arm around her.

"I'm better than good. I'd think by now you'd know that." It's almost a growl as she pulls away and walks down the hall. She throws a glance over her shoulder at me.

"Prove it and see what happens."

Damn tease of a woman.

"I can't believe we helped that asshole." Matt takes a long pull from his virgin Manhattan. We're tucked away in soft couches in the corner of Summit, a rooftop restaurant that boasts cinematic views of the Chrysler Building. The virgin drinks are in solidarity with Abby, but I'm not complaining. They are syrupy sweet and garnished with cherries as requested by goddamn Cameron because he likes to push my buttons.

He seems determined to want to share the Cherry Riddle tattoo story, making me seriously question his loyalty.

"Think of it as karma." Kennedy looks up at the tiny white bulb lights strung above us. "Your good deed for the day."

"For the year, maybe," Matt grumbles.

"I didn't mind it," Cameron chimes in. "That arrangement of 'Wild Horses' was…" He shakes his head a bit. "I kind of wish we kept that for ourselves." We all nod in agreement. That was musical magic, the four of us rearranging the classic Stones song into an edgier, bass-driven piece that's going to set the viewing audience on fire. It also helped that Ravine seemed to be impressed and pissed off in equal measure seeing us bring to life something he's incapable of.

"It's easy to see who's going to make it to the final," Matty adds. "Some of those musicians aren't cut out for this. Others are just amazing."

"You want to see amazing? Wait until you see the finalists for the music academy." I finish the last of the sugary sweet drink, setting the glass down on the table.

"I'm looking forward to that," Kennedy says.

"There are some real prodigies in there." I slide my arm across the back of the sofa, playing with the ends of Cassidy's hair. "I have a proposition."

A collective groan rises from my traitorous bandmates. "Oh, please. You all mumble and complain, but whenever I suggest we do something you always have the time of your lives."

Matt raises his hand. "That is total bullshit, and I request a redirect, your honor."

I scowl at him. "Request denied." I catch a maraschino cherry when he hurls it at me, and pop it into my mouth. The tartness has me sucking my cheeks in as I chew it down. "Now, you know that *Adventure Wars* has been on Nic to get me on the show."

"Why have they just asked for you?" Cam questions, and I shake my head.

"Gee. I wonder why that is, but not to fear, I've solved that problem. I suggested we do a Redfall show with couples and everything."

"Oh! That sounds exciting," Tess says, straightening up in her seat.

"See?" I wave my hand at Tess. "Thank you, Tess. At least someone here has a sense of adventure."

Tess gives a half bow from her seat, and Matty pipes up, "God. Don't encourage him, babe."

"I'm adventurous," Cassidy whispers against my neck and I smile, turning to drop a kiss to the top of her head.

"Of that, I am one hundred percent confident, love."

"What would we have to do?" Kennedy asks, keeping his arm around Abby.

"Well, they're starting to toss around a few ideas," I begin before Cass interrupts.

"Oh! We could do like a *Survivor* type show. All of us on an island for a couple of days."

Cam snorts, the arse. "Surviving on a deserted island with Sean? Good luck with that." He twirls the little green umbrella in his drink. Very manly.

"We've survived almost two decades together without killing each other. I would think a couple of days would be a piece of cake," I reply, seeing Sam's eyes light up.

"It does sound like fun," Sam says, glancing up at Cameron.

"Ah, I think I'm having the adventure of a lifetime right here," Abby offers, resting her hand on her stomach. "I think I'll have to pass on any remote island adventures for a while, unless they include air conditioning and twenty-four-hour room service."

Kennedy laughs, pressing a kiss to her forehead. "Momma can't be on a deserted island, Sean. Maybe after junior is born, we can talk about it." My excitement dims as I watch Kennedy settle his hand over Abby's on her belly.

I feel Cass tighten her grip against my bicep as I try to tap down the bitter taste of regret. I can't be angry at Kennedy or Abby, and I have no right to be jealous of their impending parenthood. I'm going to have to get used to just being Uncle Sean. Daddy is not in my future.

"Right. After the little one arrives then," I manage, downing the rest of my syrupy drink.

"Paparazzi at twelve o'clock," Tucker mutters, moving to take a protective stance in front of our group.

Cass leans back a bit in her seat and tilts her face away from where the leech is lurking. Sam reaches over to touch her arm, giving her a sympathetic smile. "It's okay. You get used to them after a while."

"I know. I just really don't need more exposure at the moment." Cass fiddles with the straw in her drink.

"More exposure?" Tess asks.

"Cass had the papps staked outside her shop a few times over the last couple of weeks." I slide my arm around her. The burning ball of irritation that's been living in my belly, due to the fact that we still have to hide, reignites.

"We can get security on that," Tucker says, his eyes staying firmly on the tacky intruder. He's keeping the required distance away, but the unmistakable flash of his camera lights up our cozy hideaway.

"That would probably just make it worse." Cass tugs one of the cherries off the toothpick in her drink and pops it into her tempting mouth.

"Maybe it's the pregnancy brain talking, but I'm so confused right now." Abby glances between us.

"Cassidy's father is a senator. He announced her blessed engagement six weeks ago," I broadcast a little too loudly.

Matty chokes on his drink before sputtering out, "You're engaged?"

"To another man, so the story goes. It was all a misunderstanding, but it's out there uncorrected and feeding the gossip mill whenever there's a photo of us that hits the trash mags."

"I'm right here." It's almost a growl from Cassidy. "I can speak for myself."

"Can you?" I fire back and everything stops. Total silence as the glass she's holding stills in front of her lips midsip. Her brows rise to her hairline. "Because it seems to me like you let your father do the talking."

"It's not that simple."

"It *is* that simple. Issue your own statement. In case you didn't know, we happen to have a damn fine PR guru who can help you do that." I can feel my jaw clench, unfamiliar anger firing through me. I don't like what the press is doing to her, and it burns she won't just set the record straight.

"I can't just issue a statement. How would that look for my father?"

"Better than it's making you look right now. Every time there's a photo out of you and me, the press claims you're some sort of cheating slag."

"There's only been a couple of blurry photos." Cass sets her glass on the table and frowns at me. "And here I thought you didn't care what people think."

"About me, I don't. About you? It's unacceptable, especially when it's a lie and the truth is easy to explain."

"Everything is so easy to you."

Abby pushes up from the couch, tugging down her shirt over her stomach. "You okay, baby?" Kennedy shifts forward to rub his palm over her back.

"I just need to use the ladies' room."

"I could use some fresh air," Cassidy bites out, standing up with Abby.

"We're on a rooftop full of fresh air!" I wave my arms to the open skies above.

"Yeah? Well, I could use different air, then." Her glare would set a lesser man on fire.

I feel the force of Kennedy's boot hit me in the shin across the table. "Ow! Christ, mate."

"We'll join you." Both Sam and Tess stand up, hurrying to join Cass and Abby.

Kennedy lifts his head in the direction of the girls. "Tuck."

"On it," Tucker steps up beside Abby.

"We don't need Tucker to shadow us every time we go somewhere, Kennedy," Abby says.

"You've got precious cargo on board, Mrs. Lane. I'm not taking any chances."

Abby rolls her eyes, but there's a soft smile playing at her lips before she leads the rest of the girls away from the table with Tuck following along.

I settle back in the couch, spreading my arms across the back. "The allure of the ladies' room; it's a mystery."

"It's not, really. They're going to talk about you and why you're being an ass. More than usual," Cameron says.

"Am I being an ass?"

Matt holds his thumb and index finger apart. "Just a bit. You obviously hit a nerve and whatever's going on, she clearly has her own way she wants to handle it."

"Yeah? Well, she's not handling it at all. That's the issue."

"Calling her out in front of people she's just met may not be the best way to have that conversation," Cam supplies helpfully.

Fuck. He's right. Slapping a hand on my forehead, I scrunch my eyes closed, blocking out his mocking grin. "Bloody hell. I've cocked it up." I blow out a frustrated breath.

Kennedy snorts, setting his glass down on the table. "I don't think your cock is going up any time soon, my friend."

Cassidy

Cold water splashes against my cheeks, relieving some of the heat in my face. I frown down at my wet hands in the sink before turning the water off. Abby's in a stall, while the other two, Samantha and Tessa, wash their hands at other sinks and exchange worried looks.

I suppose I shouldn't be surprised he blurted it out like that, but I wish he hadn't. It's been a fascinating and enjoyable day. From meeting his adopted "family," to the taping, and now here at one of New York's exclusive eateries; it's been an exciting peek behind the scenes at the lives of some of entertainment's elites. The best thing about it is that none of these men seems to suffer from the usual afflictions of the elites I'm used to dealing with—snobbery and narcissism. And the women are as nice as can be.

Dabbing at my face with a paper towel, I turn to face Sam and Tess, who are leaning back against the countertop. "Are you all right?" Sam asks, her musical voice sounding loud in the enclosed space. Tucker is guarding the door, ensuring we have privacy for a few minutes, at least.

"I'm fine." Tess lowers her chin and sets both hands on her hips, making me laugh. I'd better get this over with. "It's kind of a long story. My father is Senator Robert Skinner."

"From Kansas?" Abby asks as she opens the stall and walks to a sink to wash her hands.

"Wyoming." She nods, and I continue as she dries her hands and takes a place beside Tess. "My parents got some bad information and announced that I was engaged to a family friend without confirming it. It hit the media before I could stop it."

Three sets of eyes widen in shock. "They didn't talk to you first?" Tess's alto voice squeaks with outrage, and she throws her hands up.

"They thought I was just nervous about it and needed a push." I glance heavenward, realizing how ridiculous that sounds, even though it's true. "Anyway, I'm not engaged to anyone. I'd never do that to Sean."

Sam lets out a hum and nods. "I figured there had to be more to the story," she says, Tess moving beside her. "He sounded so… territorial."

"Yes! Protective. I've never seen Sean like that, except concerning one of us or the guys," Tess adds, and the others murmur in agreement.

"He's always been a ladies' man—all of them were, of course, until they met us." A tiny smile plays on Abby's lips as she runs a hand over her baby bump. "But, this, seeing him today…" She looks up, beaming at me. "I've never seen him look at a woman like he looks at you. It's adorable. He's absolutely smitten."

With a sigh, I join them, leaning against the edge of the counter on the other side of Abby. Their words warm me. "He's the most amazing man I've ever known," I admit. Then my lips twist as the irritation I felt when Sean let his gums flap earlier bubbles up. "Even when he blurts things out like a jackass."

Their laughter rings in the room. "He's a man." Tess shrugs. "They're all jackasses occasionally. Their brains get sucked down to their penises 500 times a day, and sometimes the brains don't get back in their actual heads in time when they're needed."

Abby chokes on a laugh, and I rub her back. "I guess that explains it," Sam says, her own laugh spilling over.

There's a knock, and the door opens a crack to allow Tucker's voice in. "Say, are you ladies about finished? We're going to get a queue out here in a second." He closes the door again, and we straighten up automatically, moving toward the door until I raise a hand.

"Look, I *will* get this mess sorted out. Please don't think I'm stringing Sean along. I want…" I sigh and run a hand through my hair. "For a variety of reasons, I *need* to do this face-to-face with my father, and he's been traveling." His initial trade mission was extended and my mother flew to join him. They decided to make a vacation of it and won't be back to DC until next week. I haven't heard from them, and I decided it would be better to not badger Dad about the retraction because Dale would find out I'm serious about not playing ball. So far, I've been able to dodge his calls when one of those blurry photos of Sean and I get posted to a gossip site. I hope the photographer outside didn't get a good shot. That talk with my father can't come soon enough.

Abby pauses with a hand on the handle, looking back at me with an understanding smile. "Life can be messy sometimes. Do whatever you need to do—don't worry about any of us, or the guys. We all love Sean, maniac that he is, and he obviously loves you. Let me know if you need anything—if I can help in anyway. And Sean was right; Nicole is fabulous, and I know she'd be able to help you word a statement if you'd like."

Tess echoes her offer of help, and Sam gives me a quick hug before we exit the restroom. I let them go ahead of me, Tucker moving to walk beside Abby like a benevolent guardian angel. I've barely taken a step before a hand takes mine. Sean pulls me around a corner, past a few startled diners, and into a private dining room that looks recently vacated.

"What are you doing?" I hiss, yanking my hand out of his. He holds his hands up, his expression wary.

"I'm sorry for what I said," he blurts, eyes wide and imploring. "Please tell me I haven't buggered this up already."

"Oh for the love of Pete…" I roll my eyes, wishing we could rewind the evening by about thirty minutes. Crossing my arms, I try to hide my exasperation. "Of course not. Do you really think I'm that fragile? But, damn if I don't wish you'd think before letting your mouth run sometimes."

He rocks back and forth on his heels, looking at his toes, before looking back at me with a grin. "It's just part of me charm, darlin'," he says, exaggerating his accent. Then he steps forward, taking my face between his palms, his cocky expression becoming serious. "I promise I'll do better, Cass. It's something Syd has been on about for years. But, for you, I'll try."

Pressing his lips to mine, he steals my breath, and my heart pounds. "I'm sorry I've put you in this position. I know it's difficult." I sigh softly and lean my forehead against his. "I don't want you to become a different person, Sean. Just, please be a bit more circumspect about our private lives, okay?"

I startle and try to pull away when a couple of busboys come in and start piling the dirty dishes in tubs, but Sean holds me fast. "You can count on me, love," he whispers, kissing my forehead.

"For you, miss."

Taking the glass offered by the obliging waiter, I nod in thanks and walk over to the tall windows overlooking the neighborhood to sip my champagne. People swirl about in small groups throughout the huge room, which will serve as a lounge and gathering space for the kids of the academy.

After the formal welcome by Nari, the academy's director, people were let loose to tour the building. Sydney has done an incredible job reclaiming this old building and designing something that is stylish and comfortable as well as functional and sturdy enough to stand up to hard use.

The presence of Redfall has caused quite a stir among the crowd of artsy New Yorkers and media in attendance. And Sean... I take a sip, watching the emerald-haired god across the room, surrounded by people and completely in his element. I think there's supposed to be a performance by some of the academy's kids in the auditorium downstairs in a while, but I have a feeling Sean has something else up his sleeve.

I've spent most of the time today getting to know Abby, Tess, and Sam, with some of Tucker's men dispatched to keep the media at bay. Nari and Nicole, Redfall's PR goddess, made it abundantly clear during the media gaggle that today was for the academy and its students, not "the Redfall family."

Needing some air, I take my glass and head up the stairs to the rooftop where Sean took me for our first lunch all those weeks ago. I push the door open and take a deep breath, savoring the early evening air. It's quieter up here, with only a few people talking and drinking on the chaise lounges scattered about. I stand at the edge, looking out over the city. It's not the tallest building around, but there's still a fantastic view, especially now with all the lights winking on below.

"It's lovely, isn't it?"

I look over to see a tall, angular man standing a couple feet away. He has sandy blond hair and pale blue eyes behind rectangular frames, and he's dressed impeccably in a suit. "It is," I agree. He smiles and steps closer, extending his hand.

"Philip Beckwith."

His hand is finely boned with no callouses, but his grip is firm. "Cassidy Skinner." Then my eyes widen with recognition. "Oh! You're Sydney's fiancé, aren't you?"

"Guilty." His smile warms his eyes. "And you're the miracle woman who's tamed the famously untamable Sean Murphy."

I laugh. "Not sure I'm all that miraculous." I wave a hand toward the lounge area. "Sydney has done a marvelous job designing all this. I'd say *she's* the miracle."

"I certainly think so." He smiles down into his glass of amber liquor. "I still can't believe sometimes that we found each other. She's the best thing to ever happen to me."

The quiet belief in Philip's voice touches me. It's heartwarming to see how the love in his eyes matches the gleam in Sydney's when she's talking about him. We exchange a little small talk, and then the walls break down when I get him talking about his work as a human rights attorney. His passion when speaking about some of his cases seems at odds with his mild-mannered appearance, but it's the same passion that rings in Sydney's voice when she's talking about her work. I can't think of a more well-suited couple.

Except maybe one.

"There you are!" Sydney beams at Philip as she joins us. "You've met?" She gestures between us. "Good! I'm sorry I didn't get a chance to properly introduce you earlier."

"No worries, love." Philip slips his arm around her waist, snugging her into his side. She reaches up and playfully smooths his bangs off his forehead before turning to me.

"How are you, Cass? Isn't it going well? You look fabulous!" Her cheeks are flushed, either with excitement or champagne.

"It is. And, thank you." I smooth a hand over my plum-colored cocktail dress and gesture with my glass toward her fiancé. "It's wonderful you were able to come over for the opening, Philip."

"There's nowhere I'd rather be." He presses a kiss to her temple, and Syd's smile lights up the night. God, they're cute.

"You two should come downstairs. I think they're going to announce the contest winner soon," Syd says. Philip pulls away enough so he can offer his arm to his fiancée, and then his other arm to me.

"Ladies, allow me to escort you," he says, holding himself like a stuffy lord, and we laugh. Then, arm-in-arm, the three of us head for stairs and the festivities below.

chapter fifteen

Murphy's Law No. 10: Need and want... It's a fine line.

Sean

MY LIFE USED TO EXIST IN A STEADY FLOW OF BLISSFUL UNCERTAINTY. No real focus or plans unless they centered 'round the band and whatever performance or event we had to attend. I loved it. I loved the randomness of it all. The unexpected. Craved it, even.

Now, I know I existed entirely for my own gratification and for that of our fans. Trending on the razor edge of recklessness fueled my every move. Syd was right. I had no clue what would hit me when I met her—the one who would change everything.

I get it now because all thoughts and plans have one constant focus. Cassidy has become my center. Her happiness is more important than mine. For the first time in my life, my own existence and happiness is tied to another person. That should scare the hell out of me. Commitment isn't something I've done.

Even as those words rattle my brain, I know they're a fabrication. You won't find a more committed friend, bandmate, or brother. I would literally draw blood for my sister and the guys. I *have*. But a committed relationship with a woman is virgin territory. I snort at my internal rambling as I see Cass emerge from the hallway with Philip and my sister. I'm glad that Cass and Syd get on well. I could have easily blown everything when they first met, and almost did by opening my big mouth. Their relationship has morphed into a meaningful friendship that I know is important to both of them.

My heart beats faster with each step Cass takes toward me. Blood whooshes in my ears, white noise fills the space, and everything else fades away. It's just like in the cheesy rom-coms Syd and I always end up watching. It's like Cass moves in slow motion, and when she flashes me that irresistible smile, I feel somehow more complete because I know she's happy, and by extension then, so am I.

"Sean?" I glance down at Nicole, her trusty tablet waving in front of my face.

"Mmm?"

"We're live on air in about five minutes."

"There's something I need to do first." I glance back at Cassidy when they stop beside us. I slide my arm around her and she stiffens a bit. It's not unexpected as the media is out in full force at the academy today. I've tried to give her space, and it's worked as I've been busy with meeting the families and posing for pictures, but all bets are off now. I'm not sure I could stop from touching her even if I wanted to.

Cassidy's eyes dart around the room and she takes a little step back. I feel the force of Nic's tablet against my chest. "Hey! That hurt."

"Then pay attention. Five minutes."

I take in Cassidy's wary expression. "I'm going to need ten."

Nic gets an angry look I've seen more often than not whenever she's pissed at us, or me more specifically. "What about live radio is confusing to you? You can't be late for your own event."

"I'm not late. I'm right here." Syd laughs, not helping my case at all.

"Yes, and I need you over there," Nic hisses through gritted teeth. She waves her arm in the direction of the radio station that's set up a table on the stage of the auditorium. The announcer's got headphones on and seems busy working away.

"They'll be fine for a couple of minutes. There's a room full of musicians here. Surely they can keep the radio waves entertained in my absence."

"I swear to God, Sean…"

"Matty!" I yell across the rows of seats to where he's lounging with his arm draped across the back of the chair Tess is seated in.

He turns when he hears my voice. "What's up?"

"Collect Lane and Three and keep the masses entertained for a few, yeah?" I nod in the direction of the stage, and he shrugs a shoulder at me, pushing up from his own seat.

"I'm on it."

I grin down at Nic. "See? Problem solved. Matty and the guys will hold the fort down. You can survive for a couple of minutes." I take Cassidy's hand and tug her with me down the hall.

"Sean! Ugh!" Nic's exasperated voice dies as I march down the hall with Cass hurrying to keep up.

"What are you doing?" Cassidy asks through a laugh, almost breathless as I duck into one of the rehearsal rooms at the end of the hall. It's filled with gold and black helium balloons touching the ceiling and long dark ribbons dangling in the air.

"Christ. I forgot about these." I laugh, pushing a few out of the way as I shut the door. "We're letting these off when we announce the winner."

Cass stops in the middle of the room, blowing one of the hanging ribbons out of her face. "What's going on?" She's got that little coy smile on, her blue-gray eyes almost sparkling at me. She's perfect in that deep purple dress I'm sure she designed herself. It dips and curves in all the right places, and a wave of lust rolls through me.

"I need you, Cass." It's more of a desperate growl than anything else.

She reaches up to her hair, untangling a stray ribbon that's gotten caught in her bright hairpin. I hope it's one of the ones I gave her. "What do you need?"

"You. That's all."

"So you dragged me down the hall and into the crazy balloon room to tell me that?"

"No. You don't understand. I *need* you." I'm in front of her in two quick strides, and I let my hands curve against her neck. "I've never needed anyone before." Her mouth is on mine then, and I'm kissing her as if I'll die without the taste of her lips and the feel of her body crushed to mine.

"I need you." I back her up, shoving balloon strings out of the way until she bumps into the edge of the leather sofa up against the wall. "I ache for you, all the time," I murmur against her lips between hot, wet kisses. Her tongue, fuck me standing, her perfect hot, velvet tongue glides against mine. Her delicious, sweet taste floods my senses, and I'm gone.

"I love you." We lose our balance, falling back on the cushions. "No, that's not right." She stills beneath me, her hot breath caressing against my face as she leans back.

"I'm sorry, what?"

"Love isn't big enough for what I feel." Her worry fades, her eyes become glassy. "I can't explain it, but I have to try before I blurt it out on national radio for half of America to hear." Her fingers trace the edge of my jaw, and I drop my head to lean closer. "Wouldn't your father just love that? Talk about inconvenient timing."

"I don't think love is supposed to be convenient," Cass whispers.

"It's more than love." I brace my hands on either side of her head, my fingers dig into the cool leather. "I mean, I love my parents, my sister, the guys, but it's not what I feel for you, not even remotely, because that would be really fucking weird." She shakes her head, her fingers tracing over my lips. "It's more like…" I struggle to find the words. "A supernova in my heart."

She leans back with a little laugh. "That's like the worst valentine card ever."

"We could make it a side business. Super cheesy valentine cards. I love you more than bacon, for instance."

Cassidy moves a wayward balloon string out of the way. "Well, why limit it to just valentines? We can cover all the holidays or just have generically cheesy cards, you know? A picture of a squirrel with 'I'm nuts about you' written in glittery font."

I laugh, dropping my forehead to hers. "This isn't coming out right. I wanted this to be perfect for you."

"Hey." She leans back against the cushions and takes my face between her hands. "You bring me cannoli at all hours of the day. You text me with ridiculous messages to let me know you're thinking about me. You tell me things you don't share with anyone else." There's a touch of sadness in her eyes. It's been hard these past few days with all the talk of Kennedy and Abby's impending bundle of joy, but talking about it with Cassidy has eased the void a bit. I'm still swimming in the sea of bewilderment of unanticipated loss, but every day it gets a little better thanks to her.

She lifts my hand from the couch and sets it over her heart. I feel her take a deep breath in, the swell of her breast filling my hand. "You're in here. Always. And that's not a supernova or some flashy word no one has thought of before. That, Sean, is the very definition of love."

I run my hand along her waist. "How do you always know what to say to me?"

She gives me a cheeky shrug. "It's a gift."

"I know you're right. Love isn't supposed to be convenient or make sense at all. You… This has been unpredictable, sheer madness, really, and I want to share every moment of it, of life, with you." She takes a quick breath in, and I reach for one of the black ribbons, wrapping it around her ring finger. "Marry me."

"You know, that's the second time you've asked me."

"And I'll keep asking until you say yes."

Her lips crash to mine and she grips the back of my neck to urge me forward. With a flick of her hand, she frees the ribbon and balloon from her finger and then fumbles with my belt until she gets it open. Sighing, she drops her head back to the cushion when my lips tease across her neck. That little sound is everything. She's home and my own personal heaven.

"Yes," she whispers, fisting my shirt and trying to tug it up at the same time. I attack her mouth with a groan, feeling her hands shake as she gets my jeans open and pushes them down. My cock practically cries, begging me to sink into her tight warmth.

She gives me a few slow strokes over my hard-as-titanium cock, in complete contrast with our frenzied kisses. I feel my balls tighten already. My hands find their way under her skirt, my fingers waste no time in tracing the outline of her lace knickers to slip them off.

I don't really want to tease her or take my time, I'm driven by mindless want and need, but I stroke my fingers into her, my thumb dropping a beat onto her clit. The sound she makes when I take her to the edge rides the line between bliss and agony. I know she's close already. It's like she'll cry if I don't take her.

She arches up to tug at my shirt once more, pulling me back between her thighs, and then I'm thrusting into her, not even pausing to enjoy the feel of her stretching around me. It's just raw, frenzied fucking. It's our skin slapping and her skirt bunching up between us, with the sofa groaning and bumping the wall with each snap of my hips.

She lets out a cry and my lips find hers to stifle the sound. I hear one of her shoes drop to the floor when she wraps her legs around me, grinding her hips forward. She murmurs against my ear, half of it I can't even understand. All I can register is her wanting it harder and faster, and that's exactly what I give her. When she comes, her sweet pussy milks my orgasm right out of me as I collapse on top of her.

We're a blissful wreck on the sofa, with ribbons dancing around us and a few decimated balloons in our wake. She laughs against my shoulder, softly running her fingers through my hair. I practically purr like a kitten when she does that. There's nothing like pure satisfaction.

"It's been more than ten minutes," she whispers, dropping a kiss to my chin.

"Mhmm. They'll manage." I lean back, trying to smooth out her hair. It's a lost cause. One look at her and everyone is going to know what we were up to in here, if they didn't hear us already. Can't help but feel a little cocky about that.

"You're going to be my wife."

Her hands palm over my ass. "Did I say that? I don't remember saying that." God, I love it when she's like this—blissed out and completely content.

"No getting out of it now." I pause, frowning at the balloons drifting beside us. "I should've gotten a ring first."

"I don't need a ring." She pulls at one of the ribbons. "Besides, I have this. It's all I need." Cass wraps it around her finger and holds her hand up to the light. "It's perfect."

"You're perfect." I drop a kiss to her forehead and ease out of her tight clasp. "It's going to take everything in me not blurt that out, you know."

"I need to talk to my father," she says quietly as I tug my jeans up and search for her knickers. "He's back in DC now. I was planning on going down Saturday."

"I'll go with you."

I find the enticing purple lace on the floor and hold it up in triumph. She laughs and steals them away from me. "I need to do this alone, Sean."

"Like hell you do. You're going to be my wife, and I'm not letting you have a difficult conversation like this alone." I'm aware I sound like a possessive nut job. So be it.

Her eyes widen for a moment before she steps into her knickers. "Most conversations with my father are difficult."

"All the more reason for your fiancé to be there. Your real one." She smoothes her hands over her skirt, and I pass her the shoe that fell off. "We'll take the Pink Tornado. Make a road trip out of it."

"Pink tornado?" She reaches for the shoe, but I hold it out of her reach.

"Did you not stalk me online yet?"

"Oh, I did, but I gave up after the hundredth picture of you with your arm around a different woman." Cheeky girl.

"Jealous?"

She gives me a mock pout. "Insanely."

"Well, my arms only wrap around one woman now." I pull her against my chest, and she melts against me. "The pink tornado is a vintage VW van I had tricked out and restored."

I lean back and hand over the shoe. It's high and black and, Christ, so hot. I hope I can get her to wear those later on when it's just the two of us, and we're not under some time crunch.

"It's pink?"

"Mhmm."

"That won't draw attention at all." She steps into the shoe, and my eyes stay on her legs.

"Aren't you a saucy little minx?" I take a healthy squeeze of her ass.

"You need to stop. You're already in trouble with Nicole, and we don't have time for another round of that." She glances at the sofa, her cheeks tinged soft pink.

"Fine." I hold up my hands and take a step away from her. "But tonight, you're all mine."

Her eyes run over me in a way that isn't at all innocent, and then she's laughing, pointing to my groin. "You might want to do that up."

I glance down, seeing my belt still hanging open. "Right. Don't want to draw attention to our clandestine activities." I fasten the belt and hold my arms wide. "Do I pass inspection?"

She smiles up at me with a nod. Just one look and she's got me weak-kneed. "And then some."

"I hope there's cannoli left over." She adjusts the top of her dress.

"Forget the music, just eat cannoli?" she asks, and I give her a questioning look.

"What?"

"You know? Like *The Godfather*? Leave the gun, take the cannoli?"

"I've never seen *The Godfather*."

She takes a step back like she's been singed by fire. "I'm sorry, what did you just say?" Her eyes widen in surprise.

"I've never seen it."

"How is that possible? Hasn't every man seen it?"

I lean forward to press a kiss to her nose. She scrunches it in response. "You're forgetting I'm not every man."

"As if I could forget."

"We can watch it together. Movie night. I'll set up a screen on the roof here. We'll have blankets and popcorn. I can try to get to second base." I waggle my eyebrows at her.

"Pretty sure you just passed all the bases when you swung for the fences there." She's trying hard to contain her smile.

"That can be another one of the cheesy cards brought to you by Supernova Industries. 'I'd swing for the fences for you.'"

Her laugh fills my heart to bursting, and I press a lingering kiss to her lips. "There's a loo just down the hall if you want to freshen up. I'll do the same, and then we can get this show on the road." I open the door and peek out, hearing music filtering from down the hall. "Coast is clear." I turn back to her with a whisper and find her untangling one of the ribbons.

"Can't forget this." Cass holds it up and smiles.

"Would be a crime to misplace your engagement ring." I really am going to have to get her one. Something perfect, special, unique.

"I'll guard it with my life. Now go!" She shoos me out the door, her soft laughter fading only when she ducks into the loo. It's tempting to follow her in there, but she's right. Nic is going to kick my ass already, but it's totally worth it.

It's been a frantic couple of hours, but we've finally made the announcement of our program winner, Josh Redmond. Josh is only sixteen but plays guitar like a beast. He's also been nervous as hell since the announcement. In stark contrast to some of the other students we've met tonight who were casually dressed, Josh wears a crisp white dress shirt and a thin blue tie, and constantly adjusts his round wire glasses.

The media is long gone, and there are only a few lingering students and parents left in the auditorium. Josh is still as skittish as a wide-eyed foal.

"Do you mind if we take a picture with the band?" Josh's father asks Nari and I. Josh has been nudged by his father from the corner of the stage he seemed insistent on cowering in since being showered with balloons and confetti. I have the feeling Josh doesn't have a lot of friends. I hope we can help with that. The academy is going to have forty students to start with. There's got to be some kindred spirits for him here.

"If that's okay with Josh, sure," Nari says.

Josh shrugs, looking embarrassed, his eyes trained to the floor. "I guess." He shifts uncomfortably as if he wants the ground to swallow him up.

"It's not the place for modesty here, mate." I nudge him in the side as he shuffles forward. "You totally rocked 'Rev You Up' in your audition video."

Josh looks hesitantly at his father who smiles and nods his encouragement. 'Rev You Up' is a complicated piece from one of our earlier albums that probably only a handful of seasoned guitarists could do any justice to. "That's not the easiest song you could've picked," I note.

"It's one of my favorites," he says, finally looking me in the eye. He's clearly starstruck and looking a bit baffled at all of the attention he's gotten this evening.

I give him an encouraging smile. "Mine too. How about you play it for us now?" I suggest.

"I don't... No... I mean," he stammers, his eyes as wide as dinner plates.

"Come on then." I move across the stage and lift one of Kennedy's guitars from the rack stand and turn back to him.

His mouth drops open as I stride back to him. "That's one of his Les Paul customs. I couldn't... no way," he mumbles, staring at the guitar as if it's the Holy Grail.

Kennedy pats him on the back, and I hold the guitar out to him. "You can." I watch as he looks frantically at his father.

"Come on. Out of everyone who entered this contest, you won. You know you're talented," Cam offers his own words of encouragement.

"I've never played one of these before. Mine is some cheap Gibson that used to be my grandfather's," Josh explains.

"Hey, no Gibson is cheap," Cam corrects him.

"No. I didn't mean… Are you serious?" Josh's eyes dart back to mine.

"You know, Cam and I came up with that riff using a couple of these." Kennedy nods at the Les Paul, and the two of them share a look.

"I know. I mean, I read about it in *Guitar World*," Josh mumbles. He tentatively places the thick black strap over his shoulder and turns back to his father. "Dad!" His voice is an awed whisper.

"Go ahead, bud," his dad says enthusiastically, holding his phone up. "Can I?" I nod, taking a step back so he can video his son.

Josh's shaking fingers move over the fret board almost as if he's afraid to touch it. "Before today, I've only played for my family. Dad sent the entry in."

"Wise man, your dad," Matt says. Yanking the cord to stretch from the amp behind him, he plugs it into the guitar.

"It's all yours, Josh. Let's hear it."

He takes a shaky breath, getting a feel for the strings, and then he really starts playing. The hypnotic sound fills the auditorium, his eyes fixed in concentration on his fingers as they fly through the riff. It's laced with texture and precision, and if anyone else closed their eyes and listened to it, they might think it's Kennedy playing. With a few hiccups that probably only the four of us could pick out, he's managed to copy the riff like a pro, and the kid is only sixteen years old.

"Holy shit," Cam mutters, glancing at me in disbelief.

I shake my head as I watch him work through to the ending notes. "Dude! You are amazing!" Matt practically gushes.

"You really are," I agree, moving beside Matt. Josh stares back at me, practically vibrating with excitement.

"Now, this time try to put your own spin on it," Kennedy suggests gently. "Every note doesn't have to mimic what we did; in fact, it'll be better if it doesn't."

"I don't know how… I mean…" His voice trails as he hesitates.

"You do know how." I drape my arm around his shoulder. "It's why we picked you. Close your eyes and let it take you somewhere."

"Okay," Josh mumbles, and following my words of wisdom, he closes his eyes and plays this time from his heart. We step away to give him some space, and join his father as he looks on, clearly proud.

"Your son is incredibly talented. I hope he enjoys it here," Nari says, smiling as she watches Josh.

His father can't contain his pride. "I know he is. And thank you for this. He's kind of shy, and doesn't have a lot of friends, so this is a pretty big deal for him."

"It's a big deal for us too. It's not often we see musicians with this much raw talent," I admit.

"How did that feel?" Kennedy asks him when he finishes. Josh is practically beaming.

"So awesome!"

"It sounded amazing." We move back to join him as his dad snaps off a few pictures of us all together. Josh makes a move to lift the strap from his shoulder, but Kennedy stops him. "You keep it," Kennedy offers. Josh looks as if he may pass out. "Just promise me you'll take care of it."

Cassidy

"Where the fuck do people park in this city? It's worse than New York."

I can't help my giggle at Sean's frustration. He's gripping the wheel of his beloved pink van like he wants to rip it off the steering column. We've circled the Russell Senate Office Building, where my dad's office is located, about four times in heavy afternoon traffic trying to find

262 | **B.B. MILLER** & **LESLIE CARSON**

one of the most elusive creatures in Washington, DC—a parking spot that's less than four blocks from where you want to go.

"This is why you should've let me arrange this trip," Tucker growls from the back. He insisted on accompanying us when he heard what I intended to do. I wasn't thrilled with more people being involved, but since he's the one who found all the dirt on Dale, I relented. "We could've had a nice SUV drop us off and be at our beck and call."

Sean waves a hand toward his grumpy security guard. "Pssh. Where's the fun in that?"

"Are we having fun?" I ask, as Sean swears under his breath when another driver cuts us off.

"Of course we are." He tosses a grin my way, then refocuses on his driving, turning again onto First Street. "Oh, thank fucking God!" he declares as a sedan pulls out of a spot just ahead. "See! We're even on the same block. It was meant to be."

"If you say so," Tucker mutters. As soon as we're stopped, he gets out and heads over to the parking kiosk. I let Sean get out and come around to my door. It gives me a few more seconds to swallow down the ball of nerves that has been steadily growing with every mile. I know I need to do this—I *want* to do this—but that doesn't mean it's going to be easy. My door opens, and Sean's hand appears in my field of vision.

"Come on, love." His understanding smile calms my jumpy stomach. "It'll be fine. You can do this."

I put my hand in his and give him a shaky smile. "I know. Thanks for coming." He helps me out and holds me close for a second.

"Anything for you. I've got your back." His warm lips brush against mine, and my heart swells. His reassurance means more to me than he'll ever know. I know I look brave from the outside, but sometimes I don't think I am.

"Thank you." I kiss him again, quickly. "Let's do this."

Tucker returns from paying; he buttons his suit jacket and smooths down his tie, his eyes scanning the street. I don't see anything out of the ordinary—just busy sidewalks full of people glued to their cell phones. Typical DC.

Sean purses his lips and plucks at the collar of his shirt. He's wearing a suit jacket and button-down, open at the neck, with his jeans. His emerald green hair draws a few more looks here than it does in New York, but nothing remarkable. I tug the belt of my trench coat tighter and lead the way into the building.

The Capitol Police officers give Sean's hair a suspicious look as they check our ID but let us go through the metal detectors without incident. I take Sean's hand and guide us through the marbled halls upstairs to my father's office, the click of my heels echoing off the walls. Taking a deep breath, I swing the heavy oak door open.

"Cassidy! What a lovely surprise." Sylvia, my dad's office administrator, looks up from her computer with a startled smile spreading across her face. Two staffers share a desk, crammed into the tight space behind Sylvia's desk. Built in the early 1900s, the building is impressive, but the offices are small for modern needs. Through an open door to the right, I can see a collection of aides and interns crowded around a long table, typing on laptops or with cellphones stuck to their ears. To the left are my father's and Dale's closed office doors.

"Hi, Sylvia. Sorry for bursting in without an appointment." I jerk my head toward the closed doors. "Are either of them in?"

"Dale's out somewhere, but your father's here. He should be finishing up a meeting in a few minutes, if you'd like to wait. I can squeeze you in before his next meeting." I swallow my laugh when she frowns at the emerald mop of hair adorning Sean's head. I slip my hand in his and smile when I see her eyes fly open wide.

"That'd be great. Sylvia, this is Sean Murphy, my fiancé, and our friend, Tucker Pearson."

"Your fiancé!" Her mouth drops open for an instant before she manages a strained smile. "Well, it's a pleasure to meet you both."

"Ma'am," Tucker says, his rumbling voice loud in the space. A couple of the aides in the next room observe us with drawn brows, as if trying to remember where they've seen us—probably Sean—before.

My helpful fiancé takes my coat and hangs it on a peg before stepping forward. "Sylvia," Sean purrs, taking the startled woman's hand

and giving her a smooth smile. "I hear you're the glue that keeps this whole operation together."

"Oh, um, well…" The poor woman blinks like she stared too long at the sun. I can't blame her; I frequently feel the same when he gives me that smile. I glance down at my shoes and smooth my silk shirt.

Thankfully, my father's office door opens and two men leave—one I recognize as another senator. They both frown at Sean's hair as they pass us on their way out of the office.

Sylvia waves us in, and I take a deep breath and share a look with Sean. "Okay, let's go."

"Cassidy?" My father puts down the file in his hand and frowns at me in confusion as I enter his office.

"Did you know?" I ask without preamble, striding forward on the thick carpet and planting myself, hands on my hips. He stands behind his carved oak desk, his confusion evident.

"Know what? What are you doing here, Cass?" He looks to the men behind me, a frown on his lips as Tucker closes the door with a click. "What's going on?"

"About the pictures. Or, rather, the *lack* of pictures." I ignore his questions, folding my arms over my chest. "That there were *never* any pictures. Did you know?"

"Pictures of what?" He leans forward, bracing himself with his fists on his desk. "Who are these men?"

I take a deep breath, reining in my roiling emotions enough to remember my manners. "This is Tucker Pearson, a security expert, and this…" I step closer to Sean and slip my hand in his. "This is Sean Murphy. My fiancé."

My father gapes at me, while Tucker's eyes widen in surprise. "Seriously? Congrats, man," he murmurs to Sean, nudging him with his elbow. "This is awesome—I finally won a bet with Cam." Sean returns his smirk before stepping toward my dad, his hand outstretched.

"It's a pleasure to meet you, Senator Skinner."

My father's face freezes; I'm not sure if the word fiancé or Sean's English accent is the bigger shock for him. He stares at Sean, his eyes moving slowly from his green hair down to his black Doc Martens. Cocking an eyebrow, Sean withdraws his hand my father left hanging.

"Cassidy, what the hell is going on?" Dad stands straight again, glaring at us from beneath his bushy eyebrows. "I don't have time for these games. I have to leave in a few minutes for a meeting with the majority leader."

"It can wait." I raise my chin and meet his angry gaze. "I'm not playing games. Sean is my fiancé, and I love him. I told you I'm not marrying Jack, and I meant it. There are several reasons, but Sean is the most important. However, this isn't the reason we're here." I release Sean and lean forward over the edge of Dad's desk. "I want to know if you've always known there were never any photos of what happened to me." My voice lowers. "Back then."

He rears back like I've struck him. "Photos?" With a worried frown, he looks first at Sean, then Tucker.

"They know," I inform him, and I'm not surprised to see his shock. "They know enough about what happened to me and everything about what happened when Kevin and Dale came to campus. In fact, they know more about Dale than you do."

His pale blue eyes dart between Sean and Tucker until he finally focuses back on me. "Cass, there weren't any photos," he says quietly, looking at me with consternation. "I don't know what you're talking about."

I narrow my eyes, studying him. He's telling the truth. I can see it in his eyes. This is why I needed to do this in person. A weight leaves my shoulders, and I take a shaky breath. "Dale told me there were. He told me you had him secure a special cyber team to keep a watch out all these years. Every once in a while, usually when you needed my help, I'd get a text telling me they'd found and deleted another photo. And every time, I was reminded of what you did for me, and I'd go along with whatever was needed, out of gratitude. And because I love you."

My father's eyes grow wide as I speak. With Sean's hand on my back giving me strength, I continue, "I've lived with this...this *fear* for years." I blink back the wetness in my eyes. "Always wondering if a photo would slip through, wondering if...if you'd seen them." My mouth twists with disgust, the memory of that long-ago night briefly washing over me. "I wanted to talk to you about it, but I could never find the strength. The whole thing was just so...*humiliating*. I didn't want to think about it, and I definitely didn't want you and Mom to have to think about it. I just wanted for us all to forget it and talking about it would just keep it alive." I glance at Sean, his lips mashed into a thin line as he listens.

Gritting my teeth, I press a fist to my chest and keep going. "But I haven't been able to forget it. Dale's kept me on a string, and he tugged at it whenever he wanted something." I squeeze my eyes shut for a second, hating the quaver in my voice. "I've been his puppet. *But no more.*"

Dad sucks in a breath, looking shaken, and rubs his temples. "Cassidy...I don't...I can't..." He comes around the desk and takes my hands in his. "Cass, I swear to you there were never any photos. Not one. None of them, the people who"—he glances at Sean, and lowers his voice—"did that to you, took any photos. They were too drunk and too, um, focused on what they were doing." He grimaces and glances down at his feet in embarrassment before meeting my gaze again. "It was one of my fears, but Dale and your brother ensured that it wasn't an issue. All of their devices—phones, computers, and whatnot—as well as their emails and social media were scoured and destroyed. Kevin saw to it himself. In fact, I wanted to encourage you to go to the police," he says, and it's my turn to be shocked. He was willing to risk his career for me by going to the police?

"Dale talked me out of it." His lips twist in a familiar expression of dissatisfaction. "He convinced me the press would've been too much for your mother. She was going through tests for breast cancer at the time."

What? I cling to his hands, my eyes wide. "I didn't know that! Why didn't you say anything? Did Kevin know?" If my brother knew and didn't tell me, I'll rip him a new one.

"No. Marilyn didn't want to worry either of you. It turned out to be nothing, so that was that. But that's why I agreed to not involving police." His eyes harden as he continues, "So I had him make sure those fuckers paid another way." He's talking about them ending up in the ER. "And the ones who are still alive are still paying."

Tucker grunts with approval, and I glance over to see Sean nod at my father with a smile of grim satisfaction. I pull my hands from Dad's and sweep my hair out of my eyes. "What do you mean?" I look at him as if I've never seen him before, and I guess I haven't. I can't remember the last time I saw the gleam of paternal vengeance in his eyes.

He waves a hand. "I've just kept an eye on them. Made sure they stayed the insignificant little shits they've always been. Nothing you need to worry about."

I swallow, love for my Dad mixing with my anger toward Dale. "But I *have* worried," I say, grasping the corner of his desk. "Dale has kept me in a continual state of worry for years…for *nothing*." My voice breaks at the end, and Sean slips an arm around my waist, pulling me close to his side.

"It's okay, love," he murmurs. "He won't anymore."

"Dale Canton is my chief of staff and most trusted advisor. There's got to be a misunderstanding." My father shakes his head, and then looks at me, confusion marring his face. "Politics is a family sport; you've always known that. My name is on the ballot, but we're all in this together. I've tried to keep you out of most of it, but sometimes it's advantageous if…" He spreads his hands, looking a little lost. "You've always seemed happy to help. Dale said—"

Sean snorts a harsh laugh. "I can imagine what he's said. That fucker has a lot to answer for." He suddenly leans forward, peering at the framed family photos on Dad's desk and selects one with a soft huff. "Look," he says, tapping the glass lightly. It's me as a baby, sitting on our old sofa at home in a diaper, my birthmark on full display. Ah—that's one mystery answered. Dale knows about my birthmark from this photo.

"Put that back, please." Dad frowns at Sean, and then runs a hand over his face roughly, as if he's weary of the world. "I've known Dale for years. I can't believe he'd betray us like this."

"You don't know him as well as you think," Tucker says flatly. He pulls a sheaf of pages out of his inside suit pocket and slaps it on my father's desk. Photos.

Fuck. I catch a glimpse of bare skin wrapped in some kind of black strappy harness before I pull away from Sean and walk to the far side of the office, wrapping my arms around myself.

"Is this really the sort of person you want to associate yourself with?" Tucker spreads the photos out on his desk. "Your constituents generally lean toward the conservative side, don't they? How would they feel about this?" My father leans over the pictures, uttering an oath, and grabbing at one of them with an expression of incredulous disgust.

"I'm usually the first to say 'live and let live' regarding people's private habits, and God knows my own past behavior could hardly be considered saintly," Sean says, studying the photos. "Not even in my most debauched dreams did I ever think of using a vegetable like *that*. Especially on myself. That's just fucking weird."

Suddenly, the door opens and Dale walks in. "Cassidy," he begins, his wary gaze taking in the room and my father's outraged expression. "Sylvia told me you were here. What brings you to town? Is Jack with you?"

"You…you…" My father sputters with anger. "Sylvia!" he bellows, making us all jump. His assistant's startled face appears at the door. "Call security. Now!"

Sylvia disappears, and Dale swiftly closes the door behind her. "Bob, what's going on?" He looks at Sean and Tucker. "Who the hell are these guys?"

"Truth tellers, Canton," Tucker says, his face grim. "Which is more than I can say about you."

I move without thinking.

"What are you—shit!" Dale flinches from the force of my slap and covers his cheek with his hand. "What the fuck?"

"You bastard," I spit at him, wringing my stinging palm. I draw my other hand back, but Sean catches it in his.

"Careful, love," he cautions softly. "He's not worth injuring yourself."

"You're fired." My dad stands beside his desk, quivering with barely restrained anger. I can't remember when I've ever seen him this mad. "After everything I've done for you, after everything we've been through," he growls, his jaw twitching. "You've been manipulating—torturing—my daughter for years! You've used one of the worst things that could ever happen to a person against her."

Dale sucks in a breath, eyeing each of us in turn. His accusatory gaze lingers on Sean before he faces my father. "Bob, I don't know what they've been telling you, but whatever it is, I assure you it's not true."

My father extends an arm, shaking one of the photos at us. "This girl was an intern, you sick fuck!" He stabs a finger at the others spread on his desk. "And this one's on the majority leader's staff! I don't recognize the other girls, but I'm sure the press would figure it out if they ever got their hands on these."

Dale blanches. "Where did you get those?"

"I have *real* cybersecurity people at my fingertips." Tucker straightens his shoulders. "Unlike the fake ones you've been *pretending* to work with."

Drawing himself up, Dale glares at me before looking back at my dad. "Bob, I swear to God, whatever they're showing you has been faked. That's not me. I'd never do that—you know me! And I have no idea what Cassidy's talking about!"

Sean growls and jerks toward him, but I lay a hand on his bicep, stopping him. "You know exactly what I'm talking about," I hiss at Dale. "The threats? Trying to blackmail me to go along with this sham of an engagement to Jack, and with what? *You don't have any photos, Dale.* You never did."

The color rushes back to his face. "You're talking like a crazy person!" He points a finger at me as he looks at my dad. "See this? This is what New York does to a person. That place is a cesspool!" Sean huffs a laugh, shaking his head.

"Well, you should know a cesspool when you see one, Canton, based on those photos." He gestures to the crumpled picture in my dad's fist.

"Who the fuck are you, anyway?" Dale demands, but before he can answer, my dad steps closer.

"You can't tell me this isn't you, you sonofabitch. We've been in the steam room at the gym too many times for me not to recognize the scar on your back," Dad growls. Dale's eyes widen, and he takes a step back, bumping into a bookshelf.

"You're finished, Dale," I whisper. "Crawl back under your rock, and leave me and my family the fuck alone, or I guarantee that all of DC will see you being pleasured with produce."

His eyes flare with malice. "You *bitch*." He jerks toward me and raises his hand. Sean is between us before I can blink. He grabs him by the lapels and slams him back against the wall.

"Try it, mate," he snarls. "I've wanted a go at you for weeks."

Tucker joins them and swiftly pats Dale down, ridding him of two cell phones, just as Sylvia opens the door, accompanied by Capitol Police officers. "Take his keys and building ID. He's fired." Dad's voice is like ice. "Walk him out. He doesn't get to touch his computer or any-thing else. We'll send whatever belongings you have here, including your personal cell phone, later. After we've checked them out."

Dale stares at my dad for a beat, and then his shoulders slump in shame, the fight suddenly leaving him, and he lets them lead him out. Once he's gone, my father comes to me and gathers me in his arms, hugging me like he used to when I was small. "I'm sorry, Cass," he murmurs in my hair, and I finally let a few tears of relief fall. "I'm sorry about everything. I'm sorry you didn't feel like you could talk to me about all this sooner. Your mother and I never brought it up for the same reasons—we didn't want you to have to relive it. I love you. Can you forgive me?"

I nod and smile up at him through my tears. He kisses my

forehead and says, "Will you—all of you—come over to the house so we can talk with your mother? Then we need to set the record straight concerning Jack."

"What about your meeting with the majority leader?"

He tucks my hair behind my ear. "He can wait." He turns to Sean, who's giving me a smile that warms my heart. "You protected her."

"I always will." Sean's emerald eyes glow with love, and I'm drawn to his side like a magnet. "I love her. She's everything, sir," he says, holding me close.

Dad's mouth quirks into an awkward smile; he clears his throat and extends a hand to him. "Let's start again," he says. "I'm Robert Skinner, and it's a pleasure to meet you, Sean. Welcome to the family."

chapter sixteen

Murphy's Law No. 19: *If you get really lucky,*
the reality is better than the dream.

Sean

"YOU SURE YOU DON'T WANT TO COME WITH?" I ASK TUCKER AS I OPEN the door to the Pink Tornado for Cassidy.

Tucker waves me off. "I've got an Uber coming."

"We can drop you somewhere," I offer.

"I'm good."

I narrow my eyes, regarding him. "Where exactly are you off to?"

"Wouldn't you like to know?"

"I would, actually."

"You're settled now. My work here is done. I'm going to catch a flight back to New York to pick up my stuff and then head to Cali."

"Aren't Kennedy and Abby in Minnesota?"

Tucker nods. "They are."

"And you're not going there?"

"They're laying low with his parents. They don't need me."

"But someone in California does?"

He claps me on the shoulder. "I live in California, genius. And I've got work to do."

That's a bullshit answer if there ever was one. We're not back on tour until the end of the year, and Tucker's been with us for so long, he doesn't need months to plan anything. "Mhmm. I'm not buying it, mate."

"You know, I do have a life outside of all the drama that seems to follow the four of you around."

"What's her name?" Cassidy pinches me in the side. "Ow!" I glance down at her, and she narrows her eyes at me.

"Let him be, Sean." She shoves me out of the way and wraps her arms around Tucker, surprising him a little. He gives her a stilted pat on the back in response to her heartfelt hug, and if it wasn't Tucker, I'd level any man who dare put his hands on her.

She leans back, glancing up at him. "Thank you, Tucker. You don't know how much this means to me—everything you've done."

"It's nothing." He shoves his hands into his pockets when she releases him and glances up the street.

"It's not nothing. I'm finally out from under all of this uncertainty and worry. It's been awful spending years thinking those pictures would come out. Worrying how it would affect my father, me."

I clench my fists, my anger bubbling up again when I think about that slimy, vegetable-fucker Dale. I would've loved to have tuned him up. Fucker better watch himself.

Cass closes her eyes, taking a deep breath. "Just, thank you."

"You're welcome, Cassidy. We've got eyes on him, so don't worry, okay? If he even thinks about doing something stupid, we'll know."

"That means a lot, Tuck. Thanks, mate." I slap him on the back as a silver sedan pulls up to the curb.

"If anything happens, just—"

"Call you. I know, I know." I shove him toward the curb. "Now go to this all important work you have in California."

"You're such a pain in the ass." He opens up the door to the car, pretending to be annoyed.

"Does this *work* have a name?"

Tuck leans on the frame of the door. "I'm leaving now."

"Ha!" I point a finger at him. "I knew it."

"You know nothing," he fires back at me.

"But I can find out."

"You wish." Ah, there's nothing better than a challenge.

I fold my arms across my chest. "Care to make it interesting?"

"You want to make a bet on whether you can find out what I'm doing in California?"

"You mean *who* you're doing."

His eyes flash with warning. "Watch it."

"You're so transparent." I hold out my hand, and he grips it far more tightly than he needs to. "A grand it is then."

"You're on. I'm going to enjoy spending that money." He releases my hand and taps the door before slipping into the seat. I throw my arm around Cassidy's shoulder and we wave, watching the car until it disappears around the corner.

"He's a good friend." Cassidy tightens her arm around my waist.

"That he is, love."

My boots echo on the gleaming mahogany hardwood floor as Cassidy leads me down the never-ending hallway of her parents' DC estate home. I probably should've taken them off at the door. I glance down at my well-worn Docs that have seen countless concerts and countries. Her mum is going to have heart failure when she sees me. This should be entertaining.

This house—I'm not calling it a home because nothing this perfect and spotless is a real home—is obviously a statement piece for the senator and his wife, designed for entertaining and putting on a well-crafted facade for the Washington elite. Soaring ceilings, a semicircular staircase, and probably a thousand rooms where political alliances are forged and fought. It feels stifling and staged, and I can't imagine Cass spending any time here at all.

We follow the senator into a massive sitting room. He moves to stand behind the wingback chair his wife is sitting in. It's like they're getting ready to have a portrait taken. He sets his hand on the chair and motions to Cassidy. "Marilyn, Cassidy and her fiancé, Sean," he announces like some courtly knight.

I bark out a laugh and Cassidy elbows me in the side. "Sorry, love. But I've not heard an actual announcement of my arrival like that since I had a spot of tea with Liz." I cross the room and stand in front of Marilyn Skinner. I can see traces of Cassidy in there, but her stiff posture and wary eyes are the polar opposite. Also, Cass wouldn't be caught dead in this perfectly pressed light blue suit and pearls. Good Lord, does this woman need to relax.

"Mrs. Skinner. It's a pleasure to meet you." I take her hand in both of mine as her eyes widen, flitting up to my hair. "Before this gets started, I want you to know that I don't just love your daughter. I crave her. There's not another soul on the planet I need more than Cassidy, and I will spend my life making her happy. That's the only thing that matters to me."

Marilyn's eyes soften a little, and I see a trace of a smile, but it evaporates quickly and she repurses her lips, extracting her hand from mine. "You're engaged." She glances over to her daughter, who smiles.

"I am, Mom. I love him." Cassidy's voice is quiet.

Marilyn rises from the chair, and I move out of her path as she glides toward Cass. "Let me see the ring." Cassidy's lips curl into a half smile as she reached into her pocket and holds up the black ribbon.

Marilyn's gaze darts between the ribbon and Cass. "I don't understand?"

"About that. It was a bit spur of the moment, you know? Carpe diem and all that." The senator moves from behind the chair, joining his wife and shooting me a death glare.

"Spur of the moment?" Marilyn asks.

Marilyn's hand covers her mouth and she drops her eyes to Cassidy's stomach. "You're not pregnant, are you?" Just slice me open. Her words are like a blade to my soul. She's mortified her daughter may be pregnant... out of wedlock no less. Talk about a scandal. Christ, do I wish that were possible. My stomach bottoms out, and Cassidy looks up at me with an apologetic smile. The grandfather clock in the corner ticks off each passing, painful second.

"No. I'm not pregnant," Cassidy murmurs.

"Well, then what do you mean, spur of the moment?" Cassidy's father glares at me.

"I mean. I tend to act first and worry about the consequences later."

The senator officially hates me now as evidenced by his crossed arms and half-imposing scowl he fires at me.

"This isn't coming out right. If you're worried about my commitment to your daughter, you needn't be. She's the most important person in my life. And I'll get her a ring when the right one makes itself known. But no ring, no ribbon is going to change the way I feel about her." His jaw ticks as he glances at Cassidy. "Do you have any idea how rare and precious it is to find someone who wants you not because of *who* are but because of who you *are*?" A little crease forms in his brow, similar to the one Cass gets when I say things that don't make sense to her.

"Still, you should've asked us first," Marilyn offers.

"No. I shouldn't have. For a thousand reasons, I shouldn't have. It's not 1532, she's not yours to give away, and Cass is fiercely independent, if you hadn't already realized. It's one of the things I love most about her." Marilyn and Robert apparently have been struck speechless, exchanging a questioning look.

"Would it be nice to have a medieval blessing? I suppose, but ultimately the only opinion of me that matters is your daughter's, and believe me when I tell you that's a first for me. That I care about what someone else thinks of me is terrifying. But her happiness, her joy, seeing her light up is everything to me. I'm happy when she's happy. I'm gutted when she is, and I'll bleed for her."

"Sean." It's a single word from my Cassidy that has me moving closer to take her hand in mine.

"And what happens one day when you wake up and carpe diem changes your mind?" the helpful senator asks.

"I can understand why you'd ask that. You know, I used to think my life was perfect. I'm doing what I love, perpetually moving from one city to the next, and I liked it that way. The randomness of it all was part of the thrill. Meeting Cass changed all that. The reality is: we're all just walking around in this meaningless vortex of nothingness until one day, karma or fate or serendipity or just straight-up luck taps you on the shoulder and says, 'Mate, you're up. It's your turn.'" Cass squeezes my hand, and I look down to catch her gaze. "If you're ever lucky enough to get that tap on the shoulder, you fucking grab onto that chance and you never let it go."

"I still can't believe you said all of that to my parents," Cassidy says as we turn down a dirt path in the camping RV park just outside of DC. I'm not sure the Pink Tornado actually qualifies as an official RV, but turns out the kid at the sign-in desk is a Redfall fan, so I shamelessly convinced him to let us park for the night.

Could we have grabbed a hotel? Of course. But it's forecasted to be a clear night and spending it under the stars with the woman I love seems like a no-brainer to me.

"Every word is true."

She smiles at me, sticking her arm out the window to feel the rush of warm air. "I think my mom is still in shock."

"If you're happy, she should be. That's really all there is to it."

She squeezes my thigh as I pull into site twenty-four, grinning when I throw the VW into park. "We have arrived!" There's a small patch of grass along with a fire pit and a few of those low cedar chairs crowded around it. The squeals of kids playing at the little lake to the left drift in through Cassidy's open window. I wonder if I'll always feel that twinge of sadness when little poppets are near. I hope not.

She glances out to the space before turning back to me. "It's perfect."

"That you are, love." I unbutton my seat belt and slide my hand behind her neck to pull her lips to mine. "Let's start a fire, and we can watch the stars reveal themselves." She wrinkles her nose when I kiss the tip. "You can grill your man up some of those fine burgers we bought, and I can thank you later, many times over."

I can feel her smile against my lips. "You've got yourself a deal."

A few hours later, we're by the fire, wrapped in a blanket, with Cassidy's back relaxed against my chest. Sharing s'mores from the couple in the tricked-out RV next to us who have no earthly clue who either one of us is topped off our meal.

Cass points out constellations, and I have no idea if she really knows what they are or is making it all up, but I couldn't care less. It's a perfect moment, untainted by responsibilities and expectations.

I rest my chin on top of her head, tightening my arms around her when she snuggles in closer. "My dad should've issued his statement by now."

I watch the flames flicker and snap into the darkened night. "Mmm. Did you want to take a look at it? I saw a Wi-Fi sign back at the sign-in shack."

She turns her head and presses a kiss to my jaw. "No. I don't. I'm just glad it's finally over, you know?"

"I know. I'm just sorry you've had to live under that for so long." She reaches her hand up to flutter her fingers through my hair. I close my eyes, savoring the sensation.

"I don't have to anymore."

"No. You don't." She shifts to straddle my lap and rests her forehead against mine.

"I think you said something about thanking me for burning your burgers? Something along the lines of multiple times?" She rolls her hips, and I feel a lick of pleasure roll through me. My cheeky girl. Christ, how I love her.

"Yes, ma'am." I push up, taking hold of her ass as she wraps her legs around me. Striding back to the VW, I haul open the door and it shuts with a metallic bang behind us. Her legs tighten around me before I launch us to the pullout bed in the back and thank her... multiple times over.

I've never seen Cassidy like this; nervous, fidgeting, that spark in her eyes gone and replaced with something akin to shock.

I take a step toward her, but she recoils, wrapping her arms around her waist and making a beeline for the window.

"What's wrong, love? Whatever it is, we can handle it. It's what we do." She glances at me over her shoulder before closing her eyes and turning back to the window. "You're officially scaring the shit out of me."

I can see her shoulders sag and she glances down at her fingers, wringing them together. "I'm not really sure how to have this conversation, so I'm just going to say it." She squares her shoulders, facing me. It feels like she's an ocean away. "I'm pregnant."

Time stops. Literally. There's a whoosh in my ears like a postconcert vacant buzz that lingers for hours after we've brought the house down. I glance down at her stomach and back to her face. "Wh—what?" It's a damn good thing I'm gripping the back of the sofa, or I'd be on the floor. My heart pounds in a ridiculous rhythm, my skin prickling with heat.

An eerie silence yawns between us while we stare at each other. This isn't possible. Not even remotely, according to every single test I've taken and good ole Dr. Perez has told me. "Is it mine?"

Her mouth drops open for a second, and then she unleashes on my sheer absurdity. "Are you serious right now?" She throws her hands up in the air. *"Is it yours?"*

"Cass." I step tentatively toward her, but she's having none of it. She holds her hand up.

"Don't even think about coming closer to me right now."

My knee hits the side of the sofa, and I stop. "I didn't mean that. It's just that I was told it was more likely I'd find Elvis alive than it was for me to father a child, so you're going to have to give me a minute here to process."

"No! You don't get a minute, Sean. I sure as hell didn't get a minute when I was sitting in the doctor's office after having fainted with bridezilla number four today."

"Wait, you fainted?" She waves me off; there's no stopping her rant, and rightly so. I uttered the worst words possible in this scenario. *Is it mine?* On the scale of idiotic, this surely has a place at the top.

"Riya took me to the doctor this afternoon. These last couple of weeks have been awful for me, Sean. I've got brides ranging from the ones who want their picture taken so they can get more Instagram followers to ones who are terrified to come in for fear of their picture getting splashed all over the gossip sites."

"I'm sorry, I just—You're pregnant? You're sure?"

"Yes! Yes, I'm sure. And I thought…" Her lips smash together and she shakes her head. "That your first reaction is to question whether this baby is yours or not screams of everything that's wrong with us."

"Wait… what?"

"You don't know me at all, Sean. If you did, you'd realize how moronic it is for you to even think that. I'd never do that—be with someone else. How can you even—" I can see her eyes swimming with threatening tears.

I move to take her hand but she backs up. "I don't think that. You caught me on the back foot. I just—"

"No. I can't, Sean. I can't have this stress. I haven't been sleeping properly, I've been working around the clock… It's all just too much." Tears stain her cheeks, and she quickly wipes them away. "I can't have more stress. The doctor said I need to take better care of myself." She fishes around in her pocket and pulls out a crumpled wad of paper. "She put me on prenatal vitamins, and there's a list of things I'm not supposed to eat any more." She waves the tattered pages in front of me. "I mean, no more Brie cheese? No more coffee? Some days that's all I have time for. Coffee and cheese!"

This would be funny if it wasn't happening to the woman I love. Cass in full meltdown is a sight to behold. "Cass, take a breath, love."

"Don't *love* me," she says through gritted teeth. "I just thought you should know. I don't expect anything from you. You can be as involved as you want or not, but my first priority, my only priority now is this baby."

"Cass—" She stalks to the door, shoving the paper back into her coat pocket.

"I need to go. I have a deadline, and I can't miss it."

"Cass, don't leave. Not like this. Let me take you home."

Her jaw sets as she looks up at me in defiance. "No. You need to let me go."

"I can't." I slide my hand along her neck, feeling her pulse thunder beneath my palm. "You're in my veins, woman, don't you know that?"

"I can't do this. I need time away from all of this." She motions to me, and it's like I've been slapped in the face. "I need time away from you."

I bolt awake, my heart slamming around in my chest, the sheets tangled around my legs. I glance down at Cass who stirs, her hand reaching out for me. Christ, I haven't had a nightmare in… I run a hand through my hair. I can't remember the last time I had a nightmare, likely around my rehab time, I'd hazard to say.

I roll my neck, gripping the back of it as I try to calm the hell down. "Sean?" Cass leans up, pressing her luscious, naked body to my side, her hand sliding down my chest. She's sleep-warm and perfect, a balm to madness of one fucked-up dream. "Are you okay?"

I lift her hand, turning it to kiss her palm. "I will be." My voice is all gravelly.

"What is it?"

She drops a kiss to my shoulder, and I start to relax, soaking in her comfort as only a lovesick man can. "I just need you."

"I'm right here," she whispers against my shoulder.

I turn to roll on top of her, my head spinning with the dizzying dream, with her, with too much emotion I don't know how to handle. Her hands roam over my back and then glide along my arms.

"Mmm. Arm porn," she whispers, her fingers digging into my

biceps. I can't speak. I'm a total mess from that dream. The thought of losing Cass is too painful to think about.

Our breaths mingle, and I fit myself into her warmth, threading our fingers together on the pillow. My grip is so tight, I'm afraid I'm going to break her hand. But I'd never hurt Cassidy. I might push her buttons and take her to the edge of her sanity some days, but I'd never hurt her.

After, she sleeps with her cheek on my chest, our legs tangled together, and I just listen to her breathe. My fingers trace the curve of her spine, running a circuit along her lower back up to smooth out her tangled hair.

I think about something Russell, my sponsor, said to me once early on in our relationship. Sometimes we think we're filling our lives with all of these vapid and innocuous encounters because we're searching for something. Sure, it's a lot of fun at the time, but all of those blurry nights and random hookups don't actually mean anything. They're just getting you ready for how you'll really fill your life.

Russell was right, as he always is. I wasn't really living or filling my life. Not until Cassidy fell into it.

"Do you hear something?" Cassidy glances up from her sewing machine, pushing her glasses up to the top of her head.

"What?" I look up from my tablet and over at the stack of blankets beside the bed. No-name, a four-year old Corgi I picked up this afternoon from the rescue shelter, sleeps peacefully, letting out the odd snore now and again. When I saw him in that tiny cage in the shop window, looking up at me with those big brown eyes, I knew I couldn't just leave him there. How we need rescue shelters in this day and age is beyond me. People can be total arseholes.

I brought him up to Cassidy's place while she finished her last appointment for the day, and they are both blissfully unaware of each other. Unaware because No-name probably hasn't had a proper sleep in all of his four years, and Cassidy because she's working like a mad-woman to finish up three dresses before we jet to my sister's wedding at the end of the month.

Another snore escapes from beside the bed, and Cassidy lifts her glasses off, setting them down. "That. Did you not hear that?"

"Ah…" No-name stirs at the sound when Cassidy pushes the chair back, and he's up and bounding in my direction. "Right." I lift him up, stroking his neck. "Cassidy, this is No-name."

Her eyes widen and she rushes over, gathering him up in her arms. "He's adorable! Are you a dog-sitter now in all of your spare time?" She nuzzles his fur, and I grin at her.

"No. He's mine. Well, ours. I got him from one of those rescues."

No-name licks her cheek. "Ours? Where are you planning on keeping him?" she asks, laughing as he tries to snuggle closer to her. I know the feeling, mate.

"Here? Wherever we are, I suppose."

Her hand stills on his back, and she glances up at me. "We can't keep a dog in here, Sean."

"Why not?" I can recognize the near-whine in my voice.

She balances No-name in one arm, motioning to her workspace. "Because I have hundreds of thousands of dollars in fabric in here, and I can't have dog fur on these dresses."

I glance over at her mannequins with dresses in various stages of completion, along with my suit that she's almost finished. "I didn't even think about that."

No-name lets out a little yelp of excitement and she hugs him tighter. "Did you even get everything you need for him? A leash? Toys? A bed? Dog food?"

"Ahhh." I rub the back of my neck. "I got him food and a bowl," I tell her rather triumphantly. "He really just needs love. It's all anyone needs."

"Okay there, Paul McCartney." Her lips press together and she slowly shakes her head, mumbling something else I can't hear.

"And I have a solution for his sleeping arrangements. Move in with me. We can keep No-name at my place, and when you need to work, you can just come here."

Her eyes light up, and I move over to slide my arm around her. "How about it? You, me, Mr. No-name here. Our own family."

She sets her palm against my cheek. "I think that's a perfect plan," she whispers. No-name lets out a bark between us. Life can't get much sweeter. Even the dog agrees with me.

Cassidy

"Okay, turn to the left, please." Samantha obliges me, and I quickly move my tape, calling out measurements for Riya to jot down. Sam's tall with long auburn curls and a curvy figure that would look fabulous draped in a clingy silk. "Have you decided on a date yet?"

"Next year. We're looking at the second Saturday in April, I think." She chuckles, shaking her head. "However, Victoria—Cam's mom—hasn't given up on inviting the French ambassador, and apparently there's some summit going on then. I love that woman, but she still has trouble sometimes accepting she's not always in control. Especially when it comes to Cam."

"Ah, the joys of mothers-in-laws," Riya sings, making us both chuckle. I kneel to get Sam's inseam, and the thought of my own soon-to-be mother-in-law, Anne, comes to mind. So far, I've only met her on Skype, when Sean and I announced our engagement. She seems like a lovely woman, with dark red hair and fair complexion like Sydney's. Sean's father, Joseph Murphy, CBE, is tall like his son, and with Sean's devilish twinkle in his eye. They were surprised, having all but given up hope their son would ever marry, but thrilled for us. I'll meet them formally when we fly over for Sydney's wedding in a few weeks. Thank God I won't have to deal with a woman like Victoria. From the bits I've heard about her from Sean and Samantha, she sounds like a major pain in the ass.

Since everything went down with Dale, I've felt freer, in a way I didn't expect. Without fear weighing it down, my heart is full of optimism for the future and excitement for my life with Sean. With Kevin's encouragement, my parents are getting over their reservations about my engagement, although when they found out Sean's a rock star I thought we'd have to call 911. Discovering my mother is a closet Redfall fan was almost too much for my dad.

The best news this week was from Jack. He flew to Wyoming with his partner, Adam, and came out to his father. Apparently, after Bert took a long walk on their ranch, he came back inside to a nervous couple and embraced his surprised son. He told Jack that Adam seemed like a stand-up guy, and that as long as he was happy, that was good enough for him. He also said that if anyone on their board of directors didn't like it, they could find the door. He had his son's back, as he should. I'd been thrilled for the happiness in Jack's voice when he called. My respect for his father—environmental issues aside—increased a hundred fold.

"Look, Auntie Syd, look!" Hannah's giggled command filters in from out in the reception area. Sydney is keeping an eye on her while I get her mother's measurements. Sean is out entertaining Cam somewhere, while Sam and Hannah accompanied Sydney here for her final fitting. After seeing what I've created for Syd, Sam immediately asked if I'd create her wedding gown, too. Once we're done here, we'll look through some of my sketchbooks so I can get an idea of what she likes.

Sitting back on my heels, I tell her I'm finished, and Riya hands her the robe I keep here for fittings. She shivers a little as she tugs the fluffy terrycloth closer, obviously chilled after standing in her bra and panties while I worked. I should've turned the heat up a little first. "I hope she's not driving Syd nuts out there," Sam mutters, and I snort a laugh.

"That sweet angel? I can't believe she'd drive anyone nuts," I say as Riya rolls one of our racks with sample dresses closer. When I met Sam and Cam's adorable daughter, her strawberry blond curls danced around her pretty little face, and my heart twinged at the thought of never having a little girl of my own with Sean. But I pushed it away; there are always options.

It's Sam's turn to laugh. "Yeah, right. You should've seen her when—"

"What in the ever-loving fuck?"

All three of our heads snap toward the sound of Sydney's shocked voice, an octave higher than usual. I pop up off the floor and rush with Sam and Riya to swipe aside the curtain that divides the main salon from the rest of the shop.

Hannah is on her knees, her arms wrapped around our wiggling corgi, who Sean finally decided to name after legendary drummer Gene Krupa. Cam is trying to stifle his grin as he switches Krupa's leash to his other hand. But that's obviously not the issue.

"What were you *thinking?*" Sydney demands, her hands clutching her head as she glares at her twin.

Her *bald* twin.

"Like it?" He runs a hand over his shiny scalp. "I did it for you."

"Sweet crispy Christ," I whisper, stunned, as Sam nods in silent agreement next to me, her hand covering her mouth. Realizing I'm gaping at him, I clamp my mouth shut and continue to stare in shock and disbelief as Sydney marches up to him, jabbing a finger in his chest.

"For me?" she sputters. "You've done some daft things in your life, Sean Michael Murphy, but this..." She shakes her head and takes a deep breath to rein in her anger, for Hannah's sake, I think. "My wedding is in three weeks!"

"Exactly." He takes her hands in his, probably to keep her from smacking him. "It's your wedding. Weddings always make me nostalgic. So I thought it might be nice to walk down memory lane and go back to what the good Lord gave me. For a while, at least."

"Back to bald?" Her voice quivers and she swallows thickly, trying to hold back tears. Sydney is the furthest thing from a bridezilla as possible, but today's been an emotional day for her. It's always poignant when you see yourself in your finished wedding dress for the first time. Plus, she's in that phase where brides worry about everything: the weather for her outside ceremony, the catering and guest allergies, lost invitations, and all the other myriad details a typical wedding includes. She's on the edge.

"You know how fast my hair grows." His smile is tender, his voice careful. "By the time you walk down the aisle, I should have a good half inch of flaming fabulousness. Can't you imagine Mum's face when she sees me? And Nanna?"

She huffs a weak laugh. "They'll be ecstatic." She pulls her right hand from his and gently touches his cheek. "You seriously did this for me? You hate your real hair." Her eyes take in his gleaming, stark-white head. "I didn't think we'd ever see it again. Ever."

He shrugs and shoots me a grin over Sydney's shoulder before refocusing on her. "*Someone* got me thinking that maybe it wasn't as bad as I remembered. The only way to know is to let it grow and find out."

"Oh." Bursting into tears finally, she throws her arms around her brother's neck, making him laugh. Sam grabs my forearm, exchanging a smile with me.

"Papa," Hannah's little voice breaks the tension. "Auntie Syd owes the swear jar!"

Cam and Sean's laughter rings in the room. Cam grins down at his daughter. "That she does, sweetie."

"I can't believe you did this." I rub my hand over Sean's shaved pate and chuckle to myself. I have a feeling I'll be saying that a lot during our life together. "How does it feel?"

He pulls the blankets closer around us. "Cold. I never realized how much hair keeps your head warm." We're nestled in bed, watching the stars through the skylight. Since I moved in with Sean a week ago, my life has felt more relaxed somehow. As if this was always where I was meant to be, as corny as it sounds. He eagerly helped me incorporate my things into his space, and the condo truly feels like ours now. I've never been happier; and based on the near-constant smile he wears, he feels the same.

Pressing a kiss to his lips, I slide my hand down his neck to his chest. "You made Sydney's day," I murmur, pressing my hand over his heart.

"Once she got over the shock." He grins at me. "Your face was a picture, too. What was running through that head of yours when you saw me?"

"That you'd lost a bet. Or your mind." He pouts and I take his plump lower lip between my teeth. A growl escapes him, and I let my hand slide lower as I kiss him again.

"Losing my mind doesn't seem like a bad idea just now." Reaching under the blankets, he grips my hips and pulls me atop him. "Do you like it?"

Grinding my hips against his, I feel his hardening cock between us. "This?" He groans softly, his lips moving against my jawline. "I like all of you. I can't wait to see what you look like."

He laughs through his nose. "Don't be too eager. It was such a violent color, even carrots felt sorry for me."

I can't help my giggle. "You know, it may not be that red anymore. Is Sydney's hair the same as it was when she was little?"

"No. It's much darker now." He palms one of my breasts and kneads it gently. "Did you have a good day?"

I nod, a soft sigh escaping me. God, that feels good. "I did. I got a good idea of what Sam likes and was able to make some preliminary sketches." My breath catches when his hand moves down between my legs. "I can't wait to make Hannah's dress. She'll steal the show."

"She already does." He stills, but his breath is hot against my neck. "I'm sorry we won't be able to—"

"Hush." I shift so I can look at him fully and place two fingers over his lips. "We have an incredible life ahead of us, Sean. Whatever happens, we have options. We can do anything, be anything we want. I'll always love you, regardless."

The deep emerald of his eyes softens to a mossy green. "I'll always love you, too, my Fly-girl." I squeak out a laugh when he suddenly grabs me and flips us over. Blocking out the starlight, he sheaths himself in me, and my laugh becomes a moan as his whispered words resonate in my heart. "For now, let's enjoy the ride."

epilogue

*Murphy's Ultimate Law: Don't take yourself too seriously.
Take the leap. Dance and make a fool out of yourself. Enjoy the
journey. Say yes to the things that scare you, and you'll do what
you're supposed to do—you'll live your life.*

Sean

THE OPPRESSIVE HUMIDITY OF A NEW YORK SUMMER GIVES WAY TO glorious fall, and before we know it, the leaves turn and the nights are blessedly cooler. It's a week before Syd's wedding and all that can be done has been.

I've got no idea how Syd has managed to keep it together over the last couple of weeks as she's dealt with the minutia of planning this wedding. Eloping on the down-low like Kennedy and Abby did is looking better and better by the minute.

I'm currently relaxing back on my elbows, legs stretched out in the grass with Cass resting her head on my lap whilst Krupa basks in the sun and attention he's currently getting from the Saunders family. It's become our Sunday tradition after meeting the family a few weeks ago when we had Krupa out for a walk in the park.

Nancy and Joe Saunders have two boys: Max and Chris, aged five and eight, who love life and everything dog-related. One look at Krupa, and they were all in, trying to teach him how to catch a Frisbee. Sadly, it's not to be. Krupa's little legs are way too short, and he only succeeds in tripping over the Frisbee.

The Saunders' German shepherd, Bullet, has also given up trying to show Krupa the ropes. He just lies beside Cass, enjoying a belly rub—the lucky fucker—and occasionally looking on in disbelief at the spectacle of Krupa's shocking inability.

"You okay?" Cass glances up at me. The light breeze catches her hair, and I brush it away from her face.

"I'm always okay, Fly-girl."

She gives me a dubious look. "You've been quiet since the appointment." Ah, yes, my lovely monthly check-in with Dr. Perez. Let me tell you there's truly nothing that will make you feel more capable and worthwhile than hearing, "The odds of you having a baby are remote at best."

"I think I'm going to stop seeing Dr. Perez." Cass lifts her head and sits up beside me. Bullet follows suit, trying to shove his nose between us. "At least about this baby business."

"Why would you do that?"

I watch Krupa wipe out in the grass at another failed Frisbee catch attempt. "Because I don't want this to become a thing, Cass."

Cassidy sets her hand on my cheek, coaxing me to look at her. "Sean…"

I take her hand between both of mine. "I know what you're going to say, but I need you to know something. Dwelling on this, letting it consume me or you, isn't going to change anything." She slides her hand against the back of my neck, studying me. "I don't want us to live our lives around IVF and blood tests and hormone injections, and worry about spending too much time in a hot tub." I see that little crease form on her forehead as she listens to me. "I love my life, Cass. I'm lucky to do what I love with people I truly care about. I have a wonderful and forgiving—thank Christ—family, and most importantly, I have you." She slides her free hand against my hair, fiddling with the short strands. It's just starting to grow out, and right now, mimics the burnt orange of the changing leaves in the trees.

"Yes, you do have me, and you always will." Cass presses her forehead against mine.

"I know. That's why I know that whatever happens, whether someday we have our own baby, or adopt, or decide not to, we'll be okay. Whether we get twenty more corgis, or I decide to get a parrot." She laughs, and I lean back to meet her gaze. "I know that this doesn't define who I am or who we are together."

"I know," she whispers, arranging her sweet self so she's straddling my lap. Bullet seems to take the hint and trots off to join Krupa and the Frisbee fiasco.

I tighten my arms around her, and she melts against me, clasping her hands around the back of my neck. I just breathe her in, this woman who has filled me up and fully accepted me—flaws and all. Emotion threatens to steal my breath, and I can only manage to whisper, "You're everything I need in my life."

It's dusk at a park close to my parent's place in Knightsbridge. The park has been decked out with a thousand little white lights and more pastel flowers than I knew existed. It's ethereal, dream-like, as if fairies may magically appear.

Tucker and his amped-up security have kept the crazy fans and photographers who seem to find out everything at bay. I've still not uncovered what secrets he's keeping in California, but I've not given up on this bet yet. I'm sure he's gone and got himself a girl, and I'm going to enjoy every second of proving I'm right.

The photos of the wedding are going to be stunning, and Sydney is glowing. The masterpiece of a dress designed by Cassidy is beyond perfect. Mum is a weepy mess as she hugs Syd once more.

"My baby girl." Mum sniffles, her hands fluttering about as she tries to ward off another rush of emotion.

"Mum, don't ruin your makeup," Syd says on a shaky breath. I pass Mum a handkerchief from the inside pocket of my jacket, and she lifts it from me.

"Thank you, dear." Mum does a double take at the inner lining of my suit, her eyes widening at the Union Jack pattern. Cass was the one who suggested it, saying the pin-stripe suit she created needed a pop of something.

"You look so handsome." Mum pats the lapel of my jacket.

"This old thing?" That gets a laugh out of her. "Found it lying about, thought it would do for this shindig."

"And you've gone back to basics, I see," Dad adds as he takes his place beside Syd, motioning to my hair. We're out of view from the buzzing guests, and it's almost time.

"It's good to get back to your roots now and again, you always tell me, Pops." I clap him on the shoulder and pause to give Syd another hug.

"Be happy, Syd. That's all I want for you. If Philip ever gets out of line, you tell me and I'll kick his arse." She laughs and pushes me forward as I make sure the rings are secure in Krupa's collar. He's decked out with a Union Jack vest, handmade by Cassidy. I told her she should start selling them, and she just laughed at me. I'll have to see what I can do to make that happen. People will go crazy over custom-designed outfits for their beloved pets.

"Go! Find your girl. I need a minute here." She shoos me away, and I crouch down to ruffle Hannah's hair. I'm fairly certain my eardrums busted with the squeal Hannah let out when Syd asked her to be in the wedding. She's positively angelic in the soft pink dress Cass designed.

"You've got this, Poppet." Hannah beams at me and then gives me a little shove. "You heard Auntie Syd: we need a minute." I leave her with a laugh and a gallant bow. I'm nothing if not a gentleman.

Krupa bounds up the aisle in front of me just like Cass and I trained him to do. He dutifully sits on a mound of petals and waits, preening at the ohhs and ahhs he gets—little attention whore. I wonder where he gets that from.

Finding Cassidy is easy. She's at the front with the rest of the girls and my bandmates. Cass beams at me as I take my seat beside her. "How's she doing?" Cass squeezes my hand when I take hers.

"She looks fabulous, thanks to you."

Cass waves me off. "It's just a dress. It's the bride who makes it shine."

"Spoken like a true designer, love, but don't sell yourself short." I cast a glance over her own lavender dress that she put the finishing touches on just before we flew to London. It's lace and flowy perfection, and she looks good enough to eat. I bend my head to whisper against her ear, adjusting the matching purple hairpin that holds back a few strands of her hair. "You're stunning. I can't wait to get you out of this."

She tightens her hand against my thigh, a seductive warning.

"You know," I continue, "There's a minister or whatever he is right here." I nod at the fine man of the cloth, looking stoic as he patiently waits under an intricate flowered arch that looks like it came out of Narnia. I'm sure Syd built it herself. "We could lock this down tonight."

Cass leans back, her eyes full of mischief. "You can't upstage your own sister. She'd never forgive you," she whisper-hisses. I think she's trying to be quiet, but Matty's got superhero hearing or something.

"What's this now? Who's not forgiving who?" Matty leans across the row.

I open my mouth, but Cassidy's hand comes up to cover it. "Nothing. It's nothing. He's being ridiculous," Cass answers.

Kennedy laughs. "Tell us something we don't know."

"Shhh!" Abby and Tess both scold us as a harpist starts up and all two hundred guests stand. I remember what Cassidy said about wanting to see the groom's reaction, so I watch Philip as he tries unsuccessfully to hold back tears. I may never be best mates with the man, but it's obvious he loves Sydney, and that's all I could ask for.

Hannah is the perfectly adorable flower girl, practically glowing, and gently tossing pale pink petals along the grassy aisle. Cameron gives her a thumbs-up when she stops under the arch.

There are collective gasps when Syd comes into view with Mum and Dad both walking her down the aisle. "That dress is so beautiful," Sam says in awe, and I squeeze Cassidy's hand.

What follows is simple and heartfelt; it's two people who found each other and can't imagine spending life apart.

A few hours later, the party is in full swing. We've survived teary speeches and so many photos that my cheeks actually hurt from smiling. I've ditched my jacket to the back of a chair and won a dance-off with the groom himself. Didn't think Philip had it in him, to be honest, but that's one of the wonders of life—it just keeps surprising you.

Abby currently has her feet in Kennedy's lap, and he's massaging them for her. She leans back and glances up to the star-filled sky. "God, that feels good. Why do my feet hurt so much? It's not enough I have a basketball in my stomach—I can't even see my feet! I want to see my feet again."

"Babe…" Kennedy begins. "You're in the homestretch now."

Abby grimaces at him, waving a finger in his direction. "No more sports metaphors. You're not the one who pees when you laugh. And my ankles are all swollen and huge."

"Thought you said you couldn't see your feet," Matty says like a nob, and Abby shoots him a murderous look.

"I'll go get you something from the dessert table." Tess tugs on Matt's arm. "Come with me."

"On it. We'll be back with cake; it fixes everything," Matty says with a grin.

"Some of those little éclair things," Abby calls out, and Matt waves in acknowledgement as he and Tess make their way across the park to the dessert area.

"Oh!" Abby drops her feet from Kennedy's lap, her hand on her stomach. "He's awake."

Kennedy smiles, shuffling his chair over beside her. "Must be all that talk of cake."

Abby draws his hand over her belly. "Must be. I think he's going to be a soccer player or something."

I feel Cass squeeze my shoulder, and I turn to press a kiss to her forehead. "Want to dance, Fly-girl?" I nod in the direction of the dance floor, seeing Cameron holding Hannah in one arm as he sways with Sam around the edge.

"Love to." I take her hand and tug her out of the chair.

"Save some of those éclairs for us." Kennedy gives us a salute, and I lead Cassidy to the dance floor.

She melts into my embrace like she was born to fit there with her cheek pressed against my chest. The DJ is all about old-time love ballads, likely at the request of my dad. When I offered to have the band play, Sydney flatly refused, wanting us to enjoy the day and not worry about playing. What Sydney doesn't really understand is playing for us isn't a worry. It's what we crave, and we would've gladly lit up the night for her. We compromised, playing an acoustic set at the rehearsal dinner last night that blew up the internet when one of the guests live-streamed a few songs.

Holding Cassidy in my arms and swaying to Sam Cooke as he croons about bringing sweet love home, I know now that playing isn't all my life is about anymore.

It's about loving this woman with all of my heart and soul. It's about being everything to her. It's about all the highs and lows we'll get through together. I wasn't expecting Cassidy to fall into my life, but I learned a long time ago that the unexpected is what turns your life around.

Under the lights that frame the dance floor, I brush my thumb over her chin. "If you ever change your mind…" I start singing.

Her arm tightens around my waist as she pulls me closer, staking a claim. "I never will. You're stuck with me, London. Forever."

"Works for me, Fly-girl."

Cassidy

"Aren't they lovely together?"

I grin in agreement, hiding a laugh as Sean's polite smile becomes strained. His aunt has been babbling about the wedding and everything else for hours, it seems. One of the best things about this trip has been meeting Sean's relatives. He has a huge extended family: aunts, uncles, and cousins galore. Kevin and I would've loved having cousins when we were growing up.

And all his family members have been fascinated with me. Wonderfully gracious and welcoming, but fascinated just the same. Apparently, the Redfall members aren't the only ones who've had bets against their wild musician ever settling down.

"I hear they're going to start a family right away," his aunt gushes. "Your parents are so excited to become grandparents!" She spies someone behind us and her smile brightens, oblivious to the shadow behind Sean's eyes at the mention of children. "Oh, there's Livie Babbish. I must go say hello."

She totters off, and I slip my hand in Sean's, giving it a squeeze. I know he means what he says—that our life together is all he needs. I also know that want and need are two different things.

He smiles at me in thanks, and then looks over to where Kennedy and Cameron are charming Sean's mother and some women I swear I saw among the guests at the last royal wedding. Maybe he really *has* met the queen. "She's right," he says, watching the guests swirling around laughing, talking, and eating. "My parents will be over the moon when Sydney gets pregnant." He rubs a hand over his dark, spicy red hair. God, I love his real color. So hot.

When he glances back at me, his smile is brighter. "And we'll be the most kick-ass aunt and uncle a baby could ever hope for. The little tykes will be clamoring for sleepovers with Auntie Cass and Uncle Sean."

I nod and stifle a grin. I decided this morning to wait until after the wedding, but…oh, fuck it. Carpe diem. "Yes, we will. But you'll have to get used to a different title before you become Uncle Sean."

"Oh yeah?" He laughs. "And what would that be?"

I stretch up to kiss him on his cheek, and then whisper in his ear. "Next time you see your doctor, tell him that you beat the odds." His eyes narrow in confusion for a beat until he jerks back, mouth gaping. A brilliant smile slowly lights his face, and I nod, sliding a hand over his lapel. "Daddy."

the end

acknowledgements

The biggest thank you to our families for your support and understanding, and for going on 'research' adventures when the time calls for it.

To the incredible Michelle Clay and Annette Brignac, and their amazing Book Nerd Services: we are floored by your incredible energy, support and friendship. No one rocks like these two!

Thank you to our ARC team and pre-readers for taking time to read and providing your insights!

Thanks to the Facebook Dream Team and your ongoing inspiration.

To the unbelievably talented Jada D'Lee, we are always in awe of your creativity. Thank you for sharing it with us.

Thank you to Lauren and Greg at The Write Divas. We can never promise to eliminate every raised brow, but we'll try!

A million thanks to Stacey and Champagne Book Design for making our words and chapters beautiful.

Thank you does not seem enough to the amazing community of authors and their support including Harper Bentley and Melanie Moreland.

A world of thanks to the tireless bloggers, Twitterloves, Facebook friends and groups, Goodreads friends and review sites that support Indie authors.

And thank you, the reader for taking this journey with us. We've poured our heart and soul into this series and we hope you have enjoyed it as much as we have. Until next time, rock on, friends. Rock on.

about the authors

Almost a decade ago, an American carnivore and a Canadian vegetarian bonded over their mutual love for shoes, the perfect cocktail, and swoon-worthy story telling.

From her home in Portland, B.B. Miller spends her days with friends and family in search of the perfect pear martini.

Leslie Carson lives in Ottawa, with her busy family and three cats. She's at the rink so much, Zamboni drivers know her by name.

Together, they enjoy visiting vineyards and distilleries, and writing about romantic adventures.

They would love to hear from you.

Join our Facebook team: The Dream Team.

other titles by the authors

Rock the Dream

Live Your Dream

Chase the Dream

Sneak Peek!

Coming Soon ~ A new series with three standalone novels is coming your way soon. Wine, and spirits, and men—oh my! Here's a sneak peek at book one in the Spirits Series.

CHAPTER 1

Brie

WEDDINGS OFFICIALLY SUCK.

Immediately, I'm swamped with best friend guilt. Of course this wedding doesn't suck. It's the most beautiful wedding in the history of weddings.

My best friend, Becca Holton is finally married to her very own Prince Charming, Liam Swanson, in what can only be described as a picture-perfect wedding.

Harry and Meghan? Please. A distant second.

I mean, come on. We're in Ireland at a 16th century hon-est-to-goodness castle. Five star luxury steeped in historic character.

It's picturesque and romantic. I dare say, magical. Part of Gaelic Irish royalty. It's stone walls, original oil paintings, and carved wooden trusses, mixed with every modern convenience you could want.

My suite (named after some Duke of something or other) is a dream. I had turn down service last night, complete with little choco-lates that right now, not going to lie, I could eat seventeen pounds of. The four poster bed is a virtual cloud. I could fit my apartment back in California into the bathroom. I'm in the height of luxury. I'm not used to this level of elegance and grandeur.

The nine course meal was a little over the top, but it's what Becca and Liam wanted. Quenelle (whatever the hell that is) of Irish salmon and prawn leeks, free range/organic everything, goat cheese mousse, salted caramel pear tarte. It just went on and on, and sadly I could barely stomach any of it after what I saw in the darkened hallway.

And the view? The grounds are something out of a fairy tale. Massive rock wall gardens that stretch for days, mature trees holding onto the secrets and ghosts of hundreds of years past. You can just see a harbor in the distance over the cliffs with massive sailboats and yachts bobbing in the sea, little white lights twinkling off the languid waves.

The lake that sits in front of McGuire Castle is stocked with some kind of exotic fish that earned ohs and ahs from a few of the guests. Those fish are hungry. How do I know this? I'm currently ruining my peach organza bridesmaid's dress as I wade through the middle of it, those fish nipping at my ankles.

I curse, stubbing my toe on a rock. Probably a rock from 1745 that was placed here by some courtly night as a sign of his steadfast love for a princess.

Love sucks.

I hike the bottom of the full skirt up and take another swig from the green whiskey bottle I snagged from the bar, swaying slightly. The whiskey is produced here in some sort of time honored and highly kept secret handed down through generations. It simultaneously soothes and burns my throat going down. If only it could obliterate my memories with it.

Glaring at one of the imposing stone towers in the distance, I wonder if they still have all the equipment needed for a beheading.

It would serve Laird right—the lying, cheating, surfing bastard. I should have known better. There's no way anyone with that wavy blond hair, those ocean blue eyes and that chiseled lean body could keep all that hotness to himself.

I mean 'Laird'? Seriously? His name alone should have given me a clue how this was going to end. Oh, but he loved to tell me and everyone within a five mile radius how he was named after famed, world renowned, legendary surfer Laird Hamilton.

"Come on, Brie!" he used to say to me almost every single day. "Surfing is everything. Let's share it together." He'd give me a lopsided grin, shoving his hand through his insanely wild hair, his chest bronzed from endless hours of surfing. Many of those days, I didn't make it to the beach. We spend the morning in bed until he'd disappear to the call of the ocean, his surfboard tucked under his arm. I wouldn't see him again until midnight some days.

To be fair, I did try surfing a few times. But no way, no how was surfing going to be something I was good at even with the surfing God himself helping me. There are only so many mouthfuls of ocean water you can swallow before you give up.

Also, clearly surfing isn't *everything*. No. *Everything* may now include Alison Swanson—sister of the groom and officially now on my black list—being fucked by Laird against the cold stone wall outside the master ballroom after the wedding ceremony, but it sure doesn't include me. Not anymore.

The vision of him pounding into her against that medieval wall is burned into my head. The fabric of her identical peach dress swirling around them caught me off guard when I went in search for Laird before dinner.

Maybe it was a case of mistaken identity. I mean, we did have the same dress on, and Laird wasn't at the front of the line when they were handing out brain cells.

But Alison's funky raven dark hair and endless curves are the polar opposite to my long blond hair and below average height. Even Laird's not that stupid to mistaken Alison for me.

Maybe he'd be hit by a stray bullet during clay shooting tomorrow morning. I give my head a shake, making the darkened lake blur a bit. How much of this damn whiskey have I had? I lift the bottle, squinting to study the etched sailboat on the front.

McGuire's Irish Whiskey - Chapman Reserve - Batch 41. Holy, holy hell it's strong. Strong and going down faster than it should. But I deserve it, damn it. I've supported stupid Laird and his dream of winning of the stupid US Open of Surfing in Huntington Beach for *four years*.

Four years of him not having an actual job. Four years of me cheering him on, of carting his hotness around to every surfing competition on the coast of California in my beloved Jeep that somehow slowly became his.

Four years of me finding myself stranded alone on the highway because he didn't fill said Jeep up with gas. Four years of me trying to explain to him that Vulcan wasn't a real planet.

All of those quirky conversations that I loved at the time, now only serve to rev my anger up.

I wonder how long this has been going on with Alison. We've been planning Becca's wedding for a year, and Alison and Laird have been part of the process every step of the way. The number of times the two of them went off together on some wedding emergency errand makes my head hurts to think about.

I thought it was sweet—Laird helping out and getting involved in the wedding. He would jump at the chance to go search for Irish themed decorations with Alison. What an idiot I am.

More ankle biting as I stumble a bit on the rocky lake bottom. I shouldn't be out here. Even in my slightly intoxicated haze I realize this. I should be having a ball at the ball. The band is fabulous, my best friend is married, and they are about to send up a fireworks display to top the night off.

But, I just couldn't take any more. No more of Laird's sideways glances to Alison when he thought I wasn't looking. No more lovey-dovey kisses between every single other couple in attendance. Feeling over heated and betrayed, I bolted before the first dance. Ed Sheeran is amazing, don't get me wrong, but even I have my limits.

Stupid Laird and his seaweed dick. I can only hope that somewhere along the way, all that salt water has caused permanent shrinkage. I kick my leg out at the evil fish lurking below. God, how pathetic am I? There's nothing wrong with Laird's cock. It's fine as these things go. Normal. Yes, I did come face-to-dick with some seaweed wrapped around it once, but isn't that to be expected when he spends 80% of his time in the ocean? You know, when he's not drilling a bridesmaid that's not me?

There's not enough whiskey in the world for this feeling.